NEVER GOT OVER YOU

S.L. SCOTT

S.L. SCOTT

ISBN: 978-1-940071-99-2

Cover Photographer: Regina Wamba of ReginaWamba.com

Cover Models: Claire + Noah Villalobos

Cover Designer: RBA Designs

Editing:

Marion Archer, Making Manuscripts

Jenny Sims, Editing4Indies

Proofreading: Kristen Johnson

Beta Reading: Andrea Johnston

IN THE KNOW

To keep up to date with her writing and more, visit S.L. Scott's website: www.slscottauthor.com

To receive the newsletter about all of her publishing adventures, free books, giveaways, steals and more:
www.slscottauthor.com
Audiobooks are available on major retailers

ALSO BY S.L. SCOTT

To keep up to date with her writing and more, visit her website:
www.slscottauthor.com

To receive the Scott Scoop about all of her publishing adventures,
free books, giveaways, steals and more: Visit her website:
www.slscottauthor.com

Join S.L.'s Facebook group: S.L. Scott Books

Read the Bestselling Book that's been called **"The Most Romantic
Book Ever"** by readers and have them raving. We Were Once is
now available and FREE in Kindle Unlimited.

We Were Once

Audiobooks on Audible

Complementary to Missing Grace

We Were Once

Everest

Finding Solace

Until I Met You

The Everest Brothers (Stand-Alones)

Everest - Ethan Everest

Bad Reputation - Hutton Everest

Force of Nature - Bennett Everest

The Everest Brothers Box Set

The Crow Brothers (Stand-Alones)

Spark

Tulsa

Rivers

Ridge

The Crow Brothers Box Set

Hard to Resist Series (Stand-Alones)

The Resistance

The Reckoning

The Redemption

The Revolution

The Rebellion

DARE - A Rock Star Hero (Stand-Alone)

The Kingwood Series

SAVAGE

SAVIOR

SACRED

FINDING SOLACE - Stand-Alone

The Kingwood Series Box Set

Playboy in Paradise Series

Falling for the Playboy

Redeeming the Playboy

Loving the Playboy

Playboy in Paradise Box Set

Talk to Me Duet (Stand-Alones)

Sweet Talk

Dirty Talk

Stand-Alone Books

We Were Once

Missing Grace

Until I Met You

Drunk on Love

Naturally, Charlie

A Prior Engagement

Lost in Translation

Sleeping with Mr. Sexy

Morning Glory

From the Inside Out

Never Got Over You

1

Natalie St. James

I'm the first to admit I have no business taking another shot.

Especially after the past two.

But what's a girl to do when a room full of strangers is chanting my name and a particularly wild best friend places the shot hat on my head along with a small glass of liquor in my hand?

I drink.

In a little hole-in-the-wall hidden from the main street in Avalon on Catalina Island, I down the liquid like a champ, then promptly proceed to fall from grace, also known as the barstool.

My eyes close, bracing for impact, except . . . someone catches me just before landing. With my breath caught in my throat, I hang in the balance of arms made of steel and open my eyes.

Laughter fades away with any drunken shame that threatened as I stare into the soulful eyes of a stranger.

"Hi," whispers the future hero of my dirty dreams . . . *oh, wait.*

Maybe I'm unconscious? Maybe I was knocked out cold, and I'm dreaming. I blink. Why are my eyes open? Letting my lids fall, I keep them closed long enough to pray, "Please let him be real. If he's not, I'm begging you to leave me in this dream a little longer." My lids drift back open to find him still staring at me.

"Are you okay?"

"Perfect," I reply. *I think.* I'm not sure if I actually voice the response or not. I feel pretty damn perfect in his arms, though, the response still fitting in any circumstance that involves me, him, and those arms wrapped around my body.

Naked would be nice, but I'll save that for our second date.

His brow furrows, but a smile curls the corners of his lips.

The fog of alcohol clouds my mind, creating a heavy blanket on my brain. Regardless, I try to calculate the odds of a ridiculously sexy stranger—the exact man I'd craft if Create-a-Hottie was an actual thing—being in the right place at the right time to catch me if I fell.

It's impossible, so the only logical answer to this conundrum is that either he is the best college graduation gift ever or I'm dreaming. "How are you so hot?" I ask, worried he'll disappear in a puff of smoke and mirrors. Clamping my eyes closed again, I whisper, "Dear Lord, please don't let him be a mirage."

"I'm real." *Yes!*

Does that mean my friend set up this encounter for me? She's always been a great gift giver. It is our job, after all. I squint one eye open, biting my bottom lip. "*Mm*, so real," I purr. *Too perfect to be real, though. I must be dreaming.*

His grin creates dimples that could compete with the Grand Canyon. *How did I know I liked dimples enough to add them into this delirium?* I don't know, but score one for me.

"I think you're going to be okay," my dream man says, his voice as delectable as his face.

Wait, what? No. "As for me being okay, not so fast, buddy. No need to rush toward the waking hours. Anyway . . ." I drape my hand across my forehead. "Dream or real, I'm going to need mouth-to-mouth resuscitation."

His dimples dig deeper. "Is that so?"

"*So* right," I pant.

"Do you think I should call a paramedic?"

"That's a little kinky for me, but if you're into it . . ." I press my lips into a pretty little pout to seriously consider this twist. "Nah. Changed my mind. I only want you. Just the two of us resuscitating each other."

"You want me?" he asks, surprise tingeing his tone as he cocks an eyebrow. He readjusts me in his strong, manly arms. "Circling back to the real part, you do realize you're not dreaming, right?"

I reach up and wrap my arms around his neck, wanting to melt in his arms again. Totally obsessed with how I fit so perfectly, I pull him closer and hold tight. "You do realize you're stupidly attractive, right?"

He chuckles, his grin lifting higher on one side.

That smirk would totally get me into bed, given what it's doing to me while dreaming. I close my eyes again. "I'm ready."

"For what?" His deep, dulcet tones vibrate through my body.

"Resuscitation. I'm ready. Resuscitate away."

When nothing happens, I peek one eye open. He's still

staring at me with the smirk I'm ready to kiss off his sexy face, and whispers, "I don't think you need me—"

"Trust me." Opening both eyes, I also run my fingers through his shiny, chestnut-hued hair, taking in the feel of the soft strands. "I really, *really* need you."

When he leans down, I prepare my lips with a quick lick before meeting his . . . or at least, that's the direction I hope this dream is going.

"I was thinking—"

"Yes?" My gaze floats from his mouth to his eyes again.

"We've been at this a while. Maybe we should get you off the floor?" His head tilts to the side, and the industrial lights above him shine bright in my eyes, almost like a place of business, a restaurant, or a bar would hang. My senses begin to return, starting with the stench of old beer scenting the air.

"Yuck." Next comes a wave of cedar-y cologne and salty air. That's a scent I approve of, but that's when something else hits me. *What if I'm not dreaming?*

"Up you go," he says, shadowing me again as he tries to lift me to my feet.

I don't budge. "Dream or not, I quite enjoy being horizontal with you."

"Are you always this, *should we say*, flirtatious?" he asks, laughter punctuating his question.

"Not when I'm awake, no."

As if he couldn't be more gorgeous, little lines whisker from the outer corners of his eyes, enticing me to drag my fingertip along each one. I don't, but I want to. "Are your eyes hazel or brown? It's hard to tell in this light."

"Brown."

"Brown does them a disservice. A kaleidoscope of colors

is trapped inside them. I'm going to need a closer look in the sunshine."

"The sun will be setting soon."

"Then we should hurry."

A restrained chuckle wriggles his lips. "You can stare into my eyes, but I have to warn you, once you do, you'll fall madly in love with me. And I'm leaving tomorrow, so if we're falling in love, you better get to the loving part since you've already fallen."

"Good point."

"Get up, Natalie," my best friend says, rudely barging into my fantasy and peering at me from beside his shoulder. "The floor is filthy! Now you're going to have to wash your hair."

My eyes shift her way. "Please go away and let me have this one little dream, Tatum."

Snapping her fingers twice in front of my face has me jerking my head back. "You're wide awake and making a fool of yourself."

Noise from the crowded bar filters into my consciousness. Instead of looking around to confirm, I stare into Dreamy's eyes a moment longer and then exhale as embarrassment becomes reality, returning me to the present. "You're real, aren't you?"

A slow nod accompanies a smug expression.

The heat of my cheeks has me pressing my hands to them in hopes of cooling my skin down. "Do you mind helping me up?"

"I need to know something first."

"What?" I ask, knowing I should leave before I'm sober enough to realize how absurd I've been behaving.

Still holding me in his arms as if I'm light as a feather, he leans closer with his eyes on my mouth. When his gaze rises to meet mine, he asks, "Did you fall in love?"

My heart rate spikes, and the sound of it beating whooshes in my ears. Maybe I did hit my head because I swear at that moment, the one with my dream man so close I can kiss him or even lick him if I want, I can answer honestly.

Despite all the physical signs of me feeling otherwise, I reply, "You know. I think it's time for me to go." *Before the last few minutes really sink in.*

My feet are set on solid flooring while his hands remain on the underside of my forearms to steady me. Like the perfect gentleman. "I wish—"

"Nat," Tatum says under her breath. She moves in and grabs my hand.

"What?"

Her hair catches the light when she flips it over her shoulder, an exhausted sigh following right after. Every blonde needs a brunette bestie, and Tatum Devreux was destined to be mine since our mothers exchanged silver spoons from Tiffany's as baby shower gifts. I'm not exactly the calm to her wild ways, but she can out party me any day.

"A party on a yacht down in the harbor. We have to go now, though."

Panic rises in my chest. I know I should want to hightail it out of here to save myself from further mortification, but I don't want to go. I'm perfectly content right here.

I'm not shy about it. I look straight at him, but I'm smacked with a dose of candor I wasn't ready for, my ego crushed under his expression that mirrors pity. Now I regret not making a quick getaway when I had the chance.

My stomach plummets to the floor I was just hovering above. "Yeah, it's time to go," I tell Tatum, my hand pressing to my belly in an attempt to keep myself together. My hand is grabbed, and I'm tugged after her as she calls, "Ciao, darlings."

I turn back to catch Mr . . . *Dreamy*, *Smug*, *Sexy*, *Pity-er of Drunk Girls* watching me. I'm left with two options to make an escape without further incident. I *could* blame the craziness on a head injury, or I *could* just leave. "So . . . thanks," I say awkwardly as I back toward the door. *Yes. Choosing the latter.*

"Are you sure you're okay?" His voice carries over the lively crowd.

I dust the dirt off my ass. "I'm fine. Guess I'm not a tequila girl."

"You drank rum," he replies with a lopsided smile that could sweep me off my feet again if I'm not careful.

"Rum. Tequila. Same difference." I wave off the idea because it doesn't really matter. "I'm not good with liquor." That should settle it, but I make the mistake of daring to look into his eyes again. The five feet between us virtually disappears, and mentally, I'm back in his arms again, reading the prose that makes up his features. It would take me days to interpret, capturing not only his thoughts but a history that's worn in the light lines. He makes it hard to look away.

Stepping forward, he raises his hand and then lowers it to his side again as conflict invades his expression. "You sure you're okay? You might have a concussion."

I can't say I'm not touched by his concern. Grinning, I ask, "Does a concussion involve my heart?"

"What's happening with your heart?"

"It's beating like crazy."

Smiles are exchanged. "I think you're experiencing something else, but if you'd like me to call an ambulance—"

"Nope," Tatum cuts in, yanking me toward the door again, and laughs. "He's cute, but we don't want to miss the yacht." She whips the straw hat off me and tosses it to him.

I twist to look back. "Thanks for the lift. *Literally.*"

"Anytime," he says with his eyes set on mine. When he shoves his hands in his pockets, he looks like he's posing for a Ralph Lauren ad. Tan. Rugged good looks. Tall. Those dreamy eyes and a grin that call me back to him. But life isn't a dream. It's time to return to reality.

Goodbye, dream man. It was nice hanging with . . . onto you.

2

Nick Christiansen

Two days without the worries of late-night study groups, working my ass off interning at a law firm, and the constant micromanagement of my dad. At twenty-five, I've been ready to break out from under his thumb for a long time now.

He just hasn't received the memo that I'm not a kid anymore.

A last-minute invitation for a quick getaway before graduation from Stanford Law School and the pressures of my family brought me here. That's all this was supposed to be. A night of hanging with my best friend, a day of kicking back around the resort pool, and then barhopping to celebrate my final year of school behind me, today should have been much the same.

So, what just happened?

I know. Grinning as I recall how one minute, I was finishing my beer to the sound of spinning keys around my best friend's finger, and the next, chanting was filling my ears. *"Shot. Shot. Shot."*

I saw *him* first, an asshole ready to take advantage of an opportunity. The opportunity—a certain blonde in a loose white shirt, wide open between the top two buttons. Cutoffs reveal a lot of leg—shapely tan thighs—and a brown leather belt hangs around her waist more for decoration than for a purpose. Her sandals, only noticeable if you're looking for them, don't add any height. Bracelets of silver and gold with touches of turquoise covered her wrists, and the bar's raggedy shot hat had just been placed on her head. Clearly, I spent more than a few seconds taking her in without regret.

She was a vision in any state—from New York to California, drunk or sober—but it wasn't her outfit that had me acting on instinct and running into others to get to her. It was the asshole bragging about fucking her before she realized what hit her. Sure, I could have snapped back that no one would even know he was fucking her since he has a minuscule dick. But the hard lines of his face and the anger found in his dark eyes had me believing he meant what he said, not in jest or as a threat, but as a mission he intended to complete.

I should have punched him in the fucking face, but I didn't have time. I dashed the second my attention was grabbed by the sound of a squeal, the sight of arms in the air, and the pretty woman flying toward the floor.

Because I'm good with my hands, I've caught everything from the attention of college football scouts to a swordfish on vacation. I've also been called a golden boy my whole life growing up in the Golden State. But catching this girl right before she hit the floor might be my best catch yet.

She weighed nothing but made quite the impression. I

flexed my fingers under her back to rid myself of some weird energy burning through me. *God, I sound like my mom.*

I swore I'd never believe in that New Age stuff. She did her best to preach it, but logic has to play a part in our outcomes. But there's no logical answer as to why I'm still thinking about the woman I held for so long as if more was at play than two people colliding into each other's lives without their permission.

The back of Harrison's hand lands on my chest. "Nice save, but why'd you let her get away?"

"She's free to do as she pleases."

"What?" he asks, his brow careening between his eyes. "No, I mean, why didn't you get her number? She was hot, and the way you held on to her was like you had no intention of letting her go. It was becoming awkward watching the two of you cling—"

"We weren't clinging to each other. I was—"

Shaking his head, he says, "Save it, Nick. I don't need to hear about you falling for some chick."

"Technically, *she* was the one who fell."

"Let's not make this weird." He nods toward the door. "Taylor put us on the list. We've got to go before the yacht leaves the dock."

I follow him toward the door, but not without stopping by the asshole on my way out. "Today's your lucky fucking day because if we ever cross paths or you go within thirty feet of that woman again, you'll be flat on the ground before you know what hit you. Got it, fucker?"

He stands up but quickly realizes he has to look up to meet my eyes and sits back down. "Fuck off," he grumbles through a wiry beard.

My arm is caught before I have a chance to land a hit. "He's not worth it," Harrison says.

He's right.

This fucker also isn't worth a night in jail.

As the asshole cowers on the barstool with his head lowered, flinching from a hit that won't come, I lower my arm. "Lucky fucking day."

The conversation slowly resumes as Harrison and I head for the exit. My friend laughs under his breath just outside the entrance. "What gives, Christiansen? We haven't been in a fight in a long time." Cracking his knuckles, he adds, "Don't get me wrong. I'm up for it, but why are we fighting some guy twice our age in Catalina?"

"He needs a lesson in . . ." *Blonde. Tan. Blue-eyed beauty.*

"In what?" Harrison asks as he whacks me in the arm.

Ripping my gaze away from the blue-eyed beauty kneeling beside a scooter, I glance at Harrison. "Huh?"

When I return my attention to her again, I hear him grumble. "Ah. It's all so clear now."

I seize the moment. "This is a coincidence. Hi, again," I say, raising a hand while my voice pitches like a thirteen-year-old hitting puberty. *What the fuck?* Clearing my throat, I mentally berate myself for sounding like an idiot.

Harrison and both of the women turn to look at me. The blonde stands up with a reassuring grin on her face and shoves her hands into her back pockets. "Hi again, yourself."

I'm not the only one seizing the day. Harrison saunters up and asks her friend, "What seems to be the trouble?"

"Trouble with a capital T. Hi, I'm Tatum," she says.

Harrison takes her hand. "Pleasure to meet you. I'm Harrison."

Although she appears to blush, she pulls her hand and then points at the tire. "We have a party to get to, but we have a flat, and the rental company won't be here for an hour."

"That's quite the dilemma. Maybe we can help," Harrison says.

It's funny how he was in such a hurry not three minutes prior. He moves in to take a closer look. Harrison Decker was born with two trust funds and a gaggle of nannies. He didn't exactly grow up knowing his way around mechanics. I can't judge him too harshly since my background is similar, but I can still laugh at him because at least I know how to change a tire.

He leans back, glancing up at the brunette. She's pretty but doesn't hold a candle to the beauty beside me. Speaking of . . . I walk around the Vespa and lean down. Squeezing the tire, I listen. My eyes meet Harrison's, who's stepped off to the side with his new friend. His lack of loyalty isn't a surprise when there's a pretty woman around.

Her friend called her Natalie, but since we haven't been introduced, I just say, "You have a slow leak."

"Announce it to the world, why don't ya." She can't keep a straight face and cracks up. "Sorry, I had to."

I chuckle because of how much she makes herself laugh. She still waves it off. "Sorry, as you were saying." Another giggle escapes, though.

"The company shouldn't have put you on this scooter without checking it properly."

I look to my side to find those blue eyes staring into mine. "So we're stuck?" She grabs the tire, pumps it a few times like that might bring it back to life, and then drags her hand over a few treads. Leaning awkwardly on it, she adds, "Together?"

Is she flirting? It's not the approach I'd take, but it's curiously entertaining. "Afraid so." We both stand back up.

"You don't have to be afraid. I won't bite."

Something tells me she might by how her gaze darts down my body and back up again.

"I didn't mean I was actually afraid."

"I know. I was just teasing." If I didn't know she was drunk, I'd assume she was odd. She definitely has a quirky sense of humor. Maybe I do too because when she rubs her temple, she smears black grime along the side of her face, and I have to stop myself from laughing.

I reach forward, determined to help her out, but a spark fires in her eyes, and she says, "I knew we should have rented the golf cart. Tatum insisted on the Vespa, but I don't trust anything with less than four wheels."

"Wise." That response brings her earlier smile to the surface. "I heard your friend call you—"

"The party," her friend cuts in, wearing an expression scrunched with concern. "We're not going to make the party if we don't leave now."

"We can stay—"

"That's it!" Harrison snaps his fingers. "You can stay and help with the tire, and I can give Tatum a ride. Problem solved."

"A ride? Yes, that's great," Tatum says without missing a beat, already heading for the scooter with him in tow. He pats my shoulder on the way, the message already received loud and clear. *Guess I'm staying.*

"You don't mind, right?" Tatum asks as she slips on a helmet and swings her leg over the back of the Vespa. I'm about to answer, but the beauty next to me replies instead. "What about our girls' trip?"

"It's going swimmingly, don't you think?" Tatum points at Harrison and silently mouths, "He's so hot." For Harrison's ears, she adds, "We're turning lemons into lemonade."

The beauty next to me exhales and then frowns, her eyes

reflecting her change in mood from the fun-loving girl I met inside. The sun shines in her eyes just before she rolls them. "Swell. All we need is vodka."

"Thought you didn't know much about alcohol?"

Rocking her hand back and forth, she laughs. "I'm no expert, but I've had a few lemon drops in my life." Looking right at me, she asks, "Have you had one before?"

"No."

"You should." It's as if she's forgotten about her friend altogether. "They're really good."

"Maybe we can get one together."

"Maybe." Her grin is sure and quite stunning. But that grease . . . I should really tell her about the smudge on her face, but it's sort of cute how unsuspecting she is of the mess.

Harrison backs out of the parking space and stops in front of me. "I'll see you back in the room."

"Yeah. Sure." I'm not bothered he's taking off with a chick. That's how we've always operated, not giving each other a hard time over a hookup.

Just as he pulls to the edge of the parking lot, Tatum motions to her friend's temple area, but then says, "I promise to make it up to you back in the city."

When they blend into traffic and travel around the corner, we're left in their dust. I'm more interested in the blonde next to me. She stares down the street with her hand as a sun visor and then shifts to the curb, sitting down on it. She laughs at some inside joke, then turns to me. "Guess you're stuck with me."

I sit down next to her. "There are worse people to be stuck with, I suppose," I reply, gently nudging her like we're old friends.

"You sure about that?" Her smile breaks through the

disappointed façade she briefly tried on for size, the other one never quite fitting her natural disposition. Nor her drunk one. "For all you know, I could be a nightmare to deal with."

"I'm fairly certain I'll be okay. You're not a serial killer, are you?"

Offense colors her expression but is whisked away just as quickly. "*Me?*" Her fingers swirl near my nose. "I'm not the one with that boy-next-door face."

Capturing one of her fingers, I hold it hostage and grin at her. "You say that as if it's a bad thing."

"Handsome guys are always so cocky, too."

"All I heard was handsome."

I'm granted another front-row seat to an eye roll, this one more dramatic and aimed at me. "Of course, you did." Her eyes lock on something lower. "That Omega watch was probably stolen from a victim. If it's real . . ."

"Let me get this straight. Your serial killer radar is going off because I'm wearing a *real* Omega watch? I'm no expert in detection, but I'm pretty sure that's not a reliable method." I reluctantly release her finger, but I hold onto the fact that she never once tried to pull away.

"Money is always a dead giveaway for lady killers."

"I thought we were talking about serial killers."

"Lady-killers. *Serial killers.* Tomato. *Tamahto.*" She nods. "It's all the same thing."

I chuckle. "I'm still curious about money being a give-away. Care to expound on that train of thought?"

"Money makes people mean."

"Do you know this firsthand or something you've surmised?"

"A little of both. Anyway, what other method would you suggest I figure out who the bad guys are? I can't ask because what serial killer would ever admit they're a serial killer?" The way she angles her head to the side as if I'm going to give her a meaningful response to this insanity causes me to sweat under the collar. Just a little. *I'd hate to disappoint her.*

"Serial killer conversation aside," I start, holding my hand out. "I forgot to introduce myself. I'm Nick."

She slips her hand against mine, and our fingers wrap around each other. Ah, there's the gorgeous smile from before. "Hi, Nick. I'm Natalie."

3

Natalie

I didn't know sex was possible through a handshake, but I might need a cigarette after this one. *And I don't smoke.*

Until that moment, I was content calling him Mr. Smug and Sexy. But temptation has a name, and it couldn't be more perfect. *Nick.*

Nicholas.

Nicolai.

Domi*nick.*

Although now I'm curious about the nickname, I exhale before glancing into those brown and golden-tinged eyes that made me feel safe inside the bar. I'd like to say he was better looking in the cover of the dimly lit bar, but nope. He's still ridiculously attractive in broad daylight, if not more so.

Pulling my gaze away, I ask, "So now that we have that out of the way, are you a serial killer or what?"

He bursts out laughing, rocking back on the curb and sadly causing our hands to fall from each other. I fidget awkwardly with my belt, not knowing what to do with my hand in his hand's absence. Continuing to chuckle, he says, "I'm not. What about you? Kill anyone, Natalie?"

"I have the perfect alibis regarding a few exes, but I never followed through." I wink.

When his chuckles wane, he says, "I'm not sure if you're kidding or not."

"Guess you'll have to take a chance." I rest my palms on the concrete behind me. "Between us, my best friend just topped my list of future victims." Suddenly feeling the need to stand, I pace a few feet and then return to him and prop my foot up on the curb. "You don't have to worry about me, Nick. In fact, I can wait for the rental company to show up all by my lonesome if you want to take off." I check the time on my watch and scowl, irritated when I see I still have some steps to cover to reach my daily goal.

"What's wrong?" he asks, standing up.

He's tall. I noticed that inside, but with him up on the curb and me standing lower on the parking lot, he's absurdly giant. Even my brother would be jealous of Nick's height, and my brother is no slouch. I reply, "It's dumb."

Seeing fingers flex reminds me I've caught what appears to be Nick trying to touch me several times. I would have karate-chopped his wrist, but I laugh, knowing that's a lie I can't even tell myself. I was forced out of his arms inside, so I'd wholeheartedly welcome a repeat.

Or maybe . . . Could I pull off a legit fall when standing on steady ground? Is it worth the potential injury if he doesn't catch me this time? Or even worse, thinks I'm a lost cause of a klutz? Will it matter what I think about him catching me if his lips are on mine? Or even better, he kisses me so good that I can't think at all?

Even though he's great with his hands, I blow off the crazy idea.

"Natalie?"

"Yes?" I look up into his persuasive eyes, wondering if I should put my devious plan into action. I bet his lips would make the fall worth the embarrassment.

When he continues to look at me as though he's in on some secret, which he isn't, or there's no way he would still be standing here knowing I've been daydreaming about mauling him and that mouth of his, I add, "Seriously, if you take off now you might make the party before they depart."

"I don't mind waiting."

Shrugging, I add, "It's your night."

"Nah. I'm not missing out. Actually . . ." He steps down next to me. "I think I got the better option for the night."

"Beats end of the stick. Also, if memory serves, you weren't given an option but rather a babysitting job."

His laughter bellows from his gut. "I could say so much, but . . ." He reaches toward me again—just enough to notice but not close enough to touch. Then he retreats with worry creasing his expression. "You've got—"

"Stars in my eyes? They always shine like this when I drink. Speaking of, we can wait inside and have another drink."

Glancing over his shoulder when a couple of guys come tripping out—boisterous and crude—I remember hearing them remarking on the size of the waitress's breasts. "They're horrid."

Nick turns, blocking me in his shadow. I can't see the other men, but I can hear them. My stomach tightens, but I find safety in the fact they can't see me either. "I can think of a better word." He doesn't share that word, but I get the gist.

This time, I let his hand caress my cheek, the pad of his

thumb rubbing my temple. The little gesture doesn't seem to satisfy him, but it does me, and I move closer. He asks, "How are you feeling?" His voice is as warm as his touch.

On the verge of sobering up entirely too soon for my liking, I wouldn't mind having an excuse to touch him right back. Alas, even under the influence of a few drinks, I remember my manners. "I shouldn't have drunk so much."

"Shots taken under peer pressure never end well."

The other men have carried on to the next bar, and Nick and I are alone again. Considering how busy this place is, I'm starting to feel lucky I've been given the time to sober up. The last thing I want to do is throw up in front of him.

Nick—catcher of drunk women, flat-tire determiner with all-around movie star good looks. Among everything I've already learned about him, I can't help but note his looks. What can I say besides he's hot?

When I was in his arms, I was fairly certain he was the devil sent to make me sin. Now I'm starting to think he's my guardian angel to keep me safe. I might be a little disappointed. Giggling, I add, "Truer words have never been spoken. I'm tipsy and hungry."

"Ah, those usually go hand in hand." Holding up his phone, he offers, "I can order food?"

I'm already licking my lips from the very thought of a big burger with fries. "It's okay. Thanks, though." He yanks his gaze away and stares at some nearby golf carts like they've offended him.

I try to fix that frown. "Since we have time to kill—"

He eyes me suspiciously. "Kill?"

I laugh. "Can we end the serial killer thing? Does *passing* time work better for you?"

"Much better."

He's easy to talk to, and I like that. "I kind of embarrassed myself earlier."

Shifting beside me, he keeps his eyes on our surroundings. "We all fall on our asses every once in a while." He angles his chin my way. "But you got up and dusted yourself off like a champ."

"I appreciate the vote of confidence and motivational speech."

The sweetest lopsided grin slides into place, the right side of his mouth kissing a cute dimple above it. "It was all you."

"A man who can give me credit," I reply sarcastically. "That's a first." My gut twists and not from the alcohol in my system. I've gone too far. "I shouldn't have said that."

"You wouldn't have said it if you hadn't experienced it. Sucks you had to deal with that behavior."

Rubbing my temple, I sigh. "I hate when I get emotional."

"Let's blame the alcohol and not worry about it."

I may have fixated on his looks so much that I overlooked his kindness. Inside the bar and out here, he's been nothing but a gentleman. When he grasps my hand and pulls me against him, a few heartbeats are lost in the heat of the connection. My shoulders fall, and I look up at him, sucking in a staggered breath. "I—"

"Almost got run over."

"What?"

His gaze pivots to my right, and I turn in his arms to see a golf cart skidding to a stop, not even a foot from where I was standing thirty seconds prior. Whipping my attention back to Nick, I say, "You're a regular hero, saving the day and me again."

"I wouldn't say regular. Let's try on super for size."

"*Super*hero?"

"You're right. That might be giving me too much credit. The guy was driving like a maniac."

I'm not sure what the difference is between an everyday hero and a superhero or how we even got tangled in this conversation in the first place. *Oh, yeah . . .* The guy bent over the flat tire says, "Busy night. I've had three flats, and one of our best Vespas ended up in Catalina Harbor. Not good." He looks at us. "I'll take a look, but I don't have any spare tires, so I might not be able to fix it on the fly." *Great. Just what I need.*

Big hands still protectively cover my forearms, which shifts my focus back to Nick again. "Can I blame the rum?" I ask, laughing lightly.

"For?" His answer is for only my ears, an alluring tone that has me lowering my guard.

"I thought you were going to kiss me. *Again.*" I slip out of his hold and roll my hand. "Like inside, which might have been more wishful thinking on my part, but out here, it seemed like the perfect setup for a kiss under the stars of Catalina to set a mood."

"Which mood are we trying to set? I'll see if I can arrange for your fantasy to come true."

"Fantasy?" My voice pitches. I realize I'm doing exactly what I'm not supposed to be doing. Falling prey to a great face and hot body has gotten me in trouble more times than I care to admit. So I won't admit anything to anyone, other than Tatum, of course, since she's usually with me. This trip was about having fun, but not *that* kind of fun. Throwing my arms up as a self-built barrier, I continue, "No fantasy over here. Nope. No mood. No setting. Nothing needs to be arranged. I'm good." I shove my hands out farther. "*So* good. You don't even know how good I am."

Narrowed eyes are trained on me as if I'm about to make a fast getaway. I just might, actually. It might be the only thing that saves me. "Are you okay?" he asks.

"Not really, but don't worry. It's me, not you."

"That's the first time I've heard that from someone I'm not even dating."

Raising an eyebrow, I smile because it's insane to think someone like him has experienced the same thing as me before. I mean, look at him. "You've been dumped with that line, too?"

He runs his thumb over his bottom lip, still staring unabashedly at me, but his chuckling is confusing. "No," he replies. "But—"

"It's busted. Can't fix this one, miss." The Vespa guy eyes me, and I think he waggles his eyebrows, but I'll give him the benefit of the doubt that he didn't. "Want a ride?" he asks.

His eagerness has me questioning if I want to get tangled up in that. Short answer: *I don't.* "I'm good. Thanks."

"Okay, then. Have a good night." He speeds off in the golf cart, leaving me standing here trying my best not to make it awkward for Nick.

Peeking over at him, I say, "I mean it. You don't have to worry about me. Seriously. I can call a car, or I don't know, hitch my way back."

"I can drive you back." The words rush from his mouth as if the universe's very existence hinges on them. I force my gaze away and eye the lone working scooter—turquoise with chrome accents—because it's too easy to get lost in his eyes otherwise.

He walks over, taking the helmet from the broken-down scooter, and offers it to me. "Even though you don't trust two wheels, you can trust me. I promise to drive safely."

I don't want to leap into his arms, but I'm close to jumping and straddling his body. Alas, I control my desires. "If you're sure?"

A smug grin covers his perfect face. "I'm sure."

Taking the helmet, I hug it in my arms. Tatum thinks she's won the Super Bowl with Harrison, but I'm happily grinning because she left me with a consolation prize that feels more like winning the jackpot. "We're staying at Catalina Vista. It's just down the coast from here."

Bellowing laughter overrides the end of my sentence, and he says, "That's where we're staying."

"Looks like it might not be such a coincidence, after all."

"I'm thinking it was destiny."

"Whoa. Let's not get too far ahead of ourselves, cowboy. We're still strangers."

"You're a handful, I can tell." He gets on the scooter and lifts the kickstand before righting it. "Front or back?"

"I've been called many things by guys. Handful doesn't even rank in order of the bad."

"Fuck those guys." The anger that punctuates the curse word . . . well, you guessed it—it's unexpected and definitely a turn-on.

I grin, feeling as if he just defended my honor, and pull the helmet over my head. "Back."

What? Did you miss the part where I said he was stupidly handsome, and he's been utterly charming? Add in the honor part, and I'm already halfway gone. So what do you expect me to do? Call a car? Not on my life, literally, when I have a hot guy wanting to give me a ride. My inner voice yells, "*Get on the bike.*"

The sight of Nick sends a thrill up my spine, and the thought of holding onto this big hunk of a man is sobering in a good way. It's not every day that a girl gets to go on an adventure with a hot stranger, even if it's on two wheels and not the safety of the recommended four.

My Audrey Hepburn-loving heart squeezes with excitement that my California version of *Roman Holiday* is coming true. Although the perfect chignon and makeup elude me, as well as Audrey's grace being thrown out the window, this fantasy apparently includes helmet hair and a hunky man. God, I sound like my mother.

Mental note: Never use *hunky* again.

Angling to look at me over his shoulder, he asks, "You think you can handle me, Natalie?"

"Don't worry about me, Nick. I can handle you."

"Hold on tight."

I do, as tight as I can, closing my eyes while pressed to his back. It's then that I realize my inner voice, *the responsible one*, never stood a chance against this man.

4

Natalie

Nick smells divine.

Does he have no flaws? I don't know if I'm enamored by his perfection or annoyed by it, but he smells too good to worry about the rest. With my nose stuck to his back, *technically inhaling*, he smells of bergamot and musk mingling with masculinity and great sex.

I cling to him, the wind awakening my skin just as Nick's exhilarated my insides. *I'm not sleeping with him*, I remind myself. I'm on a self-induced love embargo after my last relationship went awry. Anyway, I've never been one for vacation flings, preferring to hook up with someone I could see again. Of course, I hadn't met Nick before either, *sooooo* . .

Stop overthinking. I can hear Tatum telling me those words herself. Enjoy the ride as we zip back to the hotel. I might be on two wheels, but Nick keeps his word and drives in a way that makes me feel safe.

I straighten my back and look around the beautiful

island as we zip around it, but I keep my arms wrapped around him.

Glimmering like diamonds under the late afternoon sunlight, the tips of the ocean waves are mesmerizing. If I could bottle this sight with the wind kissing my skin to gift, I'd make millions. Not a video knock-off. The vacation itself has to be added to my catalog. Not right now though, so I put business aside and enjoy the view myself.

I couldn't ask for a better end to summer, and even though we ventured around the island today, it's been nice to relax at the pool, read a book, and drink while dancing last night away. I honestly don't care about another party on some yacht in the harbor when staring at this stunning sight.

The ride back to the hotel flies by too quick, and as soon as we pull up to the front, a valet greets us before we can even remove our helmets. While Nick tips him, I take my helmet off and fluff my hair, and then drop my hands to my sides like I wasn't being a total girl wanting to look good for him when he comes around the scooter. "Ready?" he asks.

"Actually, I'm not ready," I mumble under my breath because Nick is more than a hot guy I met at a bar.

"What was that?"

As we walk toward the door, my stomach fills with the impending goodbye, and I reluctantly reply, "Yes." Just inside the hotel doors, I stop and look around the bustling lobby. When I turn back to him, awkwardness has become a third wheel. "This has been . . ."

"This *has* been . . ." He looks down and starts laughing. A shyness has crept over his features, and his eyes find mine again. "I don't know what to say, Natalie. You?" I shake my head. He shoves his hands in his pockets and lets a few seconds pass before he rocks back on his heels. "So, we're here."

"We are." I mimic him by dipping my fingers into my pockets. "Although I had concerns, we arrived safely despite the two wheels. Thanks for that."

"Thanks for trusting me with your life."

"Two times in one day. If we're not careful, this could become a habit." When a couple walking arm in arm cuts a little close to me, I move closer to Nick. Waiting for them to pass, I keep an eye over my shoulder.

When we're alone again, he says, "Would that be such a bad thing?"

His eyes are darker in the shadows of this space between —left to the parking lot and right to the lobby—but I can still see the playfulness in the golden edges. "So far, it hasn't been."

"Give me enough time, and I'm sure I'll blow it."

"You say stuff like that, but I have a feeling that like earlier, the great Nick doesn't blow much." My hand flies to cover my mouth. Through slits of my fingers, I wince. "That did not come out how I wanted at all."

Through a restrained chuckle, he asks, "How'd you want it to come?"

I hold my finger up. "I, uh." His twist of words causes my breath to stagger, and I bite my lip. I'm not even sure he was insinuating anything, but my body reacts like he most certainly was. I cross my arms over my chest to keep them from grabbing hold of him, clinging to him like I've become a regular fixture around his parts—a new freckle or I'd even settle for a blemish, but he clearly doesn't have any of those. "Well, it's been—"

"Are we already back to impersonal goodbyes again? I was hoping for—"

Screw it. I move in, ready to show him just how personal I can be. "For something more personal." Throwing my arms around his neck, I close my eyes just as I plant my lips on his. But when nothing happens—not a peck, not a great lip embrace that leads to a tango of the tongues—I jerk back and find his eyes fixed on mine but warm like melted chocolate. *Delicious.* Except that rejection crawls under my skin and starts setting up residence.

Just when I step back, he grabs my arms, capturing me before I can escape my humiliation. "I didn't expect that."

"Pfft." I try to blow it off. I may not be able to run from him, but I can look everywhere else around him and search for cobwebs in the corners of the ceiling, a crack in the plastered walls or please Lord, give me the strength not to care that he didn't want to kiss me. "Oh God, yeah, no worries. I didn't either."

He tilts his head, and the slightest of lines creases between his brows. Even curiosity can't detract from his good looks, though. And damn those dimples that appear out of nowhere. "You don't have to be embarrassed, Natalie. I just—"

"Yeah, I just . . . too." *Wait, that makes no sense.* "You know, I think it's best if I go now. This weekend isn't about hooking up with a straight from the pages of my favorite magazine model just because I fell purposely into his arms. "

"Purposely?"

"Ignore me. I'm babbling."

"You're impossible to ignore." Speaking of impossibilities, he's hard to read. Was that a compliment or an insult?

I'm not sure. That's my cue to exit. Thumbing over my shoulder, I add, "This was a girls' trip." I snort-laugh, not even meaning to make a joke, but that one just fell into my lap. "Pun intended. Get it? I'm a girl, and I tripped?"

I like that he laughs when I'm trying to be entertaining, even if I'm not that funny. "I got it. Glad I could be a part of that trip. Pun intended." He winks, and yeah, take me out of the oven because I'm done—hot and ready to be eaten. Though I'm getting a little ahead of myself with the last part.

Ticking through the *pros* of why I should be walking away—early morning flight, the no-sex clause I agreed to, and him smelling so good that I know I'd lose all my sensibilities in a night of passion. Though that last one should go on the *con* list.

I back away, begrudgingly distancing myself, and let my gaze trail after a bellman. Two words: Love. Embargo. I clap and take another step back. "Alrighty then." Pushing my hand forward and raising my chin, I say, "It's been interesting, Nick."

"That it has." The heat and the spark of electricity between us has my heart kicking into gear. "So, this is our farewell?"

"It's probably best, don't you think?"

"Best for whom?"

Have I ever said how sexy I find it when men know how to use an objective pronoun? My knees get weak, but I manage to steady myself . . . *by latching onto his arm.* "Sorry," I reply breathlessly. "I think the alcohol has gone to my head. I should have taken you up on the offer of food."

"It's not too late. Offer still stands."

Soooo tempting.

I knead his bicep like a kitten on a scratch post and then take another step back, knowing the rum is starting to overrun all rational thought, or worse, control my libido. Only bad things happen when I follow my hormones instead of listening to my head. "I appreciate it, but I should call it a night. Early flight and all."

"That's too bad."

His gaze lingers on me before glancing over his shoulder. "I'm down this hall."

"I'm down that one."

"Opposite directions."

"Seems that way." Dread begins to deteriorate the thrill he had me feeling. I know what I should be doing, but my feet refuse to walk away. I sigh, staring down at the gold threads running through the heel of my shoes. "Yeah, I guess so."

I like that neither of us makes a quick escape, but I wish he'd give me a reason to stay. I mean other than asking to buy me dinner and keep me company. *Ugh.* I'm really starting to hate my responsible side. I swallow down my apprehension and say, "Goodbye, Nick."

The distance grows between us, but he doesn't make a move to leave. "Goodbye."

A beat or two passes before I turn to leave, walking with purpose down the corridor.

"Hey, Natalie?"

Happiness bubbles inside me, and I whip around. "Yes?"

"I'm in room 203 if you're ever in the neighborhood or need a lift."

It's so easy for him to make me smile. Not sure how he does it, but I can't let alcohol dictate my decisions. Nothing good ever comes of that, including two ex-boyfriends I wish I'd never met.

With Nick, I may not be drunk, but I do wish I'd met him under different circumstances. "I appreciate that, but I don't think I'm getting on two wheels again anytime soon."

Smugly curling in an arm, he smirks. "I meant me." It's low-key bragging, but with him, I can let it slide because if I was giggling before, now I'm full-on blushing.

My chest gives me away with heavy breaths. "I'll keep that in mind. Thanks again for the ride," I reply, memorizing that grin that gravitates to meet the dimple in his cheek and the scruff that took a solid day or two to grow. The windswept brown curls that formed from the helmet are tempting me to run my fingers through them. He's just so . . . *gah*.

When I look at him, really look at him like I am now, I know I should be embarrassed by my rejected kiss, but I think I'm the lucky one now. If he'd returned it, I'd still be lost in the feel of his fullness pressed to mine, our lips sating a desire I feel even now.

No, he won't be easy to forget.

No one-night stands with hot guys.

No man-crazy crap anymore for me. I'll leave that to Tatum. I need to focus on myself and my needs this time around. Exhaling, I'm set in my stance and start walking again. "Good night."

"Suddenly, it's not feeling so good."

I turn back, too hopeful, considering nothing can come of this. *Damn those dimples.* I knew better than to look. "What isn't?"

"The parting ways thing we're doing." The smile disappears as he looks down, seeming to search the Saltillo tiles under our feet. When his eyes find mine again, he says, "I'll see you around." It's not a question or an invitation. Just a statement put out there to settle in the air between us.

"Look on the bright side. Next time, we won't be strangers."

A light chuckle vibrates through him. "Yeah. Next time . . ."

Nodding, I wave. "See you around." We both turn away at the same time, heading in opposite directions—in the hotel and in life. Despite the burning desire to run after him, I don't. Going our separate ways is best. I'll order food and can start packing. Tatum will be back before I know it, then tomorrow, we'll catch our early flight back to Manhattan.

A quiet dinner.

A glass of wine on the patio.

Then to bed before we trek back home.

There's definitely no need to tangle a man into my plan and complicate my life. Who cares about dimples and scruffy jaws, sinful eyes and those big hands?

Not me.

Nope.

I stop in front of the door, but instead of relief, panic sets in. "Oh, no." Patting my back pockets, I search for anything that will get me into this room— the key, my phone, ID. I don't even have money or a credit card. "*No. No. No. No. No.*" I slam my hands against the wood. "Ugh!"

Tatum! *Damn her.*

I carried our stuff this afternoon when she insisted a purse ruined the look of her bikini. Tonight, she carried mine since I didn't have a purse that wouldn't get in the way of our carefree fun. A lot of good that did me. It's so out of the way it's on a yacht somewhere in the harbor.

A couple comes around the corner, drawing my attention with their laughter. I'm not exactly lost in the desert, stranded with no hope of finding civilization. But before I get wound up even more in that direction, I head for the front desk. I'll be in the room in five, ten minutes tops. I rest my hands on the cold stone counter in front of an attendant, my gaze dipping to her name tag. "Hi, Uma, my traitor of a roommate took off for a yacht party, leaving me without a key to get into the room or even a phone to call her."

She smiles so sweetly. "This isn't the first time I've heard of that happening, but it usually ends with them losing the key in the harbor. The good news is I can help. Name and room number please?"

"Natalie St. James. Room 351."

After tapping a few keys, she narrows her eyes on the screen. "All right. I see your name right here, Ms. St. James. I'll just need to see your ID."

"Oh. Well, I don't have that either. See, it was my best friend's turn to carry our stuff in her purse since I carried it to the pool." Resting my arms on the counter, I laugh from the memory. "It's actually very funny because we were out shopping for a little purse for me, but then we came across this bar, and if they put the straw hat on your head, you have to drink."

"Sounds like Later Gators."

I snap. "Yes, that's the place. *Any*how, we're sharing a suite, but the Vespa got a flat, and there were two guys so sweet and helpful." Leaning forward, I whisper, "She went with Harrison to the party, and I returned to the hotel with Nick, though I hate two-wheeled anything. Although I didn't hate being on two wheels with him. In fact—"

"Sounds very eventful, Ms. St. James—"

"You can call me Natalie," I offer since we're bonding and all.

"I'm sorry, Natalie. I can't give you a key without seeing ID. Is there anything else I can help you with today?" Despite straightening my back, my shoulders still fall under defeat as I stare at her like we're speaking different languages, and I don't have a translation app. Her smile never falters, though, making me suspicious. Suddenly, I don't think she's as sweet as she appears. She adds, "It's hotel policy for the safety of our guests."

"But I'm a guest."

Her smile zips into a straight line, and then she holds her finger up when the phone starts ringing. "My apologies again." She directs her attention toward answering the phone and turns a cold shoulder to me.

Leaving the desk, I wander to the lobby lounge. I only stand there a moment before I not only feel out of place among all the couples but my stomach also growls, garnering unwanted attention—mine to be precise.

When a certain man's room number floats through my head, I begin to believe it would be perfectly okay for me to barge in on him. *Would it?* He did invite me, after all.

Not two minutes later, I find myself standing in front of room 203. Staring at the san serif silver numbers, I take a deep breath, readying myself for battle. That's what this will be—a war waged between what I shouldn't do and what I really want to do. My hand is raised, and I knock three times before I can change my mind. The pinpoint of light seen in the peephole goes dark, and then the door swings open.

Met with his welcoming grin, I shrug. "I was in the neighborhood."

5

Nick

"Don't get any ideas." I'm poked in the chest as she passes by, and then adds, "I won't stay long." *That's disappointing.*

"Come on in," I reply sarcastically to the back of her head. Letting myself enjoy the view over my shoulder, I take in her body—the toned legs dipping out of her shorts and her obvious curves under that baggy linen shirt. "You won't be here long enough for me to get ideas? Too late for that, sweetheart."

She tries not to give me the pleasure of seeing her smile, but it was worth the effort when she turns back and reveals it. "Tatum hasn't returned, and she has the key. You don't mind if I wait here, do you? You're much more interesting than a lobby full of lovey-dovey couples."

"No problem. Lovey-dovey?" I kick the door closed and follow her into the villa's living area.

She stops and looks around before turning back to me. She tilts her head, her hair flowing in soft waves over her shoulder, and she smiles. "You know, making out, holding hands, kissing, dressed up for dinner or drinks. Basically, couples who look more like they're having an affair than together for any length of time."

"Interesting observation and assumption."

"Listen, Nick. Real love is for fairy tales. I can name a dozen couples who make things work for financial reasons or emotional stability, for the kids, or to fight the fear of loneliness. They don't put affection on display or make a production when their wife or husband enters a room." She shrugs. I'm not sure if it's a fleeting emotion of sadness or resignation I see cross her blue eyes, but it doesn't belong there.

"So what you're saying is you're a romantic?" I quirk a smirk and give her a little wink.

"Yeah, I'm just waiting for my knight in shining armor to show up and whisk me away on his white horse." She's almost convincing by the longing heard in her tone and far-off gaze.

"Where would you go?"

As if the spell is still cast, she replies, "To our castle, of course, silly. And guess what?"

"What?"

"We'd live happily ever after." Her smile is lost under the admission as if a thief has stolen her joy.

Leaning against a corner of the room, I cross my arms over my chest, finding it fascinating how animated she can be one minute and then introspective the next. "That's very romantic for a non-romantic."

"What can I say? A girl can still dream even when her feet are planted in reality." She cuts over to the bar and grabs a bottle of water. "Can I have this? I can order more for your room later."

Although she's already drinking it, I say, "It's all yours,

and what kind of host would I be if I made a guest restock the supply?"

Natalie's already moved on toward the terrace. "We have an incredible view from our room," she says, "but wow, the ocean is endless on this side of the hotel." Excitement colors her expression when she reaches for the handle of the over-sized glass door. Over her shoulder, she asks, "May I?"

"Of course. Make yourself at . . . well, it's not my home." I shrug. "But a home away from home." She smiles. God, she has a great smile, and I've enjoyed every last one of them.

"A home for a few days. Sorry for ruining it by inter-rupting whatever you were doing. First at the bar and now at the hotel. It's almost like we're becoming a thing."

"Guess we were meant to meet."

"So I could barge into your life three times? You're very optimistic, Nick." She slides the door open.

"There was no barging either time." *Quite the opposite.* "The last time, in fact, I held the door wide open."

"And you're polite enough to give cover for a girl who can't hold her rum." She sends a wink my way before firing off a list of aggravations—*stupid fashion, Tatum, purses, the hotel's response*—which solidifies my thought that, sadly, she didn't come knocking willingly. Missing a few pieces to this puzzle, I ask, "Why couldn't you get into your room?"

"I'm blaming my ex-friend Uma for that," she says with a roll of her eyes. I chuckle but bite my tongue. "Can you see anywhere on my body where I could possibly hide my ID?"

She's giving me permission to check her out, so that's what I do.

Slowly.

Taking my time, I start at the top and let my gaze slide over her until I reach the bottom.

Twice.

By the second tour of her curves, she's squirming a little, which makes me chuckle again. "Do you really want me to answer that, Natalie? Because that means I need to check every inch of you."

"You mean again? Because you just did it twice," she whips back, but I also catch her blushing. I wouldn't mind touching those cheeks to see how soft and warm they really are. She waves her arms, and then her energy deflates and they land hard at her sides. "Anyway, no ID. No room key. No phone. So, here I am."

Typically, I don't rely on astrology or New Age beliefs, but she's different from the other women I normally meet. I want to have sex with her. Sure, *naturally*. But I kind of don't mind the lead-up, the foreplay to it with her. Smirking, I tip my head down and run my fingers through my hair.

Okay, she doesn't make a ton of sense, but she's entertaining, nonetheless. The earlier far-off look in her eyes is now focused, the entire universe appearing to weigh down her shoulders as she stares into the distance, and she asks, "Think we can see the boat from here?"

Keeping some distance between us, I rest my forearms on the railing, giving her room for the thoughts hijacking her attention. She leans far enough over the railing like she just might be able to touch the ocean. Or at least one of the boats in the harbor.

"No. It was going to cruise around the island." The distant break in the waves keeps my eyes captive until I look farther out to sea, my gaze reaching the cruise ships on the horizon.

"Where are you from?"

I turn to her. "Why so serious?" I'm given a shrug, so I ask, "Should we get to know each other, Natalie?"

She laughs softly, turning her gaze my way. "We should,

Nick." The K crashes on the end of her tongue as if she's just given in but wants to make sure I'm aware.

I'm aware of her. *All of her.* She's wholly entertaining but has so many layers left to unfold. "I'm from LA, but don't hold it against me." I chuckle, inwardly shaking my head at myself. I'm making a fool of myself. *Why the hell did I say that*? God, I used to have game. Where has it gone? Lost after years of having my nose buried in books.

Angling my way, she says, "You know, I've been thinking."

"That can be dangerous."

A soft smile returns. "Especially when you're tipsy." She was definitely drunk, but I'll give her tipsy now as she begins to sober. "I don't think we properly introduced ourselves."

"No?"

Shaking her head, she purses her lips. "What do you say we start over?"

"I like our beginning."

This time, she laughs, and when the joy reaches her eyes, the blue sparkles like the ocean in the afternoon. The wind stirs her blond hair around her shoulders, and the layers seem to play favorites with where they fall. Her tan is deep enough to have settled into her skin long before her vacation. The delicate clang of the bracelets around her wrists reminds me of the wind chimes at my parents' beach house.

Natalie is captivating—fine features highlighting a heart-shaped face. I journey from her eyes and then take a quick slide down the gentle slope of her nose anchored by full pink lips. Being in LA, I know women who've paid a lot of money for the natural beauty that Natalie possesses.

A desire to kiss her surges through me, so I turn away,

distracting myself with live music drifting from somewhere down below to quell the craving. It doesn't work. I still regret not kissing her earlier. Don't think about it. Just talk. "And you?"

"I think we were born enemies. I'm a New Yorker through and through."

"Eh, there's no East Coast versus West Coast rivalry here. New York has seasons. We have sunshine. You have the Yankees. We have Hollywood. Pros and cons to both. I guess it's just what you're used to."

"I love the beaches on the Pacific, but we have the Hamptons."

"You have Katz's Delicatessen, but we have In-N-Out Burgers. It all evens out."

She scoots her foot over and taps the side of my shoe. "I've never had In-N-Out. Am I missing out?"

"Yeah, you're definitely missing out."

Sipping her water, she glances toward the setting sun before lowering the bottle and saying, "Maybe the next time I'm in LA, you can take me."

"It's a date." She's shaking her head before the words leave my mouth.

"Actually, I've sworn off dating, so let's call it a meetup."

"You're very specific with your no's. No dating? No ideas. No—"

"No sex." She's not snippy about it but more matter-of-fact. Then something comes over her, and she reaches over, resting her hand on mine like we're old friends. "Sorry if that came out wrong. That was more of a reminder for myself."

Catching her hand before it retreats, I hold it between us. "Am I that tempting?" I lean over and whisper, "C'mon, you can tell me the truth."

Her head sways to the side and then returns to its rightful place, her eyes never leaving mine. "Honestly?"

"Honesty is always the best policy." Even the soon-to-be lawyer in me doesn't believe that everything is so black and white. There's a lot of gray area to rule out before picking a team. When she gently returns her hand to the railing and her gaze to the ocean, the missing connection is felt under my skin. She carries a world of emotions in the depths of her blue eyes, and I hate that the option to read them has been taken away.

She nods.

Grinning smugly, I nudge her. "I'll take that as a yes. You're not so bad yourself, by the way."

She crosses the divide to poke me in the stomach, which makes me chuckle. I clench my abs to make it worth her while. *Of course.* She says, "I bet you say that to all the girls." It's not lost on me how a look of approval flashes across her face.

I might have been enamored with her the first time I looked into her eyes but getting to know the real Natalie feels like a reward. That she's comfortable sharing more about herself is the cherry on top.

There are hints of her socialite status, something I'm familiar with back home, though she doesn't appear to carry her worries in bags around with her—*designer or not*. She's opened her up in ways the rum hid prior. My stomach rumbles, and I rub my stomach. "I'm starved. I was about to order food before a *certain someone* barged into my room."

Laughing, she says, "And here you had me believing I'd made your night better."

"You did. So much better. I'm glad you're here, Natalie."

She moves in such a seductive way, sliding her hand

along the railing before she turns with the grace of a ballet dancer. "So am I."

Her eyes flash to mine, knocking the breath from me. If she can capture me with a look, I can only imagine what else she has in store for me. I clear my throat. "Would you like something to eat?"

"I could eat. You left me craving—"

"Touché."

"Ha! Actually, I was referring to the In-N-Out talk. I'd love a burger, cooked medium with all the toppings."

"Lettuce, tomato—"

"Everything. Even the ones that cost extra." Her little wink is cute, though the sassy side of it is more dominant. "*Oh!* And I want a mound of fries," she says, demonstrating with her hands. "Not just a side. A whole plate dedicated to them."

I'm almost afraid to ask. "Anything else?"

"Extra ketchup on the burger and for the fries. A soda—"

"Let me guess. Large?"

She nods excitedly. I can't wait to watch her eat a meal that could feed a linebacker.

"Got it." I go inside and call room service. It's then I realize that I've held the key to her presence in my pocket the whole time. What can I say? She's very distracting. I find myself smiling while watching her nose around the terrace.

When I hang up and fill the doorway, I debate for a hard few seconds, but I know telling her is the right thing to do. "I can call Harrison for you. He could let Tatum know you're locked out of the room." I regret the moment the words leave my mouth because, if I'm honest, I don't want that. If she takes me up on the offer, she'd be gone before we have a chance to get to know each other. *And I definitely want to get to know her better.*

I hold the phone out for her, wanting to see something in her eyes that tells me I'm not alone in this desire to spend more time together.

Her bottom lip is tugged under her teeth as she appears to have her own internal debate. When her gaze glides up to mine, she says, "It's fine. It's a party on a yacht. They can't make it return to shore, so I'm good waiting. She'll return eventually."

Pocketing the phone, I reply, "The island is small. I'm sure they won't be gone all night." I'm tempted to text Harrison to stay away a little longer. "But we should have time to eat before they return."

"We can still eat together even if they do," she says. "And I bet the boat doesn't have burgers."

"No," I say, enchanted by the way she thinks. "I bet it doesn't."

"What should we do in the meantime?"

"Meantime is such an interesting phrase. The space between, the time difference between the past and the future." She comes toward me. "Whatever happens in the meantime doesn't count, right?" The words are subtle, but I hear the same desire to stay.

"It's time unaccounted for."

"Under that definition, *technically*, we can do whatever we want." Her eyes brighten with possibility as she looks into mine. "What should we do with this *meantime*?"

Stretching my arm out, I signal behind her. "A dip in the plunge pool?"

A smile tugs at the corners of her lips. She comes to the door and leans against the frame, her body silhouetted in the doorway with the sun shining behind her.

I could stay there, but she's a lot tempting herself. I move just inside the villa, and since she hasn't said anything, I throw out, "Or we can watch a movie?"

Crossing her arms over her chest, she says, "You sure are forgiving considering I invaded your villa."

"We're in the meantime, so is this even happening?"

She giggles. "Good point." Her chest rises and falls with a deep inhale and huff of an exhale. Standing up straight, she adds, "I should probably be up front with you—"

"About?"

Disappointment filters through her fine features. "I can't sleep with you."

Smirking, I reply, "I wasn't going to bed, so no worries."

"You know what I mean."

"You told me not to get any ideas the moment you walked in and mentioned no dating or sex, so I figured that included tonight as well."

"Very perceptive." When she turns to the patio, her hair swings through the air. As she walks back outside, she adds, "I'm on a love embargo, so even if I wanted to have sex with you, Nick, I can't."

Completely fascinated, I return to the terrace to do some invading of her personal space. "What you're saying is that you want to, but can't?"

She plucks the front of her shirt. "It's hot."

"It sure is." *Damn, is she ever.*

I could spend the rest of the night analyzing her reaction. I'm going into law for a reason. It's concrete, set, but flexible when approached from the right angle. Psychology isn't an arena that suits me or my analytical mind. Though I still find myself wanting to impress her, which is crazy considering we live on opposite sides of the country.

There's no future for us. And there's no tonight either

due to her love embargo, which is another Natalie curiosity. Yet I can't resist flirting with her. *Wanting her.*

Unlike her cute, drunken comments earlier that she does want me, finds me sexy, and even called me her dream man, she's changing as she sobers. Still gorgeous. But less assertive.

And that's when I realize what makes her different from other women I've dated and why I'm so intrigued by the woman in front of me. "I can't read you, Natalie."

Sitting on the chaise, she leans back and kicks her feet up. Closing her eyes, she soaks in the last of the sun's rays, and says, "I'm an open book, Nick. If you can't read me, you can ask me anything."

I sit on the chair beside her. "Where do we begin?"

6

Nick

I never found fries sexy . . . *until I met Natalie.*

If the sight of her lips wrapped around the thick cuts of potatoes didn't do the trick, then hearing her moan in pleasure did. I've been uncomfortably hard ever since.

The scent of burgers still lingers in the air, but I'm over the food, wanting to be under Natalie. Imagining her on top of me, riding me with that confidence she carries like a chip on her shoulder—potato pun intended—has me wishing for more time than we'll get tonight. So far, we've had just over an hour of banter, good food, and laughter. *When was the last time I just hung with a girl and enjoyed myself so thoroughly?* I have no idea, but it's been a while.

She slips out from the chair, leaving me sitting at the table. "Do you mind if I use the bathroom?"

"Of course not. Let me show you where it is."

As I enter the bedroom, a million thoughts race through my mind of what I'm supposed to do while she's in the bathroom.

Do I wait awkwardly on the bed or divert to the chair in the corner?

Do I turn on the TV or grab a book?

Do I return to the living room and wait out there?

Or maybe I'm overthinking this, and it's not a master plan to get me into the bedroom, but she just has to use the bathroom.

I literally have no ideas when it comes to her, so her command about not getting any is technically working. And I'm not upset by that fact. It's good to live by instinct, do what feels good and what comes naturally instead of being accountable to someone else's deadline.

"That's okay," she says. "I know where it is."

Oh, so yeah, definitely overthought that one. When she disappears into the other room, I stay on the couch and look around.

8:19.

Twiddling my thumbs, I start to wonder if Harrison and Tatum will barge in and ruin my night. Two hours ago, I would have welcomed the company, but now, I quite like the time alone with Natalie.

8:21.

I stand and walk to the open door of the terrace. Shoving my hands in my pockets, I think about the job with my dad and how happy he is that I'm joining the company.

8:22.

Taking the bar exam in three months will solidify his offer. Until then, I can't have a life. Embarrassing Corbin Christiansen is out of the question. So studying is my new pastime.

8:24.

It's only been five minutes, but damn, I'm beginning to miss her. I should check on her. Cutting through the living room, I ask, "Everything okay?"

"Peachy."

When I reach the doorway, I stop and grin. Lying on the bed with her ankles crossed and her hands behind her head as if she intends to stay awhile, she adds, "What took you so long?"

With a running start, I jump on the bed, causing her to bounce. Tucking my hands behind my head, I turn my head to face her. "I was trying to give you privacy."

"Always the gentleman. It's a great quality." We lie next to each other for a few minutes, no words exchanged—no pressure, no expectations. She makes it easy to find peace in the quiet.

I can't hear the hand on my watch ticking, but I feel every second of our time together. As if she can sense my nervous energy, she glances over at me. "Hope you don't mind me resting. Day-drinking and stuffing myself with carbs was not the best idea I've had. Not if I intend to stay awake, that is."

"What's your worst?"

"My worst idea was when I left Carlton Klein alone in my room."

I shift onto my side. "I'm going to need more details on that story."

"I had the worst crush on him in tenth grade. He stopped by one day to get help with French . . ." She laughs. "I should have seen that one coming. We frenched all right. And then I went to the kitchen to get sodas, and when I returned, he was gone."

"The kissing was that bad?"

"Him showing my panties to everyone who would look the next day was that bad." Her eyelids dip closed, and brows pull together as if the pain still exists inside her. We're lying here together like a line might have already been crossed, so I caress her cheek and gently try to ease the tension with the pad of my thumb.

Her skin is soft, and the rankle of her brow relaxes. She leans into it when she opens her eyes again. "He told everyone we had sex." I can't help but notice how shyness has crept into her tone, and it's softened.

"I'm sorry that happened to you."

"The girls didn't believe him, but the guys did." The little lines disappear, and a small smile emerges. "Silver lining was that no girl would go near him after that spectacle, and I never lacked for dates."

"All's fair in love and war."

"Trust me, there was no love lost between us. We spent the next three years as mortal enemies. Last I heard, he went to Berkley to get as far from the city as possible. I hope he got the fresh start he was searching for."

I pull my hand back, resting it between us. "Do you mean that?"

She nods. "We all deserve second chances. He used me to become popular. It backfired because the avenue he chose made him lose credibility. Lies would have done the trick. The prop made it a stunt. No girl would see that and think, 'hey, that's a guy I'd like to date.' Nope. All they imagine is their panties are the next on display."

"You have a good heart, Natalie. I'm glad Carlton Klein didn't change it."

Laughter rattles her shoulders. "He's done the least amount of damage to me. He was my worst idea, not my worst decision, but that's not a story for two strangers getting to know each other."

I roll onto my back again, staring at the beams crossing the ceiling. Taking a chance, I reach over and take her hand. "I made a few bad decisions in my life." Her fingers fold between mine. I glance over and add, "You're not one of them."

That elicits another smile, not shy, but big and broad—gorgeous like her. Keeping our hands clasped together, she rolls toward me, an eagerness built into her expression. "Tell me about your day, and don't leave out the good parts. I want all the details."

As requested, I tick through my day from the sunrise surf to lunch at a food truck. She never once appears bored, but rather entirely engaged. I say, "I'm not sure why we picked to go inside that bar other than it sounded like a good time from outside."

Looking pleased as punch, she says, "It's not destiny if that's where you're going with this, Mr. Optimistic. It's . . ." She looks away, searching for some evasive explanation, then takes a deep breath. Her exhale takes a while as if measured in the confines of time. A quick glance, and then she returns her attention to the ceiling. "Nick?"

"Yes?"

"You have me rethinking my stance."

"On?" I ask, not wanting to stare at her but not even trying to find an excuse to do it anyway.

"You and the sex."

Okay, for real. How am I supposed to keep a straight face after that comment? It's impossible. "We've been dancing around this since you showed up, so here are my thoughts even though you didn't ask," I start after the laughter stops. "First, *the* sex? Did we make a pact I'm not aware of? I feel like I would remember that? Or is this a recurring theme for you to stick to the embargo you mentioned and not have sex by reminding yourself every hour or so?"

"Hm." Considering the question, she twists her lips to

the side. Her eyes narrow, and she proceeds with caution. "And second?"

"Second, I assume the sex is referring to sex with me, but you made it really clear there would be no sex, monkey business, and to keep ideas out of my head the moment you walked in. I, for one, can live by your rules, but I have to say I think it would be quite fun to find out if the same chemistry extends beyond what's currently happening between us. Just my two cents."

"That was a lot, Nick. If you were trying to woo me into bed, a simple, hey, you're hot followed by some kissing is a great start." Exasperated, she rolls her eyes as if the whole world has worn her down. "It's on the table. Geez, I'm right here lying next to you. Do I have to be naked for you to make a move?"

I grin. "That's not a terrible idea."

"Oh my God," she says, throwing her arms in the air and letting them fall heavily to the mattress again. "You're incorrigible." *Me?* "I finally give in to my whims, and now you're the impossible one. You've done your job. I'm charmed, rummed up, and dined, so why are you arguing with me instead of kissing me like you mean it?"

"As much as I loved to take credit for any of those arguments, I've actually not done anything to earn an ounce of your affections if that's how you're calculating this deal."

She sits up, her eyes volleying between the open door and the end of the bed. I tuck my hands behind my head again and wait for the comeback I can sense she's constructing. When she finally turns to me, she rests her chin on the round of her shoulder, and says, "Maybe it's naïve of me, but I feel safe with you. I have no clue why, but I like you, Nick."

"I like you, too."

"But if you don't want to have sex, I'd like to stay in bed

with you. We could talk, or I'm sure the hotel has a backgammon set."

Sliding my hand across the blanket, I rest against her hip, wanting to hear every crazy thought that comes to her head. "Be forewarned, I'm really good at backgammon."

"Only one way to find out." She slips her legs off the side of the bed and reaches for the phone on the nightstand. There's a pause, and then she says, "Do you have backgammon available? . . . Okay. Yes. Also, rum. Send that up as well, please." Whipping back to me, she asks, "What kind?"

"You were drinking Bacardi. Order a bottle of their best rum, and we should be good."

She places the order and hangs up the phone but then stands, planting her hands on her hips. "I thought for sure this was going in a different direction."

"For the record, I never said I didn't want to have sex, but I can't say I'm disappointed."

Another laugh escapes her. "You surprise me, Nick."

My name has become so familiar with her tongue that it sounds like it belongs long term. I'm kind of hoping it lasts. "How so?"

"Remember how I said not to get any ideas?"

"Very clearly."

"Did you ever get any?"

I eye her, those sexy legs, and that shirt that does her figure a disservice. "One or ten."

"Guess what?"

"You got a few ideas of your own?"

"Mm-hmm." A knock on the door grabs our attention, and she hops off the bed. "Lots of ideas on how to pass the time, so don't go anywhere."

If she only knew that I have no intention of wasting a

second I have with her. She's a breath of fresh air in a life that's become stale. "I'll be right here when you return."

She licks the corner of her mouth before nodding. "I'll be quick."

As soon as she answers the door, I jump up from the bed and dig through my backpack in search of a mint, gum, or anything that will cover burger breath. Not that I think things are leading back to kissing, but if they do, I'm not going to pass up the offer like I did back in the lobby. *What a fucking idiot I am.* I had someone I'm actually interested in kissing me, but I let that little voice in my head stop me from returning the same. She was drunk.

I don't kiss or have sex with drunk women. I'm not some beacon of integrity, but it's just a good moral to live by.

I score a piece of minty gum and rush to chew it up before spitting it back out in the wrapper when I hear the flush of the toilet. I check for any messages on my phone. There's nothing from Harrison, but I'm not bothered. I'm actually wondering if I should message him to stay gone a lot longer.

When I hear the door click closed, I drop it on the dresser and dive back onto the bed, resuming my position just as she re-enters the room. Her eyes dart between me and the disheveled blanket, and she says, "Why do you look guilty?"

"Me?" My voice goes up an octave. Damn it. I clear my throat. "I wasn't doing anything."

"*Ooookay.*" She turns and says, "I don't know if the cart will fit in here. I'll see."

I scramble out of bed and cut across the room to beat her to the door. "I got it."

Pinned to the wall, she covers her chest. "Geez almighty, you scared me."

"What can I say? I love backgammon."

"Apparently." She takes the other side of the cart, looking proud as a peacock at the table covered in bottles of soda, alcohol, waters, and three desserts. But her expression falls until her gaze reaches the lower tray, and she spots the game. "Where should we set up? Bedroom, living room, or terrace?"

"Depends on the rules."

Tapping her lips, she lowers her hand. "You're right. The bedroom it is."

I legit had no clue where she was going to choose, so I can only imagine what led her to the bed. *Guess I'm about to find out.*

She grabs the game. "Come on."

I push the cart into the bedroom and set it at the end of the mattress. She opens the leather case and starts separating the pieces to each other's perspective sides while I crack open the rum. "Tonight is a surprise."

"I know," she replies. "It's so much better than I imagined."

"You imagined it going badly?"

She looks up from the game board. "No, just figured we would have done it already. It's nice to have foreplay."

Foreplay? I crank my neck from the double take. "Is that what this is?"

"I was assuming since most guys would be bored by now."

No way could I be bored with her. "You're kidding, right?"

"What would I be kidding about?" Sure, she's been hot and cold, and hard to read at times, but having an expectation placed on the time she spends with a guy rubs me the wrong way. She doesn't owe me anything. Definitely seems like she attracts some losers, myself excluded, of course, because I'm not that guy.

Well . . . I am that guy. I've had sex with plenty of women, but sex was something mutually agreed upon, not a precursor for the date. The natural course of the night took shape, and we would have sex. That doesn't have to be the case tonight.

Just as she opens a soda, I reach over and cover her hand with mine, stilling it. "I'm going to say something I hope doesn't ruin the night."

Seriousness fills her features as she tenses. "Okay. I'm listening."

I scrub my hands over my face, not believing I'm about to say this. When I open my eyes, I say, "I'm not going to have sex with you, Natalie. I'm not using reverse psychology or asking anything of you. There are no ulterior motives. I'm simply enjoying your company enough to want to take sex off the table so we can continue this good time."

"And here I thought sex on a table *was* a good time." She's going to kill me one sexual comment at a time. Her laughter dissipates, and she looks toward the window, trying to straighten the line of her mouth. She can't and starts laughing again. When her eyes land back on me, she adds, "I appreciate what you're saying. I suddenly sound like a nymphomaniac. Believe it or not, I don't sleep with every date. I haven't slept with a lot of men, in general, but there was just something meeting you the way I did, well . . . I hate getting emotional. That's the tequila again."

"Rum."

"Yes, rum." She sits back on the bed and crawls up toward the headboard. Resting back, she asks, "Is it wrong I want to kick your ass in backgammon?"

Although she's distracting from one topic—an important one at that—her honesty is as refreshing as her personality. "Nothing like a bit of healthy competition." I chuckle and start pouring drinks. I know I need a stiff one after that discussion.

"By the way, if you're trying to woo me, you're doing a stellar job. I'm wooed."

Laughter bounces between us, and I wonder if I *am* wooing her. I don't normally woo any woman. I don't have to, but Natalie deserves it. From the things she's said, it's clear that she's been hurt in the past. But she's strong, trying to hide any vulnerability, and I'm inclined to show her that a good time with a man doesn't have to be tied to how the night ends.

Whether this turns into more than a game of backgammon, though, remains to be seen. Either way, I get to spend my night with a beautiful woman, away from the noise of a crowded boat. *It doesn't really get any better than this.*

7

Natalie

How does Nick make a pip sound sexy?

He opens his mouth and speaks. That's how. Everything he says, from cocked dice to the lover's leap, has me on the verge of spontaneously combusting. Don't even get me started on the beavers. I agreed to that before we started the first game and still have no idea what it means. But I sure do love hearing him say it.

Beavers.

Beavers.

Beavers.

"Two out of three," he says, bearing his last checker and politely not throwing his victory in my face. My brother totally would.

I fall back on the bed, arms draped above my head, and give him the credit he deserves. "Congrats on the win." I'm not a sore loser. This was only about the second or third time I've played in my life. I don't even know where the suggestion to play backgammon came from, but I'm glad it appeared. I haven't laughed this hard in a long time, especially over what my grandmother would call old-fashioned fun.

I catch his eyes skimming my body just before he clears his throat and gets up from the bed. "I should check my phone."

Secretly, I wish he wouldn't.

In the past two hours, I've decided that as much as I thought this had all the makings of a memorable one-night stand, I'm glad we didn't come back here and fall into bed. Well, we did fall into bed, but I'm glad we didn't have sex. We've kept it light with superficial stuff, not wanting to bog our night down with details that won't matter come morning. Hanging out and just getting to know him has been fun.

As for making out, that's a whole other story. Surely, it's not normal to want to kiss someone and have them return it, I might add, so badly. When I'm not caught up in the game and how to play, I'm caught up in the memory of those plush lips, the scratch of his scruff against my skin, and the undeniable rise in temperature between us when I unsuccessfully kissed him in the lobby.

The rejection stung worse than a wasp, but there was no ill intent found in his expression. I believe him. As for that foreplay? Theoretically, it's not breaking any laws—*or embargos*—if we make out before we know each other's last names.

Attempting my best Lois Lane, I stretch, flirting with the Clark Kent version of Nick as he stares at his phone. All night, I thought he'd make a move, but he's got the willpower of Superman. *Damn it.*

Becoming a limp lump on the mattress when my flirtations don't get his attention, I briefly give in to my heavy lids and close them. No, I cannot fall asleep here even though my body has decided otherwise. It's been a long day, what can I say? Well, I can say a lot to Tatum for blowing me off and leaving me stranded, but since I'm a good friend and don't mind the current view, I let it go . . . until later, of course, when she'll hear all about it.

In an effort to stay awake, I ask, "Anything interesting?"

"No," he replies, grinning to himself and sounding relieved if I'm reading him correctly. When he catches me staring, he adds, "Is it wrong to want more time with you?"

Now I'm the one with the foolish grin. "You're such a charmer."

"Like in backgammon, sometimes I win, and sometimes I lose." It's good to hear he might be having similar struggles.

Wanting to tease, I straighten my mouth for the sake of the play. "I have to be honest, Nick." I prop myself up, leaning back on my hands nonchalantly. "I might not be your best idea. You might have had a chance two hours ago, but now, I'm fading. I won't stop you from the pursuit, but you've been warned."

"As long as I've been warned, it's on me." *God, I'd like to be on him.* Is it the rejection that has me so hot for him? I'm pretty sure it's everything about him. "Since you're fading," he starts, tucking his phone in his back pocket, "you can stay here and get some rest. I'll hang out in the living room and let you know when Harrison returns."

Wait, that's not what I wanted. Not at all. Shoot, he read me all wrong. I've been hot and cold, and coming on so strong with this man, I've scared him away completely. But what do I want? Where could this possibly lead? Checking the clock, I realize I have to leave for the airport in eight hours. The fun I was having blaming the alcohol has ended. I only have myself to blame for any further embarrassment.

It seems impossible to determine in the next few seconds, so I start to believe in his plan. "It's probably best if we call it a night. Thanks for letting me borrow your bed."

"No worries."

Snuggling down, I roll to my side, but my eyes trail him as he moves to the doorway. Even with the distance between us, I can see the weight of the day beginning to drag his shoulders down. As he turns out the light, he says, "I'll let you know when I hear from the others."

"*The others* sounds like they're aliens or something."

"Go to sleep, Natalie." I may not be able to see his smile, but I can sense it in his tone.

I giggle. "Sorry, my mind goes into overdrive sometimes. Night."

"Good night."

I watch him disappear into the other room. I love that I can smell his scent around me, but I hate the emptiness filling the room.

I can be alone.

I swear I can.

My last relationship reminds me daily that I'm better off alone than being with someone who doesn't respect me. Nick is different. I can already tell because most guys would have jumped at the opportunity to have sex. Not that I'm going to declare Nick a saint just yet, but he's definitely stealing the title of Prince Charming.

Lying here, I close my eyes and think about how nice it would be to have the warmth of his body wrapped around me.

Yep. I definitely have a problem being alone. This is when I break the cycle and learn to stand on my own two feet. I don't need a man. Wanting them is the bad habit I need to break.

Readjusting, I punch the pillow to fluff the down and tug the blanket out from under me to cover my body. The room is quiet, so I listen for any sounds in the living room. Yes, I'm half-ass eavesdropping on Nick. But I'm met with silence.

Why is it so quiet? I sit up, trying harder to pick up on anything—the sound of typing a text because what psycho turns off that sound, of talking on the phone or even whispering, or the TV playing to pass the time or fall asleep on the couch while waiting. I get nothing.

The bed has lost its comfort, so I flip off the covers and pad to the door. Curiosity consumes me, so I peek out and see him standing in the doorway to the terrace. He takes a sip of the dark liquid, the melting ice taking up more space than the liquor in the glass.

Crossing my arms over my chest, I lean against the doorframe. Nick's back is to me, his shirt billowing in the wind. His curls look more natural in this setting. Maybe they weren't windblown or curled from the helmet, but natural instead. Either way, my affection for them has grown exponentially . . . just as it has for the man.

"Nick?" My voice is quiet in the spacious villa, but he hears me and turns around.

"You're up? You're not tired?"

"I am, but . . ." I chicken out, shifting my weight to the other foot and fidgeting with the hem of my shirt. "Did you hear from Harrison?" I have no idea what I'm doing. Flirting? Seducing? Biding my time until Tatum returns? *Please don't let Tatum return any time soon.*

Why does that sharp-edged jaw and shoulders broad enough to span Brooklyn to Manhattan have to be so tempting? I dance around what I really want to ask. "What do you think about us becoming friends?"

There's a quiet strength about Nick—the way he moves

so effortlessly, the comfort he embodies in his own skin, and how observant he is as if he can see right through me. The most genuine smile I've ever seen covers all other pretenses, letting them fall away and easing his muscles. "It's better than strangers."

"I agree."

"What does this friendship entail? Sharing personal information?" He cocks an eyebrow. "Phone numbers? Maybe even room numbers since you know mine?"

Quirking my lips to the side, I roll my eyes. "I got your number all right, but I was thinking more along the lines of snuggling."

"Snuggling?"

"Yes, Nick, it's another term for cuddling. My body and your body sharing heat and, I don't know, just lying in the same bed together." I sound like an idiot, but my gut also twists at the thought of being rejected again.

As if he can read my mind, he sets his glass on the coffee table and comes toward me, taking hold of my hands. "Will you snuggle with me, Natalie?"

"Are you sure?" I ask, sounding aloof.

He chuckles but still leads me back into the bedroom. "Which side of the bed do you sleep on?"

"The middle."

A wry grin, visible even in the low light, crosses his lips. "Okay, you get in, and I'll find a spot."

I scramble under the covers as he patiently waits for me to settle in. I lie in the middle of the mattress, arms and legs spread wide, but then laughter takes hold, and I bring them to my sides and move to the left—*just a little.*

His eyes catch the light, revealing his amusement as he crawls on top of the covers beside me. It's only a moment, not even a minute before I warn him, "I'm coming over."

Wordlessly, his arm goes wide, and I snuggle against his side. He's not lacking words for long, though. "Now that you got me here, what are you going to do with me?"

"*Shhh*. Snuggling also involves the quiet game." I give myself away when I giggle, my body shaking against his.

"I have to say, that's not one of my favorite games. I tend to lose when I play."

Now he chooses to talk up a storm. "Suddenly, this doesn't surprise me. If it makes you feel better, I usually lose, too. Maybe we can try together."

"Losing, or are you trying to get me to shut up?"

Patting his chest—the hard chest where his heart thunders underneath—I say, "Never. I like the sound of your voice." *I like the rhythm of your heart. I like the strength in your arms even when you're relaxed.* I very much like snuggling with Nick.

It's not just the faded scent of his cologne that I'll miss come morning. It's the slow and gentle connection we're building, the way he beat me at backgammon but didn't rub it in my face, and the look I caught in his eyes when I lay suspended in his arms at the bar. We've already shared a myriad of moments, and it's only just gone midnight.

I close my eyes, letting these growing emotions drift away like the ocean tide. No use spending energy on something that has an expiration date the next morning. I wiggle a little closer when his arm tightens around me. "Good night," I whisper.

"I like the sound of your voice, too."

And then he kisses my forehead.

In the moonlight sneaking in through the window as his breath steadies along with mine, I smile. I'm a sucker for a forehead kiss. Almost nothing is more romantic than that

caress. With my cheek pressed to his chest, I realize I'm also
a sucker for Nick.

I COULD LIE HERE in heaven forever and never want for
anything more than this weightlessness that bears no
burdens to my life. I feel free in Nick's bed, practically
purring while wrapped in his sheet in the warm and inviting
space.

And although it's so similar to our room, I feel safe
tucked in Nick's bed surrounded by his belongings. So much
of Nick invades my world that I didn't note earlier when I
was wide awake. The hints of rum coat his breath, and a
leather satchel worn enough to have traveled the world is
next to the bed. A book . . . a tangible book with a bookmark
sticking out from between the pages is on the nightstand
next to a silver travel alarm clock. These aren't the items of
any college guy I know.

The clock, book, and bag are sophisticated like the man
who owns them. Even the rum smells sexy coming from
him. I'm sure my breath is the exact opposite.

It's tempting to snoop around and learn more about this
man I've spent my night with while he sleeps. He's older but
not by much—life hasn't yet dug into his expression, leaving
its mark—yet enough to easily compare him to the guys I
dated at university, making them seem immature in comparison, especially my ex.

The breakup with Dane still hangs heavily over my
head. It's dumb, just as I was for trusting him . . . I swiftly
sweep away all thoughts of him, wanting to relish in Nick
for a bit, happy to let him consume my thoughts instead.
His kind side can't be denied. He's given me a place to rest,

eat, and wait, all without asking for a single thing in return.

Despite my desire to lounge around, I slip out of bed after a few hours of sleep, knowing I've stayed longer than I should, and tiptoe into the bathroom. I freshen up and then tuck my shirt into the front of the waistband of my shorts, leaving the tail to float behind me as I pad through the suite in bare feet. The tiles are cool against my skin, and the breeze sneaking in from outside through the door is a much-needed breath of fresh air. It cools me from the heat Nick left behind as he caressed my skin.

I find my shoes and slip them back on. I don't know where his phone is to check the messages, but there's no sign of his friend anywhere either.

Checking the time, I wonder if Tatum ever made it back. With one hour until we need to start our trek back to New York, I'm willing to take the chance and head back to our room.

The sinking feeling in my gut that I'm forgetting something isn't logical since I showed up at Nick's door with nothing. I peek into the bedroom one more time, spying him lying right where I left him. I hate leaving, wondering if I'm walking out on a good thing.

I am.

Although last night was filled with many highs, laughs, and something that I thought had the potential to bloom into more, this relationship was always meant to be strangers who bonded once on vacation. First-name basis. *And I'm okay with that.*

My life is too messy to drag someone across the country to become a part of it.

I head for the door and open it, but I'm not eager to rush out. With my life on the East Coast calling, I take a deep breath and push through my instant regret. "Thanks for being a friend for a night," I whisper as I leave Nick behind.

I didn't know how hurt I'd been prior to snuggling in his arms, the betrayal of other men wedged into my heart. Being a man of integrity, with kindness and an awesome sense of humor, Nick soothed that pain away, restoring my faith.

"Goodbye, Mr. Smug and Sexy."

8

Nick

I open my eyes and find the bed empty beside me. *Fuck.*

Jumping up, I grab my phone from the dresser and look for any sign of Natalie. But my brain is still half asleep, so I waste time on stupid things like looking for a text. "Natalie?" I call out, glancing through the open door to the bathroom and then moving into the living room. I could kick myself for falling asleep, but how could I not when I was holding her in my arms? I haven't felt that kind of peace to let my mind rest in years. I found it with her, though. "Natalie?"

Peeking out through the glass, I hold the smallest bit of hope she might be on the terrace, lounging on the chair or leaning on the railing. A deep-seated disappointment returns because I didn't even get her full name. I have no way of contacting her to tell her how much I enjoyed playing backgammon.

It was more than the game I enjoyed. I should have told her how much last night meant to me. I look at the door when I find no sign of her anywhere else. Glancing over to

Harrison's room, I notice his bed is still turned down from housekeeping, making it easy to conclude he scored with Tatum as well as a place to stay last night.

Ah, fuck it.

I put on my shoes and head out to search for Harrison. If I can find him, I can find Tatum, and that leads me back to Natalie. I hurry to the lobby, practically jumping over suitcases left near the bellhop station, but skid to a stop when I see Harrison coming toward me from the other hallway. "Where's Natalie?"

"Good to see you, too."

"Sorry, I don't have time for jokes." I look over his shoulder, hoping to see the girls coming. "I have to find her."

That surefire smirk reveals how his night ended or morning started. We don't discuss these things usually, but let's just say the dude scores a lot. But there's a sincerity about Harrison that not many see. He may not talk about it, but he's been burned by plenty—family, friends, and gold diggers. The swagger is dropped, and he asks, "What's going on with you, Christiansen?"

"I should have told her my last name. Or gotten hers. Exchanged numbers or made plans. I should have done something to keep in contact, but I didn't."

"Okay," he says, shrugging, still appearing not to catch on to why I'm panicking. "Why not?" *Why. Not?*

That's a good fucking question.

I don't know why I didn't when I felt more than lust for a woman for the first time in my life. With Natalie, I want to spend time talking with her rather than simply fucking or doing the foreplay dance leading up to it. Because I think I found someone real.

She was real with me.

She. Was. Real. And I let her fucking slip through my

fingers while I slept. Fuck. I run my hand through my hair. "We were playing games when we should have realized it was more. Last night was more." Maneuvering around him, I head in the direction from which he came, ready to bolt to their door. "What room are they in?"

He's already shaking his head before I finish asking the question. "They're already gone."

Stopping, I look toward the large exit doors, not ready to admit defeat. "I can catch up to them. How long ago did they leave?"

"At least an hour, probably longer."

"Are you sure?"

"I'm sure. Tatum said goodbye when it was still dark outside. I fell back asleep and just woke up. Figured I should get back to the room to pack."

I look down at the tile beneath my feet, the same flooring that led Natalie away from me. Should I try the ferry? Maybe call the airlines at LAX? Will anyone give me information about another traveler?

I know the answer already.

When he moves out of the way of other guests, my attention drifts to his hand. And his phone, a new option coming into play. "You can text Tatum."

His expression falls when he flips the screen toward him to look at it. "Yeah, it was kind of left back in the bedroom. We didn't exchange details. It was . . ." he says, glancing toward the exit, "nothing more than a vacation thing." Lowering his phone, he shoves it in his pocket. "I need to pack."

When he turns to leave, I say, "Are you sure about that?"

He stops to look back. "Yeah, we have to check out soon."

"I meant about Tatum."

"Doesn't matter, man. We live on opposite sides of the country, and I'm not the pen pal type."

"We just move on like last night doesn't matter? Like *they* don't?"

His brow furrows, and he hits me with a glare. "Yes."

Left standing there wondering what options I have, I sigh, wishing I could ask at the front desk about Natalie. But given she couldn't even get into her own room last night, there's no chance they'll give me any information. That'd be a fool's errand.

A fool. That's what I am. A fucking fool for letting her go.

The walk back to the villa feels longer than usual, with my feet dragging beneath me. *What can I do?* There's nothing left but to return to my life.

I let myself in, the door slamming behind me. The terrace would usually call to me, the ocean just beyond, but that's not where I spent most of my time with Natalie. I walk into the bedroom and do a quick scan to find any trace of her. Anything that would give me a clue to who she was or even if she was real.

There's nothing but a crumpled sheet. Standing there, I try to recall what sidetracked us from, as she put it, "properly introducing" ourselves. Frustration sets in when I realize it was me. I changed the topic by bringing up how much I liked our beginning. That still holds true, but I fucking hate our ending.

"HOW WAS CATALINA?" my mom asks, stirring a cup of tea when I walk in the back door that opens into the kitchen. It must be two—her routine runs like clockwork. "I always find it so relaxing there."

I close the door, dropping my bag on the floor, and go to her. I'm not sure how to reply. The truth isn't something I'm ready to acknowledge, but I also don't like to lie or worry her. Kissing her on the cheek, I say, "It was good." I go with neutral, unoffensive, and generic.

Before I turn to head upstairs, she touches my cheek. "Well, that doesn't sound like you."

"Me having a good time?"

"No, the lack of emotion behind it. What's wrong, darling son?"

Cookie Christiansen reads me like a book. I equally love and hate it. "Just a lot on my mind."

Picking up her teacup, she takes a sip, then says, "That's understandable. This is a big move. Are you ready?"

I lean against the counter. "I think I can handle walking across a stage."

She laughs. "I meant the exam and coming to work for the company."

"Do I have a choice on either?"

"Not according to your father, but at the end of the day, it's about what you want."

I've never understood her patience with him. Not that he's horrible or anything like that, but they see life so differently. She's about doing what makes you happy, and he's about making money, which makes him happy. "You and Dad are so different. How do you make it work?"

She laughs, moving around the island to sit on a barstool. "We stopped trying to make it 'work' and made it 'love' instead."

"Nope. Not going to have that conversation." I pick up my bag.

Her laughter rings louder in the bright kitchen of my childhood home. I know I'm lucky, though. My parents are a rare breed. *Still married. In love. Happy.* "Oh, Nick. I'm not talking about sex, although that's important as well. I'm talking about the little things. Changing your perspective. It's not work to love each other, so that's not a term we use. Loving each other is easy. It's life that gets in the way. We hit a bump in the road or smash into a wall sometimes. We may be different and not always agree, but we do listen." With a sweet smile, she adds, "Most of the time. But I'm okay with us being two beings with our own minds. What fun would it be if we agreed on everything?"

"I see your logic." I kiss her head as I pass behind her. "You would have made a great lawyer."

"I'll leave that to you. I'm proud of my degree, but in practice, I'm glad I chose a different path."

"You chose wisely."

Just as I round the corner to head for the stairs, she says, "I had really hoped you would meet someone, Nicholas." Although she can no longer see me, she knows I'm listening. "The new moon was in your seventh house."

All right. She's got my attention. Guess she's rubbed off on me . . . just a little. Taking a few steps back into the room, I know I shouldn't indulge in the New Age stuff she's so into, but this time, my interest is piqued because of one thing —*Natalie*. "Oh, yeah? What does that mean?"

"New beginnings. The start of a fresh relationship. That phase ends today, though." She eyes me as if she's reading the book she personally wrote. Again, I know I'm lucky. It's not just that my mom can read me. It's that she made the effort and invested the time to get to know me, even through my *lively* teenage years, as she calls them. She never backed down from showing me love.

I wouldn't want it any other way.

"Not that I'd expect you to *meet your forever love* on vacation, but you never know what can happen on an island paradise."

Natalie happened.

My heart beats to life, a heavy thud felt in my chest. I avert my gaze to the leather handles in my hand. Suddenly, every scratch on the surface of the bag is the most interesting thing I've ever seen.

She takes a deep breath and releases an exaggerated exhale. "Destiny's hand can't be forced. Fortunately, there are many other phases of the sun and moon to come in your future. Focusing on your studies is probably best."

"Yeah, probably." I don't know why my heart sinks, but its abrupt protest is felt. I trudge up the stairs and enter my bedroom. I have a good life and have been given practically anything I could ever want. But the one thing living in Beverly Hills, a bank account full of money, and endless business opportunities can't give—a real life, one of my own choosing, one that comes with a genuine connection instead of professional agreements with strings.

Natalie was the opposite of that to me.

I don't know her background and have no clue what she does with her life in Manhattan. I don't know her last name or anything about her family. I know her, though—that connection to the person she is on the inside was constructed and the foundation laid down. But maybe that doesn't matter, and I need to listen to my mother.

"Destiny's hand can't be forced."

Guess I'll never know.

9

Nick

Remorse has consumed me.

That I didn't kiss her and we didn't take the time to exchange numbers or surnames frequents the back of my mind. I regret falling asleep next to her without getting every last tidbit.

But more so, I'm beginning to regret the entire weekend altogether. Another birthday passed, graduation came and went. I officially left Stanford behind and passed the bar exam.

I'm a full-fledged practicing attorney, also known as an adult. That's how my dad refers to me these days. If adulting consists of being buried in the routine everyday of the legal department of Christiansen Wealth Management, then it sucks most days. Is it challenging? Sure, sometimes, but I'm left with generally mundane tasks like reviewing contracts and sitting in on meetings to discuss the expansion of the company. It leaves too much time for my mind to wander back to a girl I met last spring.

Four months later, it's easier to call her Natalie No-Last-Name to give our encounter some substance. Natalie doesn't seem enough for something that felt big . . . *feels* big. I only call her that in my head, of course. But the name is more fitting than I'm comfortable admitting.

Thinking about her isn't healthy. Dating no longer interests me, like somehow, I had a taste of the good life, and now I can't be bothered with anything less. Sex is still appealing, but no one holds my attention as Natalie did. I've never struggled like this—not with women or dating, finding someone to hook up with or even skipping the foreplay and just fucking. It was never a big deal before.

One night in Catalina ruined the life I was living. Not that I was content, but hell, I had a life at least. Now it feels like I've left that back in Catalina.

I try to keep my thoughts regarding Natalie to a minimum and am quick to rid them from my mind and focus on my future. That means being present instead of living in the past.

My job is always a good excuse to get out of the text invitations from girls I've hooked up with in the past and women who are interested in me now. All I have to say is, "I have to work in the morning," and that's a free pass without further explanation.

They are none the wiser.

But why can't I seem to connect with someone like I did with Natalie? Surely, there has to be someone who interests me. The few times I went out with other women, I felt as though I was betraying someone who isn't real, yet who steals my thoughts and consumes my spare time. Sometimes I can still see her so vividly that I'm delusional enough to reach out and touch her, her laughter filling my ears and the way she looked at me as though I was saving her.

From what?

Another shot?

No, it was more than that, but I need to let it go—let *her* go—once and for all. My phone lights up with a text.

Mom: *Dad will be home in ten.*

Me: *I'll be down.*

This is the weekend we celebrate the man who has provided a life of luxury by means of financial advisement to the wealthiest Angelenos. My mom goes out of her way to throw the biggest and best party for my dad, spending countless hours planning every meticulous detail. So, there's no missing it, no matter how much work we have to do. The four of us are expected to be here.

This was the perfect event to bring a date, yet not one name other than Natalie-No-Last-Name came to mind. *I'm so fucked.*

My brother and I delivered his diamond jubilee gift of cufflinks earlier this evening. He'll wear them tonight, but otherwise, they'll join the rest in his collection, rotating them out for special occasions. I imagine cufflinks have to be ranked up there with ties as the most boring gift to receive. They remind me of the life I don't want to lead.

The door opens, and Andrew leans in to judge me with just a glance. "I thought Mom wanted you in the Brooks Brothers tux?" he asks. Being fashionably late isn't something my brother and I strive for. It's an effort to blend in. We usually fail because our good looks run in the family, so we tend to stand out. "I was feeling Armani."

I shrug the jacket down by the hem and then fix my tie standing in front of the mirror.

"You should have shaved."

Rubbing my jaw, I walk past him into the hallway. "I like to keep Dad guessing."

"You mean pissed," he says, chuckling. "Those are two different things." He closes my door and then catches up with me before we descend the stairs. Andrew might be two years older, but you wouldn't know it by our height. We've measured, and we're identical down to the millimeter. *Not that we're competitive or anything.*

His hair is a few shades lighter than mine, taking more after Cookie's than Corbin's. I look more like my father, inheriting his lighter brown eyes and hair color.

If I'm the golden boy, then Andrew is pure platinum. He fails at nothing, and our dad respects the hell out of him. Andrew also has less of an ax to grind. He always wanted to join the business and followed through. He's built his own prestigious clientele of new money here in LA, impressing not only my dad but also bringing in some major bank for the company. "Yes, they are," I say, grinning.

He shakes his head as we walk downstairs. "Are you trying to give him a heart attack on his birthday, Nick?"

I, on the other hand, couldn't care less about financial strategies and the market. I also have no desire to work directly under my father, so joining the legal team—with the intention of one day running it—is the compromise we settled on, which leaves my dad's sons running the business when he retires. It's a win all around.

I stop when we land on the marble floor. "Neither a brand of tux nor me not shaving is going to give him a heart attack, stroke, or other fatal condition. It will rankle his feathers at best. I'll keep his glass of scotch full, and he'll be fine."

His jovial expression turns serious, and he asks, "I wanted to talk to you quickly about New York. What are your thoughts?"

"I can fly out, meet the heads, and get the contracts."

With the party in full swing, I move off to the side to finish this conversation in private.

Shoving his hands in his pockets, he says, "My schedule can be rearranged, and I can go with you."

"It's no big deal, Andrew."

He laughs. "It's actually a huge deal."

"I can handle it."

Nodding, he says, "I know you can. I also think it's a great opportunity. One I wish I'd been given." The noise from the crowd filters into the foyer, and Andrew looks over my shoulder. "It's getting busy."

I glance over my shoulder. "These parties always are."

When I turn back, he says, "Look, Nick, I know you never dreamed of working for the company, but having you there is an asset."

"By last name alone, but I don't do anything any other attorney couldn't do."

"It's good having you there. That's all I wanted to say." Shoulder to shoulder, he pats my back, then says, "Time to play nice."

"I'll do my best." We start walking again, and I add, "Thanks."

"You're welcome, little brother."

I just shake my head and laugh.

The house drips with crystals that sparkle like diamonds when reflecting the light from the chandeliers. With bars inside and out, a buffet as long as the Oscars red carpet, and a clear night as if she demanded nothing less of September, this might be the pinnacle to Cookie Christiansen's party planning.

Trays of champagne circulate, but I'm ready for something stronger, so Andrew and I head for the bar as party guests flow in from the terrace. I order, "Rum and Coke, and a scotch from that bottle you have stored away for the guest of honor."

With drinks in our hands, Andrew leads the way as we walk outside through the partygoers to find my parents greeting the guests as they arrive.

"Happy Birthday, Dad," I say, gifting him with a fresh cocktail.

"Thank you, son." He looks pleased by the drink and gives me a smile. "You always did have great timing." As we shake hands, he adds, "I see you dressed for the occasion." I was waiting for the dig to come but thought it would take him a few drinks to get around to it. He's a traditional guy, so maybe I intended to push a few buttons with the scruff and modern cut suit.

He'd normally dive into a game of verbal volleyball. He loves to be right, but so do Andrew and I. My mom is usually left refereeing. It's always done in fun and keeps us about our wits. He takes a gulp of his drink, not holding back. *Go, Dad.* The edges of his shoulders begin to slouch, and he appears more relaxed. "Nick brought the good stuff."

My mom smiles, a silent message of gratitude aimed at me. Rubbing my dad's shoulder, she says, "Only the best on this special day."

Covering her hand with his, he looks at her, and it's easy to see the love shared between them. Don't get me wrong, my dad can be an asshole when it comes to business, but never to my mother. "It's brilliant. You shouldn't have gone to so much trouble, Cookie."

"You know I love to spoil you."

Glancing at Andrew and then at me, he laughs. "She does. Find yourselves a woman like your mother, sons, and you'll never go a day without smiling."

Speaking of . . . While I was at law school, Andrew was

stuck in the thick of marriage and kids talk. Part of joining "the family business" entails expanding the actual family by raising future Christiansen execs to keep the line of succession going.

Andrew looks at me. "Was that Mr. and Mrs. Dalery arriving a bit ago?"

Leaning in, my mom whispers, "Dalen Dalery came with her parents. She looks . . ." She pauses and then lowers her voice even more. "Distinctive. She's really changed since high school, Andrew."

Distinctive? Wow, if that word doesn't raise a red flag, I'm not sure what would.

My mom is blind to the fact that Dalen used to be crazy. If she knew that Dalen cheated on my brother back in high school, she'd go all mama bear on her despite the cutesy baked goods name.

He looks over his shoulder like a man on the run, and asks, "How long do we have to stay?"

Since my dad is shaking hands and back to greeting guests again, my mom laughs between us. "Two hours, and then you're free from all family duties tonight."

Andrew gives her a hug. "You're a good cookie, Cookie."

"Don't I know it," she adds.

My brother and I leave them to it and make our way back inside, shaking the hands of people we know and some others who introduce themselves. Eventually, we part ways. He returns to the bar, and I head for the buffet. I don't get two cubes of Swiss cheese on my plate before I'm cornered. "Hey, Nick."

Speak of the devil. *And holy fucking whoa!*

I pop my eyes back in after they bug out. Different is an understatement. Dalen leans in, and air-kisses are exchanged. *What?* We're in LA. This is what we do. But I'm still in shock by the drastic change in her... "I, uh..."

"It's been years, Nick. How are you?" Her hair, formerly brown, has gone platinum with big curls pinned to the sides of her head. It reminds me of a centerfold from some magazines my uncle gave me when I was sixteen.

Her tits are making quite the grand entrance in the low-cut dress. Keeping my eyes above deck is going to be a testament to my willpower. She wasn't flat-chested back then, but *mountains* is the only thing that comes to mind now. Looking around me like I'm hiding my brother back there, she asks, "I haven't seen Andrew tonight. Is he here?"

"He's around." I almost feel bad for selling him out. *Almost.* But let's get real . . . pun intended, which makes me think of Natalie, Dalen has no interest in me. It's always been about my brother. It always will be until he's married with kids. And I can't say she'll even get the hint then. Since she's not in a hurry to leave, I step back from the table, out of the way of other guests trying to get to the cheese, to force my eyes to look at anything other than her chest. I ask, "Still living in LA?"

"In Hollywood, actually. I have an apartment near Sunset. Great views of the Hills and close to everything." She moves around me, touching my wrist as if she's afraid I'll leave. "I hear you're in law school. I never took you for the lawyer type when you were younger." She pops a grape in her mouth.

"What can I say? I like to surprise people and graduated last May. I'm working with my brother and dad now." With impeccable timing, I spy my friend cutting through the party and know my night is about to change. *For the better.*

Harrison barrels up, hand raised ready to smack down on mine. "Dude, bring it in."

I lay a fiver down, and we bump shoulders after that. "You made it."

"Wouldn't miss it. Cookie's parties are always worth the stop-by." When he casually looks to my side, he does a double take. "Holy—Dalen?"

Either she's changed more than her physical appearance or she's gotten better at hiding her crazy because sounding sweet as a kitten, she says, "Hi, Harrison. Look at you all grown."

I'm not sure he physically bites his tongue, but he definitely holds it. Harrison is an honorary Christiansen. You mess with one of us, you mess with all. He says, "Wow, you look . . ." He's wise to think twice about his words before sharing them. She waits, shifting in discomfort with every exaggerated second that ticks by. "Great."

She beams, his compliment feeding the need she apparently has to please. "Thanks, Harrison." She pinches his cheek. "You always were a sweetheart." Moving to the other side of us, she rubs my bicep. "It was good catching up. And if you see Andrew, will you let him know I'm here?"

"Absolutely. Have a good night."

As soon as she's out of earshot, Harrison says, "Holy shit, that's quite a look."

"Yeah, it is." But I don't want to spend my time talking about Dalen. "I promised my mom we'd stay for another hour."

"We can go upstairs to burn some time?" *See?* Harrison gets me. He also has to deal with the same rules in his family, so he's learned to work around them. "And yes, I did greet your parents. Cookie's in her element, isn't she?"

I laugh. "Ah, yes. These things don't stress her. They invigorate her." I shake my head. She has endless energy. "Grab some food, and we'll head up."

"On it."

We hang out in my room as we always did—me taking the recliner and him settling on the couch. It's an ugly-ass chair, but it's so damn comfortable that I can't get rid of it. I kick the footrest up. It feels like we're teenagers again when we hang out like this. I miss it. And I know he regrets not going to Stanford. His dad is even more of a hard-ass than my dad. *Without the benefit of having Cookie to soften the blow.* "Maybe it's time to approach your dad again."

Harrison finishes his appetizer plate and grabs the plate of desserts to polish off next. "He won't budge. I need two years of actively selling real estate under my belt in some other office before he'll bring me into his. The first two years are garbage, and he'd rather not smell the stench of my humiliation, as he puts it so kindly."

"That sucks."

After taking a drink, he lowers his glass with little left inside it. "How do things stand with you and your dad?"

"Good as long as I'm fulfilling his plan." The thought has me finishing my drink as well. "I'm flying to New York next week. Andrew says it's a good opportunity."

He studies me, searching for the cracks in my story to decipher how I really feel about it. "Why you?"

"It's a company we're in talks with to buy. They want to meet one of us, and Dad thought it would be a good job for me since I'll also be delivering the contracts."

"Ah, I see. A takeover."

Kicking back, I set my glass down on a table beside me. "No, first, we'll ask nicely."

He chuckles and starts munching on a mini piece of cheesecake. "How kind of you."

"I haven't mentioned it since there aren't a lot of details and it might fall through, but my dad and Andrew want to be in New York. They want the address and the presence. If all goes well, talk of moving me out there has been tossed around."

His eyes narrow just enough to notice as he seems to mull over what I said. "Is this something you want?"

"I'd miss surfing."

Taking a bite of cookie, he chews, and then asks, "And your best friend?"

"Let's not go that far," I reply, teasing. "Of course, man. It's not a done deal, but they'd make it worth my while to pursue."

"There's a lot of valuable real estate in New York."

That's my friend. Nodding, I add, "Sure is, and I like the way you think."

He gets up, snooping through stuff that's been sitting around since I was a preteen. Holding an MVP trophy from my junior year in high school, he asks, "Isn't New York where Tatum and Natalie were from?"

"Sure is," I repeat my earlier answer, suddenly wondering what the chances are that I would see her again. One in eight-plus million. Guess that settles it.

What's the point in hoping when the odds aren't in my favor?

My head is finally getting the message, but now I'm dealing with my stupid heart. And that hasn't received the memo.

10

Natalie

I underestimated Nick and that night in Catalina.

It's not that I didn't think twice before I walked out of that hotel room. It's that I knew nothing would come of hanging around. *What could I possibly say to him?* "We had fun playing games and having dinner together, you caught me before I hit the ground like a sexy superhero. I live in New York. You're in LA. We make perfect sense, so should we make a go of it?"

No, of course not.

1. I had just gotten out of a terrible relationship.
2. Bi-coastal should be reason enough.
3. One night does not mean we're meant to be.

It was a fantastic night, though. One of the best times I've ever had. That's why I still think about Nick, but I can't justify the time I've allowed myself to dwell on him.

Even the few crappy dates I've been on since May haven't erased him from my thoughts. *So what will?*

Fingers crossed someone comes along who can end this ridiculous man ban, once and for all. Yes, I'm still on an embargo. When I met Nick, both love and sex were off-limits. As if one has anything to do with the other. I've learned it doesn't, but I would have sacrificed that pledge to get physical with him. Now it's been so long since I've had either that I'm open to one or both these days.

My best friend is a great friend, but I'm lonely when I lie in bed. I miss being held and falling asleep in Nick's . . . *I mean,* in someone's arms.

A text lights up my phone next to me on the bed. Holding it above me in the air, I read what my brother sent.

Jackson: *Hey, you asked to let you know if I heard anything. Paperwork for your sign-on bonus crossed Dad's desk today. Financially, it's worth considering, especially since Mom and Dad created the position specifically for you.*

My parents appreciate the dedication my younger brother has shown working there all during college. I appreciate having a spy amongst the ranks.

Me: *Thanks for the heads-up.*

Jackson: *What are you thinking?*

Me: *I'm not. I'm processing what this means.*

I know what it means, but I'd like to live in denial for a few more hours.

Jackson: *I'll see you tonight.*

Me: *See you, J.*

Tossing my phone to the mattress, I sigh in frustration. How will I ever convince them for an extension when they're already making alternate plans? *For my life.*

Getting up, I pull on my sneakers, needing to go on a run. It's the only way for me to burn off this anxiety before seeing them this evening. If I don't get rid of this nervous energy, then this celebration will turn into a disaster.

I tuck my phone into the pocket of my workout pants and head for the door. "Later, Tatum," I call, and then wait.

She comes rushing from her bedroom right on schedule. "Before you go, how do I look?" She spins, her deep pink sequin minidress catching the light. I can tell how good she feels by the genuine smile.

It's easy to tell her the truth. "You look beautiful."

"Thanks." Eyeing my workout clothes, she asks, "Shouldn't you be getting dressed?"

Waving it off, I reply, "I have time. I need to fit in a run to get my thoughts straight."

"Everything okay?"

"Fine." I tighten my lips. "It will be fine. Don't worry."

"Okay. The champagne is chilling, and the hairstylist is on her way. I'll have her do my hair first." Her attention returns to the screen of her phone.

"I won't be long." I slip out. As soon as I close the door, I head to the stairwell, then rush through the lobby and feed out onto the sidewalk. The freedom of the outdoors fills me with relief the moment it hits my throat.

I start jogging, my life whirling around in my head and spinning faster with every step I take. I need to block out the constant reminder ticking I hear as soon as I wake up in the morning. I'm never able to forget that the countdown has begun.

Since graduating, I don't understand who I'm supposed to be anymore—an independent business owner or my father's daughter who makes him proud? How do I balance my dreams with everyone else's plans? Better yet, how do I not disappoint my family, who have already done so much for me?

On most days, a quick run allows me to breathe easier and loosens the knot that keeps me tied up in the stress of failing. Today, it's not working, so I run faster on my way to the park.

I was raised to believe I could do anything, but now I'm being asked to compromise what matters most to me or give it up altogether. My small company, STJ Co., combines my favorite things—shopping and spending another person's money. But with only two months left on my loan, I have to prove this can be a valuable asset to the St. James portfolio. Sure, it's not a big moneymaker—*yet*—but I'm building a solid clientele, and I'm proud that the business I started is blossoming.

But a position at Manhattan Financial Group, Inc. has been haunting me since June, so clearly, what I've achieved is not considered good enough.

How will I justify the continued operation of a business that's still in the red? I'm not used to failing, and in most people's eyes, that's exactly what I'm doing. How do I get my family to see me as more than some frivolous girl who they hope falls in line with their plan?

I stop when I reach the edge of the pond, bending over and resting my hands against my thighs. Catching my breath isn't easy, but when I see the time on my phone, I know I need to head back so I have enough time to slip back into the role of a proper St. James for the night.

A party in our honor months after graduation feels a little strange because we've moved on from that part of our lives. But with Tatum's parents traveling so much and mine running a multimillion-dollar business, this was the date they chose. Four and a half-months late. *It's the gesture that counts.*

As soon as I enter the apartment, Tatum says, "It's going to be okay, Nat. I promise." My best friend knows me well.

"Thanks."

The stylist pauses when Tatum peeks around her hips, her eyes finding me just inside the apartment. "The plan is we go to dinner, we schmooze, and we collect our gifts, then the real party begins. You only graduate from college once."

"Technically, it was months ago, though."

With the artist working her hair magic, Tatum continues like this is everyday life for us. It kind of is, but still . . . "Don't be a party pooper. We have the rest of our lives to be depressed. I know you're stressed, but maybe your parents will surprise you and offer to carry the STJ loan a little longer."

I toe off my sneakers and kick them by the door. "That would be amazing, but I have a feeling my time is up." I don't like being negative, so I fix my attitude and push off the table. Pulling the bottle of champagne from the fridge, I ask, "Who's ready for a glass?"

". . . So, here's to my big sister and her best friend. May you live your adult lives as bold as you lived your youth. Cheers!"

I stand and raise my glass, tapping it to my brother's. "Thank you, Jackson."

The sound of crystal clinking together is the making of a melody—this one officially launching Tatum and me into the world. Before I sit down, I add, "I'd also like to thank John and Martine, my amazing parents, who have supported all my endeavors from ballet at five to backing my company at twenty." Raising my glass higher, I add, "And for this lovely celebration."

I drink my champagne and take a deep breath, nervous about broaching the topic of extending the loan to keep my company afloat until we can turn a profit. Hopefully, my toast is a good segue into that conversation later.

When I sit, my dad sets an envelope down and pushes it across the table to me. "We're proud of you, Natalie. You worked hard and graduated with honors. It's good to see the St. James tradition succeed in your generation."

"Thanks, Dad." Taking the envelope, I ask, "What is this?"

My mom, looking New York chic in head-to-toe Balmain, rushes into the private room. Even breathless, she is as fashionably chic as she is late. I can only dream of being so put together. She lovingly calls my fashion sense Hamptons meets California coastal casual. Although she's never critical of me, she does encourage me to refine my style, hating that I wear cutoffs sometimes. She leans closer and whispers, "You look beautiful tonight."

"Thanks, Mom." Glancing at my dad, I add, "And thank you for the gift."

Taking advantage of the opportunity, he asks, "What are your plans after the gifting thing?"

"The 'gifting thing' is my plan. If you have time in your schedule, I'd like to talk to you this coming week about potentially extending—"

"No, Natalie. The agreement was for you to do that for a few years and then come on board with the financial group. The offer is in the envelope with details, and the contract was emailed to you this evening. Also, I've included the sign-on bonus that was promised. It's all there. All you have to do is sign your name and cash the check."

Why do I feel he still doesn't understand what I do? "You

make it sound so easy to trade doing something I love for what I promised you when I was fifteen."

"You graduated in May and turned twenty-three in July. It's time to take on some responsibility and build something that will still be around in twenty years."

"Like your career," my mother adds as if that's helping my side. It's not. *Clearly.*

"I wasn't dabbling," I start. "I was . . . I *am* building something. My clientele list has doubled in the past four months alone."

"Great. Let's get them signed up and invest this extra money they have to spend."

I wave my hand in front of my face because they're not hearing a word I'm saying. My glass is refilled just as Tatum pokes me in the hip. When I turn to her, she whispers, "Don't ruin your night with a fight."

My parents have moved on and are talking to Tatum's parents. Across the table from me, my brother frowns. He knows the last thing I want to do is be a broker. Other than that, I'm not sure where I fit into the family business. I twist my mouth to the side and shrug.

Resting her head on my shoulder, Tatum asks, "Are you ready to go?"

My mom says, "Congratulations again."

"The real world is calling come Monday," Tatum's dad adds.

Tatum sets her napkin on the table and scoots back to stand. "On that note, it's time for us to leave." We're given a round of applause, and she takes a bow. "Thank you for coming and for the lovely gifts."

I may not see eye to eye with my parents, but I'm grateful for them. I move around and hug them. "Thank you for the generous gift and for this dinner."

"You're welcome," my mom says before holding my hand. "I know you're not excited about the position, Natalie, but sleep on it. You might find it's something you can grow into enjoying."

Dad adds, "The real world isn't always sunshine and roses. It's time for you to put your degree to work." I am, but I realize they'll never accept my dreams when they have the best-laid plans in place already.

A sympathetic grin creases my mom's mouth. "I never would have thought I'd enjoy my job so much. And I'm good at it." Caressing my cheek, she adds, "You have a big advantage over me with your degree. There's nothing you can't accomplish if you put your mind to it. We'd be very fortunate to bring on such talent. That you're our daughter is the icing on top."

She makes me want to say yes, but my heart just isn't in it. "I'll sleep on it. Thank you again for everything."

We're quick with the goodbyes to the rest of the guests, friends of our parents, and a few cousins who I never speak to but who came to suck up to my parents. After we escape, Jackson comes outside and waits with us for a taxi. "Where are you going?" he asks.

"Is it that obvious we're not going home?"

"Yes, to anyone under fifty." He bumps into me. "Nice job on keeping things light tonight. They're in a great mood."

"I always have Monday to rain on their parade. No need to ruin a perfectly nice Saturday night."

"Taxi's here," Tatum says, tugging his tie. They've never hooked up, at least that I know of, but she flirts with everyone, and he eats it up. "The Delilah Hotel. I heard the bar is *the* place to be tonight. Are you coming with us?"

"Yep."

In the back of the cab, Tatum sends a few texts and then

contentedly looks out the window. My brother's attention is glued to his phone screen. I actually think he's working even though it's already past eleven. Tapping his phone, I say, "This right here is why I'm not interested in becoming a broker. You haven't even graduated from college, and the work never ends. I don't want to live to work."

He chuckles to himself. Cutting the light off, he looks at me. "Then work to live, sis. I know you don't want to hear this, but if you join the company, I know you'll be the best in the biz."

Squeezed between the two of them doesn't leave much room to wriggle out of this conversation. "I get it, everyone feels I need to put my marketing degree to use in another way." I rest my head back, the lights from outside flashing through the windows. I nudge him with my elbow. "You've done your job in recruitment. Can we give it a rest tonight?"

My worries have resurfaced with a vengeance, putting an edge to my good time. I should have paid better attention to the fine print. My parents gave me a two-year loan to start my business and months to figure out my life. I can't justify continuing STJ if I'm only breaking even.

Tatum and I have been working together, which has been fun. We're alike in so many ways, but our parents are not the same at all. She received a blank check last May and was told to travel the world before settling down.

My parents could afford the same but have always said we need to earn our way in life. I don't blame them. My dad following in his father's footsteps and taking over the business when Grandpa had a heart attack was his dream. It's even Jackson's, who happily stepped up and joined the company part-time his freshman year in high school. It's his dream to run it one day, and he's well on his way, so why are they set on me being there to play second fiddle?

Tatum wraps her arm around my shoulders. "I have no doubt you'll show everyone how determined you are. Together, we're unbeatable, but enough business talk for tonight."

"That's what I said."

"Great minds." The taxi pulls to the curb, and she adds, "It's time to party."

She flashes her phone to the doorman, bypassing a line that extends halfway down the block. He steps aside to let us go inside. We cross the Art Deco-designed lobby and enter the bar. "Welcome to The Delilah. Follow me right this way," a hostess says, leading us to a red velvet booth in the center of the room.

Tatum is quick to slip between Jackson and me to sit like the queen bee. I don't mind since she loves the attention, and I'm perfectly fine letting her own it. Celebrities hidden in corners, socialites lining the bar, and the Manhattan elite fill the dark speakeasy.

Martinis have been flowing when Tatum perches herself on the top of the booth to chat with friends she's run into. I know them as well, but Jackson's been regaling me with stories from a business trip to Chicago last weekend. "He said he prefers traditional asses—round but firm."

"Oh, my God." I laugh behind my hand, worried I'll spew an olive. "Instead of assets?"

"Exactly. I don't know how Dad kept a straight face."

"Me either." I take another sip of the dirty drink, the liquor harsh when it hits my throat. You'd think I'd be used to it since it's my third. It's not smooth like the alcohol I drank in Avalon. I cough, wanting the burning to subside, then try to take a deep breath.

"May I get you a glass of water?" The male voice doesn't contain the deep tones that harmonize to my heartbeats, but

I still whip around, hoping to see the man from Catalina again.

I'm left disappointed. The guy isn't bad looking with dark blond hair, lighter eyes, and a good build. He's actually quite cute, but that instant spark I had with Nick doesn't exist.

At what point do I move on from the best night of my life? When will I forget that I ever met Mr. Smug and Sexy? Is it even possible? I'm starting to believe it's not, and putting effort into it otherwise is fruitless to boot.

Sitting up, I reply, "I'd like that."

11

Natalie

Chad was much more interesting in the dark bar of The Delilah.

I was also on my third martini when I accepted his date invitation. His good looks can't make up for the two hours I just lost sitting across from him at dinner. It'd be one thing if I only had to look at him all night, but he lost me when all he talked about was business.

Did I mention Chad is a stockbroker?

That should say everything, but to be more clear: *Big ego. Little penis.*

Whoever said stockbrokers are sexy was wrong. Come to think of it, though, no one says that. Except, David from my dad's office once said it to me. Literally, those words. "Women find me sexy because I'm a stockbroker."

He was being more arrogant than usual because he had scored a date with a model after flashing cash in his profile pic. That was the only date they went on . . . I heard through the office gossip grapevine when I was interning two years ago. But then he tried that same line again on me, flashed his photo, and then asked me out. When I didn't reply in a timely manner—I was never going to answer—he emailed me the photo "for my personal collection." Although my dad wouldn't mind me dating a successful stockbroker, I have a feeling that wasn't what he had in mind.

Instead of replying to David's email, I forwarded it to my dad and brother and cc'd David.

He was fired that day.

As for Chad's penis, I don't know about the size first-hand, but I can tell by how he loves to brag that he's pretty proud of himself.

He's a dime a dozen in this city and boring, much like every other man I've dated in the past few months. Is it really a surprise I'm still single when this is the current pool of available men?

No.

Thank God dinner is done, and we can move on with our lives—preferably in different directions. I've learned my lesson. Embargos aren't always so bad. Sometimes they serve a purpose, and mine just became clear—do not force a connection that isn't there. If it happens, it happens, but being lonely shouldn't be a condition to lower my standards.

I know magic exists.

I experienced it once on Catalina. But maybe, it's just not my time. I have my company—*at least for now*—and a handful of good, trusted friends. And as they say, there are plenty of other fish in the sea. I just need to get rid of this one. *Stat.*

My mind ticks through this week's to-dos as we walk down the sidewalk. I glance over, politely pretending to be paying attention with the occasional nod and "ah, I see," but the latest sell-off that landed him in hot water with his boss doesn't hold my interest. The bright yellow sign for the corner bodega does, though, luring me to go inside to buy a pen and pad to jot down the extensive list I've created.

Disappointment sets in when we pass it. It would be rude for me to make the detour, so I carry on, hoping he's done talking before we reach the next corner so I can dash off. Friday night is bustling in this part of the city, and the sidewalk is crowded with people going in all directions. When some jerk passing by knocks my shoulder, I'm about to turn around and say something, but then I hear, "Sorry."

I stop and spin around just in time to catch sight of the back of him. "Thanks."

A jaw sharp enough to cliff dive off the side.

That grin that would give a rogue a run for his money.

And brown eyes that precariously balance a warm soul and mischievousness behind squinting lids. "Natalie?"

Oh.

My.

God.

"Nick?" I run into his arms without thinking twice. Not even once, if I'm being honest. Closing my eyes, I breathe him, savoring the energy flowing through my veins. It's as if my body's been dormant, and Nick's the catalyst. "God, I missed you so much," I whisper under my breath, unintentionally vocalizing my confession but not caring. I hate how we ended. *Is it wrong to want an actual chance with him?*

I instantly recognized his deep tone as if my insides had been wired to pick up on the frequency. And I could never forget those eyes and how they drank me in the first time we met. But it's those arms, the same ones wrapped so tight around me now, that I'll always remember most. Like in Avalon, he holds me like he doesn't want to lose me, quenching not only his thirst for this connection but also mine.

When I look at him, his smile is better than I remember and he whispers, "What?"

I'm not going to admit that I missed him twice, though, when he hasn't said it once. I mean, that would be embarrassing. We barely know each other. "I asked what you're doing here?"

His warmth disappears with his arms as he lowers them and takes a step back. "Business." He takes his time giving me a once-over, owning every lingering second. Goose bumps arise like a long-awaited wave covering my body. "Wow." He stares at me as though he expects to see a glitch in the system to prove I'm not real. "I never thought I'd see you again."

Holding my arms out, I say, "Here I am."

"Yes, you are."

I've missed the dulcet tones that warmed my insides. His voice makes me weak in the knees as memories of Catalina flood back.

A throat is cleared, and Chad adds, "And so am I."

Oh, right. I'd forgotten about him. I take a step back to include him in this exchange, though I'd rather just tell him good night. "Chad, this is Nick. I mean, *The*—"

"It's almost been five months," Nick says, with his eyes set on mine and ignoring my date altogether.

"Four months, three weeks," I reply with a shrug. "But who's counting?"

"I have been. Every day. God, it's good to see you, Natalie."

Suddenly, I wish I would have worn something instead of these jeans and a simple blouse that ties at my waist. If I'd know that destiny was going to play her hand tonight, I would have worn a dress, a dress with pockets, or one that's fitted. I'm not sure which dress or the style, but I would have worn something different, a dress just for Nick, is all I'm saying. "You too. *So* good."

Clearly Team Natalie, Nick comes closer, ignoring the invisible line of personal space. I can't say I mind. "I'm not here long, but we should catch up."

I'm startled by a loud clap. When I turn toward the sound, Chad says, "This has been fun, but Natalie and The Chad have plans."

Nick's face remains impartial for about point two seconds. Then he loses it. "The Chad?"

I'm right there with him on this one, but I refuse to get caught up in Nick, more than I am already, and force my eyes back to Chad. "We do?"

"Yes."

Nice enough to move on, Nick asks, "What do you think," as if it's just the two of us, "about going on a date?"

Although my gaze shifts to the man standing next to me, I can feel the heat of Nick's proximity melting me on the inside. Damn him and that, that, that electricity or chemistry. Whatever it is that feels like a fire heating a winter's night that flows between us. Cracking a small smile, I keep my voice low as if Chad might hear me if I don't, and reply, "I'm already on a date, Nick."

"Yeah, *Nick*," Chad adds loudly, awkwardly causing a scene by the wide berth people are leaving around when they walk by. "She's on a date with The Chad, so fuck off, dude."

I've had it with the third person reference. I was patient all through dinner listening to *The Chad*, but I've had enough. Just when I'm about to say something, I notice the warmth of Nick's brown eyes turn cold when he levels Chad with a glare. Stepping closer, he leaves enough room to fill the space with a new, unrecognizable emotion—the playfulness gone the moment Chad opened his mouth. "Listen . . ."

I shouldn't, but I can't help myself when Nick glances at me. I assist. "*The* Chad." Okay, maybe I'm not the most helpful, but it is funny.

"Listen, *Chad*," Nick continues, not missing a beat. "I understand you thought this was going well, but I can tell you from firsthand experience that you don't stand a chance of getting a good-night kiss, much less a second date."

Chad steps closer and scoffs. "Oh, yeah? What makes you think that?"

"Ask her." Nick's eyes only find mine a second, but it's long enough for me to see that sexy confidence I remember so well from Catalina filling his irises.

Chad turns to me, putting his back to Nick. Tilting down, he whispers, "This was going well, you and I, before he showed up, right?" When I hesitate, he adds, "Tell him. We're going back to my place uptown. We can have a nightcap—"

"Well . . ." Throwing my hand up, I place a wall between us. "Let's not get ahead of ourselves, Chad. It's been *okay*, at best—first person or third person—but not worth a nightcap." I was feeling generous with the okay rating on the date. If this were an online survey, it would rate a one star, at best.

"What are you talking about? At dinner, you said you liked the pasta."

Blinking rapidly, I try to make the connection between liking the pasta and liking him. "I did. It was great. Thank you for dinner," I say, staring at him.

Chad's eyes ping-pong between Nick and me but land in my direction again. With his mouth dropped open, he works his way up from my chest, a place he gave more attention than my personality while consuming said delicious pasta. Then he starts laughing deliriously while looking around. "This is a joke, right?"

"Ashton's not going to pop out of the bushes."

"Who?" he asks.

"Never mind." I sigh, realizing the awesomeness of the show *Punk'd* doesn't live on. Guess I'm the only one who loves to watch old shows. Clapping my hands together, I add, "I think this a good place for us to say goodbye." I offer him a friendly handshake.

"What?" With a furrowed brow, he glances at my hand and then up to me. "Wait . . . are you blowing me off?"

"No. Not at all. The date was over, so I'm saying goodbye."

"But I'm a stockbroker. I work on Wall Street."

"Please don't take this personally . . . well, I do hate lying. The fact is, it's you, Chad. We're just not a good fit, so I think goodbye is best."

"Forever?"

"Yes, forever. Goodbye, Chad."

His mouth falls open again, and then he shoots Nick a glare full of daggers. "Asshole."

Nick shrugs. "You win some. You lose some."

Chad looks back at me. "Don't call me—"

"Don't worry. I don't have your number."

The bitterness trails him as he storms away. When he's out of earshot, Nick asks, "The Chad?"

Pleading, I ask, "Can we forget this ever happened?"

"Most definitely not," he says, chuckling.

Rolling my eyes, I shake my head. "Great."

"Let me ask you, Natalie, how'd you set up a date if you don't have each other's numbers?"

"I deleted it at dinner."

"The Chad was that bad, huh?"

"Worse than you can imagine." A horn blaring from across the street draws my attention. I truly never thought I'd see Nick again, and it's not that I'm rendered mute now, but where do I start? Our first conversation was determined by the confidence attained from too much tequila. *Or was it rum?* Our next, a broken Vespa. In other words, there was no typical context to draw from, drunken or otherwise. But now? I want to know what he's been doing. Has he been back to Catalina? Is he in New York for only a short time or staying?

I want to know if he's dating someone. *Please let him be single.*

And has he thought about me as I've thought about him? Or even a little. I'd settle for a thought or two over the months since we parted ways. Although I want to know everything about him, every detail we glossed over the first time, I probably shouldn't hit him with fifty soul-searching questions, so I start with a softball. "How are you?"

"I'm good, better now." When his gaze veers to the surroundings, I take the chance to get a good look at him. Is it strange to notice that although he looks like the Nick I once met, he also appears different in the slightest of ways?

Are the lines beside his eyes a little deeper, or is it an offshoot shadow from the dry cleaner's fluorescent sign? Surely, his shoulders can't be broader. *Can they?* Has he been working out . . . more than he did before, that is? Maybe the final stages of boy to man have come to take their rightful place. *And let me tell you, it is oh, so right.*

I bite my lower lip before I even reach the superficial stuff like the stainless-steel blue-faced Omega watch wrapped around his wrist. Blue, not black. *Friendly. Business yet approachable.*

In California, he oozed the lifestyle of the West Coast in his casual but refined taste of old money. Nick said he's here on business, so the dark suit makes sense and gives off a Manhattan vibe. But the tie isn't missing because it was never a part of the look. That crisp white shirt shows no signs of wrinkling around the collar and highlights a tan that couldn't have lingered from last summer but appears to be a part of him naturally.

Why does he have to be so damn handsome? *Still.*

I'm not usually tongue-tied, but I stand there silently, admiring the man who not only remembers me but also recognized me on the street in a city of eight million people.

He shoves his hands in his pockets and rocks back on his heels. "About that date. The offer still stands if you're up for it."

"Tonight?"

"Right now."

Checking my watch, I purse my lips in thought. "I don't know. I'm coming off a bad date, so that puts a lot of pressure on you to redeem my night. If you don't, that will be two bad dates in one night. Might be a record."

"I'm up for the challenge." I knew he was, but I love that he takes the bait . . . I mean, up to the task. When he looks at me, it's as if he sees my thoughts, and my cheeks heat in response. Taking a few steps closer, so close that my eyes dip closed as if I'm about to be kissed, he says, "As I see it, we have several options."

Playing off how bad I just misread that situation—again, I might add, recalling the last rejection from him that I barely survived—I tap my eye as if dust invaded the corner. "Sorry," I reply, blinking like a crazy person. Lowering my arm, I latch my good eye onto him. "Several options, you say? Do tell."

He gives me a second full once-over and then rubs the pad of his thumb over his bottom lip as if he's devising a plan. The intensity of his eyes lands back on me. "We can get a drink at a nearby bar. Or maybe you're up to hang out at my hotel suite . . . or your place. Whatever you want to do, I'm all yours."

"Are you?"

A smirk splits his lips. "Since Catalina, but that's old news, and I want to hear about the new you."

"Like?"

"Natalie in New York versus you in California."

Undecided on what I want to do, I look down the street one way and then the other, but with him standing so close, his scent has our past trickling back into my memories. I turn back to face him and say, "I know a place not too far from here. It's low-key at this hour, but then turns into an after-hours dance club."

"I prefer low key."

"Then we have ourselves a date."

We make it to the corner before he says, "You look good, by the way."

"Thanks. You aren't so shabby yourself." The sound of his laughter is addicting, and don't get me started on that cute smile. I'd almost forgotten about those dimples.

He playfully knocks his elbow into mine. "Looking on the bright side paid off."

"How so?"

"You told me that if we look on the bright side, we won't be strangers the next time we meet. And here we are—not strangers."

"At the time, it was one of my wiser pieces of free advice."

"What about now?"

"I'd tell you to get my phone number. Much wiser, but you know, we could reintroduce ourselves and share our numbers just in case one of us goes MIA." *Hint. Hint. Hint.*

He takes hold of my hand and entwines our fingers. "We have time, but don't worry, come tomorrow, I'm not letting you slip away before we exchange the vital details."

"We're on the same wavelength." When I see the neon sign ahead, I rush toward the entrance of the bar and then spin back toward him on the sidewalk. Kicking out one of my feet, I sport jazz hands. "We're here."

He stops in front of me but glances up at the sign above the door. Smiling—big and broad, blindingly sexy like a movie star, and so *dimpliciously*—he says, "Avalon."

12

Nick

Natalie talks a lot.

Not annoyingly like some people who love to hear themselves and blather on about nothing. She holds my complete attention, covering topics from a star-less Manhattan night to Quokkas smiles not reaching their souls.

I'm not even sure what she's talking about on the latter, but I could listen to her all night. As if I reminded the universe, Natalie checks the time on her phone. "I've been talking so much I haven't heard anything about you."

"I prefer listening to you."

Her lighthearted smile disappears. "But we're running out of time."

Glancing around, I hadn't noticed how the staff had cleared away so many tables. Although I hate being the one to suggest it, I guess the night has to end sometime. "And I'm not really the nightclub type."

"I don't want the night to end."

"They're not kicking us out yet."

Soft laughter escapes her as she reaches for the wineglass, the silky material of her shirt slipping enough to expose her collarbone. I lick my lips and trace a line up to her eyes. She sips, and when she lowers the glass to the table, she spins it by the stem. "I'm rambling because you make it so easy to feel free to say anything."

I wish I were closer, wanting to inhale her scent that I only caught a waft of on the street. "Like old friends." Teasing her, I say, "Remember when we were strangers?"

"We weren't for long, only long enough for me to want to know you better," she says, laughing a little fuller. "But we were kind of forced together—"

"I don't remember it that way. I readily admit that I took advantage of the opportunity to get to know you."

Angling her chin down, she raises an eyebrow. "Confession time. Did you let the air out of our tire?"

She doesn't sound upset but looks at me in anticipation. Although I was about to take a pull from my glass, I chuckle, lowering the glass down again. "What do you think?" I'm not sure what she thinks of me, good or bad, but she gives me more credit on the conniving side than I feel is warranted.

Despite the dim glow of the candles on the table and the soft, golden light from above, I can't take my eyes off her. Back in Catalina, I tried to memorize everything about her—the curve of her waist to her hips, the way she touched me tentatively at first and then with purpose soon after.

I have relived that moment in the bar many times over the past year or so.

"How are you so hot?" She closes her eyes, and then whispers, "Dear Lord, please don't let him be a mirage." I chuckle. Who is

this girl? And why is she so sure she's dreaming. Should I burst her bubble and miss out on the fun?

"I'm real."

I nearly moan when she bites her bottom lip. "Mm, so real," she purrs. Good God, that's sexy.

But it was the way she looked at me with her ocean eyes later that night in my room—like she saw the man I wanted to be—that had me missing her the moment she left that hotel room.

Seeing her again, even though by chance, has me believing that maybe we were meant to meet again. I'm not normally a destiny kind of guy, despite being from the New Age capital of the United States, but Natalie has me wanting to believe that some things aren't left to chance.

"Not that I'm appreciative of that suit on you, but what kind of business are you doing in the city?"

I don't think I'll ever understand her train of thought, but I won't complain about it either. She keeps things inter-esting. "I'm an attorney."

Her palm sways out as if I'm evidence of this conclusion. She quirks a cunning grin, and then replies, "Lawyers aren't capable of being dangerous."

"Is that so?"

She nods. "Assholes, yes. Dangerous, no."

I balk with laughter. "Just like that, I'm lumped in with all the other assholes? That's disappointing." I take a drink, the scotch going down smoother with every sip. "What do you have against lawyers, anyway? A relationship gone bad?"

"No, they're not my type."

"That doesn't bode well for me."

Resting back, I relax in the leather wingback, watching as she tucks her legs under her, seeming to settle in for a little while longer despite the subdued atmosphere on the verge of changing. "You don't have to worry. You're boding well." I'm glad to see she's not in a hurry. Folded into a matching chair like mine, she asks, "Have you thought about me, Nick?"

"How honest are we being, Natalie?"

Sipping her wine, she follows with a small smile. "I'm conflicted."

"About?"

"This is easy between us. How much do we want to complicate it?"

It's a valid question, one I've asked myself many times. "I was under the impression we would walk away unscathed that night, but that wasn't the case when morning came. I thought I'd get another chance."

"What would you have done with it?"

"I would have made sure I could contact you again. If we're really being honest, I was left in worse condition than you found me." I could have kept joking with her all night and continued this farce we've been willfully writing since we met to protect ourselves from getting hurt. But guess what? It didn't work. The biggest distraction these past few months hasn't been the pressures of my career or my family.

It's Natalie.

Straightening her back, she slips her legs over the edge of the seat again. "Because of me?"

I sit forward, resting my forearms on my legs. This is that second chance I've been wishing for. "I made a mistake and let you go last time without telling you how much I enjoyed that night on Catalina, and I've thought of you every day since."

Her eyes lower to the glass she set back on the table. When her gaze finally latches onto mine again, she leans forward, and whispers, "I was wrong for leaving. I've regretted it every day since I left."

My heart beats against my chest. This is what living feels like, a reminder of how my life used to be. The music is louder, the lights brighter. The world awakens around us as if we've turned up the volume and are hearing our song for the first time, our confessions the melody we've been blocked from hearing. Until now.

She finishes her wine, tipping the glass back as if that will ease the reality of what she just said. When she sets the empty glass back down, questions rush from her lips, "What kind of business do you have in the city? How long are you here? A day? Maybe a few, at best?"

There's an unexpected tremble to her tone. It's not that I've been evasive to hide some secretive life, but hearing about my family and their desire to expand the firm isn't exactly exciting stuff. Not compared to hearing that Quokkas don't actually throw their young at predators. *Who knew?*

Natalie. *That's who.* It's a defense mechanism. She hides in humor, so this side is revealing of how vulnerable she really is. I won't be the one to rip the carpet out from under her. Not looking to tear down walls she's carefully constructed, I let her reside inside her fortress. *For now.*

Anyway, since I've learned of her distrust in the entirety of the profession I've chosen for my career, I think it's wise if I don't push my luck. "Trust me when I tell you that it's boring. You'd literally fall asleep on this table, and then I'd have to carry you out of here. I have no idea where you live, so that would leave me no other option than to take you to my hotel." I smirk. "And you remember what happened the last time you came to my hotel room."

I'm greeted with a smirk of her own. "I do. I remember

very well." Her eyelids dip closed, and she whispers, "Is this asleep enough?" Squinting one eye open, she adds, "Or maybe we can skip a few steps forward, and you can just tell me what will lead you to carrying me back to your room."

She's going to do me in.

I can already tell.

Just like in Catalina.

If given an inch, this woman will take a whole damn mile of my time and willpower. "I think I approached this from the wrong direction."

She sits up, her blue eyes wide open. Man, I could lose days staring into them again, not losing a second to other distractions. "Oh, yeah? Is there a better route? Or do I get options again? I know how much you love a plethora of those. Hit me with the options, Nick."

"One. We can part ways on the sidewalk with a goodbye until the universe brings us together again."

Her eyes roll, but it's undermined by laughter. "So very Californian of you."

I shrug because she's right. My mom has a directional life coach. *Need I say more?* "Two. We go to your place, play some backgammon until you're tired, and I leave, *again*, going my own way."

She shakes her head in disapproval. "Although a rousing game of backgammon is tempting, I'm holding out for option three."

"We stop playing games of any kind and go back to my hotel room."

Her eyes go wide, and her hands clasp together against her chest. "Don't leave me hanging. What happens when we get there?" *Hook. Line.* "I mean, if no games are involved, which is no fun, by the way, then what's on the agenda?"

"We could have sex?"

Her grin grows. "You're asking me?"

I nod.

There's no mulling the options for her. Nope. She's a woman who knows what she wants. "Are you in the area?" *Sinker.*

And even though I'm apparently not her type, I'm the lucky asshole she wants. *At least tonight.* But I'm up for any challenge she throws my way, including changing her mind about the kind of guy she *thinks* is her type. "Just around the corner."

She pushes up from her chair. "Then what are we waiting for?"

I won't keep her waiting. I'm on my feet, and we're out the door. But when we're holding hands walking down the street, I start to realize that this feels too good to part ways twice. Here I thought I was getting her to fall for me, but it's obvious that I'm the one who's sunk.

THE DOORMAN HOLDS the door wide for us, nodding to Natalie, and then saying, "Welcome back, Mr. Christiansen."

Though my cover's been blown, she doesn't say a peep after hearing my last name, but sensing the silence that's shrouded us, I can tell she's dying to. I tell him, "Thank you," and press my hand to Natalie's lower back, walking beside her to the elevator.

When the elevator doors slide open, we maneuver inside, slumping against the mirrored wall, and begin a round of the quiet game. Grasping the brass railing, I brace myself for the impending onslaught of questions.

Abruptly turning to face me, she asks, "Christiansen is your last name?"

I can't read her tone. Is she mad we can't continue pretending there's an iota of anonymity, or is she curious because she didn't imagine me as a Christiansen? I can't say my name in LA without instant recognition, but I don't think it holds the same weight in Manhattan. That's exactly why I'm here—to expand the business and brand. "I had no idea he'd say it. It's not going to get all weird between us, is it?"

Elbowing me in the arm, and though her expression is shaped by amusement, she replies, "Everything about us remains weird, except your name. Nick Christiansen is a great name. It's strong and classic, like a Ralph Lauren model. It suits you."

I lift her hand and kiss the inside of her wrist. Exotic with the faintest sweet scent of fragrant undernote. "I'm not sure what that means, but thank you."

"You're welcome." The elevator dings, stealing her gaze away. She starts moving, but I tug her back, wondering if she's going to share her surname.

She's captured a second wind, the renewed energy felt when she tugs me forward. "Come on, Nick Christiansen."

I want to know everything about her, but I won't pressure her for secrets she doesn't want to share. As I've learned, what's meant to be will be.

Without hesitation or questions, she gives me her trust and follows me down the hall. I unlock the suite and let her enter first. Although my steps are tentative, hers are not, and she enters like she entered the villa in Catalina—like she owns the place.

The drapes are wide open, and we're greeted by a dark cityscape dotted with lights across the wall-to-wall windows. The room has been serviced since I was here this afternoon. The king-sized bed is readied with chocolates on the pillows and blankets turned down, while a lamp in the corner gives off a hint of light.

Natalie heads straight for the window and raises her hands to press against the glass but lowers them slowly back to her sides and peers out instead. You'd think from her initial excitement she didn't live in the city, and this is a new view for her.

My gaze slinks down her back and the denim covering her lower half. Fuck me, she knows how to wear denim. Pulling myself away from her, I click on another lamp by the sofa to add more light to the situation, which seems to snap her from her thoughts.

"It's a nice view," she says.

"It is," I reply, not taking my eyes off her.

I never forgot how gorgeous she was, but seeing her again highlights details that had begun to fade from my memories—the sweet slope from her neck to her shoulders and the way the light catches in her eyes despite how dim the room is. But it's those lips—full, pink, with a sharp bow at the top, kissable lips. They're a distraction. It was more than a struggle not to stare at the bar. *Even harder not to kiss her.*

Shedding my jacket, I toss it over the chair, and ask, "Would you like something to drink?"

"Water works. Thanks."

I twist the cap off and hand her the bottle when I join her by the windows to look out. I prefer the chattier version of Natalie, finding comfort in her stories and company.

Deeper thoughts have invaded her eyes since we arrived, and I'm not sure what to say. She moves to the bed and sits on the edge, forcing a smile. "You didn't tell me how long you're in town."

Sitting on the sofa, I'm not sure what to think. Her mood

has shifted, and the last thing I want is for her to feel uncomfortable. "I can call a car for you if you'd like?"

She leans back on her hands and rolls her head to the side. "Is that what you want?"

"No. I'd rather you stay and talk to me about Quokkas or anything you want, except me. I'm not that interesting, and more so, I like hearing you talk, but small talk doesn't suit us."

Relief washes through her, and she comes over to me, nudging my feet apart with hers. She fills the space, knowing I want her here as much as she wants to be here. My eyes briefly dip closed when she runs her fingers through my hair. "No, it doesn't." It's just a whisper, but I hear other intentions in her tone.

Her confidence is on display when she sits on my lap and settles her arms around my neck. "You brought me here for a reason. How about a kiss, Christiansen?"

13

Nick

I can't say I've been an angel, but damn, she brings out the devil in me.

Cupping her face, I kiss her, not because she asked me, but because I've spent the better part of our time apart thinking about doing just this. This kiss is gentle, slow, a reconnection like our night has been so far.

Our eyes open after our lips part. She readjusts on my lap and then leans her head against mine. But I can't keep my hands off her, so I kiss her again, this time in a frenzy to make up for every kiss we missed this past summer.

Natalie has a fire inside that burns embers as fast as dynamite and then flares again before they have a chance to cool down. I'm almost afraid to look away for fear of missing out. The romantic approach I had planned walking back to the hotel goes up in smoke.

Pulling back, I run my hand along the back of her neck, and whisper, "What are we doing, Natalie?"

I lean back to look into her eyes, searching her blues for

any sign that I've crossed a line. There's nothing but green lights found in her blues signaling back at me. "Picking up where we left off." Her lips crash into mine, and her arms tighten around me as if life itself hangs in the balance.

Though I love hearing those words from her, maybe I asked the wrong question. "What happens tom—"

Through panting breaths, she says, "Don't stop, Nick."

I push my concerns to the future and live in the present. With the first kisses captured, I intend to do dirty things to that mouth of hers with the next. I send her to the cushions, and her back lands on the soft velvet. When I slide over her, her legs butterfly open for me, then wrap around my hips.

I kiss her mouth and the underside of her jaw, her neck, and trail down to the top of her chest as it rises and falls. Her quiet moans and heavy breaths build, gaining voice as I grind against her. Her legs hold me while her heels spur me on.

Sliding my hands under the hem of her shirt, I rub the tips of my fingers in delight from the softness of her skin. I kiss her shoulder and see a wave of goosebumps rise across her forearms as the slightest of shivers is felt against my middle as well. "Are you cold?" I ask.

"No." A grin with secrets to uncover graces her face. "Quite the opposite." Dragging her nails lightly over my scalp above my ears, she continues to smile. "I might not have said it before, but I want you to know that I'm glad we ran into each other."

"Date number one was that bad, huh?"

Laughter wracks her shoulders as she looks away. When her eyes return to me, she replies, "Date number two is so much better."

I lean down to kiss her again, kissing my way to her ear. "Why?"

Her lips press to my jaw, then she teases my earlobe between her teeth before she places a kiss on my neck. "Because that wasn't a match made in heaven."

Tilting my head to the side to find her eyes, I find her laden with some heavy emotion I can't decipher. "And we are?"

"That's why I'm here, Nick. To find out."

Our mouths meet, and gentle kisses turn erotic when our mouths open, and our tongues reunite, continuing a dance we began in Avalon. She tugs at the collar of my shirt, weaving her hands between us and manipulating the top buttons until they release. As much as I don't want to escape the hold this woman has on me, I stand and scoop her into my arms.

Our mouths still attached, I almost trip over the coffee table but manage to stumble over to the bed. Her fingers fumble on the remaining buttons of my shirt until she gives up the battle and rips it open, sending them bouncing across the carpet. "I'll buy you a new one," she states unapologetically.

I toss her on the bed, making her laugh, and stand at the foot of the mattress with my shirt wide open. It's only a quick pause before we both scramble to take off our clothes. Shoes are kicked off, and our tops go flying. As soon as my pants are down, I help her with her jeans that I think might have been painted on by how they refuse to come off.

One good tug on the sides and she yanks her knees up, freeing herself from the denim. We're practically out of breath from the rush, and we haven't even had sex.

As she lies there before me—her underwear barely covering anything—I ask, "Did you wear those for Chad?"

"I wore these for me."

Fuck me, she's incredible. "As it should be, but since I'm benefitting, I have to be honest."

Worry creases her brow, and she props herself up on her elbows. "What is it?"

Reaching down, I take hold of the delicate string wrapped around her right hip. "I prefer you naked." I rip that side and then the other. To the sound of her amusement, I toss the scrap behind me before hovering over her again. I kiss the skin between her tits and then look up at her. "Now we're even."

She's not shy and gives me the time and space to admire her. Not from an arrogant perspective, but the trust we established last year has carried forward. She asks, "Do you always get even?"

"Only when it comes to beautiful women teasing me with the tiniest panties I've ever seen."

She drags the tips of her fingers over my chest. "So, this is a thing you do regularly—pick up women on other dates, seduce them with good conversation and wine, and then bring them back to your hotel and rip their panties to shreds?"

Chuckling, I reply, "I'm not dangerous, remember? I'm just an attorney."

"I think I underestimated your profession."

"No, you underestimated me."

Pushing me gently to the side, she rolls on top of me and kisses me, our lips—finding, feeling, reacquainting. She pulls away just enough for our breath to release and inhale again. "I won't make that mistake again."

I caress her cheek. Her eyes close momentarily, and she leans into my touch. I still can't read her for anything, but she's a riddle I can't wait to unravel. One day, I hope to understand what every sigh, moan, and furrowed brow means, which smile is the one that comes naturally when she's smiling just for me and which is the grin she shares with the rest of the world. I'm convinced that there's something so genuine about our time together. Despite our auspicious beginning, more is developing between us.

Popping the waistband of my boxer briefs, she says, "Off. It's only fair."

"Is that what we're doing? Tit for tat?"

"Literally." She reaches behind her back and unclasps her bra. Sliding the straps slowly down her arms, she teases by wriggling the straps in her hands.

As soon as her tits are revealed, I cup them in my hands, kneading and rubbing my thumb over the buds until they bloom for me. She lifts on her knees, and says, "Your turn."

I'm quick to discard my briefs, anxious to have her settled back on top of me again. "Oh, fuck."

"What?" The alarm I feel wavers across her face.

"I don't have a condom."

Even with wide eyes and raised brows, she still manages to be stunningly beautiful. "Really? Being unprepared is so unlike an attorney," she teases, one brow cocked even when the other falls into place.

Lifting her to the side, I set her on the mattress and push off the bed. "As shocking as it may seem, I'm not the player you think I am."

I search the floor for my boxer briefs, thinking I'm going to have to run to the store down in the lobby. Natalie let me right back into her life, so I won't close that door by walking away from something she's clearly into as much as I am.

She giggles. "I never said you were a player. Judging by looks alone, you could be, though."

Smirking at her, I look at this sexy-as-fuck woman naked on my bed, wanting to memorize every freckle, curve, and mark that's uniquely her. "Thanks." Unfortunately, I can't leave her waiting, so I look around the room, wondering if I stashed a condom anywhere or left one packed in my bags from past trips.

She rests back with her hands under her head. "Any luck?"

"No, but I'm not giving up that easily." I go into the bathroom and start digging through my Dopp kit. It's not a place I've ever stashed condoms, but desperate times call for—*I can order some!* And I have plenty of ideas on how to pass the time while we wait.

When I rush back into the bedroom, I stop in my tracks when I spot Natalie holding a foil packet between her fingers. "Some of us," she says, "come prepared."

Snatching the condom from her, I say, "Good thing one of us is."

"For the record, Counselor, it doesn't upset me one bit that you're not walking around Manhattan on the prowl for a one-night stand. Other than prowling for me, of course."

I move onto the bed next to her, turning the packet over. When I look beside me, I catch her gaze. I reach over and angle her chin toward me. "You have my word that you won't be a one-night stand."

"Promise?"

Sitting up, I run my hand along the length of her thigh. *Sexy. Strong.* She's captivating in ways that had me craving her company long after she vanished last time. I lean down and kiss her, lingering to whisper, "It won't be proven in my words, but through my actions."

The sound of her gasp is almost lost under the thunder of my beating heart. *What's come over me?*

Staring into her eyes, I succumb to a force that keeps pulling us together, one that I have no say or hand in directing. I kiss her. Praying this is enough of a distraction to take her off the scent of my deeper feelings.

Natalie doesn't need to know that it's not only her outward appearance that attracts me. Anyway, talk of souls connecting is ridiculous, considering how little we know about each other. I've only been half a man since she left me. She's dangerous to my heart and well-being.

Her hands push gently against my chest, and I rise to look into her eyes. Her fingers weave through my hair, and she gives me a gentle smile. "It's okay, Nick," she whispers, kissing my temple. "You're dangerous for me, too."

I don't know if I verbalized my thoughts or she can read them, but I kiss her again and then get up and pull down my briefs while her gaze strolls leisurely down my body. She's as shameless as I am. Her unabashed quality is another one of many reasons I'm drawn to her.

Funny.

Hot as fuck.

Quick with the comebacks.

Smart and shameless.

What more does a man need?

To be inside her. That's what.

It's not hard to be . . . well, hard, when a goddess is lying naked and waiting for you. But I'm not an asshole and can wait my turn. *She comes first.*

I move down her body, leaving a trail of wet kisses. Scanning my work, I gently blow, watching her skin come alive with goose bumps. Nipples hard, hips pressing against me when her back arches. Moving lower, I reach up and take her nipples between my fingers, squeezing gently, then rubbing as I shoulder my way between her legs.

With her fingers wandering through my hair, her breathing deepens and legs spread wider, giving me access to do as I please. All I want is to make her feel so fucking good that Catalina fades into the past, and New York becomes our future.

Dragging my palm down her body, I dip a finger between her silky lower lips. Her body wriggles under my hand, telling me everything I need to know. I replace my hand with my mouth, tasting her, savoring her delicate flavor.

Hearing her pleasure forced from her mouth encourages me to go deeper. I dip the tip of my tongue into her entrance, then follow through by fucking her with it. I could take it slow and build the pleasure, but feeling her squirm is my reward. Finding her clit with my thumb, I rub sweet circles, eliciting her body to buck into me. "God, Nick." Her nails dig into my shoulders, but when I keep going, not giving her a reprieve, her moans pick up, and she grabs the sheets, fisting them.

Trapped between her thighs, I feel her back arch as I continue to devour her. She's getting close. "Nick. Nick . . ." My name rolls off her tongue as she begs for more, for me to end the sweet torture and give her the release she needs. I suck and then flatten my tongue, licking all of her over and over again until she loses control. "Oh God," she exhales just before she grabs my hair and pulls, letting her release take hold.

I pin her hips to the mattress, wanting to feel her body tremble beneath my palms and tongue. When the tremors subside, her head pops up. Through heavy breaths, she says, "That did not disappoint. I really need to rethink my whole stance on professionals." Falling back, she stares up at the ceiling with her arms wide, and adds, "Lawyers, I mean, not gigolos or whatever they call male escorts who give happy endings."

I burst out laughing. "I can't speak for male escorts or other lawyers, but I'm glad you like *my* skills."

Her head pops up again with an open mouth, tempting me to fill it. "Like? There's no liking. I *loved* it. I'm going to send you a thank-you gift for that present you just gave to me."

"That's really not necessary." I move up on the mattress beside her.

Her hand smacks flat on my chest as she twists her body to face me. "No, it's what I do. I'm a paid gift-giver."

"There's so much I want to ask about that, but maybe we can table this conversation until after—"

"Oh, of course." She grabs the foil packet and hands it back to me. "Based on that performance, I can't wait for the main act."

I rip it open, starting to think I led with my strongest skills. "No pressure." Maybe I should have saved that for last. *Nah.* Challenge accepted. I roll the condom down my length, then move over her. Natalie's legs part for me and wrap around my middle. Her hands find my shoulders, and her nails scrape across my skin. I position myself with my eyes locked on hers, the stunning blue reminding me of the floating on my surfboard in the middle of the Pacific Ocean. *Heaven.*

Kissing her, I whisper, "I promise you more than tonight." I catch a glint in her eyes and a smile that speaks to my heart. She cups my face and kisses me back.

I take it slow, pushing in just enough to watch her mouth open and hear the quick intake of air. Her lip is bit when I push in so slowly that it's painful to resist slamming into her. I do, though, because every inch I delve deeper steals another beat of my heart until it's pounding so loud that, for a brief moment, I begin to believe that Natalie holds it in her hands.

Her body envelops a part of me while parts of her own the rest. I move and thrust, needing and taking, pushing and giving.

"Yes," she sighs at the edge of losing another breath. "You feel so good." Each moan of hers urges my body for more. We move in a continuum, losing the sense of where I end and she begins. The heat between us, setting us both on fire as we thrust together and against, eventually finding our own unique rhythm.

I lower my head to taste the sheen of sweat that's formed across her shoulder, taking a lick and then sliding my tongue up her neck. Her arms lock around me, and her chest is laden with heavy breaths. I push and pull, thrust and plunge until the sound of her ecstasy drives me home. "Oh, fuck."

I don't pull out.

I don't apologize.

I fuck until every last part of me is hers for the keeping. Reaching between us, I find her clit slippery and swollen, dancing with her pleasure until she teeters over, falling into bliss right after.

When there's nothing left to give, I drop on top of her. Her frame is small under me, so I don't stay long. When I try to roll to the side, though, her arms tighten around my neck. "I like you here. Stay. Just a moment longer."

Kissing her cheek, I rest my head on the pillow under her and begin to relax. But when I hear her breath jag, I move and crash onto the mattress beside her. Her eyes are closed, the weight of the world, and me, released from her expression. "Sorry."

She turns to look at me, and I'm granted a sympathetic smile. "Don't say sorry after we make love, okay?"

It's not lost on me that she makes it sound like this will be a regular occurrence, just as I promised. I didn't know it was possible to be so wrapped up in someone. The change of heart is something new that I've only experienced with her.

Although I was referring to basically crushing her, I kiss her gently, stroking the hair stuck to her cheek and pushing it behind her ear. "Okay."

14

Nick

Panic overwhelms the good dreams I'm having, and my eyes fly open to find an empty bed beside me. *Fuck!*

Apparently, I've learned nothing since Catalina.

I sit up, the smallest bit of hope remaining as I scan the room—top to bottom, left to right—for Natalie. The bathroom door is open with no signs of her inside there either. Last night was too good to let go as if it meant nothing, but she's gone.

Slamming my fists down on the mattress, I grit my teeth and close my eyes in anger for letting this happen twice. I take a deep breath and attempt to riddle myself into rational thought. If she left, she had her reasons. Maybe last night didn't mean as much to her as it did to me.

As much as I want to take this frustration out on myself, maybe I overlooked reality. I had a few drinks, and although I wasn't drunk, not even close, did I misjudge what was happening?

Even though she remains a mystery to me, I find some

consolation in the fact she knows my last name and where I'm staying. What she does with that information remains to be seen.

What's that phrase about setting someone free, and if they never return, they weren't yours? I'm fucking this all up, kind of like my relationship with Natalie. She said she loved what I did with my mouth and tongue. One would assume that I might get a number based on that alone. Why did she make me promise her we were more than a one-night stand if she planned to disappear in the morning?

Natalie's complicated . . . to say the least, but it's one of the things that attracts me to her.

I scrub my hands over my face and get out of bed. Tugging on my briefs, I go to start the shower and grab my phone on the way. Just as I turn on the water, my screen lights up in my other hand.

I grin as everything that ran through my mind since I woke up is gone in an instant.

On the screen is a photo of her that she must have taken this morning. Her face is clean of the makeup I kissed away last night, but a fresh layer of pink lipstick has been applied. The break of day sneaking in through the window glows against her skin. She's absolutely luminous.

Her smile is mischievous as if she knew I'd wake up and freak out, or maybe that's what she planned all along. *Complicated.*

Although the shower water is still running, I leave the bathroom to snoop around for more clues that will lead me to her. I find my next one on the hotel stationery pad—a note left behind:

CHECK YOUR LAST CALL.

. . .

Love,

Natalie

SMILING. *Ear to ear.* It's been a long damn time since I've felt this happy. But I'm still quick to check my recent calls log. I chuckle when I see the last contact my phone called—Tequila Girl.

I call the number and stick in the earbud, waiting for her to answer. "You have my number now," she answers, her voice a balm to soothe my racing heart.

If I was smiling before, I'm flat-out grinning like an idiot now. "I do. Good morning, by the way."

"Good morning." There's a slight pause, and then she adds, "I would have woken you, but you looked so peaceful that I couldn't bring myself to do it."

Hoping to talk to her for longer than a few minutes, I walk back into the bathroom. "I only found peace because you were next to me, so wake me next time."

"With lines like that, I might have to keep you around."

I shut off the shower and then return to the bedroom. "They're not lines. They're truths."

"Tell me more of your truths." Her voice is a whisper.

"I'm only in town until tomorrow, and I want to wake up with you beside me."

"Are you asking me to come to a sleepover or out on a date with hopes of seeing the sunrise together?"

I know exactly what I want when it comes to her. Sitting on the edge of the bed, I reply, "Whatever gives me more time with you."

"Such a charmer." If happiness had a tone, hers embodies it. "You must have had a good night."

"The best."

"If it makes a difference, I did too."

"That makes all the difference." I don't know why I'm suddenly feeling shy. We're joking around and keeping things lighthearted, which is probably best at this hour of the morning, but this is the most I've felt for anyone in a long time . . .

I look down at the pad of paper, tracing my finger over her pretty handwriting, and ask, "Where are you?" A knock on the door draws my attention. "Hold on," I add quickly.

"Room service."

Smirking, I unlock the door and swing it open. She holds up a bag and a cup carrier with two coffee cups. I say, "I've been waiting for you," and then silently tack on *all my life*.

She moves inside the room. "Sorry I'm late."

I let the door close on its own and take her by the waist. Holding her tight, I kiss her and then tilt my head to the side to kiss her cheekbone. When I reach her ear, I whisper, "You're right on time."

Despite her hands being full, her arms come around me, and she kisses me. "Sorry I didn't make it back before you woke up. I wanted to."

When I start kissing her neck, she closes her eyes and tilts her head back. I hear the bag hit the floor, and she exhales. The palm of her hand heats the back of my neck as she holds me there. "I hope you don't have plans for breakfast."

Leaning back, I take the tray of coffees from her and pivot to set it down on the dresser. Quick to return to her, I grab her by the ass and lift her into my arms. "I absolutely have plans for breakfast, but they don't include pastries of any kind."

She cups my face, and our lips crush together. Moving toward the bed, I overshoot it, and we tumble onto the mattress. Nothing deters us, though, and she starts pulling her shirt off while I tug down my briefs. Her bra comes off, then she unsnaps her jeans. Stopping, she says, "I need a little help."

Looking down at her, I groan, "Not these damn jeans again." I hop off the bed and grab the denim at her hips. "Jesus fucking Christ, I'm going to buy you the baggiest fucking jeans to wear around me." I give a little tug, and when she slides down the bed with them, I add, "Brace yourself."

An eyebrow raises and then she grins. Fisting the sheets like she did last night, she lifts her hips into the air, digging her head into the bed. "Is this how you want me, Nick?"

Fucking hell. "Why are you so hot?" I ask rhetorically. I'm so hard for her it hurts, so it'd be nice if I could get these damn jeans off her. I get a good grip again, and this time, I'm successful.

Her bare pussy reminds me of ripping her panties last night, and my impatience to taste her again has me settling between her legs. Kissing her right there at her core, I steal her breath and cause her to squirm.

I hear my name through gasps as her heels dig into my shoulder blades. Pressing my dick against the bed, I seek relief, but nothing can replace the memory of how good she felt last night. So I study what makes her wiggle and what makes her moan, learning what she likes and what sends her over the edge to deliver exactly what she needs. Her body embraces my fingers as tremors rip through her.

Just when I'm about to slide up the bed to score another

of her orgasms and lose myself in one of my own, I turn to her. "Please tell me you have another condom on hand."

She starts laughing. "Since I've been rewarded already . . ." Pushing off the bed, she gets up and walks across the room, not one damn ounce of embarrassment found in the way she moves. Picking up the bag, she continues, "I'm not going to judge you by the lack of preparation, but if we're going to make this a regular thing . . ." She tosses me the bag. "We'd better stock up."

"On bagels or donuts?" I'm still erect from the sight of her naked body, so I shift to ease the discomfort. It won't work since there's only one true way to ease the craving.

Killing me, she takes her time crawling back onto the bed and then kisses my head. "Open it." I like that she kisses my head before she sits down.

Opening the bag, I peek inside. "I feel like it's my birthday or Christmas morning came early."

She lies down, and says, "Speaking of coming . . ." Eyeing me, she darts her tongue out over the corner of her mouth. "Where were we?"

"Right about here." Our tongues tangle in passion, and I slip my hand between us, rubbing until her body begs for more. I roll the condom down my length and push inside her, our bodies reconnecting once again.

Unlike last night, I take my time pleasuring her this morning. I want to know what she likes and how she reacts to different positions and angles. Having her turn over and raise her ass in the air, I don't push boundaries with her yet, but I enjoy watching the way her head tilts back when I dip into her entrance with a slow and calculated drive. The intensity of her heat is felt deep inside me.

The curve of her hips highlights the small size of her waist. I can't resist holding them while taking her from behind. I won't last long, no matter how I try to stave off my release. So I reach around and focus on her bliss, her release becoming mine.

Through staggered breaths, I fall to the side, and she turns over on her back, and we lie together in the aftermath. She turns to face me with a sweet smile on her face, sweet being the opposite of what we just did. "I have a confession to make."

I hate how my heart stops beating as if she's about to devastate the world we just built. "What is it?"

"There was a bagel in that bag."

Trying not to smile, I ask, "What happened to it?"

She rubs her hand over her stomach. "I ate it." Biting her lower lip, there's that mischievous look in her eyes again. "And I'm not sorry about it."

I chuckle but then put on a straight face again. "What do you suggest we do to punish you?"

"I was thinking I could meet you here later and let you have your way with me."

"Is that what you consider a punishment?" I ask, cocking an eyebrow. "Having sex with me."

"No, Counselor, but spending the day away from you will be."

Admiring the pink of her cheeks caused by the early morning workout, I say, "Who's the charmer now?" She's so gorgeous that I feel what she means deep inside me. I don't want to be away from her either. "Natalie?"

Her eyes have closed, and her breathing is even. "Yeah?"

"Sex with you is . . ." I stop, the words getting choked in my throat.

When I fail to continue, she opens her eyes and caresses my cheek before kissing my chin. "I know." Snuggling closer, she drapes her arm over my chest. I tighten my arm around her back and kiss her head. She whispers, "I feel the same," against my chest.

We lie there in the sunshine beaming through a crack in the curtains. When I'm on the verge of falling asleep again, she says, "St. James."

"St. James?"

"That's my last name."

She can't see my smile, but that doesn't matter because I'll be wearing it for the rest of the day. "Natalie St. James is a beautiful name."

15

Natalie

Nick Christiansen is the definition of swoon worthy.

Look it up.

I should be exhausted after spending the night with Nick, but I'm not. I'm full of giddiness instead. I haven't felt this good in so long and optimistic about the future professionally and personally. It's great to feel like my life is back on track again.

After locking the apartment door, I lean against the back of it and fist my hands in excitement. Not wanting to wake Tatum because she's a bear if she wakes up before ten, I squeal silently to release the energy coursing through me.

Do I go to bed to make up for the sleep I lost last night or get ready to slay the day?

Even though my parents don't expect me to come by the office before lunch, I take the opportunity to impress them. *Shower it is!* Today is the day I save my business.

Knowing my mom loves when I dress up, I plan the perfect outfit for today while showering off my night, and

Nick. His scent may be washed from my body, but my muscles ache deliciously as a reminder of him, a sensation I haven't felt in quite some time.

Dressed and ready to go, I walk out of my bedroom to find Tatum leaning over a bowl of cereal. "Good—"

"Shh!" I'm hit with a glare. I'd recognize that look anywhere—the slumped shoulders and squinting eyes even under the faintest sunlight, old makeup because she was too tired to take it off last night, and the shushing. Yeah, that's a dead giveaway.

"You have a hangover?" I whisper.

She drops her sunglasses from the top of her head to the bridge of her nose. "You could say that."

"I just did."

"Ha. Ha." Holding the large black Chanel frames up, she looks me over. "You look like a lawyer." I burst out laughing. Maybe I should wear this for Nick later. She continues, "Where are you going?"

Clasping my briefcase in my hands, I reply, "To see a man about a loan."

Her mouth quirks up at the sides. "You're going to see your dad?"

"I sure am. Wish me luck."

She slides off the barstool and comes to hug me. "I wish you all the luck in the world, my friend." Leaning back, she adds, "You got this, Nat. Don't be intimidated. Stand up for what you believe in—yourself and us."

"I will, and I hope you feel better." I open the door, but before I go, I say, "And thanks for the pep talk."

"That's what I'm here for. That and the Lucky Charms."

"They are delicious."

"Magically."

With a pep in my step, I hurry down the stairs and call

a car to deliver me to Wall Street. As soon as I arrive on the infamous street, I duck inside the building and head up to the Manhattan Financials' offices on the twenty-fifth floor.

The elevator doors slide open, and I keep walking toward the entrance, signaling to the receptionist that I'm here to see my dad. Although she's on the phone, she waves me in after buzzing me through. I spent every summer from my eleventh-grade year in high school to my junior year in college interning here. I've worked every job from mailroom to reception. I was brought into meetings with my parents to observe them in action.

Despite their best efforts to teach me financial advising and the brokerage side of the business, I never acquired a taste for either. Stockbrokers are intense, and I'd rather spend people's money than manage it. Although the gifting profession sounds easy, it takes a knack for reading people. What will have their heart racing with excitement not only to give a great present, but they seek the reward for the thought. I have to stay two steps ahead of popular gifts and know what's the next hot item.

My parents have tried to understand what I'm trying to create, but other than hiring me to sort out their corporate holiday gifts, they lose sight of the potential.

Taking a deep breath, I psych myself up for the sales pitch of a lifetime and then knock. From the other side of the door, my father calls, "Come in."

Entering his office has never intimidated me until now. "Hi, Dad."

"Natalie." He only glances up for a split second before he returns to analyze something on the computer monitor that has his face all twisted. "Have a seat and I'll be right with you."

Mom comes in before I sit down. Hugging me, she asks, "How are you, honey?"

"I'm good. Really good." I want to sing Nick Christiansen's praises, but my parents are the last people who should hear about my sexual exploits. Though they might be interested in hearing about what a gentleman he is and that he's a lawyer. Parents love lawyers for their children, especially if one of said children has no aspirations of becoming one.

"That's good to hear." My mom sits next to me. "Let's talk."

With that phrase out there, I barely have time to set down my bag. My dad turns away from the screen to look at me. "It seems the loan was calculated at the correct rate and should last you through the end of the term. Which, of course, is the end of November."

Covering my hand on the arm of the chair, my mom adds, "We know how hard you've worked on STJ, even with the heavy course load you were taking your senior year. We can see how it could turn into an exciting revenue stream. It utilizes your creativity, craftiness, and people skills. I can speak for both your father and I when I say that we do hope to have you join our team one day. But you're allowed to pursue your own dreams, which you're doing."

A glance from my mother to my father is the equivalent of a tag in the ring to take over. Without missing a beat, he folds his fingers together on the desk in front of him. "I can see you came prepared, Natalie, and I've already read over the email you sent. Not to discount the fact that you're here to defend your plans, but we support you."

Still sitting with my back stiff as a board, I nod. "Thank you. That's very much appreciated."

He continues, "Most businesses take twelve to twenty-four months to turn a profit." He clicks something on the keyboard and then squints at the monitor again. "You broke even the past three months. With two of the biggest gift-giving months ahead, we think it would be foolish to pull the plug right now." *I have worked so damn hard, and I'd almost wondered if they weren't proud of me.* But this endorsement goes a long way to heal that pain.

I try not to let my hopes get ahead of reality, but excitement ignites inside me. "What does that mean?"

"It means," my mom starts, "we'll extend the loan for another year."

"Really?" I mentally pack the pie charts and the line graphs I'd memorized away.

My dad replies, "Yes, but there are conditions because a floundering company is not a good investment. Blow it out of the water." I wait for more, assuming the agreement will be the same as before. "Get in the black and stay flush in cash. Also, you must pay back ten percent of the loan by the end of the term. You go into default if you miss one of the quarterly payments. Don't miss one, okay?"

"I won't. I promise." I finally relax back in the chair, holding tight to the slim portfolio I bought to carry my color-coded reports. I hadn't run over the figures with my accountant to be 100% sure I am in the black, but to hear such endorsement from my parents blows me away. *I can do this. They believe in me.* "Thank you for the extension. I'll make you proud. Can we go over my projections together? I'd like you to see where I think STJ is heading."

Standing, my mother heads for the door. "I can't look at them right now. Some investors from out of town have flown in to meet with us this week. We need to prepare for them." With the door in hand, she adds, "Honestly, Natalie, put your energy into your company, and don't worry about us. You're making sound business decisions."

"Thanks, Mom, I appreciate you saying that." The door closes behind her, and my dad asks, "I think that went well. You?"

"Better than well." I get up and move around the desk. When we hug, I spy his monitor. Jolting upright, I ask, "Solitaire? I thought you had my account up on the screen."

He shrugs. "Sometimes I play to take off some stress."

I laugh and then grab my leather portfolio. "I really do appreciate you both supporting this dream."

"We support you. I have a call now, so if you'll excuse me."

"Yeah, no worries. Thank you and love you."

Slipping out of the office, I do a quick fist pump, then leave before they change their minds. I pass reception and then wait for the elevator to arrive. It's such a production to get out of here, and I start to lose patience. I just want to call Tatum and share the good news, but I wait to tell her until I'm outside the building where I'm allowed to squeal with glee without embarrassing myself or family.

When I enter the lobby, I head for the revolving door and spin into it. I only take two steps forward before I'm enclosed in the pie-shape space, and it comes to an abrupt halt. I put my hands flat against the glass and push again. When I'm met with resistance, I shove the side of my arm and hip to the unyielding door. And then again, even harder.

Crap, I'm trapped.

A knock on the glass has me looking up to see a familiar face in the opposite compartment as me. Excitedly, I lift onto my tippy-toes as if I can kiss that smirk off his face. "What are you doing here, Nick?"

He points at the door in front of him and mimes for me to watch out. I'm not sure I have much of an option but to stand still and hope he can dislodge it, so we don't spend the rest of his time in New York trapped in a glass box staring at each other.

Setting his hands against the brass bar, he leans into it and then I see him angle down and shove really hard. It doesn't budge. He catches me watching out of the corners of his eyes and seems to find a new motivation to give it another try. This time, he puts a shoulder into it while looking right at me and slams against it. The momentum has him stumbling forward into the lobby just as the door behind me slams into my ass, sending me flying outside.

Despite my classic and gorgeous black Chanel "too high to run in" heels, I catch my balance within an inch of my life just as Nick grabs my middle. Phew!

I tap his chest and tease, "Your timing was off, Counselor."

He chuckles. "I guess my glory days of catching women now lie in the past."

My breathing is still a little off-kilter, but I don't care. I'll sacrifice the air I need to get another kiss from this man. I lift and kiss him with no concern for PDA in broad daylight on a Monday.

When our lips part, I reach up and rub the lipstick that transferred to his lips, and say, "What a nice surprise."

"You're telling me." Still holding me with no regard to anyone passing us on the street, he caresses my cheek and kisses me again.

He makes me feel like more than someone he met at a bar once. He makes me feel like we have a history worth building upon, as though I've made his life special, and I'm a great catch—not just physically—but for a relationship. I could wipe that lipstick that lingers near the corner of his mouth, but I have a feeling he doesn't mind the marking.

Without the words being said, I know I've found someone who makes my life special as well. *At least until he leaves tomorrow.* But we'll worry about that when the time comes.

Stepping back before I maul the man, marking him with hickeys and more red lipstick kisses, I ask, "What are you doing here?"

"I have a meeting."

How ironic. Until I remember there are dozens of companies stashed throughout the building. "Are you busy tonight? I have some celebrating to do, and I hope you'll be there, too."

"I have no plans but you. You're at the top of my to-do list if you know what I mean."

"I do and can't wait for you to tackle that task later. Since you have my number now, don't be afraid to use it."

He kisses my cheek, then reluctantly takes a step back. "I won't." Backing away, he adds, "Sorry, I have to go. I can't be late for my meeting."

I wave him off. "Don't worry about me. Go."

"See you tonight, Ms. St. James."

"Can't wait, Mr. Christiansen."

Giving me a little wink, he then turns and dashes in the manual door, skipping the revolving door altogether and leaving me standing here like a schoolgirl with a new boyfriend.

Maybe I should keep my guard up and not let him so far into my heart. But judging by how I'm floating on top of the world, is it too late to save me now?

16

Nick

"I reviewed the contract you sent to my hotel yesterday. Nothing stood out to me, and everything appears to be in order." I turn over the last page of the hard copy in front of me and then lift my attention to the legal team of Manhattan Financial. "My family understands the need for a personal touch, but I'm still curious why you wanted to meet in person."

Mrs. Singh, one of the three attorneys, rests her clasped hands on the table. Oh yes, I know that move, the technique you learn as a rookie lawyer to put the opposing team at ease and then go in for the kill. Mom's instruction in meeting protocol and psychology certainly helps, too.

"This has been a family-owned company since the beginning. We could have gone public, but that's not what our CEO wants."

"Because it no longer supports having a personal hand in the day to day when it's a commodity."

She adds, "Precisely."

"Rest assured. Christiansen Wealth Management takes pride in building relationships first and then bank accounts. This is our thirtieth year, and our reputation brings in the business, keeping our marketing budget on the slimmer side and allowing us to invest more into our employees. Our retention rate is as impressive as the names of our clientele."

Another attorney, Garrett Stans, who told me to call him by his first name, unlike Mrs. Singh, shifts in the leather chair. "So why are you a good fit for our clients?"

I could rush an answer, but I think they prefer a more thoughtful response over one of arrogance. I search the windows to the city buildings that fill it from end to end. I never get used to how dense it is—gray and brown for as far as the eyes can see, especially on this floor. There's no sky to be found.

It's a rush being a part of a place where you can feel the beat of adrenaline. But I have to say, I prefer the ocean and the peace it brings. Turning back to them, I reply, "Because we care about them as much as their needs. Each client will be given a complimentary meeting in person or via Zoom to discuss their portfolio and their goals. But we want you to know that we're not looking to let your people go. Quite the opposite. We want to keep them on if they'd like to work with us. Some will inevitably leave, but it won't be because we're closing the door on them."

"I think John will be pleased with our report." Garrett stands, and we shake hands while I stand as well. "Thank you for flying in. We wanted to meet with the potential buyer's team to get a good feel for who they represent."

"I appreciate it and look forward to hearing from you soon, hopefully with a positive outcome."

Mrs. Singh adds, "And please keep this confidential. The

last thing we want to do is make our clients or employees nervous."

"I agree. This will remain strictly between the parties involved."

"Thank you," she says with a nod.

The other attorneys say their goodbyes, but Garrett walks with me back to reception. Talking to me like we're friends, he says, "If I had to guess, I think selling to your family would be a good move for the bossman. I would be part of the transition team, and I think it would go smoothly based on what you've said."

"That's good to hear. My family is looking to get solid footing in New York, and I think the timing of Manhattan Financial selling couldn't be more perfect."

He looks around as if there are spies, then lowers his voice and says, "Selling the company isn't common knowledge. Not even a hint of it is out there. Everyone involved is under an NDA. We started with feelers and then got solid interest. Our CEO has had some health issues and wants to retire. He was hoping his kids would take on the company. His son is eager but still has another year, and his daughter hasn't shown interest. He's now ready to make a move and enjoy his retirement instead of dying on the job." He stops, seeming to bite his tongue. "I shouldn't say that. He's a great guy, really is, but you know the stress of a stockbroker. It wears on you."

"Yeah, I hear the same about attorneys."

It takes him a second to figure out I'm joking, but then he laughs. "Sure does."

Post meeting, I'm left with a lot of information to share with Andrew and my dad. Seems the timing is right to up the offer to cut out the competition and get this deal closed.

But first, there's another deal I want to close, one that specifically involves Natalie.

THE LIGHTS ARE golden and reflect against the mirrored wall full of bottles, giving the impression of a million stars lit up just for her. She deserves the stars, even in the middle of all these skyscrapers.

The band is paused as all eyes and ears are trained on the two women standing on the bar. Natalie has a bottle of champagne in her hands and a glittering tiara on her head with Tatum right next to her. I missed the speech, but I'm here for the finale.

I don't have to search for my girl. She's exactly where she should be—owning the room. In a short black skirt that fans out from her hips, it highlights her great legs. A sparkly gold top fails to disguise the shape of her fantastic tits. I'm sure that was the point when she picked it out. Jealousy strikes like lightning, and I scan the place to see what feels like a thousand guys vying for her attention.

I'm not going to waste time worrying about other guys when I only have one night left to leave an impression of my own.

This is quite the sight. She knows how to celebrate. From how she dressed to the champagne, she could be easily discounted as a party-girl socialite, but it doesn't matter what she wears. Her aura has everyone in the room mesmerized, including me.

Weaving my way through the crowd, I notice how different this bar is to the ones in LA. It's quaint, like everyone here is friends. In LA, I tend to see the same group of people, but it feels more competitive there, like we keep our enemies closer instead of our friends near.

Tatum shouts, "In celebration of my best friend, a glass of champagne for everyone."

I'm quick to cut through the cheering just before the ladies start to climb down. The band begins playing on the far side of the room, and everyone returns to their own conversations just as I reach them. Rubbing Natalie's calves to get her attention, I'm greeted with a spark in her eyes that rivals her shirt for catching the light. I'd never get tired of looking at her, but it's her personality that has me craving more time with her. "Need a lift?"

She sets the bottle on the bar and squats down, miraculously balancing on thigh high, sexy fucking-heeled, black boots. "Thought you'd never ask." Her smile is infectious, her laughter better than any melody a band could create. While she holds her tiara, I lift her by the waist and set her down safely.

I turn back to Tatum. "Would you like help?"

"Thanks." When I set her feet on the ground, she comes in to give me a hug. "It's good to see you again. It would be better if Harrison was with you."

Chuckling, I look down, rubbing my chin. "Yeah, I think he'd agree."

Natalie flies into my arms and rests her head on my shoulder. "If only destiny wasn't so wicked and would keep us abreast of her plans."

Enjoying the feel of holding her again, I rub down her back and back up again. To Tatum, I say, "I'll bring him with me next time."

She smiles, and it's easy to see why Harrison was attracted to her. Fun and easy-going. Pretty and great taste in friends. The best, actually. I kiss my girl on the forehead, and she looks up at me. "Glad to hear there's a next time planned. When is that exactly?"

"When would you like it to be?"

"Wednesday."

I start laughing. "So fly home Tuesday and return on Wednesday?" I raise an eyebrow. "I'm all in, baby, but I can't say the same for my bosses."

"I thought you worked with your family?"

"I do. They're my bosses."

Tatum hands her a glass of champagne. Natalie takes a sip and rolls her head on her neck. "I worked for my family for years as an intern. I couldn't imagine doing it full-time for my career. Not that they're bad people or bosses, but I want to do something I love."

"If you can make money at something you love, then you'll never work a day."

"That's my philosophy. And *you* need some champagne because we're celebrating. I got an extension on my loan for another year."

"Are all these people your friends?"

She laughs again, the sound as effervescent as the champagne. "No. This is just one of our favorite places to celebrate."

Tatum moves closer. "Though we probably know most of them."

Ah. It seems so by how lively the crowd is in their presence. I've always been fairly casual when it came to women. They come and go, and I let them, sometimes encouraging them to take off, and maybe we'll hook up again. I don't have to chase them, thanks to the genes I inherited, but the more laid-back I was, the more possessive some of them got. It's weird how that works.

I'm not like that with Natalie. I met an independent

woman with her own goals and dreams to accomplish. I won't be the center of her world because she doesn't cling, despite currently clinging to me. She's not alone, considering I'm doing the same to her. But I'm starting to wonder if there's more to us than a few days here and there.

It's not something I've wanted, but she makes me smile and is fun, lives life on her own terms, and is open to having me be a part of it. *So far . . .*

Tatum hands me a glass, and the three of us toast to Natalie's success. Tatum quickly disappears, not even bothering with an excuse to free herself of the burden of witnessing me kiss Natalie like I've wanted to since we left the bed this morning. "I missed you," I whisper against her cheek and then go lower to kiss her neck.

Her arms tighten around me again, and she kisses me just under my ear. "I missed you, too." Tilting back, she finds my eyes. "How did your meeting go?"

"It went well. I think we'll be making a deal, but my dad and brother have often said not to count the eggs before they hatch." She laughs.

"Yes, that makes sense."

"How long are we staying, beautiful?"

"The more drunk people get, the less they notice anyone else. Well, I say at least an hour, as it would be rude not to, don't you think?"

"For you, anything." I want to tell her that I'm all in, but it's been what? Twenty-four hours at best? Yesterday at this time, she was on another date with someone else. Maybe that's why I should hold my feelings back a bit, or maybe it's the crowded room here to celebrate her. Either way, I'll take tonight and *all* it brings.

Time doesn't matter when it comes to us.

"I'm glad you're here, Nick."

"Same here. First Catalina, then New York. And now we have each other's last names and phone numbers." We've made love and fucked, but I'm not sure here is the place to remind her of *that*. "Here's to us."

"It's like we skipped the slow ride up the tracks and met at the top of the roller coaster. Now we're shifting into warp speed, and I don't know if I'm strapped in safely."

I straighten the crown on top of her head. "Don't worry, baby. If you fall, I'll catch you."

17

Natalie

I shouldn't like being his baby as much as I do, but it's amazing how views on things like that change when with the right person.

Is Nick the right person?

He's been a great sport by staying and drinking, hanging out with Tatum and me. But there are so many people we know here that it's usually a large crowd with everyone trying to add to the conversation.

Nick just fits right in—my life, my group of friends, my heart—like he's always been a part of things. I listened to him regale everyone with stories from surfing with sharks to once falling for a girl who fell into his arms. His arm tightened around me, and I held him the same. In the brief span of a few hours here, we went from having fun to something more serious. I'm not sure if we'll label it, give this relationship a formal title, but I'm not opposed to it.

It's been a long time since I was in a committed relationship, and I wonder now if it was a good thing I waited. I know I'll hate the geographical distance between us, but who knows what tomorrow brings?

After leaving the restroom, I stop at the end of the bar when I find him and Tatum across the room. From his looks to his charming personality to being a man with a real job that pays his bills, he's perfect. Nick's not just perfect on paper, but in real life.

Even with my friends, he's a dream come true. Tatum's always been hard on my boyfriends because she was right—they were losers. But with Nick, she laughs while showing him something on her phone.

Wait . . . *photos!* Incriminating photos. I run, squeezing between groups of friends and couples, guys trying to pick up women and bachelorette partiers. With my eye on the prize, I make a Hail Mary attempt to grab the phone and make a run for it. Practically diving for it, I say, "No!"

But in my haste, I didn't calculate Tatum moving her arm to her chest and taking the phone with her. I bumble into the back of Nick, but being the wall of muscle that he is, I'm like a bouncy ball off him. Landing on the heels of my boots, I wave my arms frantically in the air to keep from tipping backward.

Tatum and Nick each are quick to grab a wrist and pull me forward so I can anchor my feet.

Angling his head, Nick stares at me in curiosity. "And I thought you falling in Catalina was a one-off. I'm reconsidering my position on this."

I shake my head. "No need for considering or reconsidering anything of the sort. I'm usually not clumsy. Well, I wasn't before you anyway."

"I'm to blame?"

Nodding with confidence, I say, "Technically, yes. There's

some kind of weird gravitational pull you have on women that makes them fall at your feet."

"Unless I catch them, of course. Don't discount my catching skills."

"I would never. *You* caught me. I'm living, breathing proof of your skills."

Tatum interrupts to ask, "What are we talking about?"

I burst out laughing. "Nothing. Just flirting with Nick."

She laughs as she glances around the bar. "That makes a lot more sense." When she turns back, she looks back and forth between Nick and me. "You know, Harrison told me he'd never seen you instantly smitten before."

Nick seems surprised. "Harrison said I was smitten? That doesn't sound like him."

"He said obsessed, but I softened it with smitten."

Nodding, Nick slinks his arm around me and pulls me to his side. "I am fairly obsessed with her."

"Fairly?" I ask, hitting him playfully in the chest.

He lifts my chin. "Utterly, head over heels, obsessed with you, Natalie."

I'm not sure if my knees go weak from his words or from how he's staring into my eyes like he can see forever for the first time, though the latter might just be me. Either way, my walls have crumbled at the feet of this man, and I'm letting him into my life like we have more than tomorrow ahead.

Tatum adds, "I'm just saying that I'm glad you two reconnected, and I know Harrison would feel the same."

With Nick's arm around me like it's now mine to parade around the place showing him off, I say, "I appreciate that, and I think we're going to take off."

I give her a hug, and then she and Nick share a friendly embrace. He says, "I'll let Harrison know I ran into you."

"Yes, tell him hi from me. I'm going to say hi to some

people I saw just walk in." She's about to dash off but stays a second longer to say, "Congrats, Nat."

"Thanks. I'm pretty excited we have a job for another year."

Thumbing toward Nick, she laughs. "I meant for him but on the loan as well." She winks and then disappears in the mass of people crowding O'Reilly's. It's hard to pass up a Monday at this bar because of the great atmosphere and live band. Except it's suddenly becoming easy to leave since Nick is here.

We hold hands as we work our way toward the exit, but talk about bad timing. I reach the door just as Dane walks in. My ex's eyes dart from my face to my hand clasped in Nick's. He glares at Nick before he turns back to me. "Nat."

"Hey," I say, my view suddenly aimed at the floor. I force my eyes up, not letting him win. I felt like shit when we were together, and though it was hard to get out from under that relationship, I did and have never felt better. My hand wraps around Nick's a lot tighter, and I say, "Bye."

Dane stands in the way, but I slink around him. Nick, though . . . he waits until Dane gives way. Out on the sidewalk, we start walking wordlessly until we reach the corner of the block. Nick stops, and says, "Don't ever cower to a man. You don't owe anyone anything. You stand up for yourself by not giving him or any other man the power to think they're in control. They're not. You are. Own it." His voice is as tense as his shoulders.

"Why are you mad at me? Because I didn't want a confrontation with an ex-boyfriend?"

"No, because you deserve better than how you just treated yourself. You don't owe him jack shit, so tell him to fuck off and move on with your night, or better yet, your life."

Anger rises inside me, the heat reaching my chest. "I have." Holding our conjoined hands, I add, "See?" But I don't feel understood, so I step back, needing the distance to get my thoughts together before speaking again. "I may have seemed weak to you, but that was me facing my demons for the first time since we broke up. What you fail to understand, Counselor, is that I don't need to wage a war with him anymore. Like you said, I don't owe him anything, not even another moment of my time. So when I told him bye, I meant it. Hopefully, it's forever this time."

I move close to a candy store entrance to get out of the pedestrian traffic and watch as he stares at me. He finally joins me under the pink and white awning, and says, "I'm sorry. I misjudged your response, your strength in that situation, and replaced it with how I thought it should go. So I was wrong, and I'm sorry for not understanding."

Pinching his shirt in the front, I tug him closer. "I expected a fight."

"I can admit when I'm wrong. In this case, I shouldn't have said anything."

I rest my forehead against his shirt. "I hope this counts as our first fight."

His brow raises and his eyes widen. "You want it to?"

"Yes, because if so, then we can move onto the last item on your to-do list."

I didn't know it was possible for his eyes to go wider, but he manages it and then balks with laughter. "I give you a taste, and you want the whole damn ice cream cone."

"You're not wrong."

Pointing toward the ice cream parlor, he adds, "Pun intended."

Taking his hand, I tug him toward the street so we can

hail a taxi. "Come on. We're running out of time, so let's get to it. Your place or mine?"

"Depends how loud you plan to be since you have a roommate."

"Your place it is." When I take off walking again, I'm pulled to a stop. Looking back at him, I ask, "What?"

"What picture did you not want me to see?"

I'd almost forgotten about that incident. "I've known Tatum all my life. She has more blackmail material than anyone else. I'm not sure which photos she was showing you, but I'm sure it involved some bad hairstyle and me looking awkward from my teenage years."

He releases my hand and pulls his phone from his pocket. Holding it up, he said, "And here I thought you looked gorgeous the day we met."

There on his phone is a photo of me in Catalina—hair blowing wildly in the wind, the ocean off in the distance behind me, and a smile that could light up Brooklyn. It's a photo I insisted she take when we walked out of the bar where I said I think I just met the man I'm going to marry.

I may have been tipsy, but that encounter with Nick is unforgettable. A lot like the man in front of me now. Why am I already missing him? I barely know him. My heart knows him best. His sweetness toward me draws me in like a bee to his honey. Don't even get me started on the sex . . . Call me shallow for loving our physical as much as the emotional connection we're building, but damn, I love that he cares to put my needs at the forefront of his pleasure. That's a first for me to experience, and now that I have, I'm not sure I want to let him go. As a matter of fact, I don't.

I return to him. "Tatum gave you that?"

"Yeah, I asked her if I could have a copy." His words are tentative as if I'll tell him no. "I hope you don't mind."

I look back at the photo again. "I don't mind. Now you have something to remember me by."

"Do I need something to remember you by?" Lowering the phone, he keeps his hands to himself when all I want is to have them touching me. "Because I've been thinking that maybe we could give a long-distance relationship a try." I open my mouth, but he's quick to put a hand up to stop me. "I know you said it's impossible because we're in two different worlds. Beaches to skyscrapers. Sunny all year to changing seasons. Hollywood to Broadway. But if I could move my world closer to you, I would in a heartbeat. I can't promise you I'll see you every weekend, but I can promise you that In-N-Out Burger is pretty damn good. So whether I come here or you fly there, I think whatever this is between us is worth giving a real shot."

"If you keep this up, Mr. Smug and Sexy, I'll be a pile of romantic mush to clean up off the sidewalk." I giggle, and say, "And I think you're playing dirty by dragging burgers into this big life decision."

"I know your Achilles heel—add in a mound of fries, not as a side, but on a plate of its own with extra ketchup on everything and all the added extras no matter the expense. That's what I'll give you if you give me . . . if you give *us* a chance."

"You're speaking my love language." If I wasn't already weak to him, he has me ready to take the leap. I hold my hand over my stomach because now I'm hungry, but there's too much to talk about to skip over and lose sight of this conversation over a plate of fries. "As much as I love talking about food, can we loop back to the long-distance dating part again?"

We clasp hands again and resume walking. "Yes, what do you want to know?"

"Where your heart lies."

"My heart has been yours since that day in Catalina."

This time when I tug him, I'm successful. "Now you're trying to steal my heart, Mr. Christiansen?"

"I thought I was smug and sexy."

I bump into his arm, knocking him off track just like he's knocked me off mine. "You're so bad. I knew you'd fixate on that part."

He shrugs. "Well, you did call me smug, although I'd prefer to hear more about the sexy part." I roll my eyes, and just when we reach the corner, he steps down into the street putting us closer to eye level. Cupping my face, he kisses me, and then says, "If I get the girl, I'll be bad every damn night if I get to spend them with you, Ms. St. James. How does that sound?"

"How can I say no to that offer?"

"I'm hoping you can't."

I press into the space left between us. Snug in his arms, I know what I want to say. I can't let fears of being dumped or, worse, not being good enough for him to keep me from trying.

Angling my head on his shoulder, I look up, catching my tiara before it slips off. "Are you asking me to be your girlfriend?"

His fingers weave into my hair, holding me close, and he kisses my forehead. "I am. Will you be my girlfriend, Natalie?"

My heart is racing, but there's nowhere I'd rather be than in his arms and work my way into his heart like he's worked his way and settled into mine. Long distance may be something new, but for him, it's worth the fight to make it work. "I'm yours, Nick, and have been since Avalon just like you said you've been mine."

We kiss, the new commitment a part of every ounce of our embrace, and two become one.

18

Nick

This fucking sucks.

It's my turn to leave, and I don't want to. How is this fair or right? We just decided to give a cross-country relationship a try and here I am walking out less than ten hours later.

Parking my suitcase at the door, I return to the bed and lean down to kiss her one more time. Natalie's eyes slowly open, and the heat from her hand warms the back of my neck. "Don't leave me."

Closing my eyes, I push down the will to stay, knowing I have to go. She pulls me close and kisses my head. When I don't say anything . . . I can't. She says, "I'll see you soon. Whether on video or in person, we'll be together."

Three little words come to mind, though I know it's too soon for that. I don't even know why they're coursing through me other than I wish I could lie down with her and stay. "Adulting sucks."

She giggles while quietly rolling onto her back to look

into my eyes. "It does, but being your girlfriend doesn't." She lifts up to steal a kiss. When she drops back down to the mattress, her hair splays over the pillow. I reach over to the nightstand and pick up the tiara she wore last night when we were out and during the second round of sex. I set it on her head, feeling like it fits her. She smiles, and my heart momentarily stops just looking at her. She's a goddess, my muse, the prettiest girl I ever did see. She says, "I'm going to miss you."

"I won't allow enough time to pass to let you."

"Promise?"

"I promise." This time, I kiss her and then push off the bed.

But she grabs my hand before I get out of her reach and pulls me back to her. She takes her phone from the night-stand, and says, "Come here." I lean down and kiss her. She takes a photo, and then says, "Say fries."

I laugh but do as I'm told. "Fries."

Typing quickly, she then drops the phone to the bed. My phone vibrates in my pocket. I pull it out and see the photo. She adds, "Now you have something to remember me by."

I could stare at this photo all day, but when I'm with her, I'd rather look at her. Nodding, I stand, knowing I've run out of time. "See you around, New York." Grabbing hold of my suitcase, I open the door and look back.

She rests up on her elbows. "See you soon, Mr. Smug and Sexy."

The door closes behind me, and I walk down the hall with a stupid grin on my face.

"I HAVE A GIRLFRIEND."

My brother never looks up from the phone in his hands. "That's great, but did you get the contracts?"

"Asshole."

"What's this about a girlfriend?" The sing-song voice has me turning on the barstool to find my mother smiling like a cat who ate the canary and can't be bothered to hide the evidence. She rubs my shoulders and gives me a squeezing hug before moving to the other side of the island. "Tell me everything about New York and start with the girlfriend."

"What?" Andrew asks, looking up from the screen. "You have a girlfriend?"

Rolling my eyes reminds me of Natalie and how cute she is when she does it. "You never listen, man."

"I listen when it matters. Your extracurricular activities generally don't interest me, but I have to admit that I'm surprised to hear this news, considering I didn't think you were dating."

My mom may not be saying anything, but she's all ears with her expression leaning more toward all-knowing. "Which planet was in what house?"

She kicks her foot behind her and rests her elbows on the quartz countertop. Conspiratorially, she replies, "I didn't want to say anything because, you know, changing fate can have a negative domino effect. But the new moon was in your fifth house and that means all kinds of good things are happening for you, Nicholas. It was the best time to take a trip. How did the meeting go?"

"I think we're getting the deal."

She smiles, her pride in me reflected in her eyes. "I knew you could do it. In business, the guides of the new moon work well for feedback. It was your time to shine."

Andrew chuckles and goes around to the other side of

the island. Wrapping his arm around her, he says, "I used to think you were weird."

She asks, "And now?"

He kisses her head. "Now I know you are, but I wouldn't have it any other way. If some spiritual or astrological current is guiding us to closing this deal, then I'm all for it."

Pushing him away playfully, she turns back to me. "Your brother is too far gone to save, so I'm going to focus on you."

"Oh yay," I tease.

She wags a finger in my direction. "You should be grateful I talked your dad and Andrew into sending you. Not only are you coming back with great business news but also a girlfriend. You can thank me later, but for now, stop stalling and give me details."

Shifting on the stool, I laugh. "Mrs. Singh was tough, but Garrett Stans, one of the other attorneys, shared an insider secret with me."

"Not that," my mom says just as Andrew says, "What is it?"

I start laughing. "Do we want the personal or the professional news first?"

"Personal."

"Professional."

I think we know who voted for what. Andrew finally caves. "Get the personal stuff out of the way so we can get down to business." He reaches into the fridge and pulls two beers out for us and a bottle of wine for my mom. She likes her white wine extra cold despite what the know-it-all LA elites think.

He pours her a glass, and I twist the tops off the beer bottles. Seems like we're going to be here a while, so I settle in after taking a long swig.

"I met her last spring actually."

My mom's grin grows. "In Catalina?"

I could lie just to throw off her game, but my mom's the best, so I'll always tell her what she wants to know. "I think you called it last May."

"But how? You were in New York."

"That's where she's from." I take another drink and then add, "You'll like this part best—I literally ran into her. Like physically ran into her on the street."

Snapping, she bolts upright and points at me. "That's fate intervening!"

"I knew you'd get a kick out of that."

She slips around to my side of the island and hugs me again. "I'm so happy for you."

I hug her back. "Me too. You'll really like her. She's smart and funny, really funny." My mom steps back but keeps a hand on my cheek. "She loves to laugh and a great pun. Mom," I start, now feeling a little shy with the next admission, "she's so pretty. Literally, like I can't take my eyes off her."

"Do you have a picture? What's her name?"

"I do." I chuckle at that, as I pull out my phone to show Mom the photo Tatum sent me. "Here. This is Natalie."

She hums with a smile on her face. "Oh, she's beautiful. So sweet. And look at that. Nick and Natalie like Corbin and Cookie."

Andrew shakes his head. My mom can't see him, thank goodness. "Kissing in a tree."

Gently laughing, she takes her glass and turns to him. "I actually have kissed your dad in a tree." Walking around him, she taps his nose. "And then nine months later—"

"Okay, that's enough," Andrew proclaims.

She's still laughing when she heads for the back door. "I think my work here is done. I've horrified one son, and the other has met his match. On that note, I'm going to enjoy a little sunshine out back and let you boys talk business."

As soon as the door closes behind her Andrew asks, "What's the secret?"

"It's not so much a secret as it's wicked skills, big brother."

My shoulder is punched. "Really? You know I'm talking about business. What did Stans tell you?"

"Ah. Yes. He told me the CEO wants to retire. He's had some health issues. He also says that they want to keep the family atmosphere and were impressed with us." I finish the beer and then continue, "I got the distinct feeling that if we padded the offer, we'd probably get a quick answer."

He drinks his beer, but I can tell by the distant gaze that he's deep in thought. "What do you think would seal the deal?"

"Obviously, we need to be in the millions. A few hundred K isn't going to impress anyone."

"We were willing to go up another three mil without approval, but I have to talk to Dad to see where he thinks we should land so we're not screwing ourselves. Manhattan Financial would have to continue to turn a profit after the acquisition. *Especially then.* But I'm not worried. We'll get our accounting team in and trim the fat. As for the health issues, what's up?"

"Not sure. It was mentioned on the down-low without too many details. He's just ready to retire and enjoy the golden years."

"Kids?"

"Yeah, but he said they're not interested in the business. I think it will be an easy transition as well. He seemed eager to lead it."

"That's good. Less we have to worry about. We can talk

to Dad in the morning and make a plan." Clapping me on the back, he says, "You did good, Nick. Making us proud." He heads for the stairs but stops and looks back at me. "As for the girlfriend, it's about damn time. And you know if we win this deal, we're going to need some people in New York. It might be something to consider."

I hadn't thought about that, but now that he's mentioned it, I have a feeling I won't think about anything else. What do I want to do? Where do I want to live? How long can I stay away from Natalie without feeling like I'm going insane?

Spinning to my feet, I grab my suitcase and head to my bedroom. I moved home after graduation to save money to eventually buy a place by the ocean. But Natalie has me thinking. Maybe I want to rent something in the meantime so when she comes to visit, we have privacy.

The next morning in the conference room bright and early, I sit beside my brother at the long table. "I typed up all the notes, including my suggestions." As we come to the end of the list, I ask, "What do you think?"

My dad angles toward me from the head of the table, rubbing his chin. "I think it's worth upping the offer and getting this deal closed. Are you up for the task, Nick?"

"I am." The answer's easy even if a little self-serving; I get to see Natalie again.

"I want this company." He stands, not minding a team of people watching his every move. "Andrew will go with you. He can handle the negotiations, but I want you to back him. As for the paperwork, make sure the legal language is in our favor. Don't let me down. Close it and come home with signed contracts."

"I'll take care of it and get us situated on the East Coast."

My dad says, "Good job on pushing this to happen.

Stans would have never confided in just anyone. It's because of you, Nick. He trusted you enough to let you know about the CEO's private situation." He looks up and grins. "Christiansen Wealth Management Manhattan has a great ring to it. Have a good day, everyone." He walks toward the door with the others.

Andrew rocks back in the office chair. "What do you say? You up to take New York by storm?"

With Natalie at the forefront of my mind, I reply, "I'm ready."

19

Natalie

"We're close to making the deal. A lot can come of it if this happens."

"I have a good feeling about it, so I'm sure it will close."

He goes quiet on the other end of the call, but then whispers, "Everything's moving so fast."

"That's good, right? It shows your family and the other execs that you're ready for whatever they throw your way."

"I mean with us."

This time, I'm the one who goes silent. Does he regret asking me to be his girlfriend? For committing to someone across the country? I know it's been a while since he's been in a relationship, but he seemed ready by his words and through his actions.

Why did I jump in heart first instead of testing the temperature with my toe? Ugh.

"Natalie?"

"What?" I ask, angry with myself for having doubted so

quickly. I guess, we're both in unfamiliar territory. *Damn those dimples.*

"I didn't mean it as a bad thing. It's the first time in a long time that I've felt content. I miss you, but knowing you're at the other end of a call or video at the end of the day is a nice feeling. I have someone I can rely on who makes me happy."

I lean against the phone, pressing it tighter to my ear, a sucker for his words and hearing him sweet-talk me. "You make me happy, too."

"No regrets?"

"Not a chance." I roll onto my back and stare up at the ceiling. "When will I get to see you again?"

Caught up in our busy lives, it's only been two weeks since I've seen him. I've started conjuring images of what it's like in his world—Nick shopping for groceries, going to the gym, hitting the beach for an early morning surfing session, as he calls it. I like to think that something exciting is always happening in his life and I get to reap the benefits of it from getting pics of his hot body or just listening to him breathe as if he's just come from a workout and lying on the couch to recover. It's all in my head, but I still like the sweaty, sexy image of him doing that.

He replies, "How's this weekend?"

"Wide open for you."

Is that a growl I hear? "I like you wide open. How about a little phone sex?"

"Oh my God, Nick," I reply, shocked. But the bed is cozy, and man, do I love my boyfriend's voice—those deep notes reaching my core when he speaks. "Go on."

A chuckle vibrates in my ear. "I can't say I mind how much you like sex."

"I hope not, but to set the record straight, I like sex, but with you I love it."

"Flattery will get you everywhere, baby. Now tell me what you're wearing, and I hope the answer is you're naked."

Having a boyfriend I can share my most intimate acts and emotions with is truly better than anything, even those sexy little dimples, but not by much.

I HUFF, setting my laptop on the couch so I can get up and pace. The client I'm working with is beyond frustrating. "This guy has dated everyone in the city, and my client thinks she can hook him with a basket of cookies."

Tatum looks up from the dining table, her mouth practically hanging open. "Is that what she requested?"

"I talked her out of it. Anyone under the age of eighty knows that cookies won't tame his ass."

She laughs and leans back in her chair. Crossing her arms over her chest, she says, "You seem to know the type."

I walk to the windows but glance back at her. "Not just the type. *The guy.* I dated him once. *Once* when you were out of town and weren't here to talk me out of it."

"Oh, so it's my fault, is it?" She sports a grin.

"Technically, it's mine, but can't you take the blame of that mistake for me for a little while."

"For you, anything. I believe I remember just that weekend. I was making a few mistakes of my own, so add your mistake to the suitcase, and I'll whisk it away so you never have to think about it, or him, again."

"You're the best. You know that? The absolute best." As far as friends go, she'll always be tops, but after last night, Nick is owning other parts of my heart. Pushing the curtains wider open than they already are, I peer outside. Night had fallen without notice, but now that it's here, my stomach rumbles. "What do you want for dinner?"

Digging through a small filing cabinet in the corner of the dining area, she pulls out a notebook of our tried and true timeless gift options and sets it on the table. "I'm not sure. What do you want? Oh! I got it. A private Michelin-starred chef prepared meal. We'll close the restaurant down. Can't get more up an arrogant asshole's alley than that."

"I take it you're referring to the client and not our dinner tonight. Correct?" Delirium has set in after working without so much as a break, and my laughter follows just after. "We've been at this all day."

She joins in laughing along with me. Definitely not at me. "No, not you."

"It's a great idea. Serves two purposes—feeds his ego and fills his belly. I'll send her an email with the concept and see if she can push her budget."

With the holidays coming up, not only are we taking corporate orders but we're also fulfilling specialized gifts to individual clients. We're busier than ever. That means fewer clients with bigger budgets would allow us to prepare properly and plan the way we need to, approaching the end of the year. "I think we need to bring a couple of people on board. What are your thoughts?"

"We have the workload to justify it, and there's no reason not to with the funding secured for another year. With more employees, we can serve more clients and continue to grow our list of regulars. We could even start adding in referral incentives. That means a potential larger reach and more profit, which they will contribute toward."

"I'm not seeing a downside when you put it like that. I need to make sure I'm covering the bases, but it sounds like we might be expanding." The thought makes me giddy. I pick up my phone to call Nick, but remember he told me he'd be in meetings until late. Lying in his hotel bed thoroughly smitten feels like a lifetime ago because I miss him. But in reality, it seems we'll not be anything but full speed ahead. *And I don't mind one bit.*

Still staring out the window, I try to act casual. "What did you think of him?"

"Oh no, Natalie. You're not dragging me into this. What did *you* think of him? That's what matters."

"I think..." His smile comes to mind. Those soulful eyes with those sunset-golden edges. And the strong arms that reveal he never wants to let me go by how he holds me. "I think Nick is pretty damn perfect."

"But you don't do perfect, Nat. You're like a magnet to damaged and troubled men, and guys who wear arrogance like a second skin." She laughs under her breath. "You sure you're feeling alright?"

No, I answer in my head. I'm love-sick for that man. "Nick is none of those things. Maybe I'm growing up and finally realized that I don't have to be emotionally battered to think someone loves me. Maybe Nick's goodness is what attracted me."

"This time."

I turn back to look at her.

"I left him in Catalina because I was in no place to see the good in anyone, much less a man. But that doesn't mean I forgot about him."

She leans against the bar, studying me. "I'm going to say something you've never heard from me before. I like your boyfriend. I think Nick is amazing, and I also think you two are pretty damn incredible together." She raises her hands.

"I know. I've hated everyone you dated, but there's always an exception to the rules."

"Nick's my exception," I say, the words seeping in as I feel their deeper meaning.

"Guess an old dog can learn a new trick."

"Hey, did you just call me an old dog?"

She shrugs unapologetically. "I'm three months older than you, so what does that make me? Ancient, that's what." Opening the fridge, she peeks inside. "There's nothing but cream cheese and a jar of cherries. Why do we even have those?"

"Last Christmas we made cherry martinis." I glance at my phone, wishing I had a text from him. It's not that I don't understand he's busy. I'm busy too, but isn't it fun to blow off obligations when you get to spend time with a new love?

Studying the jar, she asks, "Do they go bad?"

I shrug even though she's not looking at me. "Check the date."

The room is quiet while I reply to an email. I can assume she's looking for a best by date because not ten seconds later, I hear the jar hit the recycling bin. The refrigerator door closes, and she plops next to me on the couch. "Want to go out?"

"Yep. I'm starved." I set my laptop on the coffee table and stand. "I could eat a family-sized platter of pasta right now."

Heading back into her bedroom, she says, "I don't know how you stay so thin when you eat like that."

"Running three to seven miles five days a week helps." I fail to mention the intense workout Nick's given me between the sheets. How could I forget when my body remembers so well?

I know she'd love to hear all the details, but I'll save

those for now to keep the excitement of the newness to myself for a hot minute. "And good genes."

"Martine passed down those model genes all right. I can't walk by an Italian restaurant, which is damn near impossible in New York City, without gaining a pound or five from the smell alone. God, I miss fettuccine Alfredo so much."

It's true. My mom modeled for a short time in her early twenties. She was spotted in Central Park and was booked for three Paris runway shows the next week. After meeting my dad at a coffee shop in Tribeca, she quit eight months later so she could spend more time with him instead of traveling the world.

As she claims, too in love to be away from him, she also decided to help build the family business. He gives her full credit for making it a success. From marketing to financials, she's done everything to help not only build but also to create their legacy.

I feel like a failure in comparison. She makes everything look so easy. I peek into Tatum's room. "Speaking of the other jeans, can I borrow a pair of yours. A bunch of mine went to the cleaners today."

Without missing a beat, denim hits my chest. "Thanks." I toss them to my bed and then go to my closet to flip through for a shirt. Deciding I'm not in the mood to dress up, I finally just pull a red fitted tee from a hanger and toss it to the bed. After changing clothes, I slip on a pair of Gucci red heels. They're not that high at three inches. *What?* Most of mine are higher.

I'd like to say I don't worry about my makeup, but I swipe a fresh coat of mascara and lipstick on before primping my hair. Basically, I'm keeping it a low-key night.

She'll take another twenty minutes, at least, so I return

to the living room and wrap up what I was working on. Sitting there, I check my phone again, tempted to call him or text him, but I worry it will interrupt an important meeting. "He'll contact you, Natalie," I remind myself.

Remembering how he called me baby the other night, I feel warm and fuzzy. Although that thought amps up the loneliness of his absence.

I impatiently wait, wondering if I should get a glass of wine to pass the time or just sit here with nothing to do but wonder what Nick is up to. "Are you coming?"

Tatum comes out but stops in the entry to the hallway. "Don't be mad."

Popping up from the couch, I say, "You're not ready?" *As if she didn't already know this information.*

"I was thinking I would have a night in."

"What? It was your idea to go out. I got ready . . . kind of to be seen."

"You look fantastic and should go."

What the hell? "Alone?"

She goes to the door and opens it. "Totally, even if you just get us takeout. Don't put that outfit to waste. Nick would totally love it."

"But Nick won't see it."

She grabs my crossbody purse and slips it over my head. "Take a photo on the way and send it to him."

"Why are you acting so weird?"

"I'm not." Coming behind me, she shoves me toward the hallway. "I'll order the food, but you go."

"Why?"

"Go now." Her voice is hard, leaving no room for misunderstanding. "I'll call something in, but you can get a head start."

Adjusting the strap around my body, I roll my eyes and

move to the door. "God, you're so weird. If you want alone time, just say so, Tatum."

"I want alone time!"

"Okay. Okay. Geez. Calm down. I'm going. I'm going." I start walking down the hall for the stairs. Got to get a few more steps in today.

"Thanks, Nat." The door closes behind me, and I hear both locks latch. Girl needs to get some of that pent-up energy out in constructive ways instead of letting it build like anger inside her.

When I reach the lobby, I cut across the space. The doorman beats me to the door, holding it open. I step through, but then stop.

There, in front of my building, is a turquoise Vespa parked at the curb. And the most handsome man I've ever seen standing in front of it. "What took you so long?" Nick asks, holding a helmet out for me.

I look up to the sky to see Tatum leaning on our windowsill with a big smile on her face. I give her a little wave, and she sends one back. Turning to Nick, I walk closer. "I think you forgot I don't like anything with two wheels."

"Yeah, but you gave me a chance once. I was hoping you'd give me another to prove that you'll always be safe with me."

I take the helmet from him. "Well, when you put it like that, how can I say no?"

Reaching out, he takes hold of me and pulls me against him. "I hope the answer will always be yes."

My body begins to melt in his hands like a chocolate bar on a hot day. "Yes."

He chuckles. "I haven't asked you anything."

Wrapping my arms around his neck, I lift up so our

mouths are a hell of a lot closer, and reply, "The answer is always yes." Kissing him, I realize how true those words really are when it comes to him.

I'm slow to open my eyes when we part, but when I do, seeing that *dimplicious* grin is worth the wait. "What are you doing here?"

"Just in town to see my girlfriend."

He's going to do me in with his sweetness. "I'm sure she'll be thrilled to see you."

That has him laughing harder this time. "And if she's not into surprises?"

"She is." Taking a step back, I slip my helmet on. "So where are you taking me, Mr. Sexy?"

"What happened to the smug?"

"I misjudged you."

He gets on the Vespa and anchors a helmet over his head. Clasping the strap under his chin, he shrugs. "That happens to us Ralph Lauren models sometimes."

Stepping up to the side of the scooter, I shake my head. "I spoke too soon. It's official. Smug has returned to its rightful place."

"C'mon on, babe," he says, "hop on."

"I'm hungry. What about dinner?"

Turning to look at me over his shoulder, he says, "I know you're used to being the boss around here, but maybe you'll give me a chance to surprise you. What do you say?"

I get on the back of the scooter and wrap my arms around him, happy to be with him again. "I'm all in."

20

Nick

The drivers in New York are maniacs, so riding through the city with my girl didn't go exactly as planned. Flipping a cab driver off for almost killing us when he cut into our lane without signaling had Natalie on edge. I swerved into an alley to avoid running into the back of him.

The last thing I want, or need, is to be arrested for hurting a cabbie for threatening us. I promised to keep Natalie safe, and I'll do whatever it takes to keep it. *Despite her arguing that I'm doing otherwise right now.*

Pacing, she covers what has to be her fiftieth lap in front of me. "They're the worst. I mean, sure we need them, but cabbies are crazy sometimes. You can't just flip off someone because you're mad, Nick. Maybe that works in LA, but not in New York City."

She clearly has an impression that all Angelenos are chill. I don't mind her being that innocent. I'll let her believe everything is sunshine and palm trees. It is for the most part, so it's not a total lie. But I'm still not afraid of a mad cabbie.

She stops and looks around. "I need to eat. Nothing good will come of me being hangry. I can promise you that. No *sirree*, Bob."

"So I'm learning, and who's Bob?"

"You guys don't say that on the West Coast?"

Tugging her by the hand, I pull her close. "Are we back to pointing out our differences?"

Her grin has me smiling. She leans against me and gives me a kiss. "I do rather enjoy discovering our commonalities."

"We have those in spades. For instance, you like to eat, and I like to feed you. And then I like to eat you." I kick the stand up and right the Vespa under me. "Get on, babe. Let's go."

"Where to?"

"It's a surprise, something I want your opinion on."

"I love giving my opinion, that, and free advice." She winks.

Chuckling, I reply, "I'll take all your words, free or otherwise, because I'm just happy I get to hear them in person."

She pulls her helmet over her head, but then leans in and kisses me before she maneuvers to get on behind me. Resting her chin on my back, she adds, "Keep charming me, handsome, and you'll never be able to shut me up."

There are many ways I can respond to that, but I say, "Hold on," instead. I love the feel of her holding onto me, too.

I'm not familiar with the streets here, but map apps are a glorious thing. We make it to the building by taking shortcuts. When I pull into the parking garage, a valet takes our helmets before driving the moped to park it somewhere.

"I'm so excited," she says, doing a little light step shuffle with her feet. "I literally have no idea where we are or what we're doing here."

By the looks of it, she's right. We could be anywhere. The gray concrete walls and parking spot lines don't tell us anything. The name of the building—The Pressler—does, however. "Hope you like surprises." I'm not sure how this one will go over with her, and my hands start to sweat with nerves. Inside the elevator, I shove my hands in my pockets after pushing the button for the sixteenth floor.

"Especially when said surprises involve food. Does it involve food? Because I'm seriously past starved and about to eat my arm off." Her face scrunches. "That's such a gross phrase. Remind me not to use it anymore."

"Noted," I reply. "And I'm well aware of your hunger at this stage in the night, so food is, of course, a part of tonight's festivities."

She's struck with giddiness streaking up her spine. "Oh, festivities. I like the sound of this." The elevator doors open, and we step out. She's more tentative as she looks around the unfamiliar space.

I take hold of her hand again and keep walking, leading her toward the end of the hall to 1605. I open the door and let her walk in first. It helps I had a sneak peek online, but it's still good to see it in real life.

Just like the other times we've entered a space together, she heads straight for the windows. Curiosity seems to be something she carries with her, as if the city she grew up in is still shiny and new. I ask, "What do you think?"

"About?" Her gaze remains trained outside.

"I've been offered an opportunity." I throw that out there much more rushed than I planned. Clamping my mouth shut, I wait to watch her reaction, to read her thoughts and mood regarding the news. But when she remains silent for an uncomfortable few seconds, I start filling the empty space. "Here in the city . . . I was thinking about taking it."

Turning around, Natalie stares at me as if the words she heard weren't clear. "I don't understand."

"I know we just started dating, but I wouldn't be opposed to making it a full-time gig. What do you think?"

She finally comes to me, holding onto my belt loops. "I think a couple of weeks is too long to go without seeing you. But—"

"But?" It was music to my ears until that but . . .

"Are you giving up your life in California for me or a job? Maybe both?" She nods. "I'm happy to have you here, thrilled in fact, but I worry because I'm not sure it's worth trading your comfort zone for mine. What if you're not happy once you move here? Then I'll be the one you blame."

"Since we're tossing out what-ifs, what if I move and we date with intention, like we have some place to go together? A future we're working toward?"

Backing away, she leans against an exposed brick wall and then glances out the window momentarily. "It's a good thought, but I'm scared."

"Of?"

Without much light to reflect in them, her eyes are darker than usual, or maybe it's the worry taking over. "I worry you won't like me like you do now."

I didn't see that one coming. Not sure how to answer, so I use the time to memorize this new emotion that has no business settling into her posture—the dip of her shoulders at the edge, the expression caught between the happiness she wants to feel and the reality of the hurt she's experienced. "That won't happen."

"How can you be so sure?"

"Because the more time I spend with you, the more time I want to spend with you. You keep me on my toes and guessing. Life with you is an adventure, but I'd like to explore the downtime with you as well." Spying the picnic I set up earlier on the balcony and knowing how hungry she is, I realize it's a lot to spring on her. Maybe she's right, and we should talk about this after eating. I guess I was hoping for—

I'm kissed under the chin and along my jaw. Arms wrap around me, and she whispers, "I want you here, Nick. Selfishly, I want you here all the time, but it makes me feel bad for wanting you to give up your life for mine."

"This isn't a trade or an either-or situation. This is two adults figuring out how to be together. I want to find out what it's like to lie in bed with you when one of us doesn't have to leave early in the morning. What would it be like to come home from work and sit on the couch and watch bad reality TV or have sports on while you're doing your own thing somewhere in the apartment? You'd help me figure out the best neighborhood takeout and teach me how you like to fold your towels."

"Four folds total. No lazy threefold business for me."

"See? I was taught the same," I say as if this is a unique thing just for us. It feels like it is, and I like that we have something else in common to think about, even if it's mundane. This kind of stuff never crossed my mind before her, and now I want to think about it. I want to learn about her.

She gives me a good squeeze and then leans back to look up at me. "What are you really asking me?"

"I'm willing to consider moving here if you think it's a good idea."

"We've had a few phone calls and videos, lots of texts, but Nick, what if . . ."

When she pauses, I ask, "What if?" She turns away from me when I put her on the spot, hoping she takes this leap to reassure me I'm making the right decision. But apparently, I'm competing with the most fascinating city in the world outside. "Talk to me, Natalie."

Peeking at me, she says, "This apartment is nice, but whose is it?"

"I haven't bought it, but my family is thinking about it."

"Can I be honest with you?"

"I hope you'll always be honest with me."

Her bottom lip is momentarily dragged under her teeth in worry. "Sometimes I worry that I won't be what someone like you needs."

"When you say *someone like me*, what do you mean exactly?"

Concern of scaring me away is drawn into her eyes. "I've dated a lot of bad boys in my time—"

"You're twenty-three, so I'm not sure 'in your time' applies. We've both dated others. That's what we're supposed to do. That's how we find our—"

"Soul mate," she finishes as if the concept is as starry-eyed as she is right now. I'm the lucky guy on the receiving end of those ocean blues. "This isn't a fly-by-night relationship. Not for me. It may be new, but I can tell there will be damage left behind."

"Not if I have a say."

"My exes grew tired and cheated." She tosses that out there like a threat, putting distance between us as she moves across the empty room.

I call her on this bullshit. "I'm not one of them."

"No, you're accomplished and attractive, very attractive,

but you're good inside and out. You're a lawyer, for God's sake. You can have your choice of women to date, Nick." How do I get her to understand that my occupation doesn't make me the man I am? What words will convince her that in the months we were separated, my heart had felt half-full as if something—*someone*—was missing?

"I don't want other women, Natalie. I want you." *Probably forever.*

Throwing her arms into the air, she asks, "Why? Maybe that's where I'm lost. The sex is incredible, but that's not what a good foundation is built on."

"No, it's built on something deeper, something we possess—a connection like no other. I felt that connection the moment we met. So you can throw out all the reasons you think we won't work out, but what I won't let you do is put words into my mouth."

"I don't want you to find out that I'm not who you thought I was." Her voice is so soft, but I'm listening to every word.

"Who are you?"

"Catalina was frivolous fun. New York a chance encounter that led us to think we can be more." She sits on the large windowsill, so small compared to the world that's on the other side of the glass. But I hate that she feels small. I never want that for her. "I'm just a girl with her heart on the line."

I kneel in front of her. Taking her hands in mine, I say, "You've been hurt, but I won't be the one to cause you pain." Her eyes are glassy, and I'm still not fully aware of why she's upset. "Who treated you less than you deserve?"

As if I've said the magic words to unlock the Pandora's box in her heart, she replies, "Everyone." Leaning in, I wrap my arms around her back and bring her against me. She rests her head on my shoulder. "My last two boyfriends cheated on me."

"That's not about you. They're just assholes."

The slightest of smiles shapes her lips but falls just as quick again as she gazes into the distance. "My parents." I'm hit with a glare, not intuitively bad upon inspection, but a secret she's held that she's not ready to reveal.

"You can tell me anything, and I'll never feel less about you." A humorless chuckle chokes in my throat. "I feel . . . there's so much I feel and have wanted to tell you."

Cupping my face, she looks at me, reflecting the same emotion in her expression that I feel inside, pain seen in the downward turn of her mouth but so full of love in her eyes. "Me too. It feels natural, not forced. That's different and new for me, like everything with you. I've almost said it so many times after our calls or even last time you were in New York."

I find myself nodding, knowing that's when I almost said it as well. "I love you." I put it out there, tired of holding back my deep-seated feelings for her. She's ingrained inside me, a part of me that I know I'll never be able to wash away, so I'll own the emotions starting today.

Her hands fall from my face, and I miss their warmth already. "Nick . . ."

"You don't have to say it in return or anything. I know you feel it as well. That's enough to sustain me until you're ready."

"I love you." *Quick. Simple. Direct.* Like mine.

Her confession elicits my smile without permission as if my whole wiring is in tune with her words. "Well, there we have it. Two fools who fell in love too fast for the rest of the world." I sit on the sill next to her and caress her face, admiring her strength for sharing so much of herself. Her beauty is deeper than the surface of her skin. It's found in her words and how she looks at me like I'm everything.

Covering my hands, she adds, "But it's not too fast for us."

"No, I'd say we're right on time."

21

Nick

Food motivates Natalie.

She's been pretty vocal about her hunger pangs. We all get a little cranky when we're hungry. But after devouring the food I brought, we remain sprawled out on the floor of the apartment on a blanket. Fed, she's a whole new person and is back to her usual talkative self. "I love cookies as much as the next person, but can they really land a man? Asking for business purposes, of course." She laughs and waves her arm through the air expressively. "I sound like Carrie Bradshaw." *Must be one of her friends.*

"I suppose it depends on the type of cookies."

Her gaze hits me, and her lips part. I wouldn't go so far as to say her mouth falls open, but she is gawking. "The type of cookies?" She repeats me like she must've heard wrong. She crosses her legs and leans forward. "Let me get this straight. You would consider dating a woman, exclusively, I might add, by the type of cookies she gave you?"

"I think that's simplifying things a bit."

"Maybe, but I need to boil this down to the bare essence of what you're saying. It's important research—life or death of my business. Okay, that might be taking it a bit far, but this is valuable information, so humor me while I dig deeper." She sits, pulling her shoulders back. "What do cookies mean to you?"

"Sugar means I can take her home to meet my parents, but it's going to be a long wait to take it to the next level physically." Resting back on the palms of my hands, I cross my ankles of my outstretched legs. "Oatmeal signifies a homebody. It's a good thing to steer clear of if you like to party. But oatmeal raisin, that's a whole other story. That's a girl who likes adventure. Works hard, plays hard type."

Her chin lowers as she stares at me. "You're blowing my mind. Also, I think you're building up to the biggies, and I'm on pins and needles."

"What are the biggies?" She never ceases to surprise me, so I can't wait to hear this breakdown.

"Peanut butter, snickerdoodles, and gingersnaps. Chocolate chip being the top dog of the cookie world."

"Cool," I reply casually, obviously forgetting about gingersnaps. "We're on the same page." So my ego's large enough to lie a little. Does it really matter in the end that I forgot gingersnaps? *No, it does not.*

"What do snickerdoodles mean to you?"

I lay it all out in more thought than I realized I had on the topic. "It's not just to me, but I feel confident enough to speak for men as a whole." A smile tickles her lips, but she keeps her laughter detained in her throat. "Although they have a place in the biggies list, it's really just wise to steer clear. Snickerdoodles are for grandmas. Delicious, but those cookies will never get a chick a second date. Not with Grandma's dentures getting stuck in the soft snickerdoodle."

"What about peanut butter?"

"Those are tricky little bastards. If there's not an allergy involved, they conjure good things—like sex in front of a fireplace on a winter's night or staying in on Sunday morning and hanging out in bed reading the paper and then napping."

Her brow furrows, making her more adorable than she already is. "Does anyone read the paper anymore or just read the news on their phones?"

"That's what I mean. Peanut butter conjures reminiscent images of yesteryear. There's a feeling of peace, of home, with those images. Whether they happen though is still a mystery."

"This is the best conversation I've had in years. I should be taking notes."

"I'll wait while you get your phone."

I'm popped in the leg. "You're ridiculous. Now tell me about gingersnaps." Her eyebrows waggle.

"They're the cookie version of the stereotype of a redhead—fiery, passionate, that sugar taste with a bit of a kick. Great sex and fatal attraction. That's a gingersnap."

"Like the movie?"

With a somber nod, I reply, "Boiling rabbits and all."

"Yikes."

Clapping my hands together to bring this to a close, I end up startling her. She grabs over her heart. "My God—"

"You can call me Nick or sexy, even keep the smug in there for your liking."

"Ha. Very funny. Let's wrap this up. I'm now craving cookies, thanks to you."

"I'm not the one who brought this up. I'm just the one letting you into the psyche of a typical American man."

"There's nothing typical about you, or I wouldn't be here."

"I'll take the compliment. As for the king of cookies—chocolate chip—"

"Can't wait to hear your thoughts on those."

"Don't let them fool you. Most will go straight for the chocolate chip, but that's a trap. Given more thought, you should ask yourself—is it lazy or deliciously insightful? Either way, it's a risk."

"Is it, though? I mean, really? Because chocolate is always a win with me."

"But if they were sent to me, and before I tuck in, I'm asking myself the following questions: One, is this what they like or were they chosen for me? Two, are they the safe bet like the red rose or sending a message like a yellow rose for friendship? And lastly, is it basic psychology to assume everyone loves chocolate chip or reverse psychology to weed out the weirdos?"

As if she's exhausted, she lies flat on her back. Draping her arm over her head, she says, "This is way more complicated than I thought. Can't we just take cookies at face value?"

"Trust me, I never knew I had so many thoughts on cookies. I usually just eat them."

She bolts upright again. "What? Then what was all that fatal attraction and reminiscent imagery about?"

I shrug. "Thought you wanted more context to help save your business."

Laughing, she drops her head forward into her hands. When she looks back up, she has a cocked eyebrow. "I never said my business hinged on it, but I have a client who thinks she can get a player to commit by sending him a basket of baked treats."

"I'd say yes."

She crawls across the blanket, carefully avoiding the empty dishes. Settling in my lap, she leans back in my arms and stares out the window. "And here I thought I was getting insider secrets."

I wrap my arms around her middle and kiss the side of her head. "Here's an insider secret for you," I whisper. "I love you and your baked goods."

Even through the dim light filling the space, I can see her million-dollar smile. Her arms cover mine, and she says, "I love you and that nonsense cookie advice, too."

Bending down, I kiss her neck. Her eyes close, and she sighs contentedly. *Who needs cookies when one has this?* Not me.

We sit like that for a few minutes, enjoying the peace, the night, and being together again. I'm realizing that she's feeling a lot like home to my soul than when I was just in California, despite the lack of beach.

I'd rather let her roll over me than a wave any day.

Her head lulls to the side, and she says, "My parents are placating me like I'm a child who's playing house for the weekend." I've learned that given enough time and space, Natalie will share what's really on her mind. I keep my mouth shut and my ears open. "My business is low priority. If I worked for the company, though, I'd legitimize my career in their eyes."

I hate that I can hear myself swallow, but there's nothing I can do to fix such a problem. I would if I could. I'd fix it so she feels proud instead of misunderstood. Instead, I'll support her in ways that others don't. "It's a unique business, but it's legitimate. Don't let them tell you otherwise."

"My brother handles this pocket portfolio of companies. . . my brother who's still in college, if I've failed to mention that previously. He wants to follow in my father's footsteps. As for the portfolio, they're investments on their last legs that haven't made money." I hold her, and she adds, "My brother is managing my company from the loan standpoint. Reports are sent to my parents, and their input is syphoned through him to me. I haven't been a priority since they signed the extension."

"That doesn't mean you're not worth their time. It only means that they believe in you enough to continue supporting your dream. And they trust your brother to give him the hands-on experience he needs."

She turns to look at me, a smile gracing her lips. "That's a great way of looking at it."

"Just call me Mr. Positivity."

"I'd rather kiss you."

"We can do that, too." *And we do.* We kiss until the food containers are pushed to the side and we're naked in each other's arms.

Kissing. Loving. Fucking. Holding each other until the early hours of morning come. And I realize why sex with Natalie is out of this world. It's because of love. It's not just a moment in time with a hot woman to get off and get her off.

Every moment with her is richer. Every moment feels like a reward. Every moment just makes me want more, and if that means pulling up roots in California, I can see now that it's a no-brainer. *I don't want to be separated from my girl.*

I PULL up in front of her apartment building just shy of five in the morning and take off my helmet, resting it on my lap. She doesn't make a move to get off, keeping her hands on me, though she isn't wrapped around me like I prefer. "Do you want to come up?"

"I have an early meeting and my stuff is at the hotel."

She slips off, and I do the same. I look up at her building. I expected a high-rise when I met her, but this building is smaller and quaint at only ten floors compared to its neighbors. She sets the helmet down and moves against me, not quite touching, but still too far. "Next time you come to New York, if it's not for good, then I want you to stay with me." Tugging the hem of my shirt, she asks, "Okay?"

"Yes, ma'am." That brings a smile to her face. Since she won't do it herself, I take her arms and wrap them around my middle. "Would you like to come with me?"

Her laughter echoes down the quiet block of the street. She grips her hands behind my back, laughing. "Oh, now you ask me." Thoughts are racing through her eyes. She finally says, "You go to your hotel and get a few hours of sleep, and we can meet up this evening. How does that sound?"

"Lonely."

She lifts up and kisses my chin. "Good. I want you to miss me so when we're together, we don't waste a second not appreciating each other."

I rub her hips, slow circles over the denim, the urge to be inside her intense, always so strong with her. "Yes, I can't wait to appreciate you again."

Pushing off me, she frees herself from my clutches where I would have been happy to hold her all day. "Go. Do great things today, and we'll celebrate later." She blows me a kiss just as the doorman greets her.

I pick up her helmet and spin it in my hands. "I love you, Natalie St. James." I don't keep my voice down because I want the world to hear.

In the light of the entrance of her building, I can see her cheeks redden. "I love you too, Nick Christiansen."

The doorman looks back and forth between us, and then says, "I stand here all day."

"No need. I'll be seeing my girl later."

He replies, "Have a good day."

"You too."

Natalie backs in, giving me a little wave before turning and dashing toward the elevator. I understand the extra energy despite the hour. It courses through my veins as well —adrenaline, love, anticipation of what the new day will bring. All good things.

22

Nick

I get up from the waiting area and walk across the lobby when I see my brother enter the revolving door to the building. Andrew checks in at the desk before joining me by the elevator. "Good morning," I greet him with a handshake.

"You're here early."

"I've been up for a few hours, so I headed over to beat the traffic. It's quite the nightmare."

"I never was one for Manhattan. It's a lot of people crammed into a small space."

Shrugging, I punch the button to call the elevator. "It doesn't bother me so much."

He grins. It's one I'm familiar with that's been passed down from our dad to both of us. We get inside and head up to our meeting. He asks, "How's Natalie?"

Okay, fine, I'm fucking grinning like an idiot. I play it off by looking down at my shoes. "She's great."

His laughter fills the elevator. "I would like this city a lot better if I had a girlfriend waiting for me. Did I tell you I texted with Dalen last week?"

"You failed to mention it." My brother's a good guy who's made poor choices when it comes to dating. I could say the same about Dalen. So maybe it's not so surprising that they're talking again. A lot of life has been lived since they were in high school.

"I thought you'd give me shit for it." He stares at the numbers lighting up above the doors. "She's getting the implants removed." When I don't say anything, he adds, "Nothing to do with me. Just said she went through a phase but is tired of being judged by them." He glances at me just as the doors open. "She has a sweet side."

"She does."

He walks to the receptionist's desk while I hang back to wait. When he returns, he says, "Jackson St. James."

St. James. Natalie. *My Natalie.* "Funny. It's never clicked before, even when I met with the Manhattan Financial lawyers, but that's Natalie's last name."

"It's pretty common here. I've seen it on two buildings this morning. Also, solid set of investments in Monopoly."

"What?"

"Must be common here because that set of properties were New York Avenue, Tennessee Avenue, and St. James Place. I knew if I secured those, I'd kick your ass in Monopoly." Interesting. Guess he's right. I chuckle because Natalie would call it an East Coast thing.

"I can't believe you remember those names. I only remember Boardwalk and Park Avenue."

A man pushes through a door into the waiting area.

Under his breath, Andrew says, "That's why you're the lawyer, and I'm the investment broker." He's cackling when he walks ahead. *Fucker.*

"It's good to finally meet you," the man says, shaking Andrew's hand and then mine. "I'm Jackson St. James."

We introduce ourselves and then follow him back to the conference room where I pitched for our company. As soon as we're seated, Jackson says, "Thanks for flying out to hand deliver the contracts. It wasn't necessary."

Andrew looks at me. "We had other business in the city and thought we'd take advantage to sneak in some personal time while we're here. Explore a bit more. Secure a place to live."

"You're moving here?" he asks.

"Yes," I reply. "I will be. I found an apartment in lower Manhattan."

Jackson nods. "There are a lot of great buildings being built in that area. Nice views."

"Very iconic."

Andrew asks, "So you're working with your dad?"

"And Mom. They started the company together and grew it. I usually work on some smaller accounts. It was a business incubator. We've successfully launched some from the program after securing our initial investment and some were retained for the remainder of the contract."

Reminded of Natalie and how her small business is locked in a similar portfolio, I say, "That's interesting. What's been your role?"

"I'm more a numbers guy. I'm getting a finance degree." He taps the table nervously. I think he's trying to impress us, but we're well aware that junior isn't the deciding factor. He says, "There's definitely some potential worth keeping an eye on, but we'll go through everything with your transition team."

Andrew shifts in the chair, getting more comfortable. "If

we don't see the same potential, can we cut the losses before the end of the year?"

Jackson leans forward on the table. "Of course. There's a clause in the contracts, but I won't be delivering that bad news. I may want to be a shark in brokering deals after I graduate, but I'm not looking for a death wish."

"I've been curious," Andrew starts. "Why doesn't your dad hold on to the company a few more years and then let you take it over?"

"He's a 'learn from the bottom to reach the top' kind of guy. He did it and wants me to do the same. My parents have given me a big head start by letting me handle actual cases. I can't sign on them, but I understand the business."

"Hopefully you get a cut to start your own company one day. I can tell you have a drive for financing."

"I have a drive for money." *He'll fit right in with the Wall Street types.*

Chuckling, Andrew says, "That's a good motivator." He pauses and checks the time. "The team in LA will be traveling in later this week. In the meantime, do you mind giving us a tour of the company?"

"Not at all."

We follow him around the offices, impressed by how different in style it is to ours in LA—brick and warmer brown tones. Our offices are bright whites and cool blues. The similarities lie with the loyalty of the employees, who we meet one by one. It's good to know everyone when we want to keep the family environment.

After lunch is brought in and we finish, we're escorted to the office of the CEO and Jackson knocks.

We're led in to find a man, older than my dad, maybe early sixties, lines dug into his expression, but not so deep that he'd be mistaken for much older. Gray hair with a few strands of pepper still hanging on. He's sitting behind a mahogany desk, and photos of his adventures and family line the console behind him.

Introductions are made and Andrew starts talking about the framed pictures. John St. James is polished in his mannerisms, and the New England accent makes me curtail my use of slang. He reaches behind him to grab a photo of his family.

My phone buzzes in my pocket before I have a chance to get the lowdown on his kids. When I slip it from my pocket, I look down at the screen. Standing, I say, "Excuse me."

I don't answer until I reach the door, and then I whisper, "Hey Mom, what's up?"

"I was thinking about your girlfriend." *She's not alone there.* "Why don't you invite her for a visit? You can stay at the beach, and we can have her over for brunch." Although I thought it was an emergency, which is why I took the call, I'm not upset about it.

Smiling, I walk down the hall to find an empty office to finish the call. "I can ask her." I wanted to last night but felt the bombshell of me moving here was enough for one night.

"Good. How's New York, honey?"

I peek into the hallway. No one's looking for me, but I should get back. "Busy. I need to keep this brief. I ducked out of the meeting with the CEO to take your call."

"Oops. I forgot that was today. Your father just told me you were gone for most of the week. You know how vague he can be with the details. I didn't get a report back on the apartment and if it's going to work."

Thinking about lying with Natalie on the floor after the picnic, I try to muddle my way through everything that happened with Natalie and if that's an apartment where I'd want to live. I know Natalie approves, so that works for me as well. "It's great. Location and inside."

"Great. It's a competitive market, and I don't want it to slip through our hands if you approve. I'll contact the real estate agent about putting in an offer. I know you're busy, so I'll let you go, but don't forget to take deep breaths. It helps fight adrenal fatigue and will keep you in tip-top shape. Deep breaths, Nicholas."

For show, I take a deep breath and exhale loud enough for her to hear. "See, Mom. I'm breathing. Gotta run."

"Okay. Good luck and love you."

"Thanks. Love you, Mom."

When I return to the office, I meet Mrs. St. James and sit back as they go over the finer points of the contracts in detail.

Andrew studies one of the amendments and then says, "Yes, that's not something we need to discuss right now. I'll get the transition team's eyes on the incubator program."

Mrs. St. James says, "STJ remains for the duration as agreed."

"Yes, and then will be transferred back into her name." Standing up, Andrew reaches over the desk to shake his hand again. "We won't keep you. We know you must have a lot to do before you get to enjoy your retirement."

Walking us to the door, John, as he asked us to call him, says, "I hear you're moving to New York, Nick?"

"I'm the lucky guy." We move into the hall as a group toward the exit.

He adds, "Hopefully a move this big comes with a promotion."

Andrew pipes in, "It comes with the perk of a girlfriend, too."

I'm quick to interject. "That came out wrong. We didn't

hire one. I was already dating her when we signed the contracts."

Everyone laughs, including me. John says, "A woman is always good motivation. I take it it's serious?"

His wife scolds, "John."

He shrugs and still looks at me to respond. I say, "It is."

I catch Andrew's attention with my answer, but he doesn't say anything. John adds, "Maybe you'll come for dinner once your move is done and you can bring your girl-friend. It's always good to know a few people in a large city like this one when you first move. You've met Jackson, but I'm sure our daughter would be happy to show you around. I know I'd want the same for our kids if they moved interstate."

"Thank you, John, that sounds great."

I'm patted on the back.

"If she's a catch, don't waste any time getting her to the altar. We may have started later in life, but marrying Martine was the best thing I ever did. Having kids is ranked right there with it."

"Thanks for the advice."

After we leave the building, I'm tempted to punch Andrew. "Really? Did you really call my girlfriend a perk of the promotion?"

"Like you said, it came out wrong. But it was good for a laugh." We walk to the street where we see a line of cabs waiting. "He was a nice guy. Smokin' hot daughter."

I check the time, hoping we're done for the day. I wouldn't mind surprising Natalie again. "No doubt we'll meet her down the track. What are you doing the rest of the day?"

"We have a conference call with Beacon in Seattle in an

hour. We can go back to the hotel and Dad will conference us in."

"Damn, I forgot about that." There go my plans of cutting out early.

At the hotel, we convene in his suite and lose the rest of the day and then some to a discussion about the buyout of a company in the Pacific Northwest and trimming fat from Manhattan Financial. When we hang up, Andrew says, "It looks like you have your choice of cities—Seattle or Manhattan?"

"What do you mean?"

"If we buy Beacon, someone from the family has to lead the transition. You know that. That was the consensus when we started the talks on expansion two years ago."

"What did I know? I was at Berkley."

"Well now you have a seat at the grownup's table." He stands and grabs a beer from the fridge. Holding it up in offering, I shake my head, not in the mood for this bullshit. The relocation. Maybe I need the beer. "I'll go where I'm needed. Are you part of this family or—"

"Fuck you, Andrew. I'll take New York, and you can have Seattle."

"I might not be able to. Dad's been talking about me leading LA sooner rather than later." That's always been my brother's dream. Am I going to be the asshole who takes that away from him? "Listen to me, Nick. You've done a good job closing Manhattan Financial so quickly."

My dad always told me I'd feel a sense of pride from doing a job well and one that benefits my family is even better. I say, "Christiansen Wealth Management now."

He chuckles. "I stand corrected."

I walk to the door, feeling like I'm having to make a choice between what I want and what's expected of me.

Like my loyalty to my family is being questioned. I just made Natalie and me official, even told her I loved her. Was it said based on location—me being in the same city—or because I've reached a point where I don't want to be without her?

I know the answer regarding my personal life, but what have I gotten myself into professionally? Andrew's sudden change in my relocation is frustrating. Two weeks ago, he was sure I should relocate to New York due to the takeover. Now he drops Seattle into the conversation as if I wouldn't have an opinion.

"There's always room for you in management. You'd be able to buy that beach house like you want. Surf at sunrise, drive a Lamborghini, and have an office with a view of all of LA."

With my hand on the doorknob, I turn back. "I'm not the same guy I used to be."

He twists off the beer bottle cap. "Because you have a girlfriend? The Christiansen brothers could take the world by storm and grow this business internationally. What will it take, little brother? A Maserati instead?"

"We went from New York to me now moving around the world. That escalated in the blink of an eye. How about because I know what I want and will fight for it. I'm not going to be a pushover, and, Andrew, don't become another LA asshole who thinks he can buy happiness."

After taking a long drag from the bottle, he asks, "Now you're an expert?"

"No, just your brother who wants to respect his elders."

The cap is shot across the room and hits the door. "We'll make a deal. I won't be a douchebag, and you'll consider Seattle if need be."

Nodding, I take in the offer, and then say, "I'll consider it.

Later, because I need to go. I promised to take Natalie to dinner."

"Before you go, I need you to sign an amendment to the Manhattan Financial contract. We gave them a heads-up about the change we want to make. There's been a lot of back and forth with John St. James. It's going to come down to agreeing or losing a large incentive."

"I thought this deal was done?"

He goes to the console and takes a file from his briefcase. When he hands it to me, he says, "Garrett Stans helped pinpoint some smaller loans to clean up the books, and we've had Larson in corporate being the bad guy to keep our name off their tongues."

I shake my head because that makes no sense. They aren't stupid. "As if somehow, they won't know a Christiansen, or three, had anything to do with it?"

"They made this deal look golden, and we signed the offer, but once we had more detailed access to all financials, there are some issues that need to be handled. We're handling them by getting these losses off the books before year-end. But you're still the point man on the deal from our legal team, so we need you to sign this amendment."

Handing me a pen, he points at the line. "Sign here. Larson will handle the delivery since you're traveling."

"I could swing by and take them since I'm here in the city."

"Good idea. Keeps it personal. The St. Jameses should like that. Maybe they'll make this easy for us to move forward by signing."

After scanning the amendment, I sign and wrap it up in the folder. "We're good?"

"All good. See you in LA, little brother."

"See you." I leave his room and stop by my room down

the hall to drop off the file. I can take it over tomorrow before I head to the airport. With Seattle weighing me down, I don't bother changing clothes and head out to meet Natalie. I need to talk to her and hope she can talk some sense into me for even considering the idea of moving before we have a chance to be together.

I know her, though. I already know what she'll say.

She'll never want to stand in the way of something she thinks will make me happy. That means I have to make her realize that there is no happiness if I'm not with her.

23

Natalie

Nick. Christiansen.

I bite my lip just thinking about him, wishing I was biting his bottom lip instead. I'd settle for his shoulder or his bicep. Definitely his earlobe, because I notice he shivers and then always kisses me right after when I do it. I don't even think he's aware of some of his habits. I hope he never breaks them.

He has me acting like a teen again. The excitement to see him is so overwhelming that I could make a fool of myself in front of all of Manhattan and not give a damn.

And that's exactly what I do the moment I see him. I set my cocktail down and dash through the crowd. Landing against his hard body, I sigh when those strong arms lift me off the ground. A deep chuckle runs through his chest before reaching my ears, and I can readily admit I'm addicted to the sound.

I'm addicted to all of him.

I've never felt sexier than when he looks at me and

smiles like I just made his day better. Hell, his life better than before we met. It's as if the safest place in the world is in his arms because he holds me like I'm precious cargo. Unless it's sexual and then my body purrs under his touch. When he listens to me, even when I'm rambling, I feel valued by asking questions and participating. I don't have one-sided conversations with Nick. I feel so much, so strongly that I could probably die happy because he makes me feel more than good enough for the first time in my life. I'm above the bar in his eyes, and he's tops for me.

And it all came so quickly.

Does time matter when you know it's right? When your soul feels so connected to someone else that it comes alive for the first time? I've stopped worrying about timelines and what's considered responsible. I act based on how he makes me feel—*cherished*—and now live accordingly.

"He said yes," I say when Nick sets me on my feet again.

"Who?"

"Nick, your idea. It totally worked."

Chuckling, he says, "Can I take credit for an idea when I'm not sure what you're referring to?"

I take his hand and lead him back to where I left my belongings at the bar. "Our table isn't ready, so I thought we could have a drink while waiting to celebrate what a great team we make."

"I'm all for celebrating us, but fill me in on the details?"

When the bartender looks my way, I circle my finger in the air for another round and then turn back to Nick, my gorgeous boyfriend. My happiness can't be contained, and it's not just because I made a client happy, but because *we're* working. We took a chance on each other, and it's paying off. I'm not sure I can imagine life getting much better, but when he moves here full-time, I bet he proves me wrong.

I say, "The cookies. You were right. I was definitely over-thinking it. Guys aren't complicated. They love cookies, and I found out brownies go a long way toward earning points with men who can buy anything. Because what they don't do is think of the simpler things in life, the little joys, the things that make you remember something special from your childhood."

"And baked goods do that?"

"They did this time, and that's what counts. My client got the guy, the biggest player in town, and he even asked her to move in."

"That's all it took?"

"I'm sure there's more to the story, but it's fun to be a small part of making it happen. Who knew baked treats held so much power? Not me, but I do now."

He leans down and kisses my forehead. "I do love your treats."

"Stop," I say, dragging out the O a little longer. Oh, how I love a long and tingly O. Swatting his chest and then pulling him closer, I coo, "Go on . . ."

When two rum and Cokes are set on the bar before us, I'm easily distracted and hand him one. I take the other and tap the rim against his glass. "I didn't make a lot of money, but I think I've discovered an additional revenue stream. All this time, I was catering to the socialites and bigwigs of New York—millionaires, billionaires, and pretty much anyone who can afford my rates—but I was overlooking an impor-tant component of the gift-giving business. After discussing it with Tatum this afternoon, we decided we need a mid-range line of services. Sure, I can organize a private jet to the Maldives for the weekend or pick up that Lamborghini someone's husband has always dreamed of owning. The royalties are phenomenal, but those aren't as common. So if we hire somebody, we can have them cater to our wealthy clientele but offer them something they're not used to getting."

His hand is distracting as it rubs circles on my hip. *Such a tease . . .* He asks, "And what is that?"

"Home. They're so used to jet-setting that they've forgotten about the creature comforts of home. Stockings hung from the mantel on Christmas Eve, private cooking lessons for a romantic evening in. Or sharing that perfect bottle of Chateau Margaux by the fire on a cold winter's night. Though that's one hell of an expensive bottle of wine, you get where I'm going with this. My clients are used to the finer things in life, but they've forgotten what matters."

A spark of pride lies in his eyes. "And what matters, Natalie?"

"Us, and building a life together, family, friends, and being surrounded by the people you love." I don't know why embarrassment creeps through me, but I look down at the drink in my hand, wishing the heat in my cheeks would disappear. With my heart on my sleeve, I peek up at him. "Do I sound crazy?"

"No, you sound like a woman who knows what she wants and has a plan to get it."

"Why does it sound bad when women are ambitious? Like it's a dirty word or something."

"It's not to me." Brushing the backs of his fingers across my cheek, he lowers his voice, and says, "It's incredibly sexy. Your excitement is intoxicating." Tapping his glass to mine, he says, "Here's to you."

I feel his voice vibrating deep inside me, my heart clinging to the words of support.

We drink but don't have time for another before the hostess finds us to lead us to our table. After ordering our meals, I lean closer, hating that there's a table between us. I'd rather be next to him or, even better, on his lap. Why'd I insist on going out when being alone with him is so deliciously divine? To distract myself from lunging across this table and settling onto his lap, I ask, "How was your day?"

The smile I love so much doesn't bring joy to his eyes or reveal his dimples this time, making me wonder what's on his mind. After looking around the room, his hazel eyes land back on me, making me feel special like I'm the only one he truly sees.

He asks, "Can you do your job remotely, or do you need to be in New York?"

"A bit of both, and also it depends on when. Sometimes I need to be here to fine-tune details for clients, but otherwise, I do a lot over email and phone. Why?"

"Well, I want to know if you'd like to come to California? Thinking for a weekend, or if you can work remotely, however long you'd like. My family has a beach house, so I was thinking we could stay there. It's not much, more like a bungalow, but it's pretty great. That's where I go when I want to get away, or I'm looking to surf."

This time, he's the one leaning closer. Lowering his voice, he continues, "I'd like you to meet my parents and my brother." He appears to back away from the offer as he leans back in his chair. The light that flickered in his eyes when he asked has disappeared. "Only if you want."

Studying him, I can tell something is off—his eyes are wandering as much as his thoughts appear to be. The distance between us feels like it's growing larger than the wood table, but I try not to let it bother me. I'm probably reading too much into it anyway. "You want to introduce me to your family?"

"My mom is excited to meet you."

"It's so sweet that you talk to her about me."

"Have you mentioned to me to your family?"

Now I feel bad. Lowering my voice, I reply, "I'm always honest with you, so I'm not going to lie or make up an excuse. The thing is, my parents saw me go through a terrible relationship. Tatum has witnessed me at my lowest, when I believed that I was no good for anyone and lucky to have him. So the truth is, Tatum knows, as you've seen, but I was planning to introduce you to my parents and brother." When he doesn't say anything, I add, "We have a family dinner once a month, and I was going to ask if you wanted to join me in two weeks."

"But you haven't mentioned me?"

"I don't talk to them all the time. They're busy, and I'm busy. If you said yes, I was going to tell them I'd be bringing a date." I take a sip of the rum and then say, "If you said no, I'd wait until we've been dating a bit longer. I don't like to disappoint them. But to be fair, I believed we'd work out, so I haven't had a doubt about dinner with them and you meeting them then."

He smirks. "You believe we'll work out?"

I turn away, not letting him win, but when I grin, too, I know he does anyway. "Did I just open a can of worms?"

"You did." He reaches over and takes my hand. "I really don't care that you haven't talked to them about us. We're newer, and when you've been burned by someone you cared about, it's always best to take the next relationship in stride." He takes his glass in hand and says, "Here's to getting it right this time."

"To getting it right." Our eyes are fixed on each other as we drink. Lowering the glass back down, I say, "Tell me more about this beach house in California."

"It's one of my favorite places in the world. Wait until you see that water."

We eat, the conversation lighter, but I have this weird feeling he's holding back. Since he never answered prior, I ask, "What's on your mind?"

The smile I expect to see doesn't arrive. He spins the glass around with his deft fingers, the distance creeping between us. Whispering over the table, I add, "Nick, are you going to talk to me?"

"About?"

"About what's on your mind. Did something happen?"

He rearranges his napkin on his lap and then sits up again as if he remembered he was in public. "The company is expanding to the Pacific Northwest. If they get the deal they want." Adjusting the cuffs of his sleeves, he drops that bomb and then plays like that didn't just happen.

But I'm still trying to read between the lines. "If everything is going so well, why are you concerned?"

Drinking, he finishes the rest of the alcohol before setting the glass back down. "You're right. Things are going well. We targeted New York. Seattle is an unexpected opportunity, but it would poise us for the growth goals we're aiming for. Just a fast track to reaching them. I just thought . . . Well, I thought New York was enough for now."

I stare at him, noticing how little eye contact he's made. My gaze dips to his hand again to find him still spinning that glass. Nick has tells, and the glass is one of them. He's holding back, not giving me the full story. I can't help but wonder why, so I try a different tactic. "I like the apartment. When do you think you'll move in?" I ask, testing which direction the waters of his mood flow in.

The check is delivered, and he's quick to take it. "Dinner was good."

I toss my napkin on the plate. "It was. Now, what's going on?"

"I was thrown by a comment my brother made earlier."

I rest my arms on the table just as my mom taught me not to do, but stress makes me forget my proper upbringing. "Then talk to me."

"Can we talk in California after two days of nakedness?" He laughs, and I'm glad to see there isn't doubt in his eyes. I roll my eyes and giggle. *He's a sweet goof.* But he is still restless.

The bill with his credit card inside is swiped by the server from the table as she passes. "While two days of nakedness sounds amazing . . . and you want me to meet your family—"

"I do."

Rolling my eyes, I say, "You and those I do's. It's like you can't get it out of your system."

"Not until I say it for real, I suppose."

Mimicking his body language, I sit back again and cross my arms over my chest. "I'd like to meet your family on one condition." When I have his interest piqued, I say, "You have to tell me what you want to talk about in California."

He shifts forward, lowering his arms, his guard, and his voice. "I don't want it to ruin tonight since nothing's set in stone."

"Your mind's been elsewhere throughout dinner. I'd rather talk about it than leave it hanging out there between us."

He nods. "I'm sorry. You deserved better than that. We're here to celebrate—"

"We're here to be together before you have to leave again." This time, I reach over and run the tips of my fingers over the top of his hand. "I want to hear what's going on in your world. That's not ruining anything. It's communicating and sharing the burden."

Staring into my eyes, he smirks. "I'm the luckiest guy alive. You're amazing, you know that?"

"You can show me later, but right now, spill."

"My brother suggested I might be better utilized in Seattle."

I lean forward in a panic. "Versus New York?"

"Yes."

"And? What about our plans and you being here?"

"You've been honest with me, so I'll be honest with you. I'm feeling caught between you and my family. Nothing's decided yet, but that me moving there was tossed out so easily bothers me."

Sitting back, I look around at the restaurant, noticing couples and families, friends, and what appear to be business associates enjoying their meals. The atmosphere is energized with joy, making me realize Nick does that for me. I say, "I don't want you to feel caught in the middle."

"I know. It's not something you put on me. It's something I'm doing to myself." Pushing his plate out of the way, he rests his arm on the table, seemingly frustrated. "I'm a beach guy. I surf. I hang out. I'm not that hard to please, but then I met you again, and I started reevaluating things. I want to be with you, Natalie, and I'm willing to move to be with you. But where does that leave me in the long-term?"

"With a girlfriend who loves you."

The most genuine smile I've ever seen arrives just in time, soothing my frantic heart when I needed it most. He reaches around the plates and places his hand palm up. I slip mine on top, always marveling at the perfect fit. Nick says, "I love you too. That's why I want you to come to California and meet my family. I want to spend a few days with you at the beach with nothing to do but make love and cook out on the patio."

"Sounds like my kind of place, but where does Seattle stand?"

"Honestly, I don't know. It was mentioned in passing today, so I haven't really had time to ask more questions and find out whether my dad believes it's a complete relocation or something I can manage remotely at times. My guess? Whatever's decided, they'll survive without me living there full time. I can travel from here to there just as easily as I can from LA."

"Apparently, you're not familiar with our airports." He chuckles at the joke and holds my hand a little tighter. I've not ever thought about leaving Manhattan to live anywhere else other than Paris during my senior year of high school. I got over that when I realized it will always be there for me to visit. But Nick has me considering what I'd do for love, for us. "Whatever is decided, we'll make it work, and I can't wait to introduce you to my family."

24

Natalie

Two weeks later . . .

Closing my eyes, I let the sunshine warm my cheeks as the wind whips in through the window. It's not like the doom and gloom in New York. I love fall there, but for a few days, it's nice to escape to somewhere sunny that's forgotten what season it is.

I reach over and rub the back of Nick's neck, teasing him with the tips of my nails. I can tell by how he leans into the caress that he missed me as much as I did him. "It's funny how I never imagined you driving or what you might drive. I drive so little that I'm not sure my license is even valid."

"In LA, you need a vehicle to get everywhere."

"You look good in this one."

"I bought this 1974 Range Rover with my own money during my sophomore year in high school. I worked on it some, but never got it running because I was too busy with my studies to mess with it. My parents had it fully restored as a graduation gift, adding in the drop-top in the back for my surfboards."

"I like the green color and the truck. It's nice. It's very you—rugged and adventurous but has style and class."

He reaches over and rubs my thigh. "You think so highly of me." He slides his hand under my skirt. His eyes may not be on me, but I can see his chest rise with deeper breaths.

"You've not given me a reason to think otherwise."

"You're the only one. My dad's still mad at me for not delivering a file before I left New York." The tips of his fingers find the edge of my panties. "You're very distracting, beautiful, especially in the morning. I almost missed my flight."

"Hope you didn't get into too much trouble."

"I sent it that night when I arrived back in LA, but I'm not sure he'll ever let me live it down. I know hard work is the way to win him over, so that's what I've been doing."

"I noticed. I've been missing our late-night video chats."

"That's why I'm so glad you're here."

I drag my nails into his hair and slide down in the seat to put his fingers a little closer to where I want them . . . "Me too."

He takes his eyes from the road, and his gaze lands heavy on me, his intentions clear just from a look that pins me to the seat. When he continues driving, I make a suggestion instead of waiting for an invitation. "Are we meeting your family first or . . . because I have an itch that only you can scratch."

His signature smirk, the one full of confidence, lifts the edges of his lips, and he turns back to me. "I'll take you to meet my family tomorrow. I can't wait to be alone with you at the beach, or should I say inside making love while listening to the ocean waves crashing just outside the windows."

"Romantic and sexy. I like your style." I can't wait for that either, but the traffic here is insane, so it seems I'm going to have to. It takes more than an hour to get there, but the house is perfect. The little three-bedroom love nest is not too big but has all the necessities, keeping the attention on the ocean with an entire wall of accordion-style sliding glass doors bringing the outside in.

While Nick opens the place up, I snoop around, finding hints of his family everywhere. From the matte silver frames on the white oak bookshelves in the living room to the monogrammed towels in the bathrooms, it's a well-appointed home with no detail left unfinished. Joining him on the patio deck, I ask, "How long has your family owned this place?"

"Twenty years or so. It was a shack they got for a steal. My mom poured her love of decorating into it and had it redesigned and renovated. Like me and my SUV, they appreciate designs of the past, taking old things and making them new again."

"Like the apartment in Manhattan. It's an old building with new amenities." I laugh. "My mom is the opposite. She loves cutting-edge fashion and anything straight off the runway. She considers it art and collects everything from clothes to shoes and accessories. She wears them once or twice but then packs them away in archival storage containers."

"What does she do with them? Will she sell the pieces one day or—" Maybe he felt he was overstepping some imaginary boundary with me because he stops mid-sentence and returns his gaze to the crashing waves. Before I can say anything, he turns to me, and says, "I'm not really a collector. I just buy what I like and what I need."

I shouldn't be offended, but I can't help but get defensive. "Like I said, it's art. She just doesn't share it with the world. It's not on display for everyone to see, but she shares it with me, teaches me how to wear something properly."

"You have your style, and it's unpredictable like you. I like the way you look. I like how you dress for celebrations, Tuesday night, or even for me, but I really like that you dress for you and what makes you feel good."

"Why do you sound upset?"

"I'm not upset. I'm just . . ." He runs his hands through his hair and then turns to face me. Moving closer, he fills the space that existed between us and kisses my cheek and then my lips. "I want to be with you," he whispers.

"You're with me. I'm right here." Cupping his face, I ask, "What happened?"

"They want me in Seattle."

The news smacks me, sending my head to jerk back. "I thought, well, we . . ." I struggle to gather my thoughts on this. "You said you'd commute from New York. I even looked up flights from Newark and JFK. You can take the red-eye or an overnight to lessen the time away, but you don't need to be there. I need you with me."

As I start to move away, my worries becoming a reality, he grabs my waist and keeps me there. I ask, "When did you find out?"

"This afternoon. You were already on your flight."

"We'll figure it out, right? Find the best solution, one that works for us. That's a job, a paycheck. What we have is more, so whatever comes our way, we'll face it together."

He's nodding, seeming to absorb every word. "Together. We'll be together."

I smile, the certainty I have in us more powerful than the threat of being long distance. "Together, Nick. No matter what." He kisses me with all the pent-up passion from our time apart, and this talk of the future has me returning his embrace. His fingers weave into my hair, and then he's leading me back into the house and down the small hall to a bedroom facing the ocean. Although the view is incredible, his eyes never leave me as if I can compete with Mother Nature.

Sitting on the bed, he rests back, letting his gaze take a leisurely stroll along my body. I'm not sure if he's here as an observer and plans to participate until he says, "Strip for me, beautiful."

It's not the first time I've gotten naked for a man, but it's the first I've done it completely sober in broad daylight. With him, I'm not embarrassed or shy. When he looks at me like I'm the sexiest woman he's ever seen, I believe him. It feeds my ego, and I pull my shirt over my head and then start on my jeans. He's not bashful by the way he lets his eyes roam my body. The heat of his stare warms my insides, emboldening me, and I go to him. With his eyes set on me, I stand and unclasp my bra. The straps come down one by one, exposing my breasts to him.

Cupping both as if testing the weight in his hands, he then leans forward, taking my areola into his mouth and teasing my nipple with his teeth. When it's puckered hard and wet, he does the same to the other one. Sitting back, he squeezes them, kneading, and runs his thumbs over the buds.

When he kisses the skin between them, I lean in, causing his legs to spread farther as I slink in to take up space. Rubbing my hands over the back of his head, I can tell my body is ready for him, silently begging for fingers or his dick. I'd be happy with either filling me until I come. "God," I pant, helpless to letting my thoughts run wild as his lips delight in every inch of my skin.

Flipped by my hips to the mattress in a sudden swift motion, he finds the straps that keep me covered. The last scraps of fabric are pulled down over my ankles and lost in the frenzy of his mouth replacing the lace. He slides his tongue between my lower lips, causing my back to arch off the bed, and a moan escapes me.

"So fucking good." His words are warm breaths against the apex of my legs. The sensual kisses he's giving send me into bliss, and I catch up to a release that I couldn't find when we were apart. My body tightens and then tremors under his lips.

While my body recovers, he's fast and stripping off his clothes. This time, he came prepared. I'm tempted to laugh, but I feel too good to move, anticipating the second round to be better than the first.

Dropping over me, he kisses my mouth, and then whispers, "You and me, baby. Always us." My body blooms as if he's the morning sunlight, and he fills me. We're slow at first, but then I wrap my arms around him, and he starts thrusting.

"Always us," I repeat through jagged breaths. You'd think we'd been apart for months or years and not just a few weeks. Our insatiable craving caught up in each other. The push and the pull, we tumble until I'm on top. Resting my hands on his chest, I rise up and slowly sink back down. I ride him until his fingers dig into my hips, and he takes control, fucking me right back.

I feel that delicious tightening deep inside me that I know leads to a glorious release. I move back and forth, chasing it down until it catches me instead. Striking like an earthquake, it rocks my body until my insides are clenching around him. "Oh God, Nick. Yes. *Yes.* You make me feel so good."

Every last quiver is fucked from me, and then I'm held down on top of him until his release dissipates as my name is repeated. I lie down, tilting my head to the side and listening to his thundering heartbeat. It might be arrogance, but that I can make this man's heart race like he makes mine has me smiling with pride.

Tracing figure eights on his shoulder, I stretch to kiss his chin. Catching my attention, he rests back enough to make eye contact. "What if—"

"I thought we weren't doing what-ifs anymore?" I tease, still smiling like a goof.

"Bear with me." Even through the closed windows, the ocean insists on being heard. That may fill my ears, but I see Nick's Adam's apple bob in this throat from a heavy gulp, and it just about does me in. Again. Sexy bastard.

He rubs my bare back, the change in his demeanor is sudden, and his eyes full of passion. "I know this sounds crazy, but I need you to hear me out. Okay?"

I hold his hands just as tight and look into his pleading eyes. "Okay, I'm listening."

"We barely know each other in the scheme of things. We haven't met each other's families. Hell, I know you're a professional gift giver, but I don't even know the name of your company. These are things I should know. I should know your ring size and your favorite food. What's your favorite song, and if you could go anywhere, where would that be? How many kids do you want, or do you not want any at all? What movie always makes you cry, and did you grow up with pets? Are you a cat or dog person? *Fuck.*"

He squeezes his eyes closed and rubs them like he's been

asleep for his entire life until now, and he's seeing things for the first time. I lift up, not wanting to miss any of it.

When he looks at me again, he continues, "There's so much left to learn about each other, but what I do know is that I've never felt like this about anyone else before. My feelings are true and run deep, and although I'm no psychic, I'm willing to bet my future on you. I could promise you forever, and I wouldn't be lying." He sits up next to me. "We can go to Mexico or Vegas or even Catalina Island again. We can be together. I'll live wherever you want to, and we'll make it a home."

"What are you saying, Nick? Are you asking me to move in with you?"

Taking my hand, he says, "No. I should be asking you all those other questions and a million different ones to get to know you better. Instead, I'm asking if you want to get married?"

25

Natalie

Yes.

I wish I could give him that answer, but that word doesn't cross my lips. Thoughts run through my brain on overdrive, not giving me a second reprieve to catch up. *Did he just ask me to marry him?*

Still looking at me with nothing less than a desperation to love me, his fingers graze over the top of my bare ring finger. "I don't have a ring, but you can pick out anything you like, or I can surprise you. I think I have a good idea of what you'd like. I just want to be with you, tied to you in ways that no one can tear us apart. Will you marry me, Natalie?"

"You want to get married?" I ask, blindsided, the words like a fumbled football as they leave my tongue. "I don't understand why you're saying this. Are you running from the law, or did you do something wrong?"

The taste of being questioned comes out in pinched

brows as he looks at me. "Nothing's wrong, and for the record, I have no skeletons. You can run a background check. I know this is out of the blue, but my feelings aren't. I've been thinking about what I want since I left New York. I want you. It's bullshit to live in two different worlds when all I want to be is with you all of the time."

"But we don't have to be married to be with each other. You skipped a few steps, like moving in together or living in the same city."

"I love you and want to marry you, Natalie. This isn't a fly-by-night romance for me. You'll not only be the first girl I'm bringing home to meet my family. You'll be the only one. You don't have to say yes, but you should know that I'm not giving up unless you tell me no. I'll respect that, but it won't change my feelings toward you, not ever."

"I don't even know what fly by night means, but you're serious, aren't you?" I should want to tell him yes, be brave like him or bold like Tatum, but I'm so stunned I'm not sure what to say. The last thing I want to do is give a knee-jerk reaction to something that deserves thought and care.

Images of falling into his arms the first time we met and then running into him on the street in one of the most populated cities in the world come to mind. Making love that night and then the picnic in the empty apartment in lower Manhattan. His smile when we saw each other at the airport. All of these vivid memories play like a record of our love affair, making me realize I had it all wrong. *But he didn't.* "You said it was destiny the first time we met."

His grin grows, the sunlight reflecting in his eyes making them so much brighter. "I did. *It was.*" He fiddles with my fingers in his hand. What astounds me most is that we don't have all our ducks in a row. We don't know where he'll live, where my business will go, *whether it will keep growing.* Yet this incredible man sees a future with me in it, no matter where his job takes him, no matter that he doesn't know all my favorite things. And that confidence in us brings me peace. A feeling of rightness that I've only ever felt before about STJ. *Contentment amidst the chaos.*

"I don't know what I'm saying, Nick, but I think I agree with you. We were destiny. There's no other way to describe us, so who am I to argue with our fate?"

"You're saying—"

"I'll marry you." Saying it feels right and vacant of regret. "Yes, I'll marry you, Nick."

He wraps around me, and we roll to the side onto the bed. Kisses are placed all over my face under my fits of giggles, and he leaves whispers just under my ear, "I love you."

"I love you too, so much." The truth has freed itself from my chest, leaving more room for love to grow beyond my heart, spilling into all parts of me like the air I need to breathe and the blood that runs through me. Nick and I are one already, so getting married is merely a formality when thinking about destiny and the role it's played in our lives.

Lying next to him, I snuggle into the nook of his body, and say, "I love dogs."

I take the opportunity to look up at him, smiling when I see his already big enough not to contain any longer. "Me, too."

"Little dogs I can run errands with."

"I prefer bigger dogs you can play fetch with."

Running the tips of my fingers lightly over his abs, I say, "We'll compromise and get one of each or buy a medium-sized dog."

"That sounds fair." Curling his arm around me a bit tighter, he kisses my forehead. I could melt from the sweetness. Actually, I do, every time he plants one on me. I'll never turn down one of his kisses.

"I'm a six, if you're wondering about a certain ring finger. I'm not sure on the others. You already know my favorite food."

"Ketchup," he says, chuckling. "Kidding. Burgers and fries."

A sense of pride comes over me that he got it right. We could be the stars of the dating game, already well aware of the important stuff. I laugh against him. "My company is STJ Co., and I always cry during *The Notebook* whether reading the book or watching the movie. Song? *Hm.* I like some modern country artists even though I'm not supposed to admit that being from New York City and all. 'Ride' by Chase Rice is pretty sexy, though. Growing up, I loved 'Blackbird' by The Beatles or Sarah McLachlan. Either version."

The last answers he's seeking don't come as easily as the others. But he lets me work it out at my own pace. "I'm not looking to have kids just yet, but if I have to pick between a number and none, I'd go with two. It's what I'm familiar with me and my brother."

"Same," he replies quietly.

"As for anywhere I'd go if I could . . . I'm happy in your arms." This time, I lean in and kiss his chest. Looking up, I ask, "You really want to marry me?"

He quirks a smile. "I do."

"What happens next?"

"I get a ring and down on one knee to make it official."

"There goes the surprise," I tease, pushing up to look at him properly. This man and that handsome face are going to be mine forever. I can already tell he'll always make my heart race, not just from his looks but the way he touches me and how the heat lingers on my skin long after he's gone. I've never felt like this before or had someone affect me soul-deep. My past relationships feel foolish in comparison.

I love him. Our attraction may have pulled us together, but fate put the pieces in place. "I love you."

"I love you, too."

"You don't have to make a production to give me a story to tell others. I love our story best." I could snuggle all day with him, listening to the backdrop of the ocean's waves. "Feels official already."

Pushing up on one hand, he angles toward me. "It is. *We are.* I promise I'll marry you—any day, place, or time. I'll be there without hesitation. Actually, I'll show up early."

I rest my hand on his cheek. "And here I thought you were supposed to be the sensible one. You do know how crazy this is, right?"

"What can I say? Love makes people do crazy things."

"Crazy might be an understatement."

Continuing to look at me as if he'll find a crack in my decision, he says, "Speaking of crazy . . ." He runs his hand through his hair and then rubs his eyes as if pained.

"I really hate being on pins and needles."

He takes a deep breath and then looks at me again. "So my mom, she's . . ." He drags it out, and now I'm frozen to the spot with my mind filling in all the possibilities regarding his mom.

Is he going to tell me she's a movie star? Spoiler alert: *this wouldn't surprise me.* Great looks, inherited, and this so-called "bungalow" on the beach. It's not small, considering it's twice the size of my apartment, and Tatum and I have a damn nice apartment by New York standards. Or maybe she's never liked any of his girlfriends, so he's warning me. Carves pumpkins for a living or enters hot dog eating contests. Whatever she does or whoever she is, I'm starting to freak out. "What is it, Nick?"

"She's into New Age, spiritual stuff, like the zodiac signs."

"*Okaaaay*, this is not where I saw this going. Continue."

"The new moon was in my seventh house the day we met." I close my mouth and fix my expression from the shock of hearing him talk about it like he knows more than he's letting on. Is this a dirty little secret of his? *It's amazing.*

"I have to know. What does that mean?"

"It's new beginnings, the start of a new relationship."

"That's us."

He grins so big like he just won a grand prize, like a new car or something. Oh wait, he likes older cars. "It is us. According to her, we're written in the stars." *Be still my heart.*

That is the most romantic thing I've ever heard in my life. "So, when you said it was destiny that brought us together, you meant it, literally?"

He kisses my shoulder. "My analytical, reasonable side says no, but who am I to question fate? We're here as living proof, so yeah, we were destined to be together."

Moving up to rest against the headboard, I rub my toes along his muscular leg under the sheet, loving that I have full access to his body and mind for all time is exhilarating. "I like the way you think. As for our parents, though, it seems your mom will appreciate the chain of events."

"But your parents might not, so we should get our story straight."

"No alibi needed," I say, more certain than ever. "I love you, and you love me. The facts are all the evidence we need."

"You'd make a good lawyer, St. James."

"Thank you, Counselor. I'm just kind of impressed that I snagged you and didn't even have to provide you with any baked goodies."

His laughter shakes the bed, and the weight of the world is released from his chest as his lighter side returns. Grabbing my ankles, he says, "They may not have been baked, but I definitely ate your goodies," and then whisks me down to land flat on my back.

I burst out laughing. I don't even care that I gave him the perfect setup to make that comeback because I'm reaping the rewards. "You sure did, and you're welcome to them any time you're hungry."

Rolling on top of me, he slips his hand between us as he kisses my neck. "Too soon?"

I butterfly my legs open, welcoming him. "Never."

IN SOME WAYS, Nick's been a mystery. He was staying in the same kind of villa as Tatum and me in Catalina. That suite cost a few thousand a night, so I assumed he had some money. Then I was conflicted based on his job and how he's just starting out in his career. I don't mind either way, and I have plenty of my own money not to worry about his financials, but I'm getting the distinct feeling his family is wealthy judging by the neighborhood.

Large mansions populate the palm tree-lined street with blue skies overhead and birds singing. It's idyllic in that Hollywood movie star kind of way, or even for someone fresh off the Ralph Lauren runway. I mean, come on, those looks came from somewhere. I ask, "Are we in Beverly Hills?" just as he begins to slow down.

"Yes."

I angle my head to look up at the top of the walls protecting the homes from looky-loo tourists like me. "This is where you grew up?" Laughing, I add, "Like the show?"

"Nothing like the show." I notice how his fingers whiten around the steering wheel. It appears someone is sensitive about pop culture shows of yesteryear.

I cover his right hand since that's the one I can reach from the passenger's seat now, trying to contain my laughter. "Did I hit a nerve, Counselor?"

Glancing over at me, he clenches his jaw, another tell of his revealed. *He's bothered.* "Everyone thinks they know you the minute you say Beverly Hills."

"So what you're saying is that it's not all shopping, life lessons wrapped up in an hour, and hanging out at the Peach Pit? That's seriously disappointing."

He chuckles. "Okay, fine. We hung out at the Peach Pit all the time."

"You did?"

"No," he deadpans. "The diner is fictional, just like the show. Although I will say that one was built just for tourists like you."

"Can we go?"

"No."

I love pushing his buttons. It might be my new favorite thing, right after his lips on my body and how he makes me scream his name. *Twice this morning.*

I whack his arm for mocking me, though I'm not really bothered. I love old TV shows. I make no apologies. "Make fun all you want, but I bet the burger is pretty good. Hey, don't you owe me a trip to In-N-Out?"

"I do."

I almost roll my eyes from hearing him say that phrase

again, but this time it holds new meaning, and I grin instead. "You sure are comfortable with that phrase."

That finally cracks the tension I'm thinking he's feeling from bringing a girl home, his future wife to be exact, and the smile I've fallen in love with shows up.

Rubbing my leg again, he rests his arm on the console between us and leans over. "Figured I should get some practice in, so I don't fuck it up when it's showtime. And don't worry about In-N-Out." He waggles his brow. "We'll hit it up later."

The car pulls onto the entrance to a long driveway, but we're stopped at the gates. He clicks a remote, and the large iron gates open, revealing a white painted brick home with black accents—shutters, roof, and doors. "Holy crap, you're rich!" I exclaim, not meaning to be so obnoxious. The St. James are wealthy, but wow, this place is more than impressive. It's not a mansion; it's an estate. If it has a pool house like on "The OC," then I'm upping this to a compound. The place is huge, but don't get me wrong. It has a tasteful feel to it. He shifts the car into park and cuts the engine. "My parents are. I'm still saving for my beach house."

The bungalow. I'd almost forgotten they own that in Malibu too. I don't care that they bought it twenty years ago. The Christiansens are loaded and can afford it even with inflation based on this property. "Apparently, business is really good."

He chuckles and then leans over to kiss me on the cheek. "It's going well." He comes around and helps me hop from the seat. I'm not short, but the height of this SUV makes me feel that way. He adds, "Home sweet home."

"Not for long, Christiansen."

That really makes him smile. "Can't wait. You ready to meet my family?"

"As ready as I'll ever be. How do I look?"

"Beautiful, like always."

"I just realized you didn't give me any details to plan my small talk." My feet stop beneath me, my mind spinning to an abrupt halt. "Oh my God, I don't even know their names, and please tell me we aren't making any announcements."

Glancing over his shoulder, appearing to make sure the coast is clear, he then turns back to me and angles down. "No announcements today." He takes my hand, the pad of his thumb rubbing gently along the top of my hand. "That information is just for us for now. And there's no need to prepare a small talk spiel. My mom already loves you because you make me happy." We start walking again, but slowly, which is fine with me. "I'm not sure if Andrew will be here. He has an apartment downtown close to the office. And as for my dad, he's a bear to most, but Corbin Christiansen knows how to temper that side when it comes to his family."

"That's a relief." I wipe the imaginary sweat from my forehead. We reach the steps that lead to the front door, but I tug him to a stop again. "So, Dad is Corbin. Andrew is your brother. Mom's name?"

His reluctance starts to worry me. Finally, he says, "Don't make fun."

"Why would I make fun of her name?"

"It's Cookie, all right?"

"Cookie?" Gingersnaps, peanut butter, chocolate chip, and snickerdoodle. Our conversation comes barreling back. "Like what you eat, cookie?"

"One and the same. And that's her real name, not a nickname. Cookie Christiansen."

Nodding, I try to understand why that would be some-one's first name. "It's unique and unforgettable and absolutely adorable. I imagine it suits her. It does in my head, at least."

"It does." At the top of the steps, he takes a deep breath. Suddenly, I'm bracing myself for the worst. What are we walking into exactly? Because really, how bad can a Cookie be?

26

Nick

It's a big step—meeting the parents, but this is nothing compared to getting married, so I think we'll be all right. This seems like the right order to do things though I'm not stuck on old-fashioned traditions.

Thinking back to yesterday, did I ask her to be my wife on a whim, or in reaction to the news that I'm the Christiansen they're planning on shipping all over the world to represent them?

I have no idea but putting down roots with Natalie is more than appealing. I meant what I said to her. I love her. More than I should at this stage in the relationship? Hell no. I loved her the moment she fell into my arms. Being bonded to Natalie legally and otherwise is my best idea yet, making her my wife, a dream I never knew I had until I met her.

And she didn't even have to give me cookies.

I can see now that we're at a great place in life and in business. I'll help her grow that company so big that other people will be begging her for loans.

We quietly walk inside, as if we're intruders in my child-hood home. Her mouth is open as she looks up at the high ceilings and chandelier. For a California woman, Cookie has a soft spot for opulence in specific places—entryways and grand terraces that lead to a sunny and approachable garden. Go figure.

Before we enter the main living room, I whisper, "Forget about the crystal and marble. My mom is down to earth and she's going to love you."

I lead her through the living room, spying my mom at her favorite place—a barstool parked at the island near the sink. Not wanting to startle her, I say, "Hi, Mom."

She looks up from her laptop and then hops off the stool, planting her red reading glasses into her blond hair. "You're early?"

Not sure what she's asking, but I answer, "You know traffic is unpredictable."

Natalie's free hand clamps around our adjoined hands, her nervousness felt by how tight she's gripping me. "Mom, this is Natalie St. James." I add, "Natalie, this is my mom, Cookie Christiansen."

My mom's eyes light up as she comes around the island. Opening her arms wide, my mom grins like she's seeing her long-lost daughter. She always wanted a girl to bond with. "It's so nice to meet you, Natalie."

"You, too. I've heard so many great things about you and Nick's dad."

Natalie releases me, and they embrace like two friends who haven't seen each other in ages, hugging each other with genuine emotion attached. Seeing them has me feeling even more sure about our decision to move forward and get married.

When they step apart, I swear to God my mom has tears

in her eyes. She comes to me, and I hug her, whispering, "It's okay." My mom has to be the most sentimental person I've ever met.

Until I see Natalie with watery eyes as well.

When we part, she takes Natalie by the wrist, and they walk together to the other side of the island. Dropping her glasses to the bridge of her nose, my mom then poises her fingers over the laptop keyboard. "When's your birthday?"

Oh, no. I'm about to rush over to save Natalie from an astrological reading, but my dad says, "I thought I heard you come in, Nick. Come join me—*oh.* This must be your girl-friend." He forgets about me and makes a beeline for Natalie.

I remember doing the same when I saw her the first time. "This is Natalie, Dad."

"Hi," she says with a little wave. "I'm Natalie St. James."

My dad's gaze skips from her to me just before they shake hands. "St. James? That's interesting."

Instead of having a repeat of this conversation I had with Andrew, I try to end it fast. "It's a common name in New York," I reply, brushing off the coincidence.

Natalie says, "Not that common," as if I've offended her.

Great, now I've pissed her off. Introducing the love of your life to your parents is tricky business. "I meant that Andrew and I had a good laugh that there's a St. James Place in Monopoly, so we figured it must be a well-known name. Not that it's common or you're not original. You're very special—"

"Oh goodness," my mom says, cringing. "I think she gets it. It's probably best if you just end it there."

Scrubbing my hands over my face, I then look at my girl, hoping she can read the silent apology in my eyes. "Yeah, probably."

My dad says, "On that note, I need to borrow Nick if that's—"

"Take him," my mom says, wrapping an arm around Natalie. "We'll be fine."

"Geez, thanks, Mom."

She laughs. "You know what I mean."

As I come around the island, I kiss Natalie on the temple. "You'll be okay?"

"Fine. Really," she replies, and I believe her because she looks back at the screen and at my mom, and says, "June twenty-ninth."

"Oh, wow. Nick was born on August twenty-ninth, but I guess you already knew that."

I make the mistake of glancing back and am hit with a cocked eyebrow aimed at me. "Yep," she adds, "I knew that."

In my best internal narrator voice, I say, "She didn't know that."

How have we never discussed our birthdays?

We know each other's ages and other important stuff like how she's a runner. I know that because she climbed out of bed at sunrise and went for a run before I even woke up.

If I had known she had those plans, I would have hit the waves at the same time.

She drinks her coffee with just a hint of creamer and half a packet of sugar. Every time we have sex, she becomes more adventurous, slowly trying new positions, despite the confidence she has walking around completely naked, even in front of large windows where the people on the beach can get a gander.

See? I know the important stuff.

I shut the door behind me, finding my brother already sitting on the couch in my dad's home office. I take the recliner, kicking it back into position. "What's up?"

My dad sits at his desk and says, "We finally heard back on the Manhattan Financial deal. John's fought us tooth and nail on the transition team recommendations to cut some of their pet projects." He taps something on his keyboard, probably answering emails. He's always been a half-listening multi-tasker. Of course, he expects the opposite of us. Fully focused on whatever he says. You know, do as I say, not as I do kind of thing. "He's getting back to us today by five o'clock Eastern."

Andrew says, "It's the final deadline. He's agreed to cutting three of the four. He's dedicated to preserving that fourth. I have a feeling it's personal. We'll let him have it if he continues to negotiate."

"Then why not let him have it now to end this and move on?"

Sitting forward, Andrew says, "Because, Counselor, it's not good business to let your opponent win."

Hearing him call me that doesn't have the same ring to it.

Then he adds, "There's an out clause in the contracts of these business loans. We don't need his permission. We're just trying to be fair and let him walk away with the full deal. It's a brokerage house. They are a nice addition to our company, but they don't grow wealth the same way."

"Don't fuck them over. They seemed like decent people."

My dad says, "We don't fuck people over, Nick. We can't afford to humor business owners who don't have the ability to grow to the next level of sustainability. Acquiring Beacon is our next plan, not artisan pasta making or personal shopping for rich businessmen. Those aren't our specialties. We're focusing on what CWM does best. Build wealth. Business is business. If you start getting personal, you'll lose your edge."

I've done everything I was told to do growing up. Follow the Christiansen plan to a T, even down to attending Berkeley Law. But lately, I've started to second-guess what I'm even doing here. I say, "Maybe that's why I never fit into your plans. I don't have an edge."

"You have a great legal mind, son. We all have talents we bring to the table."

I keep thinking about Natalie and how much she struggles to keep her dream afloat. Given the right conditions, she's blooming like a plant. Ultimately though, business is business when money's involved, and if it doesn't fall within our guidelines, then it's time to streamline. I've heard that my whole life. "Yeah, I guess it's best to cut the losses." Not wanting to be gone from Natalie for too long, I say, "I should get back before Mom discovers Natalie and my star signs aren't compatible, and I get dumped for something ridiculous like that."

My dad chuckles. "That is a weird coincidence on the name, though. You sure there's no relation to John and Martine St. James?"

I don't rush for the door, but I'm heading for it when I reply, "I think Natalie would have mentioned if her parents just sold their family business, especially to mine."

"Natalie St. James," Andrews says, causing me to turn back. He sits forward, resting his forearms on his legs. Staring at me, he creases his brow. "Wasn't that his daughter's name?"

"Who's? John's? I'd remember that."

He says, "Natalie and Jackson St. James. You were right there, Nick, when he showed us the photo."

I try to recall John's daughter, *Jackson's sister*, but I'm drawing a blank. The call from my mom comes to mind, though. "Was this when Mom called?"

"I saw the photo. I'd recognize his daughter." Andrew stands and hurries to the door, rushing out.

Oh, shit. I run. My mind is muddled with jagged-edged pieces of the puzzle not fitting together. Praying to God we didn't just buy her family's legacy without her knowing a thing, I need to beat him there to soften the blow or explain why we're acting like maniacs.

I practically slam into the back of Andrew when he stops just inside the living room. His eyes are set on her, narrowed, and he's already shaking his head. Keeping my voice as quiet as possible, I ask, "What's the name of the company John's fighting for?"

Andrew looks at me curiously. "STJ Co. Why?"

Without taking a breath, I push past him, wanting to protect her from this news. It's going to destroy her. I don't understand how it got this far without her having prior knowledge or why her parents didn't tell her. I can only speculate that they were trying to protect her as well.

She looks at me concerned and then turns toward my brother and Dad who remain with distance between us. Andrew's solemn expression is easy to read.

Fuck. Why would her parents keep this from her? From memory, John St. James had said that his daughter wasn't interested in the company, so I guess it makes sense why she doesn't know about the takeover. *But will she feel as though she's been betrayed by being kept in the dark?* There's no way around this now that she's here. Staring at my brother and then my dad, I shake my head, pleading through the silence that's engulfing the room. "Please let me."

Natalie looks up at me innocently. "Let you what?"

My mom glances at the three of us, and then says, "What's happened?"

I reach for Natalie, thinking it might be best if I tell her alone, but then she pulls her phone from her back pocket and glances at the screen. "My mom's calling."

The four of us look at each other, and then I say, "You can take it on the terrace if you'd like privacy."

She nods, and I show her to the door, opening it for her. Just before it shuts, I hear her say, "Hi, Mom, what's up?"

Turning back to my family, I say, "What the fuck?"

"Nick!" my mom scolds, anger firing in her eyes. She rests her palms on the stone counter and angles to my dad. "What the fuck is happening, Corbin?"

Andrew is usually the first one with a smart-ass comment, but he scrubs a hand over his head and sits this one out by moving to the living room sofa.

My dad comes closer, glancing toward the terrace, and then whispers, "Natalie is the daughter of the former CEO of Manhattan Financial."

"Layman's, please," my mom says, staring at him and tapping her fingers impatiently.

He replies, "The company we just bought in New York. That's Natalie's family business."

Her mouth falls open, but then she clasps her hands in front of her chest, grinning wide as the day is long. "Destiny."

"No, Mom. Not now." My gut twists, watching my girl-friend . . . my fiancée through the windows. I'm unsure of the implications of this bombshell, but from what I have gathered, Natalie has been content in her discussions with her dad regarding business. Why would he sell it without telling her?

Will she blame me for making this deal happen? For being a part of it at all? For being the messenger or for not putting one and one together with their last names from the beginning. Although, now that I think about it, should I have questioned things more? I did see her coming out of the same building I was entering—where her family's company's offices are located. *Be rational, Nick. There are nearly nine million people in New York City.*

"I need to tell her." I start walking toward the back door, but every step has a thousand pounds weighing me down. "Without an audience."

Andrew says, "The truth is, you didn't know."

"Will that matter?"

Nodding his head, he says, "It should. Good luck, little brother."

With my hand on the doorknob, I look back. My mom says, "Destiny will always find a way through a misunderstanding."

"She's going to think I'm lying."

"You have to believe in each other, and it will always work out how it's supposed to."

Call me a New Age fanatic. I'll be anything the spiritual guides want me to be as long as I don't lose Natalie. Believing in the power of destiny and ready to fight for us to be together, I open the door.

"What?" She stops pacing, rearranging the phone against her ear as if she heard wrong. "Mom, say it again . . . No." When she turns around, her eyes land on mine. "No. *No. No.* Please tell me everything will be all right. That he'll be okay." The sunshine catches in her tear-laden eyes, and fear fills them right after. "I'll come home. I'll catch the first flight . . . I love you, too."

Her hand lowers with the phone to her side just as tears roll over the barrier of her bottom lids. "Nick . . ."

"What is it?"

She rushes against me and wraps her arms around my middle. I'm quick to envelop her body, wanting to protect her from whatever upsets her. "I have to go. He had a heart attack."

"Who?"

"My dad," she says, softly crying against my chest. *No.* "My mom said he was rushed into surgery and can't tell me anything more at this time." She looks up. "I have to go."

"I'll go with you."

I lead her back inside, and my mom hurries over, taking her into her arms. Shooting me a dirty look, she consoles Natalie. "It will be okay."

"Mom, her dad had a heart attack." I can tell my mom feels bad when her expression turns to shock. "Oh, no." She reaches for me in apology, rubs my arm as consolation for the dirty look and assumption. I say, "I'm going to fly back to New York with her tonight. Do you mind packing her stuff at the bungalow and shipping it back for her?"

She holds Natalie's face. "I'm so sorry, honey." Stepping back, she adds, "You two go, and I'll overnight your belongings."

"Thank you," Natalie replies with a wobbling lower lip. "I'm sorry to have to leave like this."

"No. No. Don't be, honey. We'll see each other again."

I hadn't noticed that my dad and brother had gathered around to lend support until Andrew says, "You guys can head out, and I'll call to arrange a flight."

After hugging my mom, I tell him, "Thanks. I appreciate it."

My dad sneaks in, "It was nice to meet you, Natalie," before we head for the door. She's polite, even when distressed, thanking them for their hospitality.

There's never a good time to head to LAX but rushing there in an emergency adds a whole new layer of stress. We're quiet in the SUV while she texts with her brother. A faded blue car with a rusted bumper that's covered in dings cuts me off, causing me to swerve. Natalie's phone flies from her hands to hit near her feet, and she braces herself against the dashboard. "What the hell?"

"Sorry. This asshole just fucking cut me off."

She stares ahead, and then asks, "Is it safe to reach down?"

We come to a stop, and I reply, "Yes."

Her fingers fly over the screen, resuming to text. When she pauses to look around, I'm tempted to tell her about the deal. I just don't know if now is the time. I'm still filled with a million questions about why her family didn't let her in on it and is still keeping her in the dark after the fact.

Technically, nothing's been confirmed. My brother saw a photo behind a guy's desk, and that's what we're basing the future of my relationship on?

He's certain she's one and the same since he noticed her enough to call her hot. As if she can read my mind, she sets her phone on her lap and rests her elbow against the window. "My brother will have a car waiting at the airport."

"Your brother . . ." I leave it open-ended, hoping she picks up the hint to fill in the rest.

"My brother, Jackson."

Well, fuck.

27

Natalie

Nick's been staring out the window for most of the flight. Granted, I told him I didn't want to talk about it, but still. I'd like him to push.

I roll my eyes at myself, mad for making him jump through hoops to read my mind. My shoulders fall because it's not a test or anything. I'd tell him anything if he asked.

I push the empty glass away because the rum didn't do anything to lift my spirits. I don't even laugh at Nick's pun about alcohol. He tried to cheer me up, knowing how much I love a double entendre and his use of alcohol and spirits. It was funny, but my heart hurts too much to laugh. If I lean into any feeling too far, I can tell I'll swing the other way and be a crying mess on the floor of this plane.

Please let my father be okay.

But Nick deserves better than what I can give, so I need to make it right. I reach over and slip my hand into his, which is on his leg. He glances over, the warmth of his soulful eyes caressing my heart in a simple exchange.

Tilting my head, I rest my cheek on his bicep. "I'm sorry."

"You don't have to be. You did nothing wrong. We all process trauma differently." He lifts the armrest and wraps his arm around me, kissing the top of my head.

I slide closer, my seat belt giving enough to let me burrow in the comfort of his warmth. Tilting my head up, I study his profile—the straightness of his nose and cut of his jaw, the several days' old scruff, and those dark lashes that make me envious. His tan skin and the raised veins running down his forearms and over his hands.

Handsome used to be the word I used most often when I thought of him. It's what fit so well from Catalina when I lingered in the memories of that weekend. But now it's loyalty and kindness, caring, and thoughtful.

Nick didn't have to fly back to Manhattan with me, but here he is without giving it a second thought. He just acted on instinct to support me. There's nothing more I can ask for in a partner than someone who puts my needs before his. It's not even something I knew to look for based on my experiences. But now that I've seen it's possible to have something even remotely close to what my parents share, I believe I can have that too.

Our fingers fold together. I promise to do the same for him—be there when he needs me, support him, love him endlessly. "I want to marry you and be your wife." Saying the words so frankly and to the point has them sounding different to my ears. It's as if I've bared some part of myself. But with Nick, I'm not vulnerable. I feel strong, ready to fight for what I want.

I want him.

A small smile works its way onto his face, and just like the sun filtering through the clouds and sneaking in the small window, it brightens my day. His arm tightens around me, and he kisses my head. *I love it when he does that.* Against the top of my head, he whispers, "I want to be married to you and to be called Natalie's husband."

Laughter, even the lighter giggles that bubble up, feels good to release as if some pressure has been taken off. I shift in my seat, draping one of my legs over his. "When do we tell our families?"

"Guess it depends on if you want to have a big ceremony or to elope."

It's nice to take my mind off my worries for a minute. "Tatum's been planning my wedding since I was seven. She'd kill me if we eloped. But having a huge New York wedding with a bunch of people I don't know, or barely at best, because we have to invite everyone my parents have ever met so they're not offended isn't appealing."

"My parents are the same way. I swear they know everyone in LA. Where does that leave us?"

Despite the nice thoughts about the future, the concerns for my dad are tightly wedged in my heart. "I don't know. I'm still trying to get my head around my dad having a heart attack. I know I want him to meet my husband, the father of his grandkids, and that is far more important than a big showy to-do for me." I undo my seat belt altogether and scoot onto his lap with my arms looped around his neck. I sigh. This is what I needed. *To be held.* Because I just don't know what we'll find upon touchdown.

I DUCK inside the limo to find Jackson sitting there. "A limousine? Really?"

"Figured if you were bringing your new boyfriend—" He goes silent when Nick ducks into the vehicle.

Figures he'd act like a weirdo in front of my boy—fiancé. *Ooohhh.* That has such a great ring to it. I wiggle my finger, ready to make it public, and nothing says engaged and taken like a ring wrapped around a certain left-hand finger. Maybe I'll pop by Tiffany's when my dad is better. Positive. I need to think positive when it comes to him. I won't be able to handle any other outcome than a full recovery. My mind and thoughts are such a mess. I wave my hand between the two of them. "Nick. Jackson. Jackson. Nick Christiansen."

"I, *uhhhh* . . . don't understand." Nonsense tumbles from Jackson's mouth.

Staring at my brother, I'm so confused as to what's wrong with him. I turn to Nick quickly, resting my hand on his leg as the car pulls away from passenger pick-up at JFK. "Ignore my brother. He can be so rude sometimes. My mom would be horrified."

"It's okay," Nick replies, quieter than usual. I was nervous to meet his family but didn't think twice about him feeling the same meeting mine. Is that what's come over him? "It's nice to meet you." His expression is tight, clearly uncomfortable.

I kick my brother's shoe. "Why'd you have to embarrass us like this? The limo was a dumb prank, Jackson." I focus on Nick and how I can make him more comfortable in this awkward situation. "I'm sorry. We used to play pranks on each other growing up." My lips tighten as I grit my teeth, glaring at my brother. "I thought we had outgrown that." Back to Nick, he doesn't seem bothered per se, but he's hard to read right now, so I keep rambling to fill the silence, "I know a bright pink limo isn't exactly cool, but—"

"It's fine. It really is." He laughs, but I've never seen a tighter smile.

What a mess. I'm so mad at my brother for making this so uncomfortable. Jackson turns away, facing the driver ahead, but I can see the downturn of his expression in the reflection of the privacy glass. "Yeah, dumb. Sorry."

"What's wrong with you?"

When my brother angles back to face us, stabbing Nick with a glare, my gaze volleys between the two of them. "What am I missing?"

Nick says, "Nothing."

Jackson grunts, "Nothing."

"Well, you're not Dad, so lower the temperature of over-protectiveness and stop trying to intimidate Nick."

"He's not intimidating," Nick clarifies before I finish.

Jackson huffs. "What the fuck is going on? This is your new boyfriend? Was this a setup all along?"

"What?" I'm hit with the words, but none of them make sense. "What are you talking about?" He signals to Nick, who I catch vigorously shaking his head. "And what are you doing?" I rub my temple, wondering if I'm going insane.

Sliding away from Nick to the other side of the seat, I complete the triangle of us, but now I can see both of them. Like they're speaking their own language, their eyes never deviate from each other. I throw my hands in the air. "Oh my God, somebody tell me what's going on."

That tantrum gets both of their attention. Jackson eyes Nick like he's about to pull a fast one and then sits back. My brother says, "Clearly, she's in the dark. Good job keeping that secret, but I'm certain she's not going to be too happy to hear how she was used."

"Jackson! Stop being rude. Nobody's using me."

He continues to eye Nick, and then asks, "Do you want to tell her, or do you want me to do the dirty deed?"

A hard stare softens when Nick looks at me. A hard swallow and fidgeting with his watch don't bring me any comfort. With my heart in my throat, I say, "Nick?" He reaches over to take my hand from the seat between us, but I pull back, needing the truth instead of being touched. "Tell me what he's talking about. *Please*."

Giving my brother the side-eye again, Nick then turns to me, and says, "I know Jackson—"

"I think the two of you have made that obvious. What happened that you're sitting here in a car unexpectedly together, and I'm being told you're using me?"

His words are tentative when he says, "I can explain—"

"I'm listening."

Jackson sits forward, and says, "It's no big deal."

"Then why are you acting this way?"

He huffs. "We've met in passing through work. That's all."

"Really? When?" My gaze slides over to Nick, who's sitting quietly listening. When I look back at my brother, I say, "This is a small world."

"Yeah, tiny," my brother adds.

I move toward Nick again, just a little. "That's pretty incredible that you guys have met before. You didn't know he was my brother?"

Clearing his throat, Nick says, "No, not until I got into this car. I guess it's not that out of the ordinary when you both work in the financial sector, but there aren't many St. Jameses who have made a name like my family has." I elbow him playfully. "Despite what you seem to think."

"Yeah, I'm finding that out."

Giving Jackson my attention again, I ask, "Why are you

so bothered, and how is he using me?"

"Just surprised." He shrugs. "Like you said, overprotective of my sister."

My heart squeezes. We've always gotten along well, but he's still my little brother although he acts like the eldest. "That's sweet, but you don't have to worry about Nick. He's amazing. You'll see."

"Incredible," he mumbles under his breath.

Being the bigger man, Nick holds out his hand in a peace offering because he's the best. "Maybe we can start over, man."

Jackson takes hold, and they shake on it. "Yeah. Sure. No hard feelings." Sure, now he's all nonchalant about it. *Annoying.*

I will never understand guys. I have to talk everything out, but they just shake hands and move on like everything's hunky-dory. *Whatever.* I don't have the energy for this. "Have you gotten an update on Dad?"

"Yeah, Mom said he's out of surgery and in recovery."

"Why didn't you tell me sooner?"

"I got the message right before you got in the car, and I was caught off guard by your boyfriend. Anyway, Dad's doing well. Mom said she'll be able to see him once he's moved into a room."

Resting my head back in relief, I close my eyes and release a deep breath. "Thank God." I know he's not in the clear, but hearing he's doing well right now is what I need to hang on to.

With the stuff between Nick and Jackson still lingering in the air, I move to sit closer to Nick again. I whisper, "You sure you want to mar—" I stop, remembering we have an audience. "To meet my parents?"

I expect a quip or nod of reassurance. That's not what I

get, though. Nick hems and then nods without saying a word. Very unlike him. But maybe the thing with my brother and being stuck in the car together is uncomfortable. "Guess we'll settle in since we caught prime time rush-hour traffic and will be here a while."

Jackson gets distracted by his phone, but Nick just stares out the window. I whisper, "I'm sorry."

"Don't be. I made a mess of things, and this is just par for the course." I lean against him and stare out the window as well.

As soon as the limo pulls up to the hospital, I climb over Nick to get out. In my rush to get inside, I notice him and Jackson speaking back at the car. "Are you guys coming?"

Jackson replies, "Tell Mom I'll be right in."

"Okay," I say to myself, thinking they're still trying to work things out. Just inside the doors, I search the waiting room with no sight of my mom anywhere.

"Natalie?" I hear my name ahead, but I barely recognize the woman coming toward me. Not that she's not her usual beautiful self, but she's not in head-to-toe designer, and she's not wearing makeup. Instead, she's in a fluffy fleece pullover and jogging pants with slip-on sneakers.

If emotions were an outfit, that's how I'm feeling as well. "Mom?" Our arms fly around each other, and the tears I'd had a brief reprieve from return and fall down my cheeks. "How is he?"

"Resting." She strokes my hair and then angles to see my face. "They gave us good news and told us everything went well."

"That's good to hear, but what happened?"

"He was supposed to be slowing down. That's what this was all about. Enjoying the rewards of our hard work." She sniffles. "We decided it was best to retire—"

"What?" Stepping to the side, out of the walkway, we hold hands. Leaning against the wall, I stand there in disbelief at what I'm hearing. "When did you retire?"

"Officially, a few days ago."

"What does that mean exactly?"

A gentle smile appears, and she tucks hair behind my ears. "It means we get to have a life again."

"No, Mom, I understand what retirement means. You just walked away from the company?"

Shrugging like a teen who got busted sneaking out, she replies, "We sold it. I know this comes as a surprise, but we were going to tell you over Sunday dinner." A million thoughts are running through my mind, but I can't seem to put a voice to them. She rubs both of my arms and then brings me into her fold. "It's a good thing, Natalie."

"If it's so good, why did Dad have a heart attack?" I snap.

"It's a long story."

"We have time."

She sighs heavily and says, "Let's get some fresh air." We walk outside and, with her arm looped with mine, stroll a few feet away from the door before I spot Nick and Jackson still talking.

Nick rubs his jaw, staring into the early evening sky while Jackson uses his hands to explain something. It's a characteristic action of a St. James. "What could they still be talking about?"

She releases me, her hands in fists. "Why is *he* here? Hasn't his family done enough damage?"

"Nick?" My head jerks from her reaction. She has to be confusing him with someone else. "That's my boyfriend, Mom. What damage could he have done?"

Scowling, she points at him. "His family caused your father's heart attack!"

28

Nick

"Are you trying to kill him?" Natalie's mom shouts at me like I've never heard from anyone before. This is a mother protecting her family, a wife protecting her husband from an attacker. From me, which makes no sense. "Leave us alone!"

"Mom," Natalie says with horror changing her tone. "Why are you yelling at him?"

Shit.

I leave Jackson on the sidewalk as I run to get Natalie out from the middle of this mess. With my hands up in surrender on approach, I say, "I can explain, Mrs. St. James. Please, just let me—"

Ignoring me completely, Martine homes in on her daughter. "Natalie, if it weren't for them, your dad wouldn't be here. He was fighting for us, for you, and look where he ended up." She grabs Natalie and pulls her behind her, using her body as a wall between us. "Get away from us, or I'll call the police."

"You don't understand."

"I understand everything. It was a good deal that wasn't good enough for you. I won't let you come near my daughter again, or my son." Her eyes glance behind me. "Jackson." It's one call of his name that has him right there when she needs him.

I plead with the only case I have left. "She doesn't know, Mrs. St. James."

Shaking her head, she says, "What are you saying?"

Natalie moves to her side but then comes to stand next to me. My gut twists that she's defending me when she doesn't have the facts. Her mom's eyes narrow. "What are you doing, Natalie? You can't be serious?"

Taking my hand, she nods. "I love him."

Blinking in disbelief, her mother takes a few steps back and then looks at her son for an ally. "Tell her. Tell her what she's choosing. Tell her who these people are and what they've done to your father."

Looking at me and then to his mom, Jackson says, "Mom—"

"Tell her!" When he fails her, she says, "Listen to me, Natalie. We sold the company to them because we trusted them to treat our companies and clients like family. But they only care about business. The contract stated they were to keep all staff and support other company interests." She moves closer again, trying to convince her daughter that I'm the devil. She jabs her finger in the air in front of me. "But these people broke that agreement when they threatened to dissolve the assets of your company."

My hand is dropped, and Natalie stands there unblinking. Jackson covers his mother's shoulder and tries to pull her back. "Mom, I think we should give Nick a chance to explain."

"He'll put poison in her ear while her dad tries to recover. I can't trust him, and neither should you." Their mother is too wound up, too angry, too emotional over her husband understandably, and looking for someone to blame. I want to butt in, to tell my side of the story, to make them understand I would never go against my word, especially where Natalie's concerned. But what can I say that will have her believing me over her own mother?

Natalie looks at me again and then steps closer, her hands so light, not taking any ownership like she usually does, as they touch my chest. "Tell them they're confused, Nick. You'd never hurt me or my family."

I stand in my own agony, not wanting to turn her against the family that she's telling me I'd defend. I would. I will . . . but why do I have to sacrifice the thing I cherish more than anything else in this world? We've barely had enough time to launch into a new life together.

Against my better judgment, my gut tells me not to reveal more than they have already.

"I wouldn't hurt or betray either." Such admissions should come easier. The words on the surface are a good thing, but buried inside the syllables is a confession that I'd give her up to keep her at peace with her parents. I lower my head while taking her hands and holding them against my stomach. Her fingers are so delicate, her wrists small. Everything about her is so breakable, even the parts of her I can't see on the outside, like her heart.

Is that what I'm doing? Breaking hearts because one of us will lose. It's me or them, so I choose to hurt myself over this beautiful woman before me.

She turns back to her mother, the same plea still residing in her eyes. "I trust him implicitly. Nick would never hurt me."

Her mom replies, "Ask him. Ask him who bought the company. Ask him who sat in our offices and promised to treat our business like it was a part of their family. Ask him, Natalie, if he went back on his word and cut loans from the portfolio that he said he would leave alone."

My love, my reason to exist, spins in confusion until she's facing me again. "Tell her she's wrong. There's been a misunderstanding." When I don't say anything, she fists my shirt. "Tell her, Nick. Tell her how much you love me," she demands, raising her voice. "Tell her,"

"I can't."

Her lips part, but I don't think she's breathing. I take hold of her waist to keep her from leaving, but her body slowly slips through my hands. "What do you mean you can't? You love me, remember?"

"I remember, and I do. I love you so much, baby, but—"

"But what?"

Martine starts crying. "What are you doing, Natalie? You're choosing him over your own family. Over your dad, who would do anything for you?"

Natalie is drawn to look at her, to see the anguish on her face. Trapped between the two of us, she replies, "I was going to marry him."

The tense has the most impact, gutting me. I ask, "Was?"

"Am," she corrects, her nerves getting the better of her as her voice begins to tremble. "Mom, Nick—"

"Christiansen," her mother adds. "Legal Counsel for Christiansen Wealth Management. Son of Corbin Christiansen, third in line of succession to CEO."

I'm stunned to the spot hearing my résumé thrown out like it was a memorization project. But Natalie furrows her brow and asks, "How do you know all of that?"

Other emotions have drained from her face, and now

just the anger remains. "Christiansen Wealth Management now owns Manhattan Financial and STJ Co. But you might want to check in with your boyfriend because they're cutting funding to your company by ending that part of the deal." The mic wasn't laid down. It was dropped like a ten-ton weight on top of my chest. She walks back to the hospital, the sliding glass doors opening as if commanded.

Jackson eyes me, and then says, "Good luck," before heading into the hospital.

But Natalie remains, standing there watching cars come and go from the ER entrance farther down the sidewalk. I'm not sure what to say, and I'm thinking Natalie feels the same way. The truth will find a way, but I have to take the first step to fix the damage. I say, "She's right. CWM bought Manhattan Financial. But she's wrong when she says I betrayed you. The truth is that I didn't put the pieces of the puzzle together. Not until today, and then it was too late. You were there with my family. You heard me assume your last name was as common as Smith in New York City."

"It's not."

"I know. Now, I know."

"My dad and mom started that company thirty years ago. They put everything into it. I can't believe they were selling it when it was still so successful."

"I only got some of the information, but your parents wanted to retire. We wanted a place with a good reputation to help with our presence in the city. It was a good match and an easy deal to close because both sides were eager."

She turns her back to me as she stares into the minimal landscaping outlining the side of the hospital. Crossing her arms over her chest, she asks, "Why wouldn't they tell me?"

"I don't know, Natalie."

She peeks at me from over her shoulder. "I don't know

what to believe or who to listen to. All I know is that my father could have died tonight, and from the sounds of it, you're partially responsible."

"I—"

"No." A wall is built, her hands standing guard to keep me from reaching her. "This is too much to digest. I think it's best if you leave, Nick. I'm going inside to be with my family." She doesn't kiss me, and there are no warm embraces. When she walks away, I'm left in the cool fall air with nothing but the memory of her looking at me like I'm the enemy.

"I didn't know." *But these people broke that agreement when they threatened to dissolve the assets of your company.* When I met with Dad earlier, yes, he was fighting for the best deal, but surely, he wouldn't be underhanded and screw them over. He said he'd keep that business, *her* business, if he was forced to. *Did he lie to me?* What am I missing?

She stops with her back to me. There are no ocean blue eyes to swim in or even a small smile to indulge my ego. She gives me nothing before the sliding glass doors open and then engulfs her.

I watch her through the glass, her family opening their arms and taking in one of their own.

But she's become my family as well, but now, I don't know where we stand with each other, other than with glass doors between us.

We may not have had a long relationship, but I knew the minute I saw her on that New York street that I wouldn't let what happened in Catalina repeat itself. And I didn't. Until now, when I have to let her be and hope she comes back to me.

Sitting outside the hospital, I don't dare go inside. Natalie needs this time with her family, and I'll respect that.

But after three hours of waiting on this bench with the chill of October setting in, I'm starting to fear that Mr. St. James is not out of the woods.

She might have told me to leave, but no way am I going anywhere. I can only hope that she knows I'm here if she needs me.

After speaking with Jackson, he seemed to understand and believed me. I hate that my entire future hinges on whether he can be a voice of reason for Natalie.

Just before midnight, I hear the doors slide open and see Natalie coming my way. I stand away from the bright lights of the hospital, hoping to find privacy from other people here for the hospital.

She says, "It's dark."

"Yeah, shortly after we arrived."

She shoves her hands in her pockets and then finally gives me the view of her deep blues. "You should go home, Nick."

My heart sinks, my hope of speaking to her tonight falling with it. "Can we talk?"

"No. Not tonight. I don't have enough energy to spare on . . ." She angles away from me as if the sight of me is too much. She sniffles but swipes at her cheeks before peering up at me again. "I don't know what to believe, Nick, but there's no reason for you to stay."

"You're my reason for staying, Natalie."

She crosses her arms over her chest, keeping an impartial face. "That's not good enough anymore."

Staring at her, I lose my words in the sliver delivered to my heart. "Love is enough."

"Not our kind."

"What kind of love are we?"

"The hopeless kind, star-crossed and tragic." I hate how definitive she makes it sound.

"I didn't know it was your family. I swear to God."

"You knew!" Rage roars through her. She slams her fists against my chest. "You knew, and you used me. You lied to me about everything." I'm hit again, but this time, she pushes so hard that she ends up stumbling backward. "And for what? A better deal? Well, that didn't happen, so move on without me."

When I reach out to catch her, she smacks my hand. "Don't you touch me. Not ever again." The anger in her eyes freezes me to the spot, and she screams, "That's why you wanted to marry me, isn't it? Isn't it?" Disgust reaches her eyes before I can answer and she adds, "You knew I'd leave you, so you thought you'd play that card. You must be pretty damn proud of yourself for tricking me."

"It wasn't a trick. There were no tricks or lies despite what your mom has been telling you."

Shock rips through her expression. "Are you calling my mom a liar?"

"No, I'm not, but this isn't black and white. She's in the gray area of understanding this situation like I am. I didn't know about your company. I had no idea that your family owned Manhattan Financial. I swear I didn't fucking know."

"I'm going to lose my company, Nick. How the hell could you *not* have known? You met with my parents. You heard me talk about STJ more than once since we found each other in New York. With the damage already done, where did you really think that would leave us?"

I move in as close as she'll let me, which isn't close enough for my liking. "We're still in love. We still have each other to rely on. *We are still us.* Don't let the lies win, because

I don't think what you've heard is correct. My father doesn't do business like that. He's—."

"Enough." She covers her forehead with her hand, and says, "I'm such an idiot for trusting a guy." Agitation sets in as she stares at me like she never knew me at all. "I wish I would have kept walking."

I reach out to touch her, but she moves away from my hand. "Then you'd be on a date with Chad—"

"At least Chad didn't lie to me."

"Neither did I, Natalie. I know there's a lot going on. You should spend time with your dad and not think about anything else. We can talk when you're rational."

"Rational?" she scoffs, planting her hands on her hips. "Wow, Nick. You know what? I'll never be rational enough to believe the lies you've been feeding me. My eyes have been opened to your deceptive practices." She walks backward. "Take Manhattan Financial and STJ Co. It's yours to do as you please just like you wanted all along, but if you care about me at all, then leave me alone." She turns her back on me and storms toward the hospital.

"I'll go to a hotel—"

Turning around, she calls back, "I don't mean just for the night, Nick. I mean forever. There's no way I can be with someone like you."

"Like me? What does that mean?"

"Someone who cares more about business than people."

I hate that I'm defending business decisions I didn't make. "Your father—"

Whipping around, she points at me. "My father is fighting for his life because he was fighting for me. Against you!" Although plenty of sidewalk stretches between us, I feel the jolt of her words.

Before the doors open for her, I say, "Natalie, I haven't

lied to you. I *won't* lie to you. I'll leave the hospital now, but please let me find out the truth and then sort this out. I love you." *Forever.*

This can't be it.

We can't be over.

She never breaks her stride, and I'm left with the remains of what could have been. I'm left dumbfounded with no clear answers to how this turned so quickly into the destruction of us.

I feel as blindsided as she does. My dad is an unscrupulous businessman, but would he so deliberately deceive a business owner in a deal? Is that how he does business? There's no getting around my role in this mess, and my intentions don't matter. I can be mad all I want or place the blame elsewhere, but the bottom line is that I'm an attorney. My job literally requires me to read contracts. I was so busy worrying about the threat of having to move to Seattle that I lost sight of what was happening in LA and New York. How could I have let something this important slip through the cracks?

And now, the woman I love is in the hospital by her father's bedside, with not only fear for her father, but the reality that her pride and joy was insolvent as of five o'clock. *Will be, thanks to my signature.*

Fuck.

I leave like she wants me to, rounding the block to find a taxi waiting. With my hand on the door handle, I debate if I should go or barge in and let her know that I'm here for her. I open the door and get in because I know the truth. *She doesn't want me anywhere near her at this time.* I head to the hotel, getting an odd look from the desk clerk. *Especially when I don't have any luggage.* Well, I don't feel like I have anything at the moment, so this is fucking fitting.

Once in the room, I start the shower with Natalie's words still rattling around my brain. I'll respect her wishes tonight —she's exhausted, so I'll chalk it up to that—but tomorrow, I hope she'll see me, and we can talk calmly. *God, I hope her father pulls through. He has to make it.*

And so do we.

As I'm learning, a life without Natalie is no life to lead. Surely, once she knows the truth and we get her company back on track with new funding, we'll be okay.

29

Natalie

Five days.

That's how long Nick sat outside the hospital.

I never saw him leave or take a break, eat, or talk on the phone. No. Every time I walked by, I stuck to the sides of the corridor or peeked out a window to find him still there as if I hadn't told him to leave.

Why?

Why does he stay?

If I left to shower and change my clothes, or even get fresh air, I used a different exit, not ready to face him. Five days of listening to how not only my dad had to fight for my loan but feeling foolish for falling for someone so calculating has me avoiding another conversation with Nick altogether.

My heart hasn't gotten the memo.

I miss him and hate myself for being a traitor to my family. But there's no longer an us in this equation. It's him, and then there's me. There's just no other way around it.

Freshly showered and in clean clothes, I'm glad to have the stale hospital off me. I park my suitcase at the door and then retrieve my laptop bag and purse. None of it's been unpacked from California. Cookie shipped it as promised, and it arrived safely the next day.

"How long do you think you'll be gone?" Tatum asks, snuggled on the couch. Her face is clear of the face paint she wore dressed as a cat for Halloween last night, and I can see how tired she is by her bloodshot eyes. It's the first Halloween we haven't spent together partying since we've known each other. I gave that up the tradition to be in California, to be with Nick. Instead, I spent it in the hospital eating bite-sized Snickers at the nurses' station every time I left my dad's room.

I haven't been on a run since the morning I snuck out of bed in LA, so not only are my emotions tattered but I also feel like crap. I sit next to her. "I don't know. At this point, we might be in the Hamptons through Thanksgiving."

"Should I ask about work?"

I rub my eyes, so tired from staying at the hospital and getting so little sleep. "I need to figure some stuff out. Just keep doing what you're doing." I grin over at her sipping her hot chocolate. "Workwise, I mean. I'll be working remotely for the time being unless I have to be in the city for anything. I'm not going to fail my clients, even if I have to work for free."

"I was practically working for free already." Grabbing a pillow, I pop her with it. "Whoa!" She starts laughing. "You almost made me spill my cocoa."

The laughter dies off, and we're left with the silence again. I know what's coming, but I can't help but feel like I'm not ready to face it. I won't hide, though. Not from her. She's always had my back . . . unless a hot guy's involved like

Harrison in Catalina. *God, why does everything have to come back to Nick?*

Oh, screw it. Might as well get it over with. "Go ahead." I curl around a big pillow. "Ask away. I know you're dying to anyway."

She blows across the top of the hot drink to cool it, and then whispers, "What are you going to do about Nick?"

I've been dreading this conversation, but I've held it in for too many days. I couldn't talk to my mom, and Jackson won't understand. Taking a deep breath, I exhale, and say, "I think it's best if Nick and I go our separate ways and never see each other again."

"That's drastic for someone you were in love with six days ago. Was that love real?" Her tone is gentle, cautious, but caring.

I nod because I can lie to the world about it. I can lie to Nick and say I never felt love soul deep like I did for him. I can lie all I want to everyone else, but that won't change the fact that I can't lie to myself. I loved him with my entire being. I love him even now. *And I hate myself for it.*

"Then why won't you talk to him?" There's no accusation or judgment in her tone, just compassion.

"My heart is so broken, like me."

"Your heart can be healed by a man who loves you so much that he's waited outside a hospital for almost a week for you without complaint. Why are you doing this? You're not just hurting him. You're hurting yourself."

"I'm trapped." I fall back into the nook of the couch and bring my knees to my chest. Rolling my head to the side, I see a crease created from concern between her brows. "My family feels betrayed by the man I'm in love with. How do I get around this? If I choose him, I hurt them. I choose my family, which I have to, I lose him. It's a no-win situation, so me dragging out a relationship with Nick won't do either of us any good."

She sits up and sets her mug on the coffee table. "It's not an either-or situation. It's hearing both sides at a minimum and then deciding what's best for you."

"You make this sound easy when it's not. I won't waste another minute on a man hell-bent on controlling my life. If the contract stands as is, I'll be answering to his family." I squeeze my eyes closed, wishing I wasn't in this mess. "Anyway, you know better than anyone the problem Dane had with my company and how hard we fought over it."

"That's because he had small-dick syndrome." Her jaw tightens as she grits her teeth. "He couldn't bear for a woman to be more successful than him."

"I wasn't even making money then. It was just the thought of me becoming successful that enraged him." I stand and start pacing, unable to sit still any longer. "Imagine the horror—a woman is more successful than a man. Sound the alarms." I'm full of restless energy that I wish I could get out of my system, run away until I'm carefree again. But I know that's not possible. I could run a thousand miles, but Nick's not going to be forgotten that easily. *Or at all.*

Looking out the window, I say, "First snow is coming."

"It's already late." She comes to lean against the window where I've perched myself on the sill.

I check my watch. "And so am I. I need to get back before he's released."

"Everyone's off to the Hamptons then?"

"Yes. My dad will have a private nurse check on him, and his doctor is out there for the holidays."

"I'm glad he's doing well."

I can't help but smile. "Me too. My dad has made a lot of

improvement over the past few days. They approved his release because they're happy with his blood pressure and other vitals. He's getting up a few minutes each day. His pain is being managed, so he's been in good spirits. He'll get to relax in the comfort and peace of the off-season at the Hamptons house."

Moving back to the door, I wrap my purse around my shoulder and the strap of the laptop bag around my body. Taking the suitcase handle, I open the door with the other hand. I'm not rushing or running. I'm hesitant to leave, worried I'm forgetting something or maybe that things will change without me around, because I already feel a change happening inside me.

"It will be good to spend time out of the hospital with my family again. We have our monthly dinners, but those are formal events. The downtime will be good."

"I know you'll be working, but think about taking some time for yourself as well. I can handle anything extra that needs to be done." She holds the door wide open, so I move into the hallway. Resting her cheek against the wood, she asks, "Will you promise me something?"

"Depends."

That causes her to smile. "If you happen to run into him, give him five minutes. It might be eye-opening." She doesn't have to explain the *him* she's talking about.

"Or heart ending."

"At least you'll be able to move on knowing the truth, and isn't that closure worth the effort?"

In all the months Nick and I have known each other, we only dated a few weeks. I *tsk*, embarrassed to admit that to myself. How did I expect something so frivolous to last? "Or pain."

She scoffs and then takes me by my upper arms, giving

me a small shake. "Stop this. You don't have to argue every little thing. The worst may happen or the best, or maybe the worst has already happened, and it will only get better from here. You have fifty scenarios swimming around in that pretty head. Instead of guessing how it will play out, take the lead and put it to bed." She squishes my cheeks together. "Or go to bed with him."

"Are those my only options?" I ask, talking through fish lips.

"Pretty much. Let me know how that all turns out."

Wrapping me in her arms, she says, "No matter what happens, you'll always be stuck with me."

I release the suitcase to hug her. "Unless you actually give a guy your number."

"Maybe if I meet the right guy." Stepping back, she adds, "The right guy at the right time, that is."

"Isn't that the truth." I tug the suitcase and start walking down the hall to the elevator. "Don't have too much fun without me."

"I never do. Take care, Nat, and send your dad my best wishes."

Still trucking to the elevator, I wave over my shoulder. "I will."

When I arrive at the hospital, the car pulls up behind Jackson's black Range Rover. I hadn't thought about the coincidence until now—Jackson's new Rover to Nick's restored model. Jackson hops out to grab my stuff from the back seat as the cab driver pulls my suitcase from the trunk.

I fold myself into the SUV and run my hand over the dash. The two vehicles couldn't be more different, but there's something sophisticated about the leather and design on the inside. My brother is more of a sports car kind of guy, but after he wrecked the last one, my parents surprised him with the SUV. This car never fit Jackson like it does Nick.

Jackson loads my luggage in the back, and I turn to ask, "Where's Mom?"

"She's riding with Dad. They left about ten minutes ago."

Irritation burns through me. "Then why didn't you pick me up?"

"You're in the opposite direction. I wasn't going to fight traffic."

Annoyed, I grit my teeth and look out the window. The bench that Nick had been occupying is empty, and disappointment fills my chest. His constant presence has surprised me, but is that it? He's gone? *Forever?* I can't say that worrying about my dad hasn't consumed me, but alongside that has been this war inside my head. *Talk to Nick* vs. *forget about him.*

I breathe what I think is a sigh of relief. Not having to face your demons is always a good thing, but I can tell it's something different. It's not relief I feel, but empty, like the bench.

Jackson gets in and starts the car. "Ready?"

I glance back one more time. Maybe he went to get something to eat or use the bathroom. Maybe he was called away or asked to move. Maybe he'll be back the moment we leave, and I'll never see him again. I pop the door open, and my seat belt flies off. Hopping out, I look everywhere, everywhere for where my heart might be.

"What are you doing, Natalie?" I hear my brother but can't bring myself to leave.

What if . . . He once tossed *what-ifs* around like he did *I do's.*

I hate that I smile thinking about him. I hate that I miss those phrases he used.

But what I really hate is that I miss him.

When there's no sign of him anywhere, I climb back in the SUV and buckle in. "I'm ready."

30

Nick

I waited.

For five days, I waited through the bad weather—light rain, cold winds, and occasional sun managed to shine, but not for long. Like my hope to see and talk to Natalie, it waned. But I would have stayed. I waited as long as I could until a hospital security guard told me to leave.

John St. James has been discharged into private care. The rest is a mystery to me. And to him. I tried my best to convince them to dig a little deeper for information at the nurses' desk. They are vaults, though, and rightly so.

Although I don't have much time, I decide to stop by her apartment. It's a risk I'm willing to take because, after this, I'm going back to LA. The car stops at the curb, and I get out. I look up at the window I remember Tatum peeking out. One. Two. Three. Four. Fourth floor left side of what I presume is an elevator.

The doorman doesn't say anything when I enter the

lobby. He stands, giving me a stern nod and disapproving once-over.

I say, "Hi, I'm here for Natalie St. James," and head for the elevator.

"She's not here. She left not forty-five minutes ago. Heading out of town by the looks of it, so you're not going to find her upstairs."

"Out of town." I repeat like the words are new to my ears. "Is Tatum around?"

"I can ring her for you."

I stand there awkwardly in the modern-styled lobby juxtaposed against the historical architecture. I walk back to the door, looking down the broad avenue, wondering which way she might have gone. "Ms. Devreux will be down momentarily."

Glancing at him as he settles back in behind the desk, I reply, "Thank you." Is this a fool's mission? Natalie's gone, and I have no idea where to even start looking.

Tatum is my last hope of reaching her again.

The ding of the elevator has me turning around. The doors open, and Tatum, dressed in a giant panda onesie, comes toward me. I cover my mouth, but the bark of laughter is still audible and echoes through the lobby.

At least she's not wearing the hood, but I'm not sure why that's where she drew the line. She says, "Ignore my outfit. I was in for the night, and trust me, this thing is not only comfortable but cozy."

She still makes no apology for it, though. You have to appreciate that about her. She stops just a few feet shy of me and leans against the side of a large leather couch. "Natalie's not here." The irritation I expected to hear from a defensive friend crossing her arms over her chest isn't found.

"She's heading out of town?"

"To be with her family."

I don't know why I feel so awkward. It's nothing Tatum's done to make me feel this way. She's done quite the opposite, actually. So much so that I dare to ask, "How is she?"

She nods toward the sitting area and moves around to claim the couch. I take a chair, resting forward on my legs. Glancing at the street through the windows, she replies, "This is tricky, Nick." Her eyes return to mine. "I'm not sure what I should reveal to you. I'd hate to betray my friend."

"I wouldn't ask that of you." Sitting up, I inwardly sigh, not sure where to go with this. I figure I have nothing to lose, and maybe, just maybe, I'll gain some insight if I'm lucky. "I love her."

Sympathy runs through her expression, turning the corners of her mouth down. "I know." Unlike me holding my feelings in as much as possible, she doesn't bother. "I like you, Nick. I like you for Natalie. I mean, even your names are cute together—Nick and Natalie. What's not to like?"

I remember my mom saying the same—*Nick and Natalie like Corbin and Cookie*—as if that could determine our destiny. For a too brief time, I believed in small signs like that, but I've started to lose faith.

Appreciating the reminder of these little coincidences, I smile. "I like Natalie and Nick as well." I sound like a kid, but Tatum makes it easy for me to feel sane with those admissions. "Is it a lost cause to hold on to hope?"

She tucks a leg under her and leans forward. After making sure the doorman isn't eavesdropping, she says, "I will always take her side. No matter what, I'll have her back. But being a good friend who's loyal also means telling her the truth, even when it's not what she wants to hear." She sits back again as if the secrets are all on the table. "I told her to talk to you."

"Thank you." The words rush out when a wave a relief comes over me.

"Not so fast, Nicky. I don't know the dirty details of what happened. All I know is her side. Let me just tell you—that side of the big picture doesn't look good for you. I'm not asking you to explain yourself to me, but I hope that if you ever have the chance to tell her your side of things, you tell her the truth." She stands and comes a little closer. "Plenty of guys have lied to her. Be the man who tells her the truth."

She walks around the couch but stops with her fingertips still on the leather. "Go back to California. Live your life, the life you've built. If you're still missing her in a few weeks or even months, you come back to see me, and I'll make sure you get to speak to her."

Bolting to my feet, I ask, "You want me to live life like she hasn't already altered it forever?"

"I want you to know for sure that you can't live without her *before* you drag her back into this mess."

"She's already in it, Tatum." And I hate that for her. I hate this whole situation, that I didn't look closer at the contracts that affect Christiansen's bottom line as well as other's. And right smack bang in the middle of this is Natalie.

I've spoken to Andrew and my dad about these contracts numerous times, and it was always *just business*. Yet Natalie thinks it was personal, an attack on her family and her company. Bottom line? I fucked up as an attorney and her boyfriend . . . *fiancé*.

"But she can find a way out."

"And you think she needs to do that alone?"

A self-assured grin covers her face. "She's not alone. She's got me and her family. We may not be you, but we can help her heal the way she needs to."

I want to argue, to keep talking so she tells me more, or feels sorry for me for the pain I feel, but as she made clear, she's Natalie's friend. Though, under the hood of her words, Tatum is also an ally of mine.

The elevator doors close, and I look at the doorman. He's shaking his head like he's heard this sad story before. Since he doesn't seem to be making a move to open the door, I head there and push it open. "Hope is only as strong as the heart that wields it," he says to my back.

I twist back with my hands still on the door and look at him. "I don't understand."

"That's the problem, son. Listen to Ms. Devreux, and you'll come to your own conclusion."

"Why can't anything be easy?"

"Most things are easy, but those aren't the things you want."

"Now there's something we can agree on. Have a good night."

Just before the door closes behind me, he says, "You too, Mr. Christiansen."

I stop again to look back. Through the glass, I can see he's already caught up in whatever's on a small TV on the desk. Checking the time, I know I should go before I miss my flight, but my curiosity gets the better of me.

I only step a foot back in. "How do you know my name?"

"You're on Ms. St. James's list of guests who don't have to check in."

I've never been inside the building, much less her apartment, but I'm on the list? Her list? I know I'm being nosy, but I've never been on a doorman's list before and feel bold after making this one. "Does she have a long list?"

He chuckles, his jowls threatening to jiggle. "You're it."

"I'm the list?"

He nods and then points at the game. I raise my hand and then go back outside again. I see the car I hired come make the block again and get in as soon as he pulls to the curb. He looks at me in the rearview mirror, and asks, "The airport?"

"I made the list." I don't know what I'm saying or why I'm telling him, but this seems like news that needs to be broadcast all over New York City. *I. Made. Her. List.*

"That's great," the driver says, not as enthusiastic as I am. Actually, there's no inflection in his tone at all. "JFK?"

Doesn't matter what he thinks. I made Natalie's guest list. *Me, myself, and I.* "Yes."

I'LL ADMIT that the high I was riding from making her list didn't last until touchdown in LA. I felt her absence growing with every mile traveled, and with a continent between us, I fear the worst—losing her altogether.

I got a text that Andrew sent a car to pick me up. I expected a ride share like Uber or Lyft, but I got Cookie's carpool instead. "What are you doing here, Mom?"

"Andrew said you needed a lift," she replies while getting back in the car. The traffic cops at LAX mean business and will make us move if we even try to say hi on the sidewalk. We'll hug in the car.

I load my leather duffel into the trunk of her Mercedes and then get in on the passenger's side. She shifts the gear into drive, but we embrace quickly before she pulls out. I say, "I did, but you didn't have to fight this traffic. A car would have been fine."

"I wanted to." She lays on her horn when a Ford F-150 cuts her off. "People are the worst."

Did I ever mention she's hell on wheels, suffering from a major case of road rage? I've had bouts of it myself in Los Angeles traffic, so I cut her some slack. I also double-check my seat belt and then hold on to the handle.

"I appreciate it."

Though she keeps her eyes focused on the road, ready to attack anyone who has the nerve to enter her lane, she asks, "How are you?"

I don't have the energy to hide my feelings anymore. "Not that great."

Her gaze finds me briefly, and she nods. "It's good to be in touch with your feelings. There's no way to change if you can't get to the root of your spiritual being."

When she deep dives into the psyche and universe stuff, I start missing the road rage mama. "I'm not sure I'm one to analyze. It's pretty obvious that I fucked up and don't know how to get her back."

"I've been worried about you, but I know sometimes we have to let our concerns run their course. I can't fix this for you, but I have a feeling you can. It's just going to take some time and innovation."

"God," I say, my head dropping against the headrest. "Does everyone have to speak in riddles? Can't someone just give me the fucking answers to make this better? First, the doorman, and now you. Just help me."

I'm glad her eyes are back on the road again when she says, "I will if I can. What did the doorman say?"

"I spent five hours on that flight, trying to figure it out

and failed. Here goes. Hope is only as strong as the heart that wields it."

Nodding, she purses her lips. "*Oooh*, that's a good one."

"Yeah, but what does it mean?"

"I'll think about it and get back to you. In the meantime, you have a lot of loose ends to wrap up."

"You're telling me."

31

Natalie

The first snow is always the most magical.

Sitting in the window seat of the library with a half-eaten piece of pumpkin pie next to me, I lean my back against the bookcase and watch as the snowflakes fall from the sky, hoping to find peace in the sight. Something is off this year.

Pressing my palm to the cold glass, I want to feel the chill seep into my skin. In a house with three fireplaces and a thermostat set at a constant seventy-three degrees, I've been missing the warmth that reaches my bones. Maybe this will remind me that it's still there. *That he's still with me.*

Numb is no way to feel, but the winter storm that blew in last night doesn't change my confusion regarding Nick. I'm still not sure I'm ready to have a conversation that finalizes our ending. What will he say but what he thinks I want to hear? Rearranging words to make them sound prettier doesn't change the meaning.

The whole situation is ugly, and I feel caught in the

middle. The thing is . . . the empty bench comes to mind again. I've struggled to get the image out of my head. I may have told him to leave for good, but I realize now that I might have acted in haste. I had other priorities at the time, the only one I should have had—my dad.

My mom comes silently into the room to drop off a glass of water for my dad, who's sleeping soundly, checks the logs in the fireplace, and smiles at me before disappearing again. My parents have always been . . . just my parents. But seeing how gentle she is with him and hearing him say it was her touch that guided him back to life puts them in a whole new light.

They aren't just the parents of Jackson and me. They aren't two powerhouses in the financial world. They're John and Martine, two lost souls who found their mate sitting in a coffee shop, and two people still in love after more than thirty years.

I've had a great example of what love looks like, how it behaves, and most importantly, how it grows through the years. How it grows even when there are disagreements and fights. Their opinions have conflicted many times, yet . . . they always come back together. That takes patience and humility . . . and deep love that weathers storms.

Is this a storm that Nick and I can weather?

I still have my company, though I'm not sure what's happening behind the scenes at CWM. Nothing has shut me down yet, not a certified letter, email, or even a voice-mail. Professionally I have no idea where I stand, so I keep going—business as usual.

Personally, I'm not having as much luck. It's hard to figure out how to move around the aftermath without getting further injured. He's said it a million times—*we moved fast.* But was it too fast, or were we moving at our own pace, one that was right for us?

The snow begins to cling to the edges of the window, and warm winter nights have me recalling eyes that held that same magic and arms that made me feel safe. Call it a momentary breakdown, but I'm tired of guessing and weak to the romantic ambiance outside my window. Picking up my phone, I decide to text Nick.

I have no idea what to say, but I think I should start with the basics. Me: *Are you still in the ci...*

Scratch that. I delete it, and then type: *I love you . . .*

There's no way I can send a mixed message like that. I backspace, ridding my screen of the words that come off as an offensive tackle in my current emotional state. The reality is, I can love him, but is it strong enough to last? Despite what he says, love can't always be the answer.

Life's too complicated for that. Hearing what Tatum once said in my head—*talk to him*—I take a deep breath to steady my shaking hands and text one question: *Did you sign that contract?*

It's the one question with an answer that can change everything. I heard about it, but I've not seen anything with my own eyes. I didn't want to, storing my faith in a secret hope chest buried in a cranny of my heart that we could be together again.

My heart drums in my chest while I stare at the screen. Please let this all be a big mistake. I can handle that Christiansen Wealth Management made a logical business decision. I understand basic economics, and the business rationale of endorsing a company if it's financially viable makes sense, too. But that addition to the contract to strip STJ of its backing just seems so personal. They didn't know me, but Nick did. That's what I can't wrap my head around.

And it will put the final nail in the coffin if he signed the document because of that.

The dots come fast as if he's been waiting for me to contact him. I guess he has since I'm the one who blocked him after the last time we spoke. Hope takes flight, and my heart is comforted by the opportunity that maybe, just maybe, we can find our way out of this tangled mess.

Nick: *Please meet me. We can discuss it.*

My heart sinks to the pit of my stomach. I guess I got my answer. Did he really choose to go along with this, to think he could take my company away without repercussions? Has he forgotten that I agreed to be his wife? *His wife?* I balk at the notion.

Instead, I'm miles away from him, two hundred or more than four thousand, I haven't a clue. I'm trying to decipher between the truth and lies, and he's not making it any easier with his response to my text. It's a simple question. His non-answer speaks volumes.

I've been through the wringer and back emotionally. I'm not sure I can take much more without losing myself completely.

Dane tried to break me.

I won't let Nick.

As angry as I am, doubt still fills me. I pause with my finger hovering over the option on the screen. I'm given some relief that it's not permanent, and then click to block his number.

I feel no satisfaction in the act. Actually, I feel worse than I did, but I'll get past it, and so will he, probably way faster than me if he hasn't already. I'm the fool who believed we were destiny. *I'll not fall for that nonsense again.*

"I can't believe November is almost over."

I turn to see my dad awake on the leather recliner by the roaring fire. "I thought you were sleeping."

"I was, but I woke up because you called me."

"No," I say, shaking my head. "I've been quiet. I didn't want to disturb you."

"You weren't disturbing me, but a father knows when his children need him. You may not have voiced my name, but you definitely needed my help. What's on your mind, dear daughter?" A smile takes hold of my lips.

My dad's voice is gentler since he had the heart attack, remaining positive and seeming to enjoy all the doting we've been doing. He's also been following his doctor's orders for calm to a T, so afternoon naps in the library have become a regular thing.

I find peace in his presence, and the surrounding books are my companions when I'm not working. I set my laptop down on the cushion next to me and angle his way, leaving out the back and forth I just had with Nick. The last thing I want to do is add my stress about men to my dad's plate. "Work."

"You used to call it fun. Now it's work?"

"I don't get to shop and match the perfect gift as much since running the company takes so much time."

"That's too bad. I've always heard that hobbies shouldn't become your source of income. Passion isn't built on monotony. When you love what you do, you suddenly look up to find that time has sped into the future."

"Very true." The darker colors of the room feel like a hug, wrapped around me and giving me comfort. Like my dad. I still have to tease, though. "I think the library is getting to you. You're becoming quite the philosopher in here."

"Maybe I should nap in the sunroom instead."

"Then you'd be telling me to look on the bright side."

He chuckles. "A sun pun. Very clever." Lowering the chair, he sits upright. "Who needs a room to give good advice. Look on the bright side."

Is there one? *Yes.* I tighten the topknot on my head while glancing out the window to find a hint of blue skies peeking through the heavy clouds. The snow has stopped, but I could use the sunshine. "I have my business, and it's going strong."

"Your mind may not be focused, but your heart is determined. There's no stopping you."

"It would be nice to have both on board at the same time."

"The universe loves to challenge us in new ways."

Getting up, I move closer, sitting in a chair across from him. "You're too young to be this wise, Dad."

"Don't I know it." He takes the glass and sips water before setting it down again. "Your mom takes good care of me."

"She does." Nothing feels hurried in this tucked-away room. It's something I've always appreciated about it.

The sound of him shifting on the leather has me looking at him—to make sure he's all right—but also, I'm seeking advice, needing my dad. I'm all over the place. He says, "I heard that you found out about Christiansen Wealth Management taking over."

"Rumors on the street."

"Or your mom."

"Yes, Mom told me when you were in the hospital."

He stares past me out the window. There's no hurry to finish this conversation, so I take the time to get a good look at him. His hair is graying, the darker strands of his natural color losing the battle to the salt and pepper. He moves with ease despite the recovery. I can't help but notice the similarities between him and the library. His whole demeanor is wrapped up in this room—worldly, comforting, and a wealth of knowledge.

His eyes connect with mine, and he says, "Not everything you hear is true, Natalie."

"Is there a record you're trying to set straight?" The twist of words reminds me of someone I used to know, so well that I can't even say *I do* without thinking of Nick.

"I think I need to consider how unhappy you are."

"You didn't make me sad. Scared me a little. Correction —*a lot*." I give him a wink. "But you're not to blame for anything else. Actually, you did so much for me, Dad. I feel like I haven't thanked you enough. Thank you."

"Come here, honey."

I get up and move closer, sitting on the wide arm of the chair. I lean down and give him a hug. "I'm so glad you're doing better."

"This is not exactly how I wanted to spend my early retirement, but this is the hand I've been dealt." He shifts to make sure that eye contact is solid. He always believed it was important to have a firm handshake and to look people in the eye. "I need to speak with your mother, but there's more to the story with the Christiansens. I've spoken to Corbin a few times."

"I didn't know you were on speaking terms with them?"

"We weren't for a few weeks, but now we're both eager to work things out. A lot has been said. Some true and some . . . let's just call it stretches of the truth."

Moving to the fire, I hold my hands down toward the flame. "Mom told me everything, Dad. We don't have to go over it again."

"I think we do."

Dread and curiosity fill me equally. As much as it's not a door I want to reopen, maybe getting his thoughts on it will help me move on. I sure hope so.

He says, "Your mom has good intentions. She's a smart woman, but she leads with her heart. I've always said it's what made her successful. People just like working with her. We were sort of a good guy/bad guy team." He rolls his eyes, and I grin, knowing where I got that bad habit from. "I was always the bad guy."

"Not to me."

"Eh, you were easy. I used to keep chocolate candy in my pocket. You very quickly figured out how to sweet-talk me right out of it. That's from your mother's side." He takes another sip of water and clears his throat.

"I can put out the fire if you're too hot."

"No, it's fine. What I was saying about your mom is that I'd just had a heart attack. She reacted from fear of losing me, looking to blame anyone but the culprit."

Leaning against the mantel, I ask, "Who's the culprit?"

"Me. I was told years ago to lower my blood pressure, work out, work less, and reduce my stressors. I worked out, ate better, but the stress was always there." He takes the blanket off and stands, stretching his legs and arms. He's not feeble by any means, thank God, but he's careful. The trajectory of his healing is helpful and inspiring. Joining me in front of the fire, he says, "I was selling the company not to only give Martine and me a new start—a slower life we can enjoy—but to also give Jackson the funding he will need to start his own venture. And for you, Natalie, to keep supporting your dreams—financially, if you needed it, and emotionally . . . if you needed that as well."

"I don't understand. Mom said you were fighting for my company, and that's what caused the heart attack."

Reaching out, he takes me by the shoulders. "That's been an awful burden you've had to bear for weeks now. I'm sorry I let it go on this long."

"But I was told Nick signed the contract. He signed a contract to dissolve my dreams. I've put everything into building a career, doing something I love, and he signed his name to a piece of paper that would end it."

"Would it? I don't ask that lightly or rhetorically. I ask that with genuine curiosity to what you truly believe."

"I don't know what you mean."

"He can't end your dreams. No one can."

Do I dig deep and admit a weakness I've carried just as long, or do I protect him by hiding the truth? Standing before me is a man I admire, one who has shown nothing but strength. He can handle it. "Through everything I was told, I never stopped loving him. But I can't get over the fact that he would do something to purposely hurt me that way."

"Facts are funny like that. The fact that you were dating Nick came as a surprise. The fact that it was serious in such a short time was another shock. But the fact that I get stuck on is why you broke up with him." He wanders to the windows to look out, shoving his hands in his pockets in quiet contemplation.

With a lump in my throat, I find it hard to speak to any of that. I've revealed more than I thought I would already, but here he is, making me want to vomit the rest of my feelings. Where will that leave me, though? Empty again.

He angles back, and says, "He signed the papers. There's no getting around that, but what I've been wrestling with is why?"

"You and me both."

"No, I don't understand why you haven't talked to him

about it, asked him directly? Why aren't you going to the source itself?"

I raise my finger into the air, my lips parting as I'm about to say something, but then I lower it down again and stare at him. *Was this the best advice ever, or did I just get the blame? My dad usually isn't one for subtlety, but I see what's he's doing in the nicest way possible.* "I should have. I should have known what was happening behind the scenes and been on top of my loan. I trust you, but that doesn't mean I could be so hands-off. STJ is my business, my baby. I need to take some of the responsibility."

"There's a lot of gray area in this matter, but the resolution rests solely in your hands." His words remind me of what Nick had said. *"This isn't black and white. She's in the gray area of understanding."*

"It seems I've been stuck in that same gray area."

"You're not alone. I've learned we weren't being represented the way we should have been. Garrett Stans saw an opportunity to weasel his way into their good graces at our expense."

"I'm not following."

"I mentioned how Corbin and I have been communicating. He was talking about how helpful Garrett's been and wanted my thoughts on promoting him. More details were shared, and we found that Garrett had not been working for our best interests. Only his own." He sits on the window seat, and says, "None of that matters where you're concerned. I just thought you should know that he was the one who put that list of companies together that would lose their funding cut. What *does* matter is that Corbin scrapped that amendment and agreed to carry the loans for their term."

I gasp, quickly covering my mouth. Lowering my hand, I feel my heart begin to race. "My loan is safe?"

He smiles, and it's the most comforting sight I've seen since . . . well, since Nick and before my dad had the attack. He continues, "It is, but we're still trying to finagle it out of the agreement. As for the details regarding Nick's role in all this, I think you should ask him yourself. Just promise me you'll be here for Thanksgiving. I have a lot to be grateful for and I know it will mean everything to your mom."

"I wouldn't miss it."

I walk out calmly, but I'm overcome with emotions. I dash to the staircase and lean against the wall, the thoughts from Nick betraying me to loving the man more than anything spin in my head. I take my phone out and look at his last message: *Please meet me. We can discuss it.*

Do I owe him that opportunity or do it for myself?

This time, I know the answer. *Both.*

I've made a commitment to my dad to stay, but my heart is already halfway to LA.

32

Natalie

"I brought you a piece of pie, Natalie," my mom says lightly as if she'll wake me. Isn't that the point of her bringing the pie? And why pie?

I glance toward the door. "It's nine in the morning. On Thanksgiving. Shouldn't we be eating that after dinner many hours from now?"

"We're too tired from the tryptophan to enjoy it." She takes a bite of *my* pie before setting it next to her when she sits down on the mattress. "And you seem like you could use some pie."

"Again, it's nine in the morning." I rub my eyes to clear away the sleep. "I haven't even seen you before now."

"Pie makes everything better." Not letting the hour or that she's sitting on my bed eating pie for breakfast like a crazy person deter her, she continues, "I was thinking about the holiday and how grateful I am for John's recovery. Also, it's been so nice to have my kids back under my roof again. I feel spoiled."

The dreary winter day is all that filters into the dark room, not providing much light. I'm too tired to overthink everything as I have for the past week. I also once heard that confessions of the heart are allowed at early hours and can't be held against you, so I whisper, "I'm grateful for Dad's recovery, but otherwise, I'm struggling." My dad made so much sense last week, but until I understand if Nick betrayed me, I don't think I can forgive him, and that has weighed me down.

I could have called him, video-chatted online, or sent a carrier pigeon. There are a million ways to communicate, but words feel empty without action. I need to see him face-to-face, the same request he made of me, to read his eyes and watch his body language.

She rubs my leg. "I'm sorry, honey. I wish I could make it better."

"I know you would if you could, but this will pass. I know it will, but why does it have to hurt so much until it does?"

"Love works like that."

Propping myself up on my hand, I ask, "Love? You say that as if you've known the loss I've felt all along."

"No, I just finally figured it out. I'm sorry for not recognizing it sooner."

"I haven't been forthcoming because I felt caught."

"Losing someone important to you is a terrible situation to be in." She looks down, shaking her head. "Before you said he was your boyfriend at the hospital, I didn't even know you were dating someone. What kind of mother doesn't know who her daughter is dating? I'm so sorry. I've been so busy with work—"

"You don't have to apologize. You're my greatest role model. Your success and how you stay so stylish even with a busy schedule. Honestly, I never felt I could live up to that."

Her smile is kind as she admires me, reaching to sweep loose strands of hair behind my ear, but she stops and doesn't do it, letting them fall back down against my cheek. "You're perfect the way you are, Natalie. I needed the strength of a partner to pursue my real dreams. You did it all on your own despite relationship obstacles and not using a dime of your trust fund."

I roll my eyes. "Technically, I couldn't. I can't touch that until I'm twenty-five, remember?" Sitting up straighter, I add, "I'm glad I couldn't, though. I'm proud of what I've created, and STJ is growing by leaps and bounds. We're covering our expenses and starting to make money."

"You're a mogul in the making." She takes another bite of the pie.

Flopping back to the mattress, I ask, "I thought that piece was for me?"

"Maybe, it's me and not you. I'm the one who needed the pie." I see a small smile, even in the dim light. She sets the fork back down and wipes it off with the napkin. Caught up in the menial task, she keeps her eyes lowered to it. "I owe Nick Christiansen an apology for treating him the way I did. It will be a tough pill to swallow, considering I'm not sure how innocent he is, but your dad seems to think things will work out how they're supposed to." When her eyes reach mine again, she adds, "Last night we finalized the deal to get your loan back. Your dad and I are your sole investors now."

"Really?" I sit up so abruptly that the fork clatters from the plate. "All ties are cut from the Christiansens?" As much as that makes me happy when it comes to business, I feel the sever to my heart over losing the last connection, even if it was a tenuous one at best.

"Yes, and now that we have cash from the sale of Manhattan Financial, we have set up a fund for you and Jackson. As for you and Nick, I met him momentarily during the contract stage, and your father has only said nice things. But Jackson has changed my mind."

Ugh. That limo ride was torture. I can only imagine what my prank-loving weasel of a brother has to say about him. "What did he say?"

She smiles. "That he's one of the good guys. That's high praise coming from him." Pausing, she searches the room as if she'll find the words she wants to use hidden in the décor. "I want to leave you with a little food for thought."

"More?" I tease. "You already brought pie."

Her laughter can be boisterous at times or quiet like now, but it's hers alone. I hope mine makes others smile the way she makes me grin. "Don't judge my pie-loving ways. As for love, Natalie, our hearts, our intuition, our souls know the truth. But the pain, the pain you're in now will make the love that much sweeter when you find the right one for you."

I study her eyes, her words music to my ears, but I'm afraid to let them sink in. "What are you saying?"

"Dad told me he talked to you." Even though Dad and I have talked a lot over the last week and shared nightly family meals together, he hasn't brought up Nick or the sale of Manhattan Financial to the Christiansens since last week. He believes in me and has given me time and space to work through my next course of action. She reaches over and covers my hand with hers and gives it a squeeze. "I was in so much pain myself. I thought I was going to lose your dad. I don't even know who I am without him, and I never want to find out."

I reach over and hug her. "I know, Mom. I'm glad he's recovering. I don't want to ever lose either of you."

"What I knew was that he'd been on the phone arguing, fighting with the CWM lawyers." I sit back, and our gazes connect again. "I wrongly assumed Nick was one of them." *Wrongly.*

I've done a lot of assuming, and it makes me wonder if it's wrongly as well. But hearing her offer the hope that maybe I can find my way through this darkness gives me a new perspective. She's able to acknowledge her errors. I think it's time for me to do the same. "The healing begins when the truth is heard. Do you think it's time to talk to him?"

"That's the million-dollar question."

Patting my leg, she then gets up and goes to the door. "Well, if nothing else comes of it but answers, then you'll get closure, and that's something we all wish for in these types of situations."

She's not wrong. "Thanks, Mom." *For the pie. The support. The love.*

Stopping as if something just occurred to her, she asks, "Before I get caught up in cooking, what do you think you'll do?"

"The pie? Eat it. Have you ever known me to pass up dessert, even at nine in the morning?"

Laughing, she says, "No, what are you going to do about Nick?"

"Ah." Lying back down, I stare up at the ceiling. The sun has started to peek through the gray day, shedding more light on everything—the room, my life, and the decisions I need to make. Tilting toward her, I finally reply, "I promised Dad I'd stay for Thanksgiving."

"He shouldn't have guilted you that way, but I'm not upset you're here." She winks.

"How crazy do I sound if I admit that I've been waiting for a sign?"

That draws her back into the room. She remains distanced at the door, but her interest appears piqued by the raised brows. "If you get a sign, how do you know it's a sign or just a coincidence?"

I recognize the skepticism in her voice. "I used to feel the same, but now I believe everything happens for a reason. We just have to learn to read the signs."

"You always were my silver lining girl. It's a great trait to have. But don't let life pass you by while you're waiting. There's nothing wrong with forcing the hand of fate sometimes. I sat at that coffee shop for two weeks, waiting for your dad to return."

My mouth falls open as I see a devious glint enter her eyes. "What? There goes my whole childhood. If you lied about that, what other lies have I been told?" *I'm teasing . . . partially.*

"I once modeled nude for an artist being compared to Jackson Pollack. He even shared the same first name."

"A painter?"

She nods. But suddenly pieces are falling into place . . . "Wait. Is my brother—"

"Natalie!" She scoffs. "No. I just liked the name."

Thank God. Images of the famous painter's work populate my mind. "Did he splatter paint on canvas because I didn't know Pollack painted figures, much less, nudes? I thought he only painted those splatters."

"I didn't say I was posing for a painting."

My gag reflex kicks in, but I keep the volume internally.

"Oh God, Mom. No. I do not need to hear this." I push the pie away, definitely not eating that. "Also, don't share any more of your lies. I'm good. Some things need to go to the grave with you. That Pollack story being one of them."

"Well, it inspired me to wait for your father. He was worth every minute I sat in that uncomfortable chair, hoping to see him again."

"Did he ever find out you did that?"

"Yes, we once confessed. That's when I found out he had been stopping by the bakery every morning at eight because that's where he had once seen me."

Throwing my arms open wide, I groan. "Why was everything so romantic back then?"

"Romance was in the air, but we definitely made it happen."

I pop upright. "You always said that you stopped modeling eight months after you met Dad to work with him, but how long did you date before getting married, and why do I not know this?"

"Thought you didn't want to know any more of my secrets?"

I roll my eyes. "Sure, use my words against me."

By how she's giggling, she's enjoying this a little too much. Or she has a sugar rush from the pie. Either way, I'm glad we're connecting like this again. She says, "It's not something I advertise because everyone has an opinion on it, but we went down to the courthouse ten months before our actual ceremony and got married." She nudges my leg. "That was the most romantic day of my life. Just us committing our lives to each other. I've not regretted it once since the day John and I met."

My heart pings to life, the gushy stuff reminding me of

lying in bed at the bungalow with Nick when he asked me if I wanted to get married. "And no one knew prior?"

"No," she replies, appearing pleased by her admission with a smile that reveals her secret. "My parents would have lost their ever-loving minds. Everyone celebrates the date of the big to-do we had at the Plaza. We celebrate our special day, just the two of us."

Trying to math through this, I finally just ask, "How long did you date before you eloped?"

She opens the door wider but stays. "Nine weeks to the day." Her finger crosses her lips. "But don't tell anyone. That's our little secret." Giving me a wink, she adds, "Let me know if you'd like me to book a flight for you." Am I that transparent? *Probably.*

"I'll keep you posted."

I'm given a reassuring smile before she closes the door behind her.

Sprawled across the middle of the bed, I'm still grinning. It's weird to think of my parents as younger and to find out they're stalkers for each other. I might die from the sweetness.

With all that was said on my mind, especially about her and Dad eloping so soon after they met, I pull the covers around me and snuggle with my thoughts. Nick would use that story to his favor. Any evidence to support his case is free game.

Taking up so much of the bed reminds me how Nick always lets me hog the middle, and he's content to settle around me. *He was good like that.*

Was?

Do I want to get caught up in wallowing? Or take action?

I roll over and see the pie. I promised I would stay for Thanksgiving, so I guess everything needs to wait a day.

I shove a big bite of pie in my mouth and then push up to get dressed. I rummage through the last few clean items in my suitcase but only find one sad pair of stretched-out, unflattering lavender running pants stuffed in the pocket of the insert. I yank them out, and a piece of paper flutters to the floor.

Bending down, I pick up the circular piece of paper and turn it over. It's an illustrated chocolate chip cookie with a bite taken out of it. "What the heck is this?"

Printed at the top reads: From the desk of Cookie Christiansen. My smile is instant. This is kind of kooky. I laugh at my pun, but with no idea what her note could possibly say, my gaze dips to her handwritten cursive. "Destiny will always find a way through a misunderstanding. Love, Cookie."

I flip it over several times, looking for more hints to what that means, but then I wonder how this even got in here. Was it meant for me, or did it somehow get caught in my belongings? She did ship this suitcase and my laptop bag to me, but would she—I inhale a hard breath when I realize what this really is.

I take off. Running downstairs, I call out, "Mom!"

"In here." I spin several times in the main entry, trying to figure out where that came from before she adds, "In the kitchen," and start running again. Flailing my arms in the air, I hold the note, and exclaim, "This is a sign."

"What is?" Her eyes narrow on the note in my hand. "That is?"

Throwing my arms around her, I say, "I'm booking a ticket to LA."

She hugs me. "You are?"

Out of breath from all the excitement, I lean against the

island where she was cutting carrots. "You inspired me, but don't tell Dad. He gave me great advice as well."

Soft laughter echoes through the kitchen area. "Oh, yeah? What did he say?"

"I talk a lot of nonsense," my dad says, coming in from the back patio. He stomps his boots on the mat. "What did I say?"

"You told me that no one can end my dreams but me. Not even heartbreak. You're right."

He nods in approval. "Sometimes I dole out a good one."

The love for her husband shines in my mom's eyes. I want that. Again. She says, "Excellent advice indeed." She turns to me, and there's no less love found. "You're going to LA?"

But that sinking feeling fills my belly again. "I'll go tomorrow. I promised—"

"Bull-cocky. You'll go when you damn well want to. You're a grown woman with whom I've had the pleasure of spending the last month. You go. Be bold and live your life to the fullest, my brilliant Natalie."

Leaning against the island, I say, "There's so much to unpack there, starting with the term bull-cocky, but there's no time." I run to hug him, closing my eyes and whispering, "Thank you."

He gives me a warm, fatherly hug, and when we part, he says, "Off you go. You need to see a man about a deal that I have a feeling he didn't make."

"I do." There's that phrase. It's all coming back to me now. "I love you both, and Happy Thanksgiving."

I run upstairs to pack, picking up the dirty clothes on the closet floor and tossing them in the suitcase before grabbing my toiletries. Grasping my phone from the bed beside the pie, I indulge and take a big bite before calling my bestie.

"Just in case you were wondering," Tatum answers as if we've been talking for hours. "I'm never giving this panda outfit back, Nat. It's the most comfortable thing I've ever worn. I want to be buried in it at this point."

"It's yours, but I need a favor before the funeral."

"Anything."

33

Nick

Take the scenic route.

They said.

It will clear your head. Andrew and my mom carried on, convincing me to make this ridiculously long journey. I should have bought a first-class ticket to Sea-Tac and had my car shipped to Seattle.

After two days of driving, I'm over it and would be fine never seeing another pine tree again.

Seventeen hours of driving should have done what they said—cleared my head— but if being one with the ocean and surfing every chance I got this last month didn't do it, then I'm not sure how an endless drive to the Pacific Northwest will cure me.

Fucking hell, I finally pull into the underground parking garage of my new building and take one of my bags from the back of my SUV. With shiny new keys in hand, I head up to the eighteenth floor and enter the ... *apartment? Place to live?*

I don't know what to call this place, but I know what it's not
—*home*.

Dropping the bag on the bed in the main bedroom, I log
on to the app on my phone and start opening the place up.
The blinds slide up, and as I pad through the penthouse, the
other blinds are already rising, letting the sunshine in
throughout the rooms.

A push of a button has the coffeemaker perking to life. I
usually hit a wall of exhaustion around three o'clock, but
because of the drive, it hits early, and I need a jolt of energy.
Sitting down on the couch, I text my mom because I know
she's worrying: *Just got here.*

Mom: *Glad you made it safely. Does everything look in
order? Should be stocked for you.*

Me: *Yes, you didn't have to do that, but I appreciate it.*

Mom: *It's what moms do. Let me know if you need anything
else. Congrats again on the promotion, Nicholas. Proud of you.
Love you.*

My chest hurts, my heart suddenly pounding for no
reason. The feeling has become a constant, but sometimes it
likes to remind me it's still here instead of the numbness I
typically experience.

Me: *Thanks. Love you, too.*

I make a cup of coffee and move to the windows to look
out, that pride my mom feels weighing on me. It's a fear of
disappointing them that has me sticking to their plan. I once
thought I might change my life's direction and leave that
damn plan behind.

Then I met Natalie, and she made me feel I could take
that plan and make it my own—create my own path—using
the opportunities I'd been given. When I started thinking
about moving to New York, I can admit it was for her, but it
also gave me time to realize that I could still have my dream

of a house on the beach. It didn't have to be in LA. If the beach has waves, I can surf anywhere, even on the East Coast.

Hell, I ordered a wetsuit for the nearby freezing waters. If I can surf along the Washington coastline, I can surf in the Atlantic. With her, it never felt like a tradeoff. I was getting to be with Natalie full-time. That was winning the grand prize and the Super Bowl all in one.

My mom found the apartment online, but it looked fine to me. Does it matter? It's a place to sleep and work when I'm not in the office. It's temporary. Six months, maybe a year. The possibility of it being permanent has been floated, but we'll take things one step at a time.

Any other time, this view would be a masterpiece. I can see far beyond the surrounding high-rises and skyscrapers of downtown Seattle. I put my hand flat to the window. The cold from outside is trying to get in through the glass. As a guy from Southern California, this cold weather is going to take some getting used to. Unlike Manhattan, which had an incentive to be there.

A promotion to Seattle to lead my own legal team, the apartment, and the money are what everyone dreams about when planning their careers. I'm getting it before the age of twenty-seven. There was no logical reason to turn down the offer, except one, and she's blocked me from reaching her.

Give Natalie time to herself, to focus on her father, and then explain how this whole mess came about. But the last text exchange didn't go as planned, so I've been confused about how we move through to find ourselves together again. Her blocking me gave me the answer I needed to make decisions regarding my future, but Tatum's offer to help is still on the table. *A few weeks to months.* That was her requirement, and I've met the minimum.

But I've been debating while going through the loss of Natalie. The pain is still a constant ache, but it's time for me to live again. Even though it's only a few weeks, I can't bear to continue living like everything's going to be fine.

It's not.

She blocked me. That tells me more than she will. Now I need to take a cue from her book and move on without her.

Despite the coffee's temperature, it doesn't do much to warm me like Natalie used to. She was my personal addiction, a zap to my system reviving a heart that had lost interest in relationships.

Everything with her was in turbo drive, but I don't regret a minute, except all the ones we were apart. I turn my back to the world and return to the kitchen to drop off the mug. I can wallow here all I want, but that won't bring Natalie back to me.

I unload my SUV and drop the boxes and luggage in the bedroom closet. Finding what I need, I get dressed and then head to the office. I've been here a couple of times over the past few weeks to make sure the transition goes smoothly, but it's time for me to settle in as well.

A WEEK DRAGS BY, and even a quick trip to LA for Thanksgiving doesn't fix my mood. I finally have an office ready to move into, so I figure Friday is a great day to officially begin.

Like in New York, the team remains intact from the previous leaders. I walk into the office in a tailored charcoal-colored suit. I fit the part of a successful lawyer down to my shoes even though I haven't done my time. Being born into the right family deserves the credit, not me. I'm not naïve to the fact that my co-workers believe I have no business being here. I'm also up for the challenge of proving them wrong.

I'm not just a handsome face with great taste in suits. I'm ready to tackle my job.

I'll leave the office politics and gossip for Andrew to handle. I'm here to ensure we're protected, legally, as we move into the next level of expansion.

I'm led to my office by a pretty assistant. I shouldn't note her appearance like that. I won't out loud, but by looking at Emily, it's obvious. Did the universe place her in my path to distract me from the heartache I can't seem to shake?

For some reason, I don't think my mom would agree. This is different. *She is.* Emily's not in my house—seventh, zodiac, or otherwise. *Only Natalie is, remaining there sprawled out, staking claims to all corners of my heart like she does the bed.*

The rush I had with Natalie still courses through me when I least expect it as if she won't let me forget her or even let her go. "Fuck."

"I can order a different chair." I turn to find Emily still standing in the office, ready to wheel the chair out from behind the desk.

"No," I say, putting my hand out. "It's not the chair."

"I'll get you whatever you need, Mr. Christiansen. Just tell me what you like."

I don't mean to stare at her blankly, but that difference is growing more apparent. "It's not the chair. It's me."

A move to a new city, just like a chair, isn't going to change things for the better. This relocation may give me a corner-office view, but I miss the one of Natalie—the skyline dotted with lights behind her when we picnicked in an empty apartment. Seeing her standing outside my hotel room in Catalina with that quirked grin, annoyed at herself for having to knock on my door because she was locked out.

Her lying in bed when I had to leave for the airport, too beautiful to walk away without another kiss. The sun shining in her eyes as she stared out to sea on the patio of the bungalow. But all those views pale compared to the one of her in my arms, thinking she was dreaming.

The first time our eyes met, I knew I was a goner. I knew I was hers. It didn't matter that we hadn't even exchanged names. My soul held hers, and that was it.

That.

Was.

It.

My mom's words return—*Destiny will always find a way through a misunderstanding.*

I'm no good for anyone else. I walk past Emily and out the door toward the exit. "Mr. Christiansen?" she calls behind me.

I keep running until I'm at the elevators, then call Tatum. She answers just when I think it's about to go to voicemail. "Took you long enough."

"I need to see her. I need to talk to Natalie. Will you help me?"

Without hesitation, she replies, "Let me work my magic."

Falling against the wall, I slump down, holding the phone to my ear. "Thank you, Tatum."

"Hurt her again, though, Nick, and I'll hurt you."

Her threat doesn't sound empty. I may not be afraid of what Tatum would do, but I won't cause Natalie any more pain, so it's easy to agree. "I won't. I promise."

"Stand by." The line goes silent. I look at the screen to verify that she did, indeed, just hang up on me. *Yep, she sure did.*

And I'm left wondering what stand by means, not by definition, but how long do I wait?

I need to get out of here because I'm too anxious to wait around for Tatum to call me back while surrounded by an office of strangers with their eyes glued to the new guy. Acting like a crazy person in front of Emily won't help those rumors. Natalie would have laughed. Emily looked ready to call security.

Taking the elevator to the lobby, I set my sights on the set of doors in front of me. I chuckle under my breath as every last thing seems to be a reminder of Natalie, especially revolving doors.

Do I push through the side door or attempt the revolving doors again?

I vote for certainty, not willing to take any more risks. Where did that leave me before now? Alone and across the country in cold weather. *That's where.*

The wind whips up, chilling me to the bone. I pull the lapels of my jacket closed in the front just as my phone rings. Moving off to the side, using a small concrete wall that juts out to block the wind, I look at the screen when it rings again.

The photo Natalie took the morning after finding each other again stays steady on the screen. My heart squeezes in my chest at seeing her beautiful face, but seeing this photo only means one thing. "Hello?"

34

Natalie

"Hi," I whisper into the phone, huddling it to my ear as if some stranger in the coffee shop will overhear.

"Hey." That tinge of hope that I've been holding onto for all this time is heard in his voice as well.

I'm not sure what to say now that I'm talking to him again. "You sound well."

"Well?" He pauses. "No, I'm not well."

I fight through the lump forming in my throat, and whisper, "You're not well?"

"No, I'm terrible, actually." The sound of wind travels the line, trying its best to keep me from hearing his deep tone that used to reach my core. But I'm here, pressing my phone to my ear to listen to anything he has to tell me. He says, "How's your dad? My dad said he's on the mend, but I haven't heard anything else."

Tilting my head down, I see the foam on the coffee is melting, the leaf design fading away. But I don't care about that. Nick asking about my dad means the world to me.

"He's doing a lot better. He's learning to relax. It's a struggle, but he's getting quite good at it."

The lightest of chuckles comes across, then he says, "That's good to hear."

"Yeah." We both seem to be suffering from the same issue—a hesitancy to drop our walls—though I have to say he had a head start. I probably shouldn't ask, unsure if I'm crossing some imaginary boundary I shouldn't. "What's wrong?" I do it anyway to satisfy my own curiosity.

"I . . . I came to realize today that I'm no good without you. Call me selfish, smug, or whatever else you want, but I'm in love with you, Natalie."

My breath catches somewhere in my chest, a knot near my heart as I digest what he just said. That wasn't what I expected. I expected a hard day at work, or his pipes are busted at the bungalow, or even that he never meant to hurt me. Those things crossed my mind before he just unleashed the love lines.

I won't cheapen the words by second-guessing him. He literally has nothing to lose at this point. He said the right thing, though, to gain my attention. "Go on."

"I miss you so much that it aches to have been away from you for so long." His voice catches this time. "I love you so much. Will you see me? I'll catch the red-eye and be there in the morning. I'll explain everything."

When I look up, the weather has gotten worse, and the wind causes a few people to move inside after their napkins are swept away from their tables. They're easy to ignore when I see a charcoal suit on a man who I swear could have walked right off a runway. I smile to myself, enjoying the sight of Nick taking cover against the corner of the building.

Tatum sets her cup on the table, and asks, "How long are you going to leave him out there?"

I place my hand over the phone, and whisper, "A little longer."

She laughs. "You're naughty."

Shrugging, I bring the phone back to my ear. "Save yourself the trip. What would you tell me if I was in front of you now, Nick?"

I watch him position himself to avoid the wind, giving me a good view of him. His hair is darker as if the sun refused to shine on him any longer. I can't see his eyes well, but those lashes are visible as he squints into the distance in deep thought. His suit fits those broad shoulders as if it was tailored to him. He says, "I was brought in at the tail end of negotiations to meet with your mom and dad when Andrew had to cancel at the last minute. I was representing my family as much as the company, scoping them out as much as they were me."

"St. James, Nick. How did you not put two and two together? We even ran into each other that morning at the building. The revolving door from hell. I won't even go in one of those contraptions again because of getting stuck in it." That's actually one of my favorite memories, but I have so many if I allow myself to still enjoy them. I find myself smiling and glance around the coffee shop, wondering if I look like a fool. But I notice I'm not the only one staring out the window at him, and jealousy spikes when I see how pretty the competition is.

"I don't have a good reason for that. They all sound like excuses, but I think I was ignoring the evidence in front of me on some level. I didn't want to see what was so obvious."

Rolling my eyes at these poor souls thinking they can get his attention through a window if they apply fresh lipstick and bat their eyelashes, I look back at him. He's barely staying put with the wind gusting around him. Pulling my shoulders back, I stick out my chest and flip my hair. "This is part of the problem we had. Everything was so fast that important details slipped through the cracks. And the thing about secrets is they always come out."

"They do. I just wished there were none between us."

"When did you find out about my company being short-listed for ending the funding?"

"When we went to my parents' house for brunch. In the meeting with my dad and Andrew. But I swear I came to tell you. You took the call from your mom on the terrace. I told my family I needed to be the one to talk to you. That's when you found out about your dad's heart attack."

"That morning is a blur to me now." Trying to remember how it played out, I finally land on his mom's expression when we came inside. "Your mom was mad at you like you were the one who made me cry."

"Yes," he says, running his hand through his hair. One of his tells I've become familiar with. We keep saying we don't know each other, but that right there reminds me that I do. I do know him. And he also loves to say I do, as I just did twice. "She gave me the dirtiest look for hurting you."

I smile. "She took my side without even knowing what made me cry." I wish he could see how that makes me feel. Just when I start to admire him again, he turns in my direction. "Oh, shit." I drop to the floor, hitting the table on my way down and rattling the mugs on their saucers.

"What is it?"

Spying on him through some guy's denim-covered legs, I see him with his back to the coffee shop again. *Phew.* "Nothing. We were just saying how Cookie loves me more than you." A smug grin rides high on my right cheek. I exhale and climb back up while Tatum laughs her ass off.

He chuckles. "I wouldn't go that far."

"I already did." As much as I want to indulge in the sound of his laughter or how handsome he is, I still need answers. "So, let's get to the details. Why did you sign a contract that effectively dissolved my company?"

"I sign as legal counsel representing our party, Christiansen Wealth Management. I had met with Manhattan Financial's legal team, so I signed, which is standard. It was boilerplate stuff. My dad even mentioned that your father was fighting for one of the companies, and we were happy to let him have it. I didn't know, at the time, that it was yours."

Pinning him to the wall with a glare, I ask, "Does that mean you would have kept it to control me?"

"No. No, not at all. If it were up to me, I would have freed you from the burden of the loan and reworked your contract."

Legal speak has to be missing love language. Like a sixth sense, it's the sixth language to getting laid. Another is the phrase "Freed you from the burden." Five of the hottest words ever heard.

Okay, so maybe I'm not thinking clearly. How can I when he looks so damn handsome in the middle of what looks like a tornado brewing? Add snow into the mix, and I say, "You should come inside."

"Come?" he asks, and my tummy clenches, just hearing him say it.

"I mean, go inside." Eyeing Tatum, she nods her approval. She picks up her cup and nods to the corner by the fire where she's heading. "The wind sounds strong. You should find a coffee shop and wait it out."

"I should. Not sure if it's getting better or worse. It's unpredictable. I see a coffee shop across the street."

Bolting to my feet, I yell, "No!"

"Why not?"

"Surely, there's a closer one than across the street. Look around, Nick."

I sit down, trying to catch my breath, not caring that I'm getting a few dirty looks for startling some table neighbors. He says, "You're right. There's one closer. I just don't care for their coffee."

"Me either." I push mine away as if it personally offended me. "We can get something else."

"We?" The bell above the door chimes, and I look up.

Standing again, I lower the phone to my side. A smug smirk is set on his stupid sexy face. I shrug. "Figured some conversations should be had face-to-face."

"I couldn't agree more." He cuts through two tables but stops on the other side of mine. "What are you doing here?"

I'm not upset that his natural instinct had him ready to embrace me, to kiss with the passion we always shared. Okay, the last part is just my fantasy, but I remember those kisses well. Reaching into my pocket, I pull the note out, and reply, "Cookie brought me here."

I know my company is safe and under a new deal with my parents, so I'm not stressed about that. But we're standing here like two fools who don't know what to do with themselves when not attached at the hip. I say, "Before this goes any further, I have to know the truth."

"I promise to tell you anything you want to know."

"Look me in the eyes, and tell me that your family wasn't trying to take advantage of my dad and that none of you knew anything regarding my company until that morning of the brunch."

We sit down, remaining across from each other. Holding his hand up like a Boy Scout, he says, "I swear to God, we wanted a clean and honest transaction. I wouldn't be working there—*hell,* I wouldn't be speaking to my family if they had planned something underhanded. I've seen enough movies to know it's always the lawyer who's taken down first." I manage a halfhearted smile. It's all I have to give right now. "None of us knew STJ was yours until you told me, then we figured the rest out when we met that morning."

He doesn't hold back the plea that fills each word. By how he's still staring at me, unblinkingly, I believe him.

"I signed the paperwork. Guilty as charged. I can't take it back, but I would in a heartbeat. I was distracted in New York when I signed them, trying to get out the door to meet you for dinner and again when I was supposed to deliver them to the offices."

Surprised how he looped that around, I ask, "Are you blaming me?"

"No. Not at all, but you are so bad for my career." A humorless laugh escapes him.

"Am I bad for you?"

"No. You're so right for me. Fuck my career. I'll find another like worshipping at the altar of Natalie." He dares to breach the invisible boundary between us and takes my hand. "We're better together."

My soul knew the truth the moment I laid eyes on him, but I'm so glad to hear him verbalize it. I scoot my chair around the table and invade his personal space. "What are your theories on coincidences these days?" I blurt, resting my chin on my hand. "I think everything happens for a reason."

Much to his delight, he replies, "Sounds like you might believe in destiny."

"Destiny with a little helping hand." I close the gap and take a deep breath. This doesn't feel like I'm giving in. I'm receiving love, his to be precise, and I have so much to give in return to him. "I missed you."

"I missed you so much. I felt lost without you."

My heart feels free, knowing I haven't lost him. "I also love you." But there's one more thing I have to do before I can open my arms for him. "I need to apologize, Nick. For my reaction at the hospital—"

"God, no, Natalie, you didn't. You don't—"

"No, I do. And my mom wants to as well. There's no excuse, really, but we were so blinded by pain and fear, and well, as my mom said to me yesterday, we were just looking for someone to blame."

"I can understand that. And I am sorry that this . . . miscommunication happened, but in some ways, it was a good thing. The time without you just felt so, so wrong. Moving here, going into my new office . . . I should have felt excited about the challenge ahead of me, but I just felt empty." *I love this man.* He's just mirrored my thoughts exactly. *Empty.*

But enough words for now. Feeling that the weight of the world is off my shoulders, I get up and do what I've been wanting to—sit on his lap and stake claim to those lips. Wrapping my arms around his neck, I lean my forehead against his. I love the way his hand rubs my hip, just like old times. "Question. How long are we going to drag this out? Because I'm really ready to be kissed again."

"By anyone or me?"

"You. Only ever you, Mr. Smug and Sexy."

His grin grows, dimples showing. "I'm going to kiss you, Natalie St. James. Are you ready for it?"

"I was born ready for you, Nick Christiansen." Before I have a chance to add some wisecrack, he cups my cheeks and kisses me with passion—his lips on mine and our tongues falling back into their rhythm again.

Ripping my lips away before we're arrested for public obscenity, I catch my breath, and then with the next, I ask, "Want to come back to my room and start this relationship on the right foot?"

"Given a second chance—"

I hold my finger up. "Third, to be accurate."

"Given a third chance at this relationship and you want to skip to the main event? No dinner?"

"I know it's hard to believe, but I'm not hungry." Tilting my head to the side, I add, "For food, that is."

"No drinks?" Waggling his eyebrows, he asks, "Rum and Cokes?"

"I'm good, all caffeinated and ready to go."

"You just want to skip to the main event?"

I shrug. "We never did adhere to other people's dating timelines. Why start now?"

He kisses me again before setting me on my feet and taking my hand. We head to the door, but before we leave, he looks across the room, and says, "I owe you one, Tatum."

She raises her mug. I give her a little wave, and mouth, "Thank you," for *everything* she did to help me track Nick down. If I had followed my assumptions, I'd be sitting in LA alone, instead of back in his arms.

At the hotel, there's no wasting time. We fumble into my room, our clothes coming off and landing on the floor like a breadcrumb trail leading to the bed. His lips embrace mine while his hands roam my body. Grunts and growls escape him as he kneels before me and kisses down the center of my body. Moans of pleasure wisp through my lips as I weave my fingers through his hair. He mentioned worshipping earlier, and I'm feeling like a goddess because of him.

But then I'm lifted and kissed on the mouth again as we fall onto the bed, our bodies tangling as we tousle in the covers. I roll onto my back and help pull the sheet from between us. As soon as my legs are freed, Nick lifts the covers and is quick to disappear under them, leaving me with the image of those dimples and mischievous eyes before he reminds me how magical his mouth is.

"Oh God, yes. So magical."

My eyes roll back in my head as I fist his hair in one hand and the sheet in the other. "I missed this . . ." I pant heavily. "So much."

My body succumbs to the sensations, and as soon as the vibrations calm, I pull him up to kiss me again. He does too, like no one's ever kissed me before—*passion, love, and forever* built into each caress of our lips.

Before I return from floating from the bliss, he slips away. When he returns, he kisses my collarbone, keeping our words out of this, needing to feel instead of thinking for a while. Covered, he fills me, pulling me into his world to be consumed again. I willingly go, craving that connection deeper than our bodies could ever reach. We make love and create it, nothing lost in the month we were apart but even more intense.

We both find our ecstasy unapologetically quick.

There's no rush to get up as we lie in each other's arms right after. It's the opposite, a desire to lie here forever. Just as my eyes dare to close, his body rattles the bed with laughter, and he asks, "What is that?"

I follow his gaze, and suddenly, a giggle helps to invigorate me again. "That would be a cookie basket."

He glances at me out of the corners of his eyes before returning to eye the treats. "Is that for me?"

"It was part of my evil plan to get you back."

Even in the darkened room, I can see his roguish smile —the charmer. Caressing my cheek with the back of his fingers, he leans down and kisses my forehead. "I was always yours, so you didn't need it."

"It's more of a *just in case* to seal the deal present."

"Can't wait to see what kind of cookies you put in there."

Sliding my arms around his neck again, I bring him to me, and we kiss. "I'm not done with you quite yet."

"Although I can't wait until tomorrow—"

"Wait? What happens tomorrow?"

He kisses me gently, and then whispers against my lips, "We start our new life."

35

Nick

Six months later . . .

TOMORROW TURNED INTO FOREVER.

Not legally. At least not yet. Emotionally. Universally. Spiritually. Our souls have already committed. Sure, we skipped a few steps in the making-up process. I don't think anyone is surprised by that.

Something else that won't come as a shock is that we didn't pass over reconnecting physically. We've ended up right back where we started—in each other's arms. But Natalie has a theory—we were great before the contract debacle. So I've promised not to let her distract me when dealing with business, and she's promised not to walk around naked when I'm working from home.

Seemed like a good deal at the time. As she would say, spoiler alert: *It sucks.* I miss her gracing me with her bare body while I'm working. She has always been a fantastic distraction. It may have gotten us in trouble, but the time apart made us realize that we were worth fighting for and that we're in this for the long haul of life, plus forever.

I can't think of a better way to spend eternity than holding this beauty in my arms. Her fingers trace letters on my chest. I'm supposed to be guessing what she's spelling, but my lids are heavy, exhausted from a long day at the office and then our activity tonight. She asks, "Any guesses?"

"No," I reply, half-asleep.

"With you."

I like her answer. Peeking an eye open, I look down at her snuggled to my side. "What was the question?"

"You once asked me where I want to live. My answer is *with you*, wherever that may be. That's the only place I care to be." She's the most forgiving person I know. I know that wound of betrayal ran deep, but she believed me, and I'll never forget that. I'd never purposely hurt her, though, and she realizes that as well.

"I discovered where I'm meant to be. That's with you."

"Sweet-talker."

"Sweet on you, but can we sneak in a nap? I have plans for you later and I'm hoping to wake up early to go for a run with you in the morning. All this pasta you've been cooking is packing on the pounds."

Her hand runs over my abs. I tense them for her. She lifts up to see my eyes and says, "You literally don't have an ounce of fat on you."

"I'm hard for you."

"And here I thought I did a good job of wearing you out." She sits up to get out of bed, but I catch her hand.

"Don't leave me."

"Ever, or just not to the bathroom? I'm hoping you mean in the forever sense because I really need to go."

I release her, chuckling, and ogle that incredible ass of hers. Grabbing her pillow, I cover my face and inhale her lingering scent deep into my lungs. If the perfect wave had a scent, it would smell like Natalie. I don't even care how creepy that seems.

She's gone just long enough for me to doze off. When she climbs back into the middle of the bed, I turn to hold her. It's our favorite way to fall asleep, and just like in Catalina, I find peace with her.

"Nick?"

"Hm?" I mumble.

"I don't want to go back to New York without you."

Lifting my head from the mattress, I crack my eyes open again. "I wanted to talk to you about that." I'm exhausted, but I hate that look of worry in her eyes.

She replies, "Now, if you're not too tired."

"I'm never too tired for you." I rub the corners of my eyes and sneak out a yawn before moving to sit up. I had hoped for a nap before the big plan, but this is more important. *She is more important than anything else.*

She slides up next to me, and we rest against the headboard with the sheet covering us. I take her hand, and our fingers fall, locking together. I ask, "Do you want to start, or do you want me to go first?"

"You go first." The quiet manner isn't fitting for a woman so vividly Technicolor to my bland world.

"I'm supposed to have a call with Andrew and my father this week to discuss if they want me to stay in Seattle or if it's time to go. Do you want to share your thoughts with me?"

"You know I want you in New York. There's never been a question about that. It's just a matter of if you want to live on the West or East Coast and the pros and cons of that."

"Maybe we need to do a pros and cons list for moving to

New York. Pro: we'll be together all the time. Another pro is your job. It's important to you and to me. I don't know if you want to relocate and take your company with you or expand into new territory. I'll help you no matter what you decide."

"Con: you don't have the Pacific Ocean to surf in every morning. Con: you don't have the Pacific Ocean to surf in every morning. Con: you won't need your Range Rover in the city. Con: you'll be away from your family."

I bring her hand to my mouth and kiss it. "Look, the pros for me are cons for you. The cons for me are pros for you. Let's forget lists. I don't care about the Pacific, but I'm madly in love with you, Natalie. And if you're in Manhattan, then that's where I'll be."

"This is all well and good, but I want you happy. Does the New York office even have an opening?"

Smirking, I reply, "It just so happens they never filled Garrett Stans's position."

Her lips are tugged to the side and pursed. Shaking her head, she glares as if he's right in front of her. "That rat bastard."

I get the anger, but I've let it go more than she has. I don't blame her. I've had more time to live with the truth of what really happened. "I might have inquired about the job last month and suggested they leave it open a while longer."

She curls around me, draping her leg over mine and leaning against me. "Love makes people do crazy things." Looking up at me, she adds, "We've done the long-distance thing, me working from here as much as possible, spending every long weekend we could together. I don't want to spend my days apart anymore. This might be the most selfish thing I've ever said, but I want you with me in New York. All the time."

I tap her nose. "Be careful what you wish for."

"Oh no, no. I'm not letting wishes, destiny determine anything, and I'm not leaving it up to fate any longer." Sitting up, she cups my face, squishing my cheeks. "I love you, Nick. I'm ready for the next stage with you."

That's good to hear. She may have given up on destiny, but I'm a firm believer.

I didn't give Natalie the love story she deserved the first or second time around, but destiny gave me a helpful shove in the ass the third time, and I won't mess it up. I reach over to the nightstand and pull out the small velvet box.

"This may not be the top of the Empire State Building or on the beach in Malibu. But this is me, nude at the moment, but let's overlook that aspect."

Sitting up a little straighter to get a good gander, she dips her gaze down my body, and says, "That's not easy to do. Compliments to you." She chef kisses her fingers and winks.

"Though I appreciate the accolade, I saw this going differently." I start to open the box. But she leans forward, the sheet slipping down, revealing her torso. *So beautifully distracting.* "You know, I have bad timing." *What was I thinking?* I'm sex drunk and all feely. She deserves more. I snap the box closed, refusing to blow my plan. "Let's do this another time."

"What? No!" She practically lunges across the bed, grappling for the ring. "Let's do it now. I'll be good. No nudity. No jokes. I'm listening."

I set it on the dresser. "It's not you. It's me. I got caught up in the moment." Grabbing my boxers from the floor, I pull them on.

"It's okay," she says, eyeing me.

Her hair is messy, sexy, and her makeup-free face has me wishing I could steal a few more minutes kissing her, but we need to get going. "We have dinner reservations in an hour. We should probably start getting ready."

That perks her up, and a big smile is flashed. "We do?" She peeks at the ring box and then nods with a squinted eye. "Oh, all right. Yes, I see now." Clicking her tongue, she adds, "Gotcha."

"Do you? Because it looks like something is in your eye."

She rolls her eyes and climbs out of bed. "Very funny. I get the shower first for that comment."

Rubbing my thumb over my bottom lip, I admire her backside. "My pleasure. Truly."

Maybe I'm an asshole for making her wait, but she has me doing the stupidest shit without thinking. This time, I want to do it right.

HOLDING her hand in the elevator, I can't take my eyes off her. She's stunning—her blond hair reminiscent of old Hollywood—sleek with a soft wave cascading in the front, meeting a deep blue spaghetti-strap top that matches her eyes.

And there are those damn tight jeans I thought we burned on the beach one night at the bungalow. Burning her favorite pair was an accident. She didn't forgive me until I tracked down another pair in Paris and had them shipped over.

Her pink lips and eyes with dark eye shadow have captivated me. I'm tempted to skip the evening affair and take her back upstairs. But the doors slide open, and we're already walking.

Stopping shy of the revolving door, I glance at her. She's already staring at me, and asks, "I say we do. What's the worst that can happen? We get stuck for a few minutes?" She wraps her arm around mine, and says, "Come on. Time to conquer this fear."

She steps right into it as if she has something to prove. Since I don't want to squash her, I let the glass slide behind her and step into the next compartment. All is great and we're moving.

Until we're not, and I run into the glass, smacking my chin on it. "Damn it."

Whipping around to find me, she's like a mime stuck in a box, palming the glass looking to escape. "Nick?"

"It's okay. It's okay. Stand in the middle." I give the brass railing a hard shove. The door gives and then seems to lock back.

A security guard races over and tries to pull the next door. When he's unsuccessful, I hold up my phone and point at it, not sure if he can hear me well or not. "Can you call maintenance, please?"

He runs to the desk and picks up the phone.

THIS IS NOT how I saw our night going. In the next compartment, Natalie sits on the ground leaning her back to the curved glass wall. We've been sending each other memes to pass the time until help arrives. *It's been over an hour.*

I already canceled our reservation since they couldn't hold it and had nothing else available.

Natalie's gone to spelling things on the glass and having me guess. I say, "Will."

She shakes her head and starts spelling another word. I guess, "You."

Annoyed, she says, "Watch my fingers, Nick."

I watch, but to her dismay, my next guess of marry doesn't work for her. And she still doesn't get it. I've given up trying for something unforgettable to ask for her hand in marriage. Being stuck in this damn revolving door is pretty unforgettable. "Me?" I ask.

"Nick, are you playing or not? You're totally wrong."

"Depends who you ask. It's will you marry me, Natalie?"

"No, it's *Saved by the Bell*, the TV show." Covering her mouth, she stares at me through the glass. She raises her palm, and I press mine to hers, the glass between us. Tears fill her eyes, and she finally lowers her hand from her mouth. As her shoulders rock with her soft cries, I get up on one knee.

Those tears fall down her cheeks, and she presses both hands to the glass. "The stars realigned for us. We fought our destiny and made the mistake of walking away. But I've learned that every time we follow our hearts, we're never led astray." Holding the box open, the three-carat, Asher-cut diamond sparkles under the bright lights of the revolving door.

I take it out of the box and tuck it under the space between the glass wall and the door that separates us. She takes the ring and stares in awe. When her eyes return to me, I say, "I love you more than anything. Will you marry me, Natalie?"

Slipping the ring on her finger, she says, "Yes."

EPILOGUE

Natalie

We're not the most traditional couple out there. We live by our own rules, and that's what I love about us. Today, we humored our loved ones and had a ceremony for them to share in the day.

Sure, we could have jetted off to Timbuktu to get the perfect social media-worthy wedding photo, walked down a long aisle at an historical church in Manhattan, or followed in my parents' footsteps and said our *I do's* at The Plaza.

Eloping would have been romantic, but every night, I go to bed next to this handsome, once-stranger, now husband is like living a fairy tale. I wouldn't trade it for anything. So, returning to the scene of the crime on Catalina—the island, not the hotel room, though I wouldn't have minded that if I can be frank with you—fit us best.

Standing beneath a pink Nick & Natalie neon sign, my husband caresses my face. It doesn't matter that we're surrounded by friends and family. He comes so close that I forget we're not alone. I tilt my head up ready to be kissed by this incredible man. For only my ears, he whispers, "You were the best catch I ever made."

Happiness isn't a word that covers how I'm feeling. I smile, staring into the sunrise of his golden-brown eyes. "I love you."

"I love you, too."

When his smile grows even wider, those dimples digging deep into his cheeks, he says, "You know what comes next?"

I want to roll my eyes, but I don't. I embrace him even tighter, and reply, "Go ahead and say it. You know you've been dying to."

"I do. I do, baby." Slipping his arms around my waist, he says, "I do forever with you."

"Good. I do, too."

Under sunset skies on the edge of an Avalon cliff, we kiss, sealing our fates forever together before heading to our reception up the hill.

Inside the bar where we met, I sit on the tablecloth-covered counter and take a bite of my first In-N-Out burger. Did anyone really expect us to have our reception catered by another place? Instead of a chocolate fountain, we have a french fry tower, and a buffet table with every variety of cookie imaginable. Though my husband's favorite is the double chocolate chunk. I'm thinking those are the cookies that led to the proposal. I've taken notes for my clients.

Nick stands in front of me, biting his lip nervously as though I'm performing surgery. I rest a hand on his shoulder, and say, "It's delicious."

Like a proud papa, he announces, "She likes it." Everyone carries on with their celebrating, not worried with our antics.

Tugging him by the lapels of his tuxedo, I say, "Come here. Let me kiss you, dear husband."

Our kisses are NSFW, not suitable for weddings . . . *or receptions.* "I can't wait for our honeymoon."

"A week at *our* bungalow, totally unplugged from the rest of the world. Only you and me, babe." I pick up my cocktail and take a sip, the rum going down way too smoothly.

"Sounds like heaven."

"It's the best gift ever. I don't know that thank you is enough. Your parents were very generous."

Clinking his glass against mine, he says, "Don't fall for their tricks, dear wife. Cookie wants grandkids while she's young."

"The plot thickens." I giggle. Glancing over at his brother and date, I ask, "How does Andrew feel about us getting the beach house?"

Nick turns to locate him. "He gets their house. They're downsizing. It may be bigger, but real estate on the beach in Malibu is more valuable, so they're about even."

"Tatum already told me not to throw the bouquet to her, so maybe I'll toss it to Dalen."

"It took us three times to get it right."

"Third time's a charm."

"He'll probably do it in two, marrying her on their second chance." He chuckles. "My brother is competitive like that." As he caresses my cheek, the amusement disappears and is replaced with sincerity. "We aren't lucky, Natalie, and charm had nothing to do with it. We're destiny."

I release a breath and then lean against him. "I should send *The Chad* a thank-you gift. If it hadn't been such an awful date, I wouldn't have been heading home."

Bending down to kiss that spot just below my ear that makes me weak in the knees, he then says, "Yeah, I'm not that big of a man. Let's just leave him in the past."

I laugh. "Already forgotten."

My best friend comes over with the shot hat. When she holds it up, I say, "Nope. That gets me in trouble every time." I kiss Nick's scruffy cheek, because he's so damn sexy, and he's all mine.

His arm wraps around my waist and he kisses me right back. "I'm just the kind of trouble you need." He helps me from the bar.

"If I put that hat on, we're going to end up making Cookie's wish a reality."

Twirling me out, he brings me back in, holding me tight against him. Dipping me, he asks, "Would that be so bad?"

"I still want to have two kids with you, but I'm thinking we have some fun for a few years, build the business, and grow your career. What do you say?"

"I already said it in front of the world." I'm whipped up against him, eye to eye. "I do." I kiss him, and when he sets me down on my feet, he adds, "We have time for a family." Cheek to cheek, we slow dance. "I'm happy we're returning to New York together. No more long-distance. You're stuck with me now, Mrs. Christiansen."

Harrison comes over and says, "The bar's opening up to the public soon, so we have to wrap it up."

A two-hour window to celebrate marriage to this man is not long enough. Good thing I have the rest of my life with him. Nick asks, "You ready to start that honeymoon?"

"Definitely."

As we hug everyone goodbye and thank them for being here, I see Harrison trying to talk to Tatum and her effectively blowing him off. I'm curious what happened between them, considering how well they hit it off last time we were here. If that's not a story in the making, I don't know what is.

Hugging my dad, I rest my head on his shoulder. It's not

but a few seconds, but we sway together. He says, "You owe me a father-daughter dance."

"I promise we'll get one when I'm back in New York." He looks good. Healthy and happy. My mother's never been more relaxed, even talking to Cookie about astrology and the moon phases of women. I'm not sure what that means, but I love that they get along so well.

While everyone goes outside, Nick and I stand there, holding hands. He's still Mr. Sexy, but there's no smug found in his smile. Just pure, unadulterated joy. It looks good on him. Our guests start chanting our names. Nick kisses my bare shoulder and then offers his arm. I wrap mine around his, and we rush through the doors into bubbles being blown. The bubbles fill the air as we pop a few running toward the parking lot.

Nick stops and then laughs so hard that he holds his stomach. When he turns back to me, he says, "Is this the actual scooter we rode on?"

"It is. And now it's all ours."

"You're very good. The strings of cans and just-married sign are a nice touch."

"What can I say? I strive to bring smiles."

He comes to me and lifts me into the air. "Mission accomplished." Lowering me slowly, he takes advantage and kisses me from my collarbone to my lips, until my feet are firmly back on the ground. He achieves an impossible feat, considering I'm floating on cloud nine.

Taking the helmet with my new name—*Mrs. Christiansen*—on the back of it, he carefully places it on my head and snaps the strap under my chin before putting his on. I pull my skirt up to my thighs and slip onto the seat. When he gets on the scooter, he asks, "I thought you hated everything on two wheels?"

I wrap my arms around him, holding on for the ride of my life. "I did, but I hadn't met you yet, and here we are now married. How are we so lucky to have found our way back to each other in a city of almost nine million people?"

"It's not luck, baby." Starting the engine, he revs it a few times before looking at me over his shoulder with a big grin. "I would have found you again one way or another because the truth is, I never got over you."

The End.

Make sure to check out the sneak peek I included for We Were Once. Turn the page.

YOU MIGHT ALSO ENJOY

__Recommendations__ - Three books I think you'll enjoy reading after Never Got Over You and all are stand-alones that will grab your heart and carry it through the story.

READ FOR FREE IN KINDLE UNLIMITED

We Were Once - Read the Bestselling Book that's been called **"The Most Romantic Book Ever"** by readers and have them raving. Turn the page for a sneak peek or jump right in and read on Amazon.

Missing Grace - You will be on the edge of your seat with your heart on the line as two soul mates fight for the future stolen from them.

Finding Solace - This second chance, small town romance that will have you falling for the bad boy. "A dazzling second-chance love story that has all the heart feels. Heartbreaking, heart wrenching, heart melting, heart throbbing and heartfelt." - Gin, Amazon Review

Spark - Lucky's Bar was playing The Crow Brothers' music. Meet these up-and-coming rock star brothers and the fierce women they fall for. Spark is all the heart and passion, depth of characters, and originality of We Were Once.

WE WERE ONCE PROLOGUE

I've never died before, but I recognize the feeling.

WE WERE ONCE CHAPTER 1

Chloe Fox

"Promise me you'll protect Frankie with your life, Chloe."

Glancing sideways, I find it hard to take this seriously. "Um..."

My mom hugs Frankie to her chest like the son she never had. "You'll give him a good home, feed him, and nurture him?"

I think this is taking it a little too far. "It's a plant, Mom, not a human."

"It's not just a plant. It's a bonsai tree. They're fickle creatures—"

"Technically, it's not a creature. It's a miniature tree."

"Creature or not, promise me you'll take care of it, Chloe. This isn't just a plant. This little guy can provide harmony and calm to your place."

"Mom, I got it." I attempt to pry the potted plant from her, but when she resists, I ask, "Do you want to keep Frankie? He'd love New York City. You can take him to

Central Park or a show on Broadway. A quick trip to MoMA or the Statue of Liberty—"

"Very funny." She shoves him toward me. "Take him. I bought him for you."

"We can set up a visitation schedule if you'd like?"

That earns me an eye roll that's punctuated with laughter. "You might think I'm being dramatic, but I can already tell this is what your apartment is missing. I wish you'd let me decorate it more. So, mock me if you must, but that little guy is going to bring balance to your life."

"It's a lot of pressure to put on a plant, don't you think?"

"Little tree," she corrects stubbornly as if I've insulted the thing. Crossing her arms over her chest, she raises a perfectly shaped eyebrow. "You want to be a doctor, Chloe. Treat it like a patient. Water, attention, and care. The basics."

Holding the plant in front of me, I admire the pretty curve to the trunk and branches. It's easy to see why my mom picked this one. "I'll try not to kill it like the plant you gave me last year." I set the plastic pot down on top of a stack of textbooks on the coffee table. "But you have to admit that I gave that ivy a great send-off."

"You did. Right down the trash shoot." She laughs again, but I hear the sadness trickling in.

"Why are you getting upset?"

The green of my mom's eyes matches the rich color of the leaves when she cries, just like mine. "I think the bonsai has had enough water for one day. Don't you think?" I ask teasingly to hide how much I hate the impending goodbye.

She laughs, caressing my cheek. The support she's always shown me is felt in her touch. "I've had the best time with you over the past few weeks. I'm going to miss you, honey."

Leaning into it, I say, "If everything goes to plan, I'll be in the city next year, and we can see each other all the time."

"You've worked hard. Now it's time to enjoy your senior year." Her departure pending, we embrace.

"I enjoy working hard, and my grades still matter this year if I want to get into med school."

A sympathetic smile creases her lips when she steps back. "I'm sorry you feel you have to be perfect all the time or that you feel medical school is the only option for you. It's not. You can do—"

"It's what *I* want." This subject was the final blow to her marriage to my dad. They disagreed about a lot, but my schooling and future were the sticking points. I don't want to relive it.

Moving to the couch, she fluffs a pillow, but I have a feeling it's only out of habit. "Seeking perfection is the easiest way to find disappointment." She eyes the pillow, satisfaction never reaching her eyes. Standing back, she swings her gaze my way. "Happiness is a much nobler mission."

After she divorced my father, she put it into practice. After leaving Newport for Manhattan two years ago, she's happier than ever. "I know you have big plans, Chloe, but you're only young once. Go out with Ruby. Have fun. Kiss boys. You're allowed to do what you want instead of what others want for you. You're allowed to be you."

Be me? The words strike me oddly. "Who am I?"

"Ah, sweet girl, whoever you want to be. New experiences will allow you to see yourself through a new lens."

I sit on the couch, blocking her view of the pillow she just fixed. "Is that why you left Newport?"

"Yes, I wanted to discover me again. In Manhattan, I'm not Norman's wife or the chair of the preservation society.

I'm not running an eight-thousand-square-foot house or hosting garden parties. In New York, I get to be Cat Fox and Chloe's mother. Those are my favorite roles I've ever had."

Working with my father might have been great for my résumé, but back home, I'll always be compared to the great Norman Fox. I'll live in his shadow if I return to Rhode Island and won't ever stand on my own accomplishments. So I understand what she means a little too well. She seems to think she was saved. *Is it too late for me?*

"Do you know who you are?"

"I'm learning every day. All I'm saying is life is happening all around you. Look up from the books every now and then."

Turning around, she takes one last glance around the apartment. "You need a pop of color in here. I can send sofa pillows."

I get what she's saying. She's the queen of décor and has strong opinions regarding my life. She'd love to not only throw some pillows on my couch but also put a man in my life.

She never understood that good grades are much more rewarding than spending time with boys who want nothing more than a one-night stand. "Don't send pillows," I say, grinning.

A sly grin rolls across her face. "You can snuggle with them, or a guy—"

"You want me to date." I sigh. "I get it."

"College guys aren't the same as high school boys." She takes her purse from the couch and situates it on her shoulder as she moves to the door.

I roll my eyes. "Could have fooled me."

"You just haven't met someone who makes your heart flutter."

"You're such a romantic."

Kissing my cheek, she opens the door, and says, "Take care of yourself, honey. I love you."

"Love you, too." I close the door and rest against the back of it, exhaling. After two months of working at my father's clinic and then staying with her in the city for the past two weeks, I'd almost forgotten what it was like to have time to myself and silence. Pure, unadulterated—

Knock. Knock.

I jump, startled from the banging against my back. Spinning around, I squint to look through the peephole, and my chin jerks back.

A guy holding a bag outside my door says, "Food delivery."

"I didn't order food," I say, palms pressed to the door as I spy on him.

A smirk plays on his lips. Yup, he flat-out stares into the peephole with a smug grin on his face. Plucking the receipt from the bag, he adds, "Chloe?" The e is drawn out in his dulcet tone as if it's possible to make such a common name sound special. He managed it.

I unlock the deadbolt but leave the chain in place. When I open the door, I peek out, keeping my body and weight against it for safety.

Met with brown eyes that catch the setting sun streaming in from the window in the hall, there's no hiding the amusement shining in them. "Hi," he says, his gaze dipping to my mouth and back up. "Chloe?"

"I'm Chloe, but as I said, I didn't order food."

He glances toward the stairs, the tension in his shoulders dropping before his eyes return to mine. "I have the right address, the correct apartment, and name. I'm pretty sure it's for you." He holds it out after a casual shrug. "Anyway, it's getting cold, and it's chicken and dumplings, my mom's specialty that she only makes on Sundays. Trust me, it's better hot, though I've had it cold, and it was still good."

He makes a solid argument. All the information is correct. I shift, my guard dropping. I'm still curious, though. "Your mom made it?"

Thumbing over his shoulder as though the restaurant is behind him, he replies, "Only on Sundays. Me and T cook the rest of the time."

"Who's T?"

"The other cook." He turns the bag around. Patty's Diner is printed on the white paper. Then he points at his worn shirt, the logo barely visible from all the washings.

"And Patty is your mother?"

He swivels the bag around and nods. "Patty is my mom."

My stomach growls from the sound of the bag crinkling in his hands, reminding me that I haven't eaten in hours, and chicken and dumplings sounds amazing. Only "culinary cuisine," as my dad would call it, was acceptable when I was growing up. Comfort food didn't qualify because anything with gravy instead of some kind of reduction was a no-no.

Grinning, he pushes the bag closer. "As much as I'd love to stay here all night and chat about the mystery of this delivery, I have other food getting cold down in the car. You're hungry. Take the bag and enjoy." He says it like we're friends, and I'm starting to think we've spent enough time together to consider it.

I unchain the door and open it to take the bag from him. Holding up a finger, I ask, "Do you mind waiting? I'll get you a tip."

As if he won the war, two dimples appear as his grin grows. The cockiness reflected in his eyes doesn't take away from the fact that he's more handsome than I initially gave him credit for.

Handsome is a dime a dozen in Newport. Good genes passed down long before the Golden Age run in the prestigious family trees of Rhode Island. So good-looking guys don't do much beyond catch my eye.

He says, "I can wait." I pull my purse from the hook near the door and dig out my wallet. He fills the doorway, snooping over my shoulder. "Where are you running to?"

Huh? I look up, confused by the question. "Nowhere."

Following his line of sight, I realize what he's referring to just as he says, "The treadmill. That's the point. You never get anywhere."

"It's good exercise."

"Yeah," he says, his tone tipping toward judgmental. "You're just running in a circle. Stuck in place."

"I'm not trying to go anywhere. I'm—"

"Sure, you are."

When I answered the door, I wasn't expecting to have my life scrutinized under a microscope. "Why do I feel like you're speaking in metaphors?"

"I don't know. Why *do* you feel like I'm speaking in metaphors?" His tongue is slick and his wit dry, which is something I can appreciate, even when it's at my expense.

Handing him a ten, I say, "Hopefully, this covers the therapy."

He chuckles. "I'm always happy to dole out free advice, but I'll take the ten. Thanks." Still looking around, the detective moves his attention elsewhere. "Nice bonsai."

"Thanks. My mom gave me Frankie."

"Frankie?"

I tuck my wallet back in my purse and return it to the hook. "The little tree?"

Eyeing the plant, I can tell he wants to get a closer look by how he's inching in. He says, "Bonsais aren't miniature trees. They're just pruned to be that way. It's actually an art form."

"You seem to know a lot more about it than I do," I reply, stepping sideways to cut off his path. "Are you a plant guy?"

"I like to know all kinds of things about plants. Mainly the ones we eat. I wouldn't suggest sautéing Frankie, though."

"Why would I sauté Frankie?" I catch his deadpan expression. "Ah. You're making a joke. Gotcha." I laugh under my breath. "You're referring to food."

"Yeah."

I take the door in hand as a not so subtle hint. "I should get back to . . ." I just end it before the lie leaves my lips. I have no plans but to study, and that sounds boring even to me. "Thanks again." I'm surprised, though, when he doesn't move. "Don't let me keep you from those other deliveries." *Hint. Hint. Hint.*

He remains inches from me, and I look up when he says, "Thanks for the tip."

"You're welcome."

Shoving the money in his pocket, he rocks back on his heels. "Hope you enjoy the food."

Pulling the door with me as he passes, I remain with it pressed to my backside. "I'm sure I will."

"Anytime." I barely glimpse his grin before he turns abruptly to leave. Then he stops just shy of maneuvering down the stairs and looks back. "You need balance in your life."

Shock bolts my eyes wide open, and my mouth drops open as offense takes over. Standing in my discomfort, I consider closing the door and ending this conversation. But

I step forward instead, leaning halfway out. "Maybe you need balance."

Through a chuckle, he replies, "The bonsai. You said your mom gave you the plant. She thinks you need balance in your life. Mine gave me calm. Mom knows best. That's all I'm saying."

Pulling the door, I take a step back, glancing at him one last time. "Thanks, professor," I remark.

"Have a good life, Chloe." His laughter bounces off the walls of the hallway.

I shut the door, bolting the lock and attaching the chain, not needing the last word. "I will," I say to myself. After a quick peek out of the peephole again to verify he left, I set the bag next to the stack of books and take a second look at the plant. "By the way he was looking at you, I thought he was going to plant-nap you, Frankie." He sure was all up in this little guy's business.

Must be a biology major.

I begin to unpack the bag, trying to ignore how his presence and the faint scent of his cologne still linger but notice how it feels a few degrees warmer. "I wouldn't blame him," I tell Frankie. "You're a beautiful specimen."

Getting up, I lower the thermostat before trying to figure out who sent the food. With perfect timing, my phone begins buzzing across the coffee table. I race back to catch a text from my best friend: *If you hear from me in ten minutes, call me right back.*

Quick to respond, I type: *Another bad date?*

Ruby Darrow, the heiress to the Darrow Enterprises, and I have been close since we roomed together freshman year. I can't wait for her to move into her apartment next door. Her return message reads: *I'm not sure. If you hear from me, then yes. Yes, it is.*

Me: *I'm on standby.*

Ruby: *Because you're the best.*

I take my duties as her friend very seriously, so I set the phone down next to the bag and pop open the plasticware. When my phone buzzes again, I'm fully prepared to make the call, but this time it's not Ruby.

Mom: *I had food delivered for you. Did you get it? Chicken and dumplings. I'm in the mood for comfort food and thought you might be, too.*

I wish I would have known ten minutes ago. Eyeing the bag, I smile. I can't argue with her choice of dish, but I'm just not sure if the pain in the ass delivery was worth the trouble.

Even a baseball cap flipped backward didn't hinder his appearance because, apparently, I just discovered I have a type. Small-town hero with a side of arrogance. *Jesus.* This is Connecticut, not Texas.

Despite his appearance, I wasn't impressed. Dating cute guys has not worked out well for me in the past. The local bad boy doesn't fit into my plans or help with my "balance" as he points out I evidently need.

So rude.

I balance just fine. School. Trying to think of more, I get frustrated. I'm at Yale for one reason and one reason only—to get into the medical school of my choice—and to do that, I need to keep my brain in the game. The school game, not the dating game. "What does he know anyway, Frankie?"

Returning my mom's text, I type: *Got it. Thank you.*

Mom: *Promise me you'll live a little, or a lot, if you're so inclined.*

She's become a wild woman in the past two years. I'm happy for her, but that doesn't mean I have to change my ways to fit her new outlook on life.

As I look around my new apartment, the cleanliness brings a sense of calm to me. After living in my parents' homes over the summer, it feels good to be back at school and on my own again.

Me: *That's a lot of promises. First, caring for Frankie, and now for my own well-being.* I laugh at my joke, but I know she'll misinterpret it, so I'm quick to add: *Kidding. I will. Love you.*

Mom: *Hope so. Live fearlessly, dear daughter. Love you.*

Feeling like I dodged another lecture on "you're only young once," I smile like a kid on Christmas when I find a chocolate chip cookie in the bag. With just one bite of the food, I close my eyes, savoring the flavor. "Patty sure knows how to cook."

I click on a trivia game show and spend the time kicking the other contestants' butts as I eat.

Soon, I'm stuffed but feeling antsy about the dough sitting at the bottom of my stomach, so I get up and slip my sneakers on before hopping on the treadmill. I warm up for a mile with that bag and the red logo staring back at me, so I pick up the pace until I'm sprinting. "I'm not trying to go anywhere. It's good exercise," I grumble, still bothered by what the delivery guy said. A bleacher seat therapist is the last thing I need.

I start into a jog and then a faster speed, though my gaze keeps gravitating toward the bag and the red printing on the front—Patty's Diner. The food might have been delicious, but I can't make a habit out of eating food that heavy or I won't be able to wear the new clothes my mom and I just spent two weeks shopping for.

I barely make four miles before my tired muscles start to ache. I'm not surprised after a day of moving, but I still wished I could have hit five. I hit the stop button and give in to the exhaustion.

I take a shower and change into my pajamas before going through my nightly routine—brushing teeth, checking locks, turning out the lights, and getting a glass of water. I only take a few sips before I see Frankie in the living room all alone. My mom's guilt was well-placed. I dump water in the pot and bring it with me into the bedroom. "Don't get too comfortable. You're not staying here."

Returning to the living room to grab my study guide for the MCAT, I hurry back to bed and climb under the covers. But after a while, I set the guide aside, behavioral sciences not able to hold my attention against my mom's parting words.

Classes. Study. Rest. Routines are good. They're the backbone of success. I click off the lamp, not needing my mom's words—*live fearlessly*—filling my head. Those thoughts are only a distraction to my grand plan. *Like that delivery guy.*

If you'd like to continue reading, We Were Once is Free in KU and available here in ebook, audio, and paperback.

ABOUT THE AUTHOR

To keep up to date with her writing and more, her website is
www.slscottauthor.com to receive her newsletter with all of
her publishing adventures and giveaways.

THANK YOU

Thank you for reading my books and for the lovely support.

I have the most amazing team helping me bring my books to life. From editing to narration, these are the incredible individuals who not only support my career journey, helping me to achieve my goals, but are my friends.

Thank You All!

Adriana Locke - for the talks, and more talking, the laughs, planning, dreaming, and then extra talking through all the things from life to business.
Andrea Johnston - for dropping everything to fit me in from a personal conversation to listening to a narration for me. Also, for always making me smile and the optimism.
Erin Spencer - You make it easy to produce top notch audiobooks. Thank you for always working with me, even when I'm stressing and working to the last minute of my deadline.
Jenny Sims - you work so hard and so last minute for me

always. Thank you for working all hours to help me hit my deadlines.

Kristen Johnson - you're the best, always helping me with anything I need and always up for my crazy ideas in the group.

Marion Archer - we've been together a long time now. Thank you for always fitting me in and for helping me sort through all the chaos in my head to find the magic in the story. I'm so glad to have you in my corner.

Made in the USA
Middletown, DE
27 April 2021